THE GAMBIT

A Ben Lewis Thriller

David N Robinson

PEACH PUBLISHING

ISBN 978-1-78036-282-3

Published by
Peach Publishing

gambit

noun

1. an opening move (in chess) in which a player risks one or
more minor pieces in order to gain a favourable position

Dedicated to everyone working so hard to make London a safe and great city

Prologue

The space was dark, the atmosphere heavy and laden with cigar smoke. It was difficult to see across the room. Discarded beer and vodka bottles littered the table. Space was at a premium: several ashtrays were full to bursting with the detritus of a lengthy session.

"Let's kill this bastard Ukrainian once and for all," the man with the thick round spectacles was saying. There was considered nodding from around the table. "He's made complete fools out of all of us. So far, no one's been able to lay a finger on him. Even our Kremlin politicians are baying for his blood."

Viktor Plushenko sat back and thought about this for a moment. He had the most to gain from the Ukrainian's demise, both on a personal and professional business level. The man in question had cost him dearly over the years, none more so than over the recent deal that Plushenko had thought had been in the bag – until Western sanctions had kicked in and rendered the Russian oligarch's position impotent.

"This is the fucker from Donetsk who has just stolen five billion dollars of my future profits," Plushenko said. "Before anyone else drags him into the Siberian wastelands and murders him, I want the opportunity to squeeze every last dollar and cent out of him first."

There were murmurs of assent from around the table.

"I'd like to see the man spliced open, his entrails left for the wolves to pick at." This time, it was another grossly overweight man speaking. His rasping voice was barely audible above his heavy breathing. "Arkady Nemikov's crime syndicates have been fleecing good honest Russian citizens for too long. No one will be sad to see the back of him."

"What do you propose, Viktor?" It was a statement of support, albeit delivered with an air of menace by a different

Russian: someone who had, until then, been sitting in silence, gauging the mood in the room.

"I propose we commission a little private enterprise," Plushenko said. "The Kremlin doesn't want this to be an official Russian operation. They'd prefer it to be kept 'off balance sheet'."

"Do you have anyone in particular in mind?" the same man probed him.

"As a matter of fact, I do: a retired professional, restless to get back into the field. He's a patriot, back from the dead, discharged from active service on 'medical grounds' as the Kremlin bullshitters have recently informed him. Someone eager to settle old scores."

"Anyone we know?" It was now the man with the thick, round, spectacles speaking, his words beginning to slur from the effects of several drinks too many.

"Perhaps. In his day, he was something of a legend. His name," he said, taking a large swig of vodka and pausing for dramatic effect, "is Oleg Panich."

1

It is the third weekend in November. Clear skies and an overnight frost have brought an autumnal chill to the capital. A few solitary pedestrians are up and about at this hour. All are wrapped up against the cold. The early sun is casting orange shadows on buildings. Those leaves that stubbornly remain on the trees around Parliament Square reflect wonderfully in the weak morning sunlight. What is there not to like about London at this time of the year, Ben Lewis muses? He is tailing a young Asian male who has been walking from the Houses of Parliament towards Victoria.

Lewis is on an errand for a man he has only recently met by the name of Jake Sullivan. Sullivan is a senior case officer in Britain's security service, MI5. Lewis doesn't work for MI5 in an official capacity – rather, he is on trial: so that Sullivan and his crew can work out if Lewis has what it takes. Sullivan had been passed Lewis's name on a strong recommendation from a Metropolitan Police Detective Inspector, Saul Zeltinger. Lewis and MI5 are in the 'getting to know each other' phase. It is a mutually convenient arrangement.

The man Lewis is following is in his early twenties. He goes by the name of Jaleel Ashraf. Ashraf is a British-born Pakistani who has travelled to London in the early hours from the flat he rents just outside Luton, to the north of the capital. Sullivan wants Lewis to find out where Ashraf is going: in particular, the names and photographs of anyone he meets. MI5 are interested because Ashraf recently returned to the UK from a visit to the Middle East. The Pakistani had been ticketed to travel to Dubai, and back, on Emirates. Once in the UAE, intelligence sources discovered that he had paid cash for onward flight connections, firstly to Cairo, and then ultimately Damascus. Whilst in Syria, he was observed meeting with several thought to be closely connected with Islamic State.

Today's is not the most taxing errand that Lewis has had to perform. On the one hand, Lewis knows that Sullivan is simply testing him: on the other, Lewis isn't actually convinced that he wants to be part of MI5. For the time being, he is happy to play the role of occasional contractor. Besides, Sullivan is paying him a useful daily rate.

Ashraf is not a difficult person to follow. The Pakistani has been oblivious to most things going on around him since emerging from Westminster underground station. A mobile phone remains glued to his ear, as it has for the whole time since leaving the station. The two of them have circled around the western side of Parliament Square, past St Margaret's church and Westminster Abbey, now heading in the direction of Victoria Station several minutes' walk away. The area is deserted at this hour on a Saturday morning: Westminster politicians have gone home to their constituencies for the weekend; traffic on the roads is light.

Lewis's phone buzzes in his pocket. He takes it out and looks at the caller ID. Removing a thin earpiece from his brown leather jacket, he places it in his ear, pressing the button on the side to take the call.

"Hello," is all he says.

"Your man is speaking to someone called Khan. They are making arrangements to meet. Keep your eyes open. We're increasingly troubled by Khan. I'll send you his picture by text." With that the line goes dead.

Overshadowed by Westminster Abbey, its much older near neighbour, Westminster Cathedral is the leading Roman Catholic place of worship in London. It is a grand edifice, set back about a hundred metres from Victoria Street; often mistaken for a mosque due to the large campanile bell tower and its unusual coloured brickwork. The large, square-shaped, area in front is paved and open. Normally, pedestrians mix and mingle freely in this piazza without being bothered by traffic; early on a Saturday morning, it is deserted. Apart from Ashraf and Kahn, there are no pedestrians. Nearest the road, the piazza is flanked on two sides by office buildings with shops at ground floor level. Lewis positions himself in the shadows of one of these, leaning against a grey, granite-clad, supporting pillar.

Khan, from a distance, looks agitated and impatient. He and Ashraf are stomping around the area immediately in front of the Cathedral. They are nervously shuffling their feet and looking at their watches. Lewis is out of their line of sight. The two Asians appear to be waiting for something or someone. They look anxious, glancing repeatedly towards the small side streets that flank the Cathedral. There is tension in the air. Lewis can feel it from where he is standing: something is about to go down. Lewis takes photographs with his camera phone; surveillance is, after all, part of the Sullivan mission brief.

A white van arrives at speed into the turning loop to one side of the Cathedral's main entrance. Khan and Ashraf spring into action. The former is quickly around the back of the van and opening its double doors. Seconds later, they are both dragging a white male in his twenties from the back. The new arrival is in handcuffs and wears a black cape over his upper body. Khan and Ashraf grab the man by each arm and march him a short distance to the middle of the piazza, immediately in front of the Cathedral's main entrance. The driver of the van is not one to hang around. He closes the van doors, jumps back in the driver's seat and accelerates away.

According to the MI5 rulebook, Lewis should probably be calling for help and backup. He considers this, briefly, but rejects it: the cavalry are never going to arrive in time. Something bad is definitely about to happen: the only person with a chance to stop it is Lewis.

The two Asians force their frightened prisoner to kneel. Khan then removes the captive's black cape and puts it on himself. At the same time he dons a thin black balaclava so that only Khan's eyes, nose and mouth are visible. As soon as the cape is removed, Lewis gets what is about to happen. They have dressed the young man in a loose-fitting orange jumpsuit. Khan is going to be this man's Islamic State executioner. Ashraf, now holding a small video camera, will be the person filming it for social media posterity. With the front entrance to the Cathedral so clearly visible in the background, a public execution such as this in the heart of central London has the potential to send chilling shockwaves across the world.

Khan removes a silver-bladed knife from under his cape. He holds it against the throat of his kneeling prisoner, posing for the camera and smiling like a man possessed. The young man on his knees pleads for mercy. Khan orders him to be silent, pressing the edge of the steel blade against the young man's neck and drawing blood. Khan begins a well-prepared speech. He talks directly to the camera, all the while the knife blade is held close to the terrified young man's face.

Lewis listens with growing contempt and disgust to the frenzied outpouring of anti-British, pro-Islamic State, propaganda. The time for him to act has come.

The distance to where Ashraf, the cameraman, is standing with his back to him is fifteen metres: Khan and his kneeling prisoner are another three metres beyond. Fifteen metres will require eighteen of Lewis's paces: at a fast walk. Nine seconds in total. Lewis steps around the pillar and starts walking.

Walking, and not running, is an unexpected decision; however, Lewis knows there is advantage in doing the unexpected. He knows that attackers usually run when they plan a violent assault. Fast movement stands out. Someone walking, albeit rapidly, isn't nearly such an obvious threat. Lewis is banking on this earning him a valuable second – perhaps two – of time advantage. For the first five seconds,

Lewis hopes that neither Ashraf nor Khan will react at all. Ordinarily, they should both be too preoccupied by their own theatre of the absurd to comprehend what may be about to unfold.

It will be Khan who will see Lewis first. Ashraf, although nearer, has his back to Lewis: he is holding the video camera. Because everything is being recorded, it will take another second, probably two, before Khan decides to stop speaking. At that stage, the surprise should begin to show on his face sufficient to cause Ashraf to turn around and notice Lewis for the first time. Which, by then, will give Ashraf probably no more than a second to react: one, single, crucial second before the express train, that will be Lewis advancing at full tilt, hits him. If the plan works, Khan, let alone Ashraf, is not going to stand a chance.

Lewis lengthens his stride. His one hundred and seventy pound body mass builds momentum as he picks up speed. He heads straight towards where Ashraf is holding the camcorder. Lewis deliberately avoids making eye contact. If he does, Khan will see the menace in his eyes and could be tempted to do something precipitous with the knife. So Lewis advances with his head down, looking at the floor at an angle of about forty-five degrees. He is a charging bull, albeit one that is walking not running. He counts the seconds in thousands in his head. He gets to seven thousand before he hears Khan stop speaking. Less than two seconds to go before first contact.

As predicted, it takes Ashraf about a second to figure out what might be happening before he decides to turn around. By then Lewis's left shoulder is connecting heavily with Ashraf's right upper forearm, causing the camcorder to go flying. Forward momentum isn't lost at the point of impact; instead Lewis rotates his upper left forearm through one hundred and eighty degrees at the elbow. The rotational movement, being in a vertical plane, enables him to swing his clenched left fist with massive force directly onto the bridge of Ashraf's nose:

without missing a beat, Lewis continues charging forward. In his wake, there is a sickening sound of broken bone and splintered nose cartilage.

One down.

The distance between Lewis and the knife-wielding Khan is less than two metres and closing fast. Khan is by now screaming angrily at Lewis. For a split second he dithers, contemplating whether to press his knife blade more firmly against his victim's throat. Time is not on his side. He wakes up to the fact that unless he does something dramatic, Lewis is about to collide with him head on. So Khan does what Lewis always knew he was going to do. He moves the knife: away from the man kneeling beside him; attempting instead to stab Lewis's advancing body directly in the chest. Except that Lewis's chest is no longer where Khan expects it to be. At the moment immediately before contact, Lewis sidesteps to his left. He grabs Ashraf's knife hand and twists it hard, spinning Khan's body around, as he executes a rapid arm lock. Aided by the torque generated by this manoeuvre, Lewis uses the power and strength inherent in his right hand to snap several bones in Khan's wrist. With his left, he grabs the knife, discarding it well out of reach. Khan screams in pain but Lewis is not in the mood for listening. Still holding on to Khan's broken wrist he uses Khan's body weight as an anchor to slow his momentum down. This way he is able to spin his own body through one hundred and eighty degrees: Lewis ends up with his face close to Khan's. Not yet finished, he head-butts Khan between the eyes, followed by an upper cut from his right fist directly onto Khan's jawbone. The man sinks to the floor, writhing in pain.

Two down.

One, at least, will be on a liquids-only diet for a while.

2

Oleg Panich had not had a great year. He had been shot twice, both times whilst on active service in Europe early in the year. One of the bullets had caused surgeons at the Military Hospital Burdenko in Moscow to amputate his right arm below the shoulder. As if losing an arm wasn't enough, the injuries had also caused the chain-smoking field agent to lose his job.

The cause of Panich's pain and suffering had been down to one man: former Royal Marine commando Ben Lewis. Panich had been pursuing Lewis in a lethal race against the clock that had begun in London, crossed the English Channel into France, before finally taking them both to Switzerland. Panich had been charged with safeguarding the existence of a Russian mole: Lewis had been trying to lay his hands on a missing, and highly explosive, dossier that risked the mole's exposure. Along the way, Lewis had escaped death and Panich had taken two bullets: once when Lewis had shot the Russian agent in the elbow at a disused airfield near Epérnay; and a second time high in the Swiss Alps. Assuming the Russian was fatally wounded, Lewis had left him for dead. It had been the former Marine's biggest mistake. All alone, and thought to be dying, Panich had somehow struggled to remain conscious. He had dug deep, finding an inner reserve of strength before summoning a Russian evacuation team. The badly wounded agent had then been spirited away over a high mountain pass beyond Martigny, to the relative safety of France.

Panich's rehabilitation had been protracted and depressing for such an active man. The bullet he had taken in his chest had passed clean through his body. It had caused only superficial damage to nerves and ligaments. Surgery had been followed by a period of rest and then gruelling physiotherapy to restore movement in his left shoulder and arm. The loss of his right arm had been more problematic. Once the skin had healed over the newly created stump, the Russian doctors had moulded a suction-fitting inner liner to fit over it; the end of the liner contained a notched pin for attaching to his new prosthetic arm. The good news had been that his superiors back at the *Sluzhba Vneshney Razvedki* – the former first directorate of the KGB more commonly known as the SVR – had authorised the procurement of the very latest carbon fibre prosthesis: a powerful and lightweight model that was state of the art. Movement was controlled by tiny microprocessors that received instructions to bend at the elbow, or to move the wrist and finger joints, myoelectrically, from the residual muscles in Panich's upper forearm. The bad news had been the lengthy process of rehabilitation: time, and yet more gym work, had been needed to restore muscles in his upper right arm sufficiently to allow him to become dextrous with his new prosthesis.

As if all this hadn't been enough, during his period in hospital Panich had been diagnosed with an advanced form of lung cancer. Doubtless exacerbated by years of incessant smoking as well as his former, highly stressful, lifestyle, overnight it changed his whole outlook on life. The message had been clear: without any chemotherapy he would have six, possibly twelve, months left to live. With chemotherapy, assuming his body tolerated the treatment, he might earn some remission: but there could be no guarantees. Having faced potential death so many times in his career, the decision had been easy: Panich had refused chemotherapy. He had decided to take his chances and make the best of the rest of his life. Irrespective of his cancer, the senior staffers back at SVR headquarters in Yasenevo had concluded that his other field injuries precluded Panich from remaining on active service. They had therefore given him a big thank you and a small, derisory pension. Panich didn't really care. He didn't have that long to live whatever happened.

Oleg Panich had always been a private man. During the days of his active field duty, outside his work he had chosen to live a solitary existence. Now, no longer called upon to disappear abroad for unspecified periods of time, he had withdrawn to the meagre comforts of his tiny apartment in the Taganskaya district of Moscow. He had found himself in unfamiliar territory, overnight becoming an ordinary Moscow citizen. Week after week in those early days, his principal focus had been on the slow process of recovery and rehabilitation. Spending hours in the gym had not been something he found either enjoyable or interesting. Up until his cancer diagnosis, he had not been aware of any of the symptoms that might ordinarily have indicated that he had the disease. He had previously put the occasional pain in his chest and shortness of breath down to the rigours of the day job. Once he had been told of his affliction and had refused chemotherapy, his reaction had been typically Panich: complete denial whilst attempting to carry on as normal. He had certainly not been about to quit smoking.

Although not outrageously rich by Russian standards, he had saved enough from his days as a field agent to be able to afford two specific luxuries that made his enforced period of recuperation and rehabilitation bearable. One was a specialist coffee maker, able to dispense endless amounts of the strong, black, liquid that his body continued to crave. The other was one of the best music and loudspeaker systems his hard-earned savings could afford. Thus it was that the former field agent would spend his days: lifting weights; drinking numerous cups of freshly ground black coffee; chain smoking his foul-smelling Turkish cigarettes; and listening to the complete operatic works of his two favourite composers, Verdi and Puccini, usually at full volume. Often he would do this whilst hunched over a large chessboard in the centre of his apartment. Panich had become hooked on chess, liking to copy the moves of Russian grandmasters in some of their more famous games. He had memorised whole segments of gameplay, trying to get inside the heads of various grandmasters in order to discover their strategies for winning so consistently. It had kept him occupied: and it had also kept him sane.

In time, he became confident about using his right arm again. It was never going to be as dextrous as previously. There were some things he could still only do with his left hand – such as firing a gun. In many respects the prosthesis function compared favourably with what he had before. In one aspect it had been a significant improvement: the strength of his grip.

Panich had always been a big proponent of violent acts of retribution. During his daily, high intensity workouts, he would imagine his new hand closing around Ben Lewis's throat. With the carbon fibre digits jammed hard against the former Marine's neck, Panich would imagine sending electrical signals from the muscles in his arm. These, in turn, would cause the tiny electric motors in his fingers and thumb to close tightly. Lewis's windpipe would be slowly crushed; the strength in his prosthetic hand would continue building until the vertebrae in his neck separated: until finally, they would snap. Panich would imagine the sickening sound of it all, the grizzly gasping noise as Lewis struggled pathetically to utter a few final sounds before a very painful death consumed him.

The thought of exacting retribution against Ben Lewis had been one of the deciding factors in Panich not accepting chemotherapy. He wanted to be fit and well, relatively, in order to see Lewis suffer and die before he did.

It had been one of the things making the whole rehabilitation process bearable.

3

Paddington Green police station is, as the name suggests, located close to the mainline railway terminus that serves the west and south west of England. It is situated on London's Edgware Road, just to the north of the Westway flyover. It does function as a normal police station. However, deep below the unattractive and utilitarian 1960's building, there are sixteen special police cells reserved for prisoners suspected of terrorism awaiting trial. Each of the twelve-foot square cells has no access to natural light and contains the bare minimum of facilities.

Ben Lewis knows about the cells, not because he has been placed in one; he has just returned from a visit to the basement and seen them for himself. A short while ago, two guards led him from his holding room on the ground floor to the basement cellblock. Here he had been required to make a positive identification of the two suspects, Ashraf and Khan. Several hours have passed since the incident at Westminster Cathedral. By this time, both men have had their broken noses set in crude splints. Lewis has seen that Khan's jaw is heavily bandaged, his face and eyes puffy and swollen. They are being kept in separate cells. Lewis has noted, with some satisfaction, that the accommodation being provided by their Metropolitan Police hosts would at best be described as meagre, and certainly basic. In what Lewis thought was a pointless, if futile, gesture, he had made a positive identification of both men before being escorted back to his holding cell on the ground floor.

Thus far, the questions from various officers from the Metropolitan Police's Counter Terrorism Command, SO15, continue to be repetitive and routine. They seem interested in his reasons for being in the vicinity of Ashraf and Khan in the first place. That no one, ostensibly from MI5, deigns to make an appearance to corroborate his story and expedite his release seems curious, if not bizarre. The interrogation team treat him with reasonable courtesy despite that, even bringing him a slice of tepid, soggy pizza at one stage.

Sometime after nightfall during a lull in the questioning, Lewis manages to sleep. He lays his head on his arms on the small square table in front of him and drifts off. He is unaware of how long he has been dozing before the door is flung open. A familiar face enters the room. This particular visitor walks across to an empty chair immediately opposite Lewis. With an air of authority, he removes his coat and drops it on the table.

"Couldn't keep away from all the fun and excitement, is that it, Ben?"

Lewis looks up and smiles, getting briefly to his feet.

"Something like that, Saul. It's good to see you."

There is an air of mutual respect between the pair of them. They shake hands. Saul Zeltinger looks tired, but then Lewis is hardly at his best either. Despite the hour, the half-German Detective Inspector is smartly turned out in a navy suit, blue shirt and a nondescript tie: what Lewis thinks of as Zeltinger's standard uniform. In point of fact, Lewis has never seen Zeltinger wear anything else.

"What brings you here?"

"Why, you, of course, Ben. You're the Metropolitan Police's latest celebrity guest. Quite the hero of the hour, or so it would seem."

"I didn't think Paddington Green was your patch, Saul."

"It's not really. But then Detective Inspectors have this habit of poking their noses into things that don't immediately concern them."

Zeltinger places his well-worn raincoat on the table before sitting down and facing Lewis. There is more than a hint of Germanic precision about the way Zeltinger speaks. Born to a German-Jewish father who, as a young metal trader, had come

14

to England and met an English nurse whom he had later married, Saul still occasionally speaks with a slight German inflection, something that he attributes to his father.

"Not so very long ago, Ben, when you were a wanted man, you had me running around all over Europe trying to keep up with you. Now that's all over, I find it ironic to discover you as an uninvited guest at one of our humble police stations."

"It's not exactly the Ritz, you know, Saul."

"I should hope not."

"Why am I being detained, by the way? Your lot are not about to arrest me, are they?"

"I shouldn't think so. No, as I understand it you're being kept here for your own protection – as much as anything to keep you out of the public eye. Jake Sullivan thought it better to put you in a place where no one would find you. There is some logic in that."

Lewis pulls a face.

"It's a bit twisted, that kind of logic. Besides, I can usually take care of myself. Whilst it's good to see you, isn't it a bit late in the day for you to be making social calls? I thought you were a family man, with a beautiful wife and twin boys to lure you home at nights."

"The capital has been on a heightened state of alert since this morning. There's been a lot going on today. Several other arrests have been made. The man who was about to be beheaded: he was an RAF Tornado pilot. Back from Afghanistan and on home leave, visiting friends and family in Luton."

"Doesn't sound like your normal line of work, though, Saul – or are you doing different things these days?"

"No, I was interviewing someone else here earlier this evening when I discovered that you were on the premises."

"Small world, isn't it? Perhaps we should have that game of chess you've been promising me, if you've got the time?"

Zeltinger looks at his watch and shakes his head.

"I need to get back to the office."

15

"Another all-nighter, is it, Saul?"

"London has the Islamic State jitters all of a sudden. The world's gone mad. Come to think of it, I never seem to have the time to play chess. I'm surprised you do."

"You should make time, Saul. I've downloaded this great chess app on my phone. Hardly a day goes past when I don't play. Why don't you try it?"

Saul shakes his head slowly.

"I'm too busy. Tell you what, though, why not come over for supper? The day after tomorrow could be good, if that works for you? It's meant to be my night off – in theory. You can meet Hattie and the twins, and the two of us can play a little chess. I need to find out whether you're as good as you seem to think you are." He smiles at Lewis as he says this, his head on one side.

"Okay, it's a deal. As long as I'm not still cooped up in here. How long are they planning on keeping me?"

"Probably until morning. I'll see if we can find you somewhere better to sleep."

"You mean an upgrade? Like on the airlines?"

"I'll have to pull rank," he says getting to his feet. "Business Class cells are hard to wrangle in the Metropolitan Police these days."

They shake hands and Zeltinger grabs his coat before heading towards the door.

"No promises, Ben, but I'll see what I can do."

4

Viktor Plushenko, one of the most powerful and wealthy businessmen in Russia, drew heavily on his *Cohiba Splendido* cigar, the brand that reputedly was Fidel Castro's personal favourite. Hand-rolled exclusively by Cuban women, for many ordinary Russians such an expensive cigar was an outrageous luxury. Most could only dream of spending so much money on something that was firstly set fire to, before ultimately being reduced to ash and smoke. Lying sprawled on the luxurious sofa in his Moscow penthouse waiting for his visitor to arrive, Plushenko briefly considered that there wasn't much in life that he couldn't afford: the finest food and wines; the best cigars; the biggest and most luxurious super yachts; and most important of all, the most expensive and prettiest young women that his hard-earned Russian money could acquire. Just like his present companion, most were blonde, most wore the latest Parisian *haute couture*, and most were more than willing to do anything that was likely to be asked of them. Making money made Viktor childishly happy. Which was why, at that particular moment, he was becoming childishly excited about the prospect of stealing several billion dollars from his arch-rival, Arkady Nemikov.

For over fifteen years, whilst both Russia and Ukraine had been part of the former Soviet Union, the two young Soviet entrepreneurs had been business partners. Their organised crime, prostitution and gambling interests had stretched in a complex triangular web: from Moscow in the east; through to Donetsk in the eastern Ukraine; and as far North as Minsk in Belarus. It had paid both men significant cash dividends over many years. Then in 1994, not long after the break up of the Soviet Union when Ukraine had made its historic deal with Russia to hand back its nuclear missiles in exchange for a peaceful co-existence with its neighbour, the partnership with Nemikov had turned sour overnight. Out of what had been friendship, there grew bitterness and mutual animosity. Each had accused the other of stealing networks and money. Nemikov withdrew to Donetsk, Plushenko to Moscow, the shutters between once-friends permanently lowered. All dialogue and friendship had ceased. Now on his own, Plushenko began to make new investments in gas, mineral extraction and transportation businesses. Arguably just to spite him, so did Nemikov. The two often bid head to head for large contracts and mining concessions, stretching from Moscow, the Baltic States, and finally into Europe as well.

Nemikov moved to London to take his business empire public; in the process raising many billions of dollars in cash. In retaliation, Plushenko had paid several billions more to buy up a London-listed mining conglomerate and take it private. His friends thought it was a tactical coup. In Plushenko's mind, he was just making a point: whatever Nemikov could do, he could do better. Although they had once been partners, as rivals Plushenko was determined to prove that he was more successful and more ruthless than Nemikov.

They had played games with each other, of course. Nemikov frequently sent spies to try and infiltrate Plushenko's business interests. Usually posing as new employees, often women, their goal was to steal the Russian's secrets and get the inside scoop on deals that were in the pipeline. In return, Plushenko had a small but dedicated team of cyber-criminals who had made it their life's work to hack Nemikov's firewalls: their goal – to learn about, and often sabotage, what the Ukrainian was up to.

They had even tried to kill each other. A car bomb in Kiev had nearly taken Nemikov's life about three years ago. It had been in direct retaliation for a drive-by machine gun attack on Plushenko as he was about to enter a Moscow restaurant. Shortly afterwards, the two of them had met and declared a truce – of sorts. On a private terrace at the Dolder Grand hotel in Zurich, overlooking the lake and sipping chilled Bollinger, they had shaken hands stiffly and declared a cessation of hostilities. Neither party really believed it would last: it had, however, saved them both from a degree of unnecessary unpleasantness. Temporarily at least, it had also extended their life expectancy.

Somehow this unstable truce had lasted. All that was in the process of changing as a direct result of the recent political madness: Western sanctions against certain Russians and their financial interests. Plushenko had watched, initially in horror, then in a blinding rage, as several of his bank accounts had been frozen and his ability to conduct deals in the West had been withdrawn. He, Viktor Plushenko, together with much of his business empire outside Russia, had been blacklisted by both the US and the EU states. What had been worse had been seeing Nemikov sitting in London unaffected by it all. Why had Nemikov become the blue-eyed boy all of a sudden, seemingly able to go about his life as normal? Then, the bastard Ukrainian had announced that he had signed the contract worth billions of dollars to build a new gas pipeline. This was the much-coveted deal that would provide an alternate, non-Russian, gas supply route from the Baltics into parts of Western Europe. It was terrible for Russia strategically, and disastrous for Plushenko personally. The Russian's business empire was likely to lose several billion dollars of future profits as a consequence of Europe having an alternative supply source. What was worse was that Plushenko had coveted that deal for himself. He had been working behind the scenes to secure it for months, knowing that winning would secure his monopoly over access to gas for many millions of people across Europe. He had invested heavily in sweeteners and extravagant gifts for the key decision makers: luxurious holidays; expensive watches; top of the range high-performance cars; and even much sought after caviar and Cuban cigars. All liberally sprinkled with copious amounts of free alcohol, pretty women and spending money for use in his casinos. Overnight, before anyone – let alone Plushenko – had had any time to react, the sanctions had been suddenly announced. This had been the trigger enabling the 'Shit from Donetsk', as he now liked to call Nemikov, to sneak in and steal the contract from under his nose. Plushenko had been unable to do a thing about it.

It had been the final straw. All of Plushenko's friends, those fellow oligarchs and businessmen who themselves had been subjected to similar sanctions, had been in agreement. The time had come to deal with the issue once and for all. Nemikov needed to pay: both with his money and with his life.

From the window of his penthouse, Plushenko had a clear view of the multi-coloured onion-domes of St. Basil's Cathedral: beyond these, to the Kremlin itself, the place where the bastards really responsible for his current plight were located. He blew smoke from his expensive cigar into the air, letting his stubby left hand caress the breast of the pretty blonde nestled next to him on the sofa. Quiet knocking on the office door interrupted their thoughts. Plushenko looked up with anticipation, his left hand already shooing the girl away from the sofa, beckoning her to be gone. Straightening her skirt as she stood, she blew Plushenko a silent air kiss before hurrying out of the office through a secret side door.

"*Da*," the overweight Russian said, rising unsteadily to his feet, getting ready to meet his visitor. It wasn't every day that one came face to face with such a legendary killer as former SVR agent, Oleg Panich.

5

The meeting with Plushenko had been short and to the point. The money Oleg Panich had been offered was more than he would have officially earned at the SVR if he had stayed working there for the rest of his life – ignoring any reduction in life expectancy due to his cancer: a two hundred thousand US dollar fee, half in advance; all reasonable and necessary expenses paid; and a completion bonus of one million dollars. All paid offshore, to a place – and in a manner – where no one from the tax authorities would be able to find it.

What had been more extraordinary had been the subsequent summons he'd had, to meet with his former SVR controller, Mikhail Volkov. That meeting had taken place not at Volkov's office, but at his small family dacha. This was located at Peredelkino, a short distance from Yasenevo but another world away deep in the forest, some twenty kilometres to the southwest of Moscow. Panich had taken the suburban train from Kiyevskaya Metro station. The snow had already begun to fall when he had arrived thirty minutes later. Volkov had sent a driver in a very old and battered Lada Niva to collect him. The Russian-made off-road vehicle had slid and lumbered uncomfortably along snowy forest trails, eventually reaching the modest old building set in its small woodland clearing.

Volkov had been waiting on the steps to meet his former colleague. Inside the datcha, the open fire had been lit; plates of food had been laid out on a circular wooden table in the centre of the room; and most importantly, there had been copious supplies of vodka on ice. Volkov, a diminutive man with a neatly trimmed beard that some had thought had been modelled after Lenin himself, had been as Panich had never seen him before: warm, welcoming and attentive to Panich's

21

every need. If he'd been suffering from any guilt at having recently dismissed Panich from the SVR on medical grounds, then such feelings appeared long-since forgotten. That day Volkov had been the perfect host.

"Oleg, come in, how are you? You look so well! Let me look at your hand."

So it had begun, small talk at first, the atmosphere full of pleasantries, the first few glasses of vodka readily poured and drunk. The mood had been entirely convivial. They had discussed Panich's health, his former operations, and toasted his successes in particular. Neither party had made any mention of Panich's cancer: as such, it had been elevated to the rank of a State secret, strictly off limits to both comrades for the duration. As true Muscovites, they had turned instead to putting the world to rights. As the light had faded and their speech had become slurred, Panich had sensed that the time was approaching when he would learn what this summons had been all about.

"Oleg Dmitriyevich," Volkov had said finally, pouring yet another glass of ice-cold vodka into their glass. He had used the patronymic out of respect and to be polite. It was the signal that they had been about to turn to a more serious subject.

"You are something of a national hero, you know that?"

Panich had shaken his head in denial. He, like Volkov, had become slumped in his chair. The stuffing had long-since been displaced, the chair's leather-clad cushion moulded into a permanent body shape that made movement difficult.

"No, it is true. Even our illustrious President," his voice had turned to a whisper, as if the man in the Kremlin had hidden microphones out here in the forest, "sings your praises." He had laughed at the disbelief on Panich's face. "I tell you it is true, my friend. Only this week our President spoke with great pride when he heard that Plushenko had chosen to work with you on this project against Nemikov. '*Only a true patriot like Oleg Dmitriyevich could be entrusted with such an important*

22

assignment.' Those were his exact words, I promise."

Again Panich had said nothing, simply shaking his head and watching the room spin as the effects of the vodka began taking their toll.

"We live in strange times. The Russian people are suffering because of Western sanctions; the price of oil has fallen through the floor; and now the rouble is being slaughtered on the foreign exchange markets. These are dark days. Personally, I would prefer to see Russia come out fighting: let Crimea be the start of a new, stronger and enlarged Mother Russia! But our President is in enough trouble with the West. At the moment, he needs to be steering a careful line between strong rhetoric and cautious actions. The downfall and demise of Arkady Nemikov must not be a Russian state sponsored operation. These are orders coming from the absolute highest level, do you hear what I am saying, Oleg? Yasenevo can help with equipment and logistics. But none of our fingerprints must be in evidence." He had reached across and thrown a new log on the fire, sending sparks flying in all directions as the heavy log landed on top of the ash pile in the grate.

"Fortunately, we Russians have always been the masters of subterfuge. We practically invented the word. So, to plant a seed: how about this, Oleg? What if certain fanatics, planning hideous acts of revenge against the West, were to do our job for us? Certain religious fanatics, for example. Perhaps even the nutcases who call themselves Islamic State? It would be unfortunate, wouldn't you agree, if one or two Nemikov family members happened to become innocent victims of such terrible crimes?" Volkov had begun slurring his words badly in places, but his meaning had been crystal clear.

"Similar to the games we played with the West during the Cold War, don't you mean?" Panich had said.

"Don't be under any misconception, my friend. The same game is being played all over again." He had sighed, the vodka finally catching up with him. "If some well-chosen acts of terrorism helped spread fear and panic in parts of the West right now, a lot of Russians might feel that the damage caused was timely and welcome." They had sat in silence, listening to the sap from the pine logs spit and crackle in the fire.

"I can see that," was all that Panich had said finally.

"Good!" He had reached across to refill Panich's glass.

"One final piece of advice, Oleg, if you'll permit me?" He had placed his left hand deliberately on top of Panich's new prosthesis. "Plushenko will doubtless be paying you handsomely. Much more than we would ever have done, for sure. Don't be tempted to go off-piste whilst you are in London. Forget about trying to seek retribution against the man who did this to you." He had patted Panich's arm as he had been speaking, the message abundantly clear.

Panich had nodded in silence. Volkov would have been hoping that it had been a sign of agreement on Panich's part. On the matter of Ben Lewis, however, Panich already had ideas of his own.

Volkov's cautionary words of warning were not about to change that, regardless of how well-intentioned they might have been.

6

Unlike MI6, its close relation that occupies a glamorous building on the south bank of the river Thames at Vauxhall Cross, the UK's domestic Security Service, MI5, has its headquarters in a more anonymous building. Thames House was formerly the headquarters of one of the UK's, then largest, manufacturing businesses, ICI. It is a grand edifice, situated on the north side of the river on Millbank.

Ben Lewis is shown to a private meeting room on the second floor by a male security officer. The door automatically locks behind him as soon as the guard leaves. It is a cold, functional room with no windows. Lewis helps himself to a bottle of mineral water while he waits for Jake Sullivan to arrive.

Ten minutes later, the door flings wide open and Sullivan rushes in, full of apologies. Following close behind are a man and a woman, neither of whom Lewis recognises.

"Ben." He shakes Lewis's hand. Sullivan is about ten years older than Lewis. Unlike Lewis's jeans and brown leather jacket look, his host arrives wearing a shirt and tie. Sullivan waves a hand at his female colleague.

"This is Laura. I don't think you've met before?"

It is a question, but Sullivan delivers it as a statement of fact.

Laura gives Lewis a cold smile and a perfunctory handshake before sitting herself down. In no time at all, she is busying herself sorting out various papers on the desk in front of her. There is no warmth in her greeting. Lewis's first impressions are coloured by this. She has short, black hair, naturally curly and wears oval-shaped tortoiseshell glasses. Lewis guesses she is slightly older than him.

"And this is Bret," he says, pointing to the other man. Bret says nothing, simply nodding a silent greeting at Lewis before helping himself to a diet cola from a fridge in the corner. He pops the ring pull, takes a swig direct from the can and then sits down. He is older than the other two: most likely in his fifties, as far as Lewis can tell. He has mainly dark hair with a splash of silver to one side and wears a navy jacket over an open necked pink shirt.

"Sorry to keep you hanging around, Ben."

Sullivan pours himself a cup of coffee from a flask and sits down in the seat adjacent to Laura.

"Doubtless everyone's had a lot on their plates since yesterday's events near Victoria."

"How long did the boys and girls at Paddington Green detain you?"

Lewis shakes his head: "Too long! I had thought someone from here might have expedited my release. They finally let me go about an hour ago. I picked up your text and came straight over. I've had officers from SO15 all over me like a rash this last twenty-four hours."

"I'm sorry about that, Ben. We were simply following due process. There has been a lot going on behind the scenes, as I am sure you can imagine. We work together often, SO15 and ourselves."

Lewis smiles thinly but says nothing. Sullivan has called this meeting, not him. He is looking forward to heading home and a change of clothing.

"It caught us all by surprise, to tell you the truth. No one had seen Khan coming. We owe you, Ben, in case you hadn't guessed. It was above and beyond what you were asked to do. It was impressive."

Lewis shrugs his shoulders and looks blankly at Sullivan. He is still trying to fathom what the meeting is really about. He gets no reaction from either Laura or Bret, but that is of no concern to him.

"The Home Secretary wants me to convey her personal thanks and gratitude. She's authorised a small bonus payment to be made. It's not a lot, but there is hardly any money in the system these days."

"It's not necessary," Lewis says. "Most would have done the same thing in my shoes."

"I doubt that very much."

"If the Home Secretary really wants to help, she can keep my picture out of the newspapers."

"It might be a bit late for that, I'm afraid, Ben. A passer-by recorded most of what you did on her camera phone. It's already up on YouTube. You've become quite the media sensation. How many views has it had, Laura?"

"Over forty thousand."

Laura doesn't look up when she says this, busily reading a document from the pile in front of her, reciting the number from memory.

"That's all I need," Lewis says. "'Ex-Marine Ben Lewis thwarts Islamic State executioner.' It's hardly likely to improve my life expectancy."

"Everyone loves a hero."

"Not me."

"So far your name's been kept out of the press. Not many seem to know yet who you are, or so it would seem."

"I'd very much like to keep it that way."

"We have, however, been picking up certain chatter amongst the Asian Muslim community. Not surprisingly, there's officially a price on your head."

"I can look after myself."

"I'm sure you can, but a very small minority are fanatical."

"Do you know who these people are? Perhaps I should pay them a visit?"

"Yes and no. Yes, we know who they are and no, you don't need to go calling."

"Because?"

"Because, let's just say that we have something going down ourselves, currently. Something that should take care of the

27

problem."

"I usually prefer to do my own clearing up. It helps to ensure that there are no loose ends."

"I hear you, Ben, but for now the answer is no. We'll let you know if that changes. In point of fact, we'd be much happier if you were to join our team permanently. What would you say to that?"

"Is that a job offer?"

"About as near as it gets."

"So that you can keep an eye on me and make sure I don't go doing any private enterprise of my own?"

"Something like that. You'd be a great addition to our ranks. I'd love you to say yes. It's actually why I've asked Laura to join this meeting today. Laura is a section head in my department. She's actively recruiting at present."

Across the table, Laura looks up from where she has been adding items to a 'to do' list on a pad of paper in front of her. She stares at Lewis without blinking. They hold each other's gaze for a few moments.

"If you have any questions, now would be the time to ask them," she says eventually. It is a dusky, gravelly voice spoken without warmth or intonation. Like a game of chess, she is playing her opening moves carefully, not wanting to give away anything about herself that she might later regret. Her whole demeanour is purely business. It's too bad for her that Lewis is such a good chess player.

He looks at her and smiles thinly. If this was about to become a quasi-job interview, then he is going to disappoint. It's time to play a different opening gambit. Still looking at Laura, his facial expression suitably blank and non-committal, he too waits a few seconds.

"I appreciate the offer, thanks," he says eventually. "Let me sleep on it a bit and I'll get back to you."

"Sure, take your time," Sullivan says, almost too quickly. "Don't make any hasty decisions. In the meantime, best be watching your back, okay?"

"I appreciate the warning, thanks."

"Anticipating that might have been your answer, there is one other thing that you might be interested in; *pro tem*, that is, and because of what happened in Victoria yesterday. There's someone who's anxious to meet you all of a sudden."

Lewis looks up from fiddling with the plastic top from the mineral water bottle, his head to one side and with one eyebrow raised.

"A Ukrainian multi-billionaire, name of Arkady Nemikov. He finds himself something of a high profile target for the Russians at the moment, given who he is and how he appears to have made his money. He's concerned about the kidnap threat to himself and his family. Needs a professional to help with the babysitting. Ordinarily, we'd offer to help. The UK government, however, are a bit touchy currently about how overtly it shows the hand of friendship to certain Ukrainians. It doesn't want to piss off the Russians any more than we already appear to have been doing. Having a third party like you stepping in to lend a hand could be helpful. When Nemikov learned about what happened at Westminster Cathedral yesterday over a private dinner with the Home Secretary, he asked to meet you."

"Surely he must have security of his own. Why does he need me as well?"

"He's been seriously upsetting a lot of powerful people recently, so it would seem. And he has a lot of money."

"How big is the family?"

"There's a wife and two grown up children: one daughter and a son."

"How old are they?"

"The daughter is twenty-four, and about to finish a post graduate medical degree at Cambridge."

"And the son?"

"Twenty-one. Also at Cambridge, studying law."

"When can I get to meet them all?"

"One step at a time. First off, Arkady Nemikov has asked to meet you in person. His private helicopter is waiting for you at Battersea heliport as we speak."

7

Lewis is directed into one of four luxurious leather armchairs. Each is able to swivel so as to allow unrestricted views out of the windows on either side of the helicopter. He sits down and buckles up as the engines begin their muted start up.

He has the sensation of having an out of body experience. The Sikorsky S-92 is most definitely a helicopter, but not as he remembers them. For a start, there is no crewman hustling him on board, shouting at him above the noise to strap in and keep his helmet on. The inside is strangely luxurious: there is carpet everywhere and the fittings are sleek and plush. Lewis can find no evidence that he might actually be dreaming. However, he finds it strange that he is not sitting in a bare metal cabin on hard seats with hooks on the floor and places on the walls to clip onto. There aren't thirty other soldiers in full battle gear all jostling to sit at the same time. No one is struggling with their equipment and fumbling to get earplugs inserted before the noise from the engines rises to levels that can cause permanent deafness. The hard deck is not littered with various items of equipment, both strapped and loose, preventing feet or legs from stretching. Most surprising of all is that once the rotors are cranked and the aircraft rises, this particular luxury helicopter is quiet. It feels surreal. Relatively speaking, there is hardly a sound: certainly no deafening vibration that rattles the body so intensely that every bone and sinew feels shaken and battered. On board the CH-47 Chinook, Lewis always expected the fillings in his teeth to shake loose. Today's experience is such a contrast to what flying in a military helicopter is all about. As the aircraft performs a banked turn away from the Battersea heliport, heading towards the Oxfordshire countryside to the north and west, Lewis feels a rush of exhilaration. It is as if he is flying for the very first time. Because of it, he stares in schoolboy-like fascination at the views from both windows.

As the London suburbs flash by beneath him in a blur, he is momentarily lost in thought. He has never heard of Arkady Nemikov. A short-term contract working for a Ukrainian oligarch could be an interesting and welcome project. It might certainly keep Jake Sullivan and now this new woman, Laura, off his back. Lewis reflects that he is in a good space with his life once more. A recent, brief, romance with his sister-in-law, Holly, did help him lay some old ghosts to rest. Now that that is over, the two of them just friends, Lewis feels ready for a new challenge.

The last five years have been strange. Once, not that long ago, Lewis had been a rising star in the Marines. A King's badge winner no less. Then, after his wife's death, Lewis found that he could blame no one but himself. He, a well-trained Marine, unable to save his young bride from drowning – in the sea of all places: why continue? So, after much wrangling, he decides not to. To the sadness of many, including his Commanding Officer at the time, Lewis simply hands back his hard-won Green Beret and goes walkabout. To distract himself, he skies each winter, occasionally providing the wealthy with private tuition to earn money. In the summers he relocates to the beaches of the Côte d'Azur. He keeps fit and stays out of trouble. All the while he is aware that he should be doing more with his life than just drift – but he can't yet work out what.

Time heals. Five years eventually provides him with answers: who he really is, what makes him tick, and what he wants to do with his life.

He knows that he's been well trained. He wouldn't be a past King's badge winner without above-average toughness, fitness, and tenacity. But time and space allow him to realise that he might be more than just an above-average ex-Marine. He might be good. Perhaps even very good.

In unarmed combat, he might even be exceptional.

Above all, he is a high achiever, excellent at getting things done – especially when it requires thinking outside the box: Lewis's *MO* usually being to break a problem down, step-by-step; and then creating solutions along the way where others often fail or give up. In the field, this makes him cunning and unpredictable. As in chess – a game at which he excels – this makes him a tough, if not ruthless, adversary.

His one weakness – it is almost an obsession – is fear of failure to deliver on his promises. This is what he has learnt the hard way. Six years ago, he gave his former father-in-law, dying of cancer, a promise: to protect his daughter, to keep her safe and out of harm. Then, weeks later, he fails to deliver: on his honeymoon, on that beach in Mawgan Porth in Cornwall. Ever since, he's been trying to comprehend why it had hurt so much. It has taken five years of going walkabout to get to the answer: to come to terms with the fact that it wasn't his fault, to stop blaming himself – that he hasn't failed. He gets this, now that he's a bit older and wiser. The realisation rejuvenates him: it puts him in the mood for making new promises to worthy causes that might come his way: exactly as he did with the Iranian journalist in Hanover Square a few months ago.

Lewis definitely misses the Military; several times in the last five years he has toyed with returning to active service. However, he enjoys too much being a sole operator: a man with no ties, no responsibilities, and no commitments. Assuming that he finds ways to get the best of both worlds – finding worthy-enough causes where his talents and skills can be put to good use whilst still operating on his own – then he will be in his element.

Indeed, a short-term contract working for a Ukrainian oligarch could most definitely be just the kind of opportunity that Lewis is looking for.

Surprisingly quickly, the engine noise changes. Lewis looks

33

out of the window and sees a large expanse of green parkland rising gently towards them: the two pilots are slowing the helicopter for a controlled landing. On this ride, there is no flaring to decelerate the aircraft such that the nose is raised and the rear ramp lowered to allow a quick ejection of the payload. On one memorable mission with US Special Forces in Iraq, Lewis had been inside one of two HMMWV 'Humvees' that had been squeezed so tightly inside the specially converted MH-47 Night Stalker that everyone had to remain inside the Hummers for the duration of the flight. When they had arrived at the drop zone, the driver of each vehicle had started their engines even before the aircraft had slowed to a halt, the Sikorsky's nose not even, at that stage, yet raised in preparation for landing. As the tailgate descended towards the ground, they had simply driven out the back. Today's landing is more sedate. The helicopter settles smoothly on to a perfectly mown circle of green grass, a short distance from a large Jacobean-style country house.

There is a welcoming committee of one, a large muscular man who introduces himself as Sergei Fedorov. He is of indeterminate age but in all probability about five years older than Lewis. Fedorov greets the new arrival with an iron-fisted handshake. He beckons silently for Lewis to follow. Despite being overweight, the man has a lightness of touch about the way he walks. It is a boxer's walk, the weight forward on the balls of the feet. The movement is fluid and without effort. This is someone who uses the skipping rope as part of his routine in the gym. Lewis is escorted in silence from the landing pad. They pass along a short path leading to a gravel drive, towards the front entrance of the main house itself.

Out of habit, Lewis keeps two paces behind Fedorov, on the man's right hand side. It is possibly a needless precaution. However, Lewis is in unfamiliar territory. Well over seventy per cent of people in the world are right-handed. Lewis knows that the odds are thus also stacked in favour of Fedorov also being a right-hander. The best place to position oneself when following such a person is behind them and to their right. That way, when they try and swing an unexpected punch to their rear they either have to swivel around on their heel clockwise and use their left hand; or else they swivel in the other direction through at least two-hundred and forty degrees before their punch can connect. Lewis is not expecting any trouble from Fedorov. However, when a seriously powerful Ukrainian oligarch sends his private helicopter to offer a job protecting his family, Lewis feels he needs to be prepared for any eventuality.

They are about forty metres in front of the main entrance to the house when Fedorov comes to an abrupt halt and swivels quickly around on his heel in the middle of the gravel drive. He spins to his left, through two hundred and forty degrees. The man has to be a right-hander. Lewis files this away for future reference. For the moment, Fedorov's hands are by his side. He is not about to swing any punches.

"Now we search, please."

Fedorov's accent is Slavic, the English words poorly pronounced. Lewis moves his legs apart and bends his knees, his weight distributed forward. He keeps his hands and arms hanging by his side, all the time staring expressionlessly into Fedorov's eyes. The man comes forward and pats Lewis down. Rough hands search around and under the shoulders, down the arms and lower legs. There is an odour of garlic and bad breath but no alcohol that Lewis can discern. It is a perfunctory search, not nearly as thorough as Lewis is expecting. The man then steps back and jerks his head for Lewis to continue to follow him. Lewis decides it is time to play an unexpected move.

"You missed something."

Fedorov looks momentarily confused. He scowls at Lewis, fixing him with a cold stare. Then, saying nothing, he simply shrugs his shoulders and turns to begin walking in the direction of the front door once again. Lewis counts to five, then follows.

Too bad: he won't be able to say later that he wasn't warned.

8

The rectangular-shaped drawing room is large, the space filled with numerous sofas and tables. Rich fabrics and curtains are much in evidence, as are copious books, neatly stacked in floor to ceiling bookcases on three sides. On prominent display, adorned with various silver photo frames, is a grand piano. A conservatory at one end floods the interior with sunlight. Ceiling-mounted security cameras, their tiny lenses hidden behind small, semi-circular, smoked glass covers are positioned at each corner of the room.

Fedorov indicates for Lewis to approach the only other person in the room, a man who is sitting alone at a square-shaped table close to a window. Fedorov then withdraws. As if only becoming aware of Lewis when he hears the door being closed, the other man looks up and springs to his feet energetically.

"You must be Ben Lewis," he says smiling, advancing with his hand extended in greeting. "Arkady Nemikov. I am delighted you were able to join me here this morning."

Strikingly, the Ukrainian is tall, slender and almost completely bald. The face is suntanned and clean-shaven, the handshake firm and confident. Lewis feels strength in the man's forearm. It suggests that he, like his security man, Fedorov, frequents the gym. The Ukrainian's dark-brown eyes never once leave Lewis's gaze.

"Not everyone offers their private helicopter to collect invited guests."

"The Sikorsky is probably a step up from what you might have been used to in the Military."

"Certainly in terms of luxury."

"I am hosting a small, private, shoot later today otherwise we could have met in London. I hope you'll forgive me dragging you all the way out here."

In the middle of the square table where Nemikov had been sitting is a large chessboard. Nemikov sees Lewis looking at the game he has in progress.

"You play, don't you?" the Ukrainian asks him.

"Not a great deal. At one time I used to be reasonably good."

"Perhaps even a junior champion? Or maybe that was just a false rumour?"

Lewis smiles. Nemikov has done his homework.

"Let's talk over a game." Nemikov indicates for Lewis to take a seat. He busies himself resetting the pieces to their starting positions.

"I was impressed when I heard what happened outside Westminster Cathedral."

Nemikov holds out two closed fists in front of Lewis to allow him to pick one: Lewis choses the empty hand. Nemikov swivels the chessboard around so that the black pieces are in front of Lewis.

"They were both amateur."

"It would have shocked the entire nation if they had succeeded – amateur or not." Nemikov is quick to make his first move. It is a classic opener: pawn to e4.

"Quite." Lewis plays a less conventional black pawn to c5.

Nemikov looks at Lewis and smiles.

"Do I sense a touch of Kasparov in your opening moves here, Ben?"

Lewis shrugs. "Bobby Fischer was also a fan of the Najdorf variation."

"Impressive. You do know your chess. A man after my own heart. Kasparov was the better player, though. Surely you have to concede that?"

"Even given that he is a Russian and not a Ukrainian?"

"Well, no one can be completely perfect, Ben, and Kasparov has spent the last ten years publically denouncing the ruling

Kremlin political elite at almost every opportunity. He has been particularly vocal about Russia's illegal annexation of the Crimea. I think of him as almost Ukrainian."

"Another man after your own heart?"

Nemikov smiles. "I think I'm going to like you, Ben Lewis."

He moves another pawn and Lewis quickly takes the white piece with one of his own.

"Kasparov did arguably play one of the best chess moves of all time, though, I will concede you that. Somewhere unpronounceable in the Netherlands in 1999 against the Bulgarian Topalov." Ben moves another piece as he talks.

"Ah, yes! The twenty-fourth move. Rook takes d4. A master class in forward thinking. I am actually inclined to agree with you, Ben. Shirov or Spassky might be close contenders for that second place. But for me Kasparov has the edge."

Lewis doesn't respond. They continue in silence for a few moves until Lewis makes a surprise play and captures Nemikov's rook with a bishop. "Check."

Nemikov exhales loudly.

"You are good. I never saw that coming."

Lewis looks up and smiles.

"Perhaps I may not have been as rusty as I had thought. Why don't we cut through the pleasantries and you tell me exactly why I am here and what you'd like me to do?"

9

With his elbows on the small table in front of him, Nemikov steeples his hands and places his chin on his thumbs. The ends of his fingers are resting beneath his nose, his eyes staring straight at Lewis's, deep in thought. He is on the verge of speaking when the main door to the room is flung wide open. In walks one of the most strikingly beautiful women that Lewis has ever seen.

"Ah, Valentyna," Nemikov says suddenly on his feet. "Perfect timing. Come and meet my guest. This is Ben Lewis, former British Royal Marine Commando and Saviour of the British people. This is the man who prevented a small Islamic State massacre in London yesterday."

Lewis gets to his feet and watches with genuine pleasure as Nemikov's wife walks across the room to greet him. Lewis can feel the warmth of her hazel-brown eyes on his. She has the most perfect skin. It is wrinkle-free: the bare minimum of make-up, not even lipstick. In her wake, long, blonde, slightly curly locks flow freely. She seems well aware of the effect she creates as she glides across the room. An expensive mid-tan cashmere dress hugs her body perfectly as she walks: she also has shoes to match, with heels that are elegant, but not impossibly high. Valentyna smiles at Lewis and extends a long thin hand. Lewis is smitten and it shows on his face.

"Valentyna has the same effect on all the men she meets, don't you, my darling?" He drapes an arm around her shoulder as she in turn shakes Lewis's hand. "Ben, meet my wife, Valentyna."

"It is a pleasure to meet you," he says.

"The pleasure is all mine, Ben. What brings you here? Are you going to come and work with us?"

She looks at her husband and her eyes dance with his

momentarily. He, in turn, raises an eyebrow and tilts his head to one side.

"Arkady, surely we could make use of someone with Ben's background?" she says, turning once more to smile at Lewis, winking at him in a conspiratorial manner. "I rather like the sound of having a former Marine looking after the family. It would certainly make a welcome change from Sergei Fedorov and some of the oafs he seems to employ."

"If you'd only let me have a few minutes with Ben here, we might perhaps get around to discussing some of that."

Valentyna smiles at him and then looks down at the chessboard.

"I am sorry about my husband, Ben. He's so wrapped up in winning at absolutely everything he does. He can't help himself from asking each and every houseguest to play chess with him. Are you good at chess, Ben?"

"Ben here is a former junior champion. He's giving me a run for my money and we've barely just begun."

"Good. Well, that serves you right, Darling. Ben, I am about to head to Venice for a few days. If, by the time I am back, you have been persuaded to come and work with us, perhaps you might find some time to teach me chess? Arkady is too impatient with my lack of progress. Everyone else in the family seems to play apart from me."

"I'd be happy to."

"Perfect. Now, Arkady, I am off to Luton Airport to take the private jet to Venice. Can I have the Sikorsky fly me there? I do so hate travelling on the M25 motorway with all that ghastly traffic."

"Sure. Ben and I will be at least another hour or so before he needs to head back to London. Who's accompanying you on the trip? Is it Sergei?"

"No, it's Gregor. I don't care for him much, as you know. I find him rather creepy, to tell the truth. I'd much rather have someone like Ben here." She smiles at Lewis and once more

41

winks at him.

Nemikov laughs. "One step at a time, Valentyna. Take Gregor, go in the helicopter and enjoy Venice. I am sorry I won't be joining you." They kiss warmly and then Valentyna turns toward Lewis.

"Until next time, Ben. I hope my husband manages to persuade you to work with us. I would enjoy very much spending some time with you on my return."

With that, she turns and glides gracefully out of the room.

10

It had been a joint operation between MI5 and the Metropolitan Police's Counter Terrorism Command. Laura, the MI5 section head whose team was responsible for covert intelligence gathering, usually disliked joint operations. They had the propensity to be complex and were often impeded by ego, if not testosterone. Working with SO15, however, was different. Officers attached to this specialist police unit were part of a very small elite. They were all highly trained professionals, most of whom regularly went on joint exercises with the Special Forces. On standby twenty-four hours a day, seven days a week, their role was to deal with all manner of terrorism threats. They were all skilled in the use of weapons and ordinances.

Following the arrest of both Ashraf and Khan, Laura's agent handlers had been tasked with probing their networks. The question they urgently sought answers to was simple: had the thwarted beheading outside Westminster Cathedral been a one off? Or was it part of an orchestrated campaign of increased violence and terror being implemented across the UK – and London in particular?

It had been an MI5 deep cover asset who went by the code name 'Alpha' who had supplied the raw intelligence leading up to that evening's operation.

Over many months, Alpha, a Karachi-born Pakistani by birth, had been infiltrating a London-based cell: this comprised three fellow Pakistani men, originally from Lahore and now living in North London. Alpha had met one of them whilst working as a casual labourer on a building site in Wembley. All three had been single; all had seemed to share common interests. Relatively quickly, Alpha had started socialising with them after work and at weekends. In time, he was joining them at their prayer meetings at a North London mosque. Finally becoming accepted, it had been at that stage that he'd been introduced to the leader of their cell, Fouad Bitar. Fouad immediately took to Alpha, in no time suggesting how beneficial it might be if Alpha and one or two of the others joined him on an education visit back to northern Pakistan. Appearing to be easily persuaded, he had accepted. Independently, he had therefore travelled via Qatar and Karachi to Islamabad. On arrival at the capital, a jeep had been waiting to transfer him to a training camp not far from Peshawar in the north-west corner of the country.

Making contact with deep cover assets usually took time and patience. Each MI5 handler used a pre-agreed contact mechanism if a crash meeting was being requested. Alpha's handler was a thirty-two year old MI5 officer called Jonathan. Jonathan had posted an innocent-looking tweet on Twitter. It was his request to Alpha for such a meeting: the timing of the post, at nine thirty-three that first morning after the Westminster Cathedral incident, was significant: every proposed meet was always exactly six hours after when it was posted. If Alpha 'favourited' Jonathan's tweet, it meant that the meeting was on. To Jonathan's surprise, Alpha had confirmed the meeting almost immediately. They already had their pre-agreed meeting place: it was a betting shop on the Kilburn High Road.

By three-thirty that same afternoon when Alpha had casually walked into the shop, Jonathan had been in position for almost thirty minutes. He had been busy, giving the appearance of someone watching the afternoon race meeting from York on the widescreen television. On the small counter in front of him had been three crumpled betting slips, evidence that his chosen horses thus far had failed to be winners.

Alpha had studied the form for the next race at York, before placing a modest each-way bet on a particular horse, Orchid

Bloom. He had then wandered over to the small counter that Jonathan had been standing next to, so as to watch the race on the television screen. Both had watched in silence as the three-thirty race drew to its close. Once all the horses had crossed the finish line, Jonathan had scrunched his betting slip into a ball before throwing it in disgust onto the counter, next to all of his others.

"No luck?" Alpha had asked innocently.

"Nothing so far," was all Jonathan had said. "Unless you've got an inside tip or two to share?" he had added as an afterthought.

Alpha had not replied at first. Like Jonathan, he'd been checking who else was in the shop. A variety of men and women of mixed ages and race had been coming and going: several Asian men; a few elderly white males who had looked like permanent fixtures. There had been no one who had seemed particularly interested in the two of them.

"What's up?" Alpha had eventually asked, still staring at the television screen showing the horses and jockeys for the next race being saddled up.

"The beheading that nearly happened yesterday. You must have heard about it."

"Everyone has. There's been talk of nothing else."

"Was it a one off or the start of something more orchestrated, that's what we'd like to know?" Jonathan had whispered.

Alpha had listened to this impassively, staring at the screen as his horse for the next race, Orchid Bloom, was shown being escorted out of the saddling enclosure. Only once the horse had begun its slow walk up to the starting gate had he spoken.

"There's something about to happen. I'm not exactly sure what and I'm not sure when, but it feels big. There's some funny stuff happening that I'm not privy to. The buzz, amongst the other three, is that it's going to be a co-ordinated attack, aimed at London commuters. They keep talking as if hundreds are going to die."

"Timescales, realistically?"

"They've already made a video. They intend to post it any time now, to begin their campaign of terror."

"What's your role?"

"To be a martyr, of course. Today, tomorrow, whenever."

"Can you give me any names: of the high-ups, the people pulling the strings? We need something to work on."

Alpha had looked around again before replying. Still no one appeared to be taking any notice.

"There are two of them. You need to be watching both. One's called Fouad Bitar and the other is his supposed cousin, Hakim. Both are in their late twenties. Fouad lives not far from here: in Kensal Rise, on Mount Pleasant Road. He's the one who arranged for me to go to Pakistan recently."

"We know about him. Who's Hakim?"

"I'm not sure. I've never met him. He's apparently connected to the upper echelons, or at least that's what they all say. I don't know where he's based. He's never around much, or that's what whispered. I think he's the one who's ultimately been planning whatever it is."

The horses for the next race were at the starting gates. As the tape had risen and the race had gotten underway, Alpha had looked directly at Jonathan.

"You need to act fast if you're going to stop them. Since the failed beheading yesterday, the heat's definitely been turned up. The timeframe is being compressed, I am sure of it." He had looked at his watch. "I ought to go."

He had left his betting slip on the counter and walked back out into the street without looking back. Jonathan had remained, thinking about what he had heard, staring blankly at the screen as, a few minutes later, Orchid Bloom had romped home in first place by several lengths.

Back at Thames House later that same afternoon, they had begun planning the operation. Officers from SO15 and a man simply described as 'an operational expert from Hereford' had squashed into a secure basement meeting room with the doors locked. It was to be a police-led, MI5 supported, operation and not the other way around. One of their first tasks had been to navigate their way through the legal minefield that governed - and indeed restricted – police powers of search and arrest, as defined by the Protection of Freedoms Act. Since two separate properties in different locations were to be raided, a magistrate local to each had to be consulted before the relevant search warrants could be obtained.

The operation had been timed to begin at four-fifteen the following morning, with both properties being raided simultaneously. The first was a flat above a shop front on Buckley Road in Kilburn, where Alpha and his three Pakistani 'friends' were based; and the other, a two-up, two-down, terraced house on Mount Pleasant Road near to Kensal Rise, where Fouad Bitar was meant to be living. At that time, they had no data on Hakim's whereabouts.

At the appointed hour, a four-man assault team, each wearing night vision glasses, had used a ram to break open the front door at the Buckley Road property. A sniper from the Met's CO19 specialist firearm unit on the rooftop of a nearby building had been keeping watch in case of any unforeseen difficulties. The raiders, climbing the stairs to the first floor, had found Alpha, and two other Pakistani men, asleep on mattresses strewn about a first floor bedroom. There was a fourth mattress on the floor, but it had been empty and had not been slept in. Dazed, confused and disoriented, all three had been arrested, handcuffed and swiftly led away to a police van waiting outside. A short time later, forensic officers with sniffer dogs had uncovered the explosives: a stash of RDX in the form of rectangular blocks of C-4 plastic. They had been cleverly disguised: split into pairs, each had been stuffed inside a hessian bag, the bag topped up with sand and made to look like ordinary sandbags. Along with various detonators and timers, it had been sufficient plastic, as one officer had later commented, to start a small war.

Over at Kensal Rise, all did not go smoothly. At four-fifteen in the morning, Fouad had not been asleep. In fact, he had been fully awake, in the process of taking a Skype call with his cousin Hakim, at that moment back in Jordan. On hearing the sound of the front door being rammed off its hinges, Fouad had tried to escape from an upper second floor window. Unfortunately for him, he had lost his footing in the dark and slipped. He had fallen two stories to the ground and broken his neck. There had been no one else in the house at the time. When they discovered Fouad's open and unlocked laptop computer, they soon found the video that Alpha had alluded to earlier. It had shown Fouad, dressed in black with an IS flag behind him, vowing to wage a war of terror on London to assuage for British crimes against Islam. It had promised a bombing campaign against the capital's transport system, intended to drive terror into the heart of every man, woman and child living, or visiting, the city.

If they had been able to keep the content of the video out of the public eye, events might have turned out differently. Sadly for them, Hakim had a duplicate copy. He also intended to broadcast it. As soon as he sensed that cousin Fouad's UK house was being raided, he ended the Skype call. There and then he had decided to post the video online himself. Using an untraceable webserver based in Bahrain, that same morning the video had gone viral. Within hours, although most Western social media channels quickly blocked access to it, its message had been disseminated far and wide.

London was officially a high-risk IS terror target.

London's transport system in particular was under threat.

11

"Is that you, honey?" Hattie Zeltinger yelled down from the top of the house upon hearing the front door slam downstairs.

Saul Zeltinger removed his wet overcoat. He shook it a little before hanging it on one of the hooks in the hallway.

"Only me, Hats."

He looked at the small pile of post that had been left for him on a silver tray and flicked through them. Most were bills and junk, although two folded scraps of A4 paper caught his eye. They were drawings produced by his six-year old twins. One depicted a stick-like person with a large truncheon in his hand attacking someone else. The words, 'Got you punk,' were written inside a speech balloon coming from the truncheon holder's mouth. He looked up as Hattie came bounding down the stairs to greet him. They kissed briefly, she smiling radiantly when she saw that Saul had found the drawings.

"Aren't they great? The one you're holding is from Zach. The man you're beating up is, Zach informs me, 'the master criminal'."

She giggled as she said it and Saul looked up at her. She was as pretty as the day they had first met: flowing blonde hair, sparkly bright blue eyes and a wonderful smile that was rarely turned off.

"Where does he learn words like 'punk' from?" Saul asked.

"Darling, it's the school playground. Don't tell me you didn't say those sorts of thing at the same age? Anyway, look at Nate's."

Zeltinger opened the second picture and laughed. It was much more detailed than the other, with various squiggly lines in all directions. In the middle was someone with what looked like a gun in his hand, the word 'superhero' written on his chest.

"I think I ought to explain," Hattie said, still laughing. "You, the world famous super hero, are in amongst all the baddies here," she pointed to several people who appeared to be lying on the ground. "They are all dead and all this other stuff," she pointed at the wiggly lines everywhere, "is, and I quote, 'gun smoke, Mummy. I mean obviously'!"

"They're terrific. You're terrific too, Hats. I'm sorry about last night. The world started going crazy. People trying to kill one another left, right and centre."

"Not you I hope?" Hattie followed him into the kitchen at the back of the house. It was a family room, with toys and books stacked away neatly on various shelves.

He turned to look at her.

"Not me, thankfully."

They held each other close for a moment. He then seemed to remember something and broke away.

"I can't stop, however tempting. I hardly slept a wink last night. I could so easily fall into bed right this minute."

"Now that's sounds like right up my street," Hattie said, starting to undo his tie.

"It's eleven in the morning, the boys are at school and I was only about to do yet more washing. Distract me, my Detective Inspector.

"Hatts, I'd love to, I really would, but I have to get back to the office. I'm only supposed to be here to grab a quick shower, shave and change of clothing before heading back to the mayhem."

"Are you sure I can't tempt you?" she said, rubbing her body against his. 'You do look very poorly. You should call in sick."

"I mustn't," he said ruefully.

"So, no time for a quick coffee before you go?" she asked him.

"Well now," he said smiling, "is the rabbi Jewish?" and with that, headed off to take his shower.

"How's school?" Zeltinger asked. He was freshly shaved and laundered and sitting at the kitchen table nursing a mug of coffee.

"Fine. Nate got into a fight yesterday. Apparently it was nothing serious and his teacher told me that it was all brought under control quickly. Zach has decided he wants to be a footballer when he grows up. Apart from that, nothing much has changed."

"How about you?" he said, taking a sip of his coffee.

"Oh, I'm fine," she said, fiddling with one of the large buttons on the front of her cardigan. "Just a bit bored, if I'm honest. I have been thinking about going back to my old teaching job. They'll have me back part-time, I've asked. That could work, couldn't it, Darling?"

Zeltinger was very conservative, quite the traditionalist, especially ever since Hattie had given birth to twins. But he knew that Hattie had loved being a nursery school teacher and that she missed her working life considerably.

"If that's what you want, Darling. Let's discuss this later, if that's okay? I'm exhausted and I don't want to say the wrong thing." He leaned over and kissed her cheek. "I've asked Ben Lewis round for a game of chess tomorrow evening, by the way. I said he could join us for supper, if that's all right?"

"Isn't he the one who took you on that wild goose chase to Switzerland recently?"

"That's him. He also, and I probably oughtn't be telling you this, was the person who single-handedly foiled the attempted beheading outside Westminster Cathedral yesterday. I actually quite like him. He's meant to be a pretty good chess player."

"Is he good looking?"

"He's a former Marine. You know, all muscles and withering looks."

"I shall very much look forward to meeting him, then! I

might get my hair done especially."

Zeltinger knew she was teasing him and pretended not to be taken in. Looking at his watch, he finished his coffee in one gulp.

"I must go. I'll try my hardest to be home early. Give my love to the boys. Please thank them for the paintings."

12

"When you make a lot of money, you find that, along the way, you also tend to make a lot of enemies."

"I can believe that." Lewis studies the chessboard for a few seconds before taking Nemikov's white knight with his bishop. "What about friends?"

"Rich people rarely have true friends, Ben. Most so-called friends are scroungers and bottom feeders, tagging along for the ride to feed off any scraps that fall."

"Who or what exactly are you most fearful of at the present time?"

Nemikov once more steeples his fingers together under his nose and contemplates the chess game.

"Well, for one thing, I fear I am about to lose this game to you, Ben."

He moves his queen to b3. It is a defensive move, designed to protect his one remaining knight. It is a weak play and both he and Lewis know it.

"Actually it is the Russians who have the most to gain by my death and financial demise. They view me as a Ukrainian interloper, someone who has deprived them of what they see as their God-given right to earn a decent living from their fellow Russians. I am a thief and a renegade, someone who in their eyes needs to be punished."

"Anyone in particular?" Lewis moves his own queen diagonally across the board and positions it adjacent to a white bishop.

"There is one individual in particular who'd like to see me get my come-uppance, as you English like to say. He used to be my business partner. A certain Muscovite named Viktor Plushenko. Viktor would love nothing more than to see my life in tatters, if not ended rapidly. Probably both, knowing him."

"Is the feeling mutual?" Lewis asks.

"That's a smart question," Nemikov answers, moving his queen two squares to his left so as to put him in an attacking position on Lewis's rook in the corner. Nemikov sighs, looking at Lewis as if wondering how much to tell him.

"Viktor and I have done some crazy things together in our time, both as business partners and more recently as adversaries. Sure, there are times when we may have both wished each other dead. Perhaps more than wished. Nowadays I prefer to outsmart him. I enjoy seeing the pain in his eyes when I am doing better than him. That gives me more pleasure than would staring at his lifeless body in a coffin."

"What makes you think you are more at risk right now? What's happened to inflame the situation?"

"Sanctions have happened, Ben. There are some seriously pissed off people in Russia currently. A small number have had access to their money, their freedom of movement, their ability to make money, all severely curtailed. From the Russian President downwards, there is anger brewing. They see this crazy Ukrainian doing deals here and there, winning contracts they would like to have had. I was awarded a big gas pipeline concession recently. It is going to make me lots and lots of money. Viktor was unable to participate and that will have made him really angry. The Russian bear has woken and is in a severe mood. Suddenly I am the Bad Boy that it sees in its sights."

Lewis studies the chess pieces in quiet contemplation. He peers up at Nemikov, a half smile on his lips.

"My apologies," is all he says before moving his bishop to d2. "Checkmate."

Nemikov stares at the board for a few seconds. He then shakes his head, smiles, and reaches across the table to shake Lewis's hand.

"You beat me fair and square, Ben. You're good."

"Sometimes by losing one battle you learn a new way to win the war."

Nemikov stands up and walks over to the window.

"That is very profound, Ben."

The Sikorsky rotors are turning, the two pilots in the cockpit preparing for the short trip to Luton airfield. He turns and looks Lewis directly in the eyes.

"Come and work with me, Ben. I would love you on my team, helping to protect my family and me. I can make you a wealthy man."

"What about Fedorov? How is he going to react to having a British interloper appear on the scene?"

"Sergei? He's been with me for years. He'll do as he's told and accept it. What did you make of him, by the way?"

He continues fixing Lewis with a stare that, even across the room, is penetrating.

Lewis hesitates before replying. Then he too stands up and walks across the room towards Nemikov. Reaching behind his back, beneath his jacket and shirt, he moves his hand into the small recess at the base of his spine. Moments later, he withdraws a small knife with a retractable blade that he places in the palm of his hand.

"Fedorov looks and acts the part. However, as a security guard he needs to be a lot more thorough. He searched me earlier and missed this. If I'd wanted to, by now you would be dead and I would be long gone."

Lewis puts the knife back in his rear waistband and adjusts the belt on his trousers.

Nemikov closes his eyes and shakes his head from side to side, pinching the bridge of his nose with his fingers as he takes this in.

"I shall have to speak to Sergei," he says eventually.

"You should let me do it. If you speak to him, then my relationship with him is forever going to be toast."

"Perhaps. Let me think about that. Meanwhile, come with

me. I want to show you something." He leads the way out of the room but this time heading towards a small door set to one side.

The fish is nibbling the bait. All that remains is for Nemikov to reel it in.

Nemikov's study is spacious, light and has views that draw the eye on a journey: down through rolling green lawns bordered by chestnut trees, and across to a private lake in the middle distance.

"This is my special place. No one comes here but me. Now," he waves his hand towards the lake, "you can perhaps understand why I love it here so much." They are sitting at chairs around a big round table made of solid oak. Nemikov has a photograph album on the table next to him.

"I'd like to take some time to introduce my family to you, Ben." He opens the album and starts to turn the pages. "Firstly, my wife, Valentyna, whom you have just met. She is the only woman I have ever married and I love her dearly. She is an independent lady. By training she is, just as our daughter Olena soon hopes to be, a qualified doctor. We lead separate but connected lives. Our principal points of connection other than our children are our house here; our main residence in London; the yacht that we keep fuelled and ready to sail at a moment's notice in the Mediterranean; and several other properties mainly across Europe, that we visit from time to time. People have tried, and continue to try, to get to me through her; sometimes through coercion and sometime via the bedroom, if we can speak frankly?"

Lewis nods but says nothing, unsure where this is all heading.

"Valentyna is a beautiful woman. You have seen the charm she possesses. No one can be a saint all the time. Despite the occasional affair that I know she has had, I trust her with my life and respect her independence."

"That sounds a challenge, from a security point of view."

"Perhaps, but she always has one of Sergei's team with her the whole time. As much as possible, that is. Being a Nemikov is a risky business, which is why I have taken certain precautions that I'd like to share with you in a moment."

He turns the pages in the album and stops a short while later.

"Now, this is my daughter, Olena. You can see, she looks a lot like her mother."

Lewis stares at the photographs and marvels at the similarity between Valentyna and her daughter. He can feel Nemikov look at him.

"Beautiful, isn't she?"

"Very. You are a lucky father. How old?"

"Twenty-five next March. You and she could make a perfect couple."

Lewis chooses to ignore the comment.

"Where is she training to be a doctor?" Lewis knows the answer to this from his earlier briefing with Jake Sullivan but wants to hear it from Nemikov himself.

"Cambridge. She's due to qualify next summer."

"Boyfriends?"

"None that I know of."

"You mentioned that you had a son as well. What's he doing and where?"

Nemikov turns another page of the album and photos of a younger version of himself but with long scraggy black hair stares back at them.

"Borys is also at Cambridge, in his final year as an undergraduate Law student at Christ's College."

"Girlfriends?"

"Nothing serious."

"Do they get on, as brother and sister?"

"For the moment, yes. They share a large duplex apartment right in the very centre of the city. Sergei has a member of his team who lives with them permanently."

"Close protection work with students is exceptionally hard. The whole university environment poses massive security risks." Lewis leafs through the pages committing their faces to memory. After a while, he closes the album and looks at Nemikov. "So, what about yourself? What do you do and where do you go to do it?"

"Me? I am constantly on the move and very difficult to pin down. I have the Sikorsky, a private jet, various cars and drivers at my exclusive disposal dotted around the world. My usual office is located at our Kensington house. I have a very efficient secretary who runs both my diary and plans my trips with meticulous care. Normally I have Sergei as my personal protection, but that can, and does, change from time to time."

"So what job would you like me to do that isn't already being covered by your own team?"

"Olena and Borys are my Achilles heel, Ben. I may at times be a cold and ruthless bastard. However, if anything were to happen to either of them, I would cave in the moment I was put under pressure. I'd do anything to protect them, including paying money: even offering my own life in exchange for theirs."

"The current arrangements aren't good enough, is that it?"

"However much I try to protect my family, the current arrangements can never be fool-proof. It's for that reason that I've recently put certain procedures in place that I hope will help. No one other than Valentyna, Olena, Borys and my Swiss lawyer, Rudi, know anything about any of this. Not even Fedorov. I am taking a risk telling you. If I am to earn your trust, though, and ask you to help in protecting my family, I owe it to you to tell you what I've done and why."

He pauses, his fingers once more steepled under his nose whilst he composes his thoughts.

"Let's talk about money for a moment. I never know the precise amounts and in any event, it hardly matters.

Conservatively, having paid off all outstanding debts, I probably have amassed perhaps over fifteen billion US Dollars worth of assets to my name, give or take some. A lot of this is tied up in property and shares of various companies that I have invested in. Stripping all that out, there is perhaps well over eight and a half billion dollars in both cash and near cash assets scattered amongst various banks and investment institutions around the world."

If Lewis looks surprised, he keeps it well hidden.

"I employ a small, close-knit team in a tiny private bank based in Zurich to look after my private office. They manage this portfolio of cash and liquid investments and help me move money around the world as, and when, required. The lead banker there is a lawyer called Rudi Hildebrandt. Hildebrandt is one hundred per cent discreet and one hundred per cent reliable. I trust him with my money and thus, by default, I entrust him with my life."

He pauses to see if Lewis has any questions, then carries on.

"A couple of weeks ago, just after I had officially been awarded the contract to build the new gas pipeline that Plushenko so coveted, it began to dawn on me that I needed to do something to protect my wife and family from certain jealous and aggrieved parties. Together with Rudi Hildebrandt, we concocted a scheme of arrangement: if I was to die or disappear, assumed kidnapped or otherwise coerced, then all my assets would immediately be frozen. The only people able to allow this freezing order to be unblocked would be the combined agreement of my wife, Olena and Borys. All three have each been given a unique code that they have committed to memory. They have also sworn that they will, under no circumstances, reveal their code to anyone, especially not to each other. The arrangement requires that Hildebrandt has to be given each of the three codes before he is able to release any of the Nemikov assets from the freezing order."

"Your logic being," Lewis says, beginning to understand the reasons behind the complexity, "that by giving your wife and children these codes, it should guarantee their lives in the event of you being killed or captured."

"Correct."

"Is that really a possibility?"

Nemikov stares at Lewis and decides to say something more.

"I think it is more than a possibility. You see, Ben, I am currently negotiating a game-changing deal with the new cash-starved government in Ukraine. The proposal is that I provide them with several billions of dollars of much-needed cash. In return, they grant me exclusive rights to various Ukrainian oil and mineral concessions. If this deal goes ahead, it will completely alter the balance of power that Russia believes it currently has over the Ukrainian people. I know this because my spies tell me that word has already started to filter back to Moscow. They are, perhaps understandably, becoming extremely anxious. You asked me about the possibility that Moscow will try and kill me? I don't think it is a possibility any more. I think it is almost a certainty."

13

Rafiq Virenque had led a troubled life from an early age. His father had been an Algerian who had had a casual affair with the woman who became his mother, Nadine. The Algerian had fled back home to North Africa as soon as he learned that Nadine had become pregnant. Virenque and he had, therefore, never met. Nadine had raised her son as best she could as a single parent struggling to make ends meet. They lived in Marseilles in a small apartment in a rough neighbourhood. The majority of residents had been either North African or, like Virenque, of mixed race. Whilst his mother had worked in a local supermarket, young Virenque, at the age of eight, had been doing his best to skip school. Rather than attend class, he had instead joined the street gangs that had roamed the streets, in particular picking the pockets of unsuspecting tourists. In his teens, he had dropped out of school altogether, becoming ensnared by drugs: initially as a user; and latterly as a small time crack dealer.

The day he had grown up and realised that he had been wasting his life was the day his mother had been killed by a drunk driver in a hit and run incident. Suddenly he had been on his own in a very dangerous and scary world. It had been a wake-up call. He had resolved there and then that he would try and do something positive with his life that would have made his mother proud. Absent any academic qualifications and otherwise at a loss to know what this might be, he had decided to enrol with the French Foreign Legion. It was a decision from which he never looked back.

Nearly a quarter of those who enlist in the Foreign Legion are French citizens; the rest come from all walks of life in whatever countries of the world they happened to be born in. People join for different reasons: for many it is to ground them in something useful that pays them a modest wage over a pre-determined period of time. For Virenque, part French, part Algerian, the discipline and camaraderie of army life had suited him perfectly. During the initial five-year term that all recruits had to sign up for, he had served in numerous countries across Africa and the Middle East. The legionnaire officers in charge of his unit had earmarked him as a possible candidate for commando selection.

The French Army's talent spotters aren't the only people trawling the volunteer soldiers in the Legion, scouting for talent. It is a little known fact that the Russian Special Forces, often referred to as Spetsnaz, also recruit selected individuals from outside Russia to undergo their intensive training programme. Typically needing people with a fluency in at least two out of the three languages of English, Arabic and French – and thus able to operate across a wide spectrum of Middle Eastern countries – Virenque had been a logical person to come to the attention of Spetsnaz talent spotters. When they had put him through selection and he had passed the gruelling assessment with relative ease, they realised that they had made a good choice. What they hadn't fully appreciated until a few years later was how ruthless Rafiq could be at killing people. Which was why, after only four years involved in various covert operations all over the world, he had very quietly been tapped on the shoulder. The KGB's Spetsbureau 13 – the highly secretive unit that specialised in 'wet work' – wanted him to come and work for them.

Since then, Oleg Panich had, on at least three occasions, worked with Virenque whilst the latter had been on attachment to Spetsbureau 13. Each time, Panich had found him to be independent minded, reliable, and thorough. Never once had he questioned the mission brief that Panich had given him. Which was why, before Panich had left Volkov's dacha, he had asked his former boss one small favour: find Virenque and get him released from his other duties. Panich needed him working on the Nemikov assignment. Having someone of Arab extraction on the team would give further credence to the subterfuge that Islamic State, and not Russia, might be pulling the strings.

There was one other person Panich wanted on his team: a man who knew Panich's way of working and in whom he had complete trust; a safe pair of hands able to assist with surveillance and mission logistics. Alexei Polunin. A fellow patriot who, like himself, had recently found himself out of the service, pensioned off with injuries sustained in the field by none other than Ben Lewis. Someone who, like Panich, would relish the opportunity for some retribution, regardless of what Volkov may have advised.

14

Olena is flirtatious, charming, and every bit as beautiful as her mother. From the moment she skips down the maisonette staircase to see the man that her father has sent to look after her, Lewis senses a potential for matters to become complicated.

"Ben Lewis," he says offering her his hand. She looks momentarily surprised by Lewis's formality.

"Nice to meet you, Ben," she says, finally shaking his hand. "My father speaks very highly of you. I'm not sure what you did to make that happen so quickly. It normally takes much longer."

She has long flowing blonde hair, just like her mother. It is slightly curly and gleams in the beam of a small LED downlighter immediately above her head.

"I managed to beat him at chess."

"Wow, that's a first. Have you met my brother, Borys, yet?"

Lewis shakes his head.

"Not yet. He's still at lectures. Are you all set to go?"

Lewis has agreed to escort Olena down to London. She is on her way to a charity event later that evening with her father.

"I will be shortly. I assume we are going by train?"

"I did ask to borrow the Sikorsky but your father wouldn't hear of it."

She looks at him to check whether he is being serious. When she senses that he is joking, she laughs.

"Dad says that you are a former Marine. I guess that qualifies you for the yacht but not the helicopter."

This time Lewis smiles but says nothing.

"Give me five minutes, okay?"

They take a taxi to the station and find themselves in good

time for the fast train to London. Olena buys them both a ticket and surprises Lewis by paying to travel second class. Once through the barrier, she strides out towards the platform to the southern end of the station where the fast train is waiting and is shortly to depart. Lewis walks briskly to catch her up, considering how alike Olena and her mother appear to be. The station is busy. It isn't yet the end of the school day but children are nonetheless milling around the platform. Olena climbs aboard the rear carriage of the train and finds a seat and sits down. She chooses a rear-facing seat in the middle of the carriage. It is in an area designed for four people: two facing forward and two backwards. There is a thin, narrow, apology of a table that juts out from the side in between the two window seats. Lewis opts to stand rather than sit, positioning himself by the door-well. This is a good position to watch people getting on and off the train as well as being still able to maintain occasional eye contact with Olena. For one brief moment he looks at her, catching her eye and winking. She smiles back before burrowing within the depths of a small bag in search of a book to read.

The train's public address system chimes and the driver's voice comes over the intercom. There is a problem with the train: one of the doors has become jammed. An engineer has been called but, for the moment, the fast train to London is going nowhere. The driver recommends that passengers take the slower, stopping, service to London leaving from the adjacent platform. It will add thirty minutes to their journey but Olena will still be in plenty of time for her evening appointment. A short time later, therefore, she finds herself sitting in exactly the same seat as she had on the previous train. Once again Lewis is content to remain standing on his own by the door.

15

The *vaporetto* inched its way into Venice's Grand Canal, jostling for space with numerous water taxis and gondolas cutting in and out of its path. This particular Number 2 water bus was on a clockwise journey. It was fighting its way from in front of St. Mark's Square into the mouth of the canal, close by the Gritti Palace hotel. From here it would head northwards in a gentle meander to Accademia and beyond to the Rialto Bridge. Batches of red and white, as well as blue and white, striped poles lay interspersed along the canal route, adding colour to an already picturesque scene of ancient buildings that were rapidly being bathed by the pink and crimson hues of the setting sun.

Valentyna Nemikov had chosen to take the *vaporetto* precisely because it was such a public and anonymous form of transport. Ordinarily she would have used the private launch from her husband's mega-yacht moored at the quayside beyond Arsenale to the east of the city. Unfortunately, that would have meant that Gregor, her tiresome security chaperone, would have had to be in on her secret tryst. That would never have done. Instead she had contrived to give Gregor the slip, purporting to have to respond to an urgent call of nature. As they had passed the Hotel Danieli, she had dashed inside leaving a surprised Gregor waiting for her in the foyer. She, in turn, had promptly slipped out of the side entrance and made her way back to the *vaporetto* pier at nearby San Zaccaria. Waiting inside the shelter was her current paramour, private tennis coach to the rich and famous, André Diday. On the *vaporetto*, the two of them had found vacant adjacent seats towards the front of the boat. With one arm draped casually around her shoulders as she had nestled close to him, they became like many others, two lovers enjoying a sunset boat trip together on the Venetian waterways. Diday had rented a private apartment overlooking the Grand Canal. It was situated beyond Rialto and it had been to there that they had both been heading.

At Accademia, as with most stops along the route, a rush of people had clambered ashore as soon as the rope moorings with the floating pier had been secured. Then, with a flick of the wrist from the boatman, a second onslaught of different people fought their way back onto the ferry. Everybody jostled for space on the crowded decks before a resigned calm descended as the ferry began its onward journey.

Immediately in front of the boatman's wheelhouse, in the centre of the boat, was a small space reserved for large items of luggage, pushchairs and the occasional wheelchair. One of the passengers who had come aboard at Accademia had been pushing a black suitcase on wheels. The owner had been a man of medium height, wearing mirrored sunglasses and black leather gloves. No one had paid either him or his suitcase any special attention: tourists and their luggage were a common sight on the *vaporetto*. Many who departed Venice by train used the cheap ferries to make their way to Ferrovia at the north end of the island where the main railway terminus was situated. In any event, it had been approaching the hour for an *aperitivo*. People's minds had begun to drift, decisions shortly to be made about where and what to eat that evening.

The ferry had slid to a gentle halt at San Tomà, the stop just before Rialto. On the crowded deck there had been more jostling as departing passengers had fought to get off the ferry, pushing their way past others who were continuing towards Rialto and beyond. No one had taken much, if any, notice of who had disembarked the boat: even less so whether the man with the mirrored sunglasses and gloves, who had been part of the departing crowd, had with him his rolling black suitcase or not.

Which had, in hindsight, been a missed opportunity.

16

Virenque had not been happy. Everything about the plan had reeked of risk and complication. If this had been a Spetsbureau 13 operation, it would have been much simpler. It would also have been better planned. Nothing would have been left to chance. Most importantly, there would have been only one person calling the shots: himself. When Virenque set out to kill someone it was quite simple: they ended up dead. No one else got in the way: there wasn't collateral damage; and unexpected things didn't make it necessary to implement a plan B. A good example had been the previous night. He had received an urgent call from Yasenevo: they had wanted a young Pakistani male eliminated – a night worker on London's underground rail network. For some reason it had been deemed urgent. Virenque had been in sole control from start to finish, exactly the way he liked it. Three hours into the man's night shift, he had suffered a fatal accident. The crushed body had later been recovered from underneath the wheels of a maintenance train. It had been deemed an unfortunate, workplace accident; no foul play had been suspected.

Today's operation had originally been Panich's idea. There had been far too many moving parts for Virenque's liking; too many unknowns; too many things that could go wrong; too many people – and thus potential witnesses – who were going to find themselves part of the mayhem that was being planned. To cap it all, Panich hadn't been around to help. He'd had to disappear abroad at short notice, leaving Virenque with Panich's former field agent, Alexei Polunin, to carry out the operation.

In order for the smokescreen part of the operation to work, Panich had required Lewis and the girl both to take the slow London train together. This alone, in Virenque's view, had been an unnecessary, complication. Then Polunin had had the idea to immobilise the fast train. The Russian had done his research: there was usually a slow train departing shortly after a fast one. Thankfully, it had all come together pretty much the way that they had hoped it might. Virenque had been in the ticket hall watching for the arrival of Lewis and the girl. Polunin had been standing at the far end of the station platform alongside the waiting fast train to London. As soon as Lewis and the girl arrived at the station, Virenque had called Polunin on his mobile. The former SVR agent had then stepped onto the second carriage from the front of the train. It had been relatively easy to slip the small, tapered, device into the slender gap between the open train door and the outer body of the train. Once in position, the doors on the train were going to remain jammed in the open position for some time to come. Sure enough, when the driver had tried to close them prior to departure, he had been unable to do so. Various railway employees in orange high visibility vest had descended on the scene to resolve the problem. They had failed. The driver had used the tannoy to advise passengers to take the slow train from the adjacent platform. Once everyone, Lewis and Olena included, had switched trains, all that remained was for Virenque to choose his moment to board the same train.

That part, at least, he had supreme confidence in his abilities to get right.

17

The final passenger about to board Lewis's train is carrying a black rucksack. He is tall and stocky in a powerful, muscular, way. Lewis is unable to get a good look at the man's face: he is wearing a hooded sweatshirt, its hood raised, and mirrored sunglasses. Something about him catches Lewis's attention. It is the way he carries himself. When you march for twenty-four hours across Dartmoor with an eighty-pound Bergen on your back, you develop a walking style that stays with you for life. It is a confident, ever so slightly forward-slanted, posture that, regardless of load, never varies. Usually it is accompanied by a steady, rhythmical, stride. Lewis still walks this way even though he handed back his Green Beret five years ago. The man about to board the train is either a past or present soldier. Most likely specialised infantry: either a Marine or Special Forces. Lewis would put money on it.

An electronic warbling sound indicates that the doors are ready to close. The man with the rucksack times it to perfection. Effortlessly he steps on board without any noticeable change in pace. Passing directly in front of Lewis, he heads inside the carriage, momentarily looking up as the doors close behind him. Lewis can't see much of the man's face because of the sunglasses. What little he does see is deeply suntanned, the skin weatherworn. The same effect one gets from living rough in the desert for prolonged periods. Lewis can still recall those days all too vividly.

The man heads into the carriage. He chooses a forward-facing seat, directly opposite Olena. He has to inch his large frame around the tiny table that juts out from the window: the other two seats nearest the aisle, in the same small cluster of four, are occupied. This slower train is almost full, with limited space for a rucksack in the overhead rack. In the course of sitting down, he is therefore compelled to place the rucksack on the floor in front of his empty seat. He then squashes his legs around either side of it as he sinks into the seat cushion.

Thirty minutes into the journey and the train is packed. Similar to Lewis, many are standing: sardines in a can. Most of those travelling wear headphones, passing the time by listening to music or watching a video on a flat screen device. Lewis's body is turned so that he is looking directly into the inner carriage. As the train pulls away from Knebworth station, the man in the hooded sweatshirt gets to his feet. Picking the rucksack from off the floor, he lifts it onto his seat. It is a precautionary measure, Lewis notes, preventing anyone from taking his place while he heads into the next carriage – presumably in search of the toilet. Lewis still can't see the man's face. There is a nagging feeling that he ought to know this person, however insane that might be. Especially given how many trained soldiers, past and present – whether Marines or Special Forces or not – there happen to be on the planet.

It is an itch that Lewis feels the need to scratch. Despite there being no obvious signs of recognition from the other man when he boarded the train, Lewis still wants to make sure. He shuffles his way past several people, eventually squeezing into the interior of the carriage to a new position, about halfway down. It feels less crowded here. Lewis leans against the edge of two single seats that are set back to back. The other man will have no option but to pass directly in front of Lewis before returning to his seat. Noticing that Lewis has moved, Olena turns around to see where he is. She raises her eyebrows in silent greeting when she spots him just behind her. They both smile: she then looks away, immersing herself in her book once more.

The train slows to stop at another station: Welwyn North. Beyond this point, the line reduces to a single track in each direction. It is about to pass over the narrow Digswell viaduct,

71

immediately to the south of the station platform. This is a Victorian brick construction over a mile in length, a strategic rail bottleneck: trains, fast or slow, to or from London to parts of Norfolk, East Anglia and the North East of England – they all have to wait their turn to cross it.

Something is badly wrong. Lewis picks up on the warning signals almost immediately. It is only as the train starts pulling out of Welwyn North station that he works out what.

It is the man, standing on the station platform, who is triggering alarm bells.

Lewis feels the blood running cold in the pit of his stomach. Olena, himself – and indeed everyone in the carriage – are suddenly in grave danger.

Lewis hardly knows the man; however, as of thirty minutes ago, he is no longer a complete stranger either. His posture – erect and slightly bent forward, with an air of the Military most definitely in evidence – is instantly familiar. So are the mirrored sunglasses and the hooded sweatshirt. This is someone who, by any rational measure, should be returning to this carriage following his bathroom break; about to pass close by Lewis; shortly to resume sitting in the seat directly opposite from Olena – the one which still has the rucksack on it.

Most definitely not waving goodbye to the departing train – and his rucksack – from his current position out on the station platform.

Lewis stoops to get a better look. As he does so, any lingering doubts soon vanish. When the man sees Lewis peering at him, a thin smile forms on the weatherworn face. He has something small in his hand, something that he points directly towards the carriage as the train picks up speed.

It is then that Lewis hears it: a distinctive 'click'. The sounds emanates from somewhere deep within the rucksack. It is quite loud. Olena hears it also. A dawning concern shows on her face as well.

Lewis knows that noise.

More specifically, he knows the type of device that makes it.

Soldiers use such a device when they want to prime a detonator to explode, at some time in the not-too distant future.

Terrorists also use it. When they have placed a bomb *in situ*, wanting to make a rapid escape before an explosion is triggered.

The rucksack has to contain a bomb.

How long the likely fuse delay is, Lewis can only guess. Doubtless it will be short – perhaps just sufficient to allow the train to reach the middle of the large expanse of viaduct?

Which Lewis estimates will be sometime in the next sixty seconds.

18

'*If you think before you act, most times you'll end up dead before you get started.*' Lewis's colour sergeant had loved his mottos. Good or bad, the words stick. Ever since, Lewis has been big on personal autopilot.

Time is critical. Lewis has, at best, seconds remaining to get the rucksack off the train before the device explodes. Lifting the heavy bag off the seat, he aggressively and urgently pushes past people standing in the aisle, heading for the rear doors. People standing in the door-well see the driven look in his eyes and make space for him. Lewis grabs the red emergency handle immediately by the exit and pulls hard. Adjacent to it is a green square panel, fronted by glass that covers an emergency door release mechanism. With his fist clenched, he punches a hole in the glass, pushing the button underneath. The train is already braking hard. Panic and confusion is beginning to spread throughout the carriage.

Lewis asks a teenage boy who has been standing, leaning against the door, to help. Together they slide one of the two double doors into the 'open' position. It creates a gap of sufficient width to allow Lewis to take the rucksack by its strap, swing it backwards behind him, and then hurl it with all his might outside of the carriage. The train is now stationary, its position on the viaduct about one third of the way across. Time stands still as the bag travels slowly in an upward arc into the open space to the side of the train. The distance to the flat grassy area below the track is about thirty metres. Lewis yells to everyone in the carriage to keep their heads down and avoid looking out of the glass windows. He counts down in his head as first the rucksack reaches the top of its meagre upward trajectory, then begins its descent towards the ground at the foot of the viaduct. Less than three seconds later there is a massive explosion. The train rocks vigorously from side to side, the strength of the viaduct's brickwork put to the test by the blast.

Inside the train several passengers have begun shouting and screaming. No one is hurt. Even the glass windows have, amazingly, remained intact.

Lewis senses an opportunity: if he is quick, he might have a chance of catching the bomber back at Welwyn North station: the station platform is, after all, only a few hundred metres behind the train. Asking the teenage boy to hold open the door for him once more, he yells back into the carriage for Olena to follow. Without waiting to see if she hears, he jumps down, sprinting along the tracks to the rear of the train for all he is worth.

19

As soon as he heard the explosion, Virenque knew that something had gone wrong. The sound had been different in both pitch and intensity from what he'd been expecting. He had chosen the amount of C-4 to use with great care. He liked using C-4. The RDX-based plastic explosive was, absent the detonator, almost completely inert. He had moulded and shaped the putty-like substance carefully, positioning it within the rucksack in a way that he knew would create a massive downwards blast once detonated. The relatively small amount of explosive he had been carrying was never going to be sufficient to destroy the viaduct completely. However, when Virenque had planned the detonation, set to go off forty-five seconds after it had been primed, the idea had been that it would nonetheless cause significant damage to the bridge. The shape and quantity of the charge should have created a huge blast wave: rendering the viaduct weakened, if not unusable – not simply killing those passengers on the train in the bomb's immediate vicinity. Panich had been most insistent on the need to damage the viaduct. It was part of the smokescreen: the subterfuge of making the bomb appear to have a different primary purpose other than killing people on the train.

Even if one of them did happen to be Olena Nemikov.

Not to mention the former Marine, Ben Lewis.

The detonation complete, Virenque's priority was getting away from the area as rapidly as possible. Earlier that morning he had driven to the station in a six-year old Volkswagen Golf. The car had been acquired the previous afternoon – he had paid cash to a delighted mother who'd been advertising it for sale on the Internet. Walking at a brisk pace to where he had parked the car, he wondered what might have gone wrong.

He was confident that he had used the correct amount of explosive; and, over the years, he had learned enough about explosive charges to be equally confident that he had shaped the plastic appropriately. So what had happened?

Out of the corner of one eye, something caught his attention. It was a man, running along the train tracks, heading from the viaduct towards the station platform. Without changing his stride, Virenque clicked the remote control on his key fob. The silver Golf's indicator lights flashed a couple of rows of cars ahead of him. He climbed into the driver's seat and switched on the ignition. Once seated, Virenque could more clearly observe as the man sprinted up the stairs of the station footbridge. Virenque recognised who it was. In an instant, he understood everything. It was the ex-Marine, the man on the train. The one Panich had also wanted killed.

Ben Lewis.

Lewis must have seen him get off the train: known, or guessed, that the rucksack contained a bomb. More likely, he had heard the tell-tale sound of the primer being set as the train had left the station platform. What a lucky bastard!

The man was using the height of the bridge to gain a better vantage point: if the roles were reversed, it was arguably what he would have done himself.

Then he saw something else. Another person: also running along the track; also heading towards the station platform. As Virenque put the car into gear and began driving away from the car park, he could see who it was.

The Nemikov girl.

Which gave him an idea.

When he'd arrived at the station that morning, he'd scouted the area around the viaduct before parking his car at the station. If he took care to let both Lewis and the girl see him leave in the Golf, there was a chance that he might be able at least to finish one part of his, now, failed mission.

A few hundred yards around the corner was a place that

had looked ideal.

20

As Lewis sprints, he tries putting himself in the bomber's shoes: what is his next move likely to be? Almost certainly, he will have planned his getaway. That means there is probably a car or motorbike parked somewhere: in a place that allows for a quick exit. Either that, or there will have been someone waiting for him at the station. Lewis thinks this is unlikely. It creates an unnecessary additional link in a chain by which someone might trace him. No, he concludes, it will be a vehicle of some description, parked in the car park – a car most likely: something quick and reliable; and nothing too flashy. Most London-centric commuter railway stations had car parks on both sides of the tracks. The bomber had been travelling on a London-bound train, heading from north to south, the station platform on the left-hand side. In all probability, therefore, his getaway vehicle is parked on the east side of the tracks. Up ahead of him, getting closer by the second, is a pedestrian footbridge that crosses from one side of the railway to the other. The view from the top will give the best vantage point.

Lewis checks his watch. Less than three minutes have elapsed since the train first pulled out of Welwyn North station. The bomber is still in the vicinity, Lewis feels sure. This man will be playing it cool. He won't be sprinting or jogging to his getaway vehicle: it risks drawing undue attention to himself.

He takes the footbridge stairs two at a time, at the top stopping and listening, his heart pounding loudly in his ears. He checks in all directions. At first he sees or hears nothing. Then, from the east-side car park, he spots it: a 2008 registered silver-coloured Volkswagen Golf.

In the driving seat is the man: complete with mirrored-sunglasses and a hooded sweatshirt.

21

Sprinting down the stairs of the footbridge, Lewis arrives on the station forecourt just as the Golf leaves the car park, heading southwards. He searches frantically for a suitable vehicle to beg, borrow or steal. This is the time he wishes he had his lovingly restored Honda CB750 to hand. Olena appears, gasping and out of breath from having tried to keep up with Lewis.

"What the hell is going on, Ben?"

"We've got to follow that silver car," he says pointing in the Golf's wake.

A couple on a Honda motor scooter pull into the station forecourt. The rear passenger, a woman, climbs off the back of the scooter, heading towards the ticket office. A moped isn't a perfect choice, but it is the only option immediately to hand.

"Follow me. When I call, simply climb on the back and say nothing."

The driver, a man in his early forties, is wearing a half-face helmet with goggles. Lewis approaches him from behind at an oblique angle to his left such he has no idea what is about to happen. Wasting no time, Lewis jabs the man firmly in the ribs with his right elbow. Using the strength in his other hand, he then pulls the unsuspecting victim off his seat whilst holding the scooter with the other hand. The man falls to the tarmac, winded and confused, but not seriously hurt.

"Come on," Lewis shouts at Olena. As soon as she is sitting behind him, he accelerates away sharply in search of the Golf.

The Honda is no match for the Golf in terms of speed. Lewis's immediate concern is where the bomber might be heading. Accelerating in the same general direction, his mental compass tells him that the road will veer around in a broad loop directly towards the viaduct itself. Sure enough, a short distance later, the Victorian bridge's massive brickwork arches come into view, across to their right. One minute they are travelling at over fifty miles an hour, the next Lewis is jamming on the brakes, the machine coming to an abrupt halt. Just ahead is a mini-roundabout. A few metres in front is a small driveway: a silver Golf has pulled in, the driver's door wide open. It is the same car. The bomber is nowhere to be seen. It appears as if the vehicle has been abandoned and the man is making a run for it. Most probably, heading down the small lane running immediately behind where the car is parked. Either that or he has just switched vehicles with another that had been lying in wait.

"What do we do now?" Olena asks.

"Wait here. I'm going to take a look down the track."

"What if he comes back when you're away?"

Lewis is already off the bike, starting to run down the narrow lane.

"He won't," he calls over his shoulder. "If he does, just holler. I'm not going far."

22

Lewis's mistake had been thinking that Virenque had disappeared down the small lane. In fact, the Frenchman had chosen the location with care. It was a place where anyone following would readily have been duped. Immediately adjacent to the lane entrance, nearest the road and hidden by the parked Golf, was a small driveway. It belonged to a private residence. There were two brick pillars on either side, it once having been a gated entrance. Virenque was crouched behind one of these. From here, he was able to watch from the shadows as Lewis fell for his simple trap, running off down the lane, away from the parked Golf.

Olena, still sitting astride the motor scooter, never heard or saw Virenque when he crept up behind her. As a skilled practitioner of the Russian martial art of *Systema*, he knew exactly where and how to execute the perfect neck chop. Aimed directly at Olena's vagus nerve, the cranial connection that links brain and body, the blow temporarily immobilised her, causing her to pass out. As she fell to one side, he hoisted her on to his shoulder, silently carrying her limp form across to the Golf. He opened the boot and placed her unceremoniously inside. Then, closing the rear tailgate without a sound, he climbed into the driver's seat and restarted the engine. He was now in a position to atone for his earlier failure. All that remained was to drive to a private, secluded, location before killing the Ukrainian woman, expertly, at his leisure. It was, after all, what he was particularly good at.

Putting the car into reverse, he lined up the driver's side front bumper so that, as he drove away, he would knock over, and immobilise, the scooter. The sound of the car starting had caused Lewis to turn around. Virenque could see him in the rear view mirror, sprinting back towards him. Virenque was tempted to take a shot: however, the angle was difficult and it was an unnecessary additional risk.

Instead, this time he simply put his foot on the accelerator and sped away.

23

Lewis is fifty metres down the lane when he hears the car starting. Cursing, he spins around and starts sprinting back towards where he left Olena and the Honda.

Except that Olena is no longer there.

From a standing start, fifty metres at Lewis's personal best of eight metres a second takes him almost six and a half seconds. It is nowhere near quick enough. The Golf is accelerating away towards the Digswell viaduct by the time he covers the distance. The stolen motor scooter lies immobilised on the roadside next to where the car had been, its front wheel badly buckled. How could he have been so stupid?

'*Commiserating over battles lost will never win you the war, solider.*'

It is Lewis's colour sergeant once again. It is small consolation but he is right – and Lewis knows it.

There is a car park in the distance, close to the viaduct and next to a school. It is the time of day when parents are collecting children. The car park is half full, with more cars arriving. Lewis runs across the road, focusing, in particular, on a black Mercedes four-by-four that is parked in the middle of the lot with its engine running. The owner is out of the car, talking with another parent a short distance away. They are staring at the viaduct and pointing, doubtless discussing the recent explosion.

It is the break Lewis needs.

Judging the moment finely, Lewis climbs into the driver's seat and begins accelerating away. In the rear view mirror, the owner continues talking to her friend, for the time being unaware her car has been stolen.

Once on the main road, Lewis floors the accelerator,

content to be driving a car with a powerful three-litre diesel engine beneath its bonnet. He checks the fuel gauge: the tank is nearly full. His current location is close to where the rucksack bomb exploded, the road about to pass immediately beneath one of the arches of the viaduct. Two cars have pulled to one side, their drivers – now curious spectators – also out of their cars and gesticulating in various directions. Lewis swerves around them, trying to close the gap on the Golf. A helicopter appears to his left, slowing to a hover directly above the railway viaduct. Lewis snatches a brief look. The machine bears the navy blue livery of a police helicopter.

The road continues in a north-westerly direction. Lewis is fast approaching a decision point: whether or not to turn onto the A1M motorway – and, if so, in which direction does he need to go?

24

Digswell viaduct is located less than three miles from the headquarters of the Hertfordshire Police constabulary at Stanborough Park to the south of Welwyn Garden City. Within minutes of the bomb exploding, the Chief Constable for Hertfordshire had been informed. The decision had been taken to invoke the county's multi-agency Emergency Response Plan. Under the terms of the plan, jurisdiction of major incidents passes to a consortium of interested agencies known as 'Hertfordshire Resilience' – chaired by the Hertfordshire Constabulary.

Like a well-oiled machine, the emergency response centre at Welwyn's Police Headquarters began the process of initiating various strands of connected activity relating to the incident. The National Police Air Service had been contacted at their headquarters location in West Yorkshire and two helicopters had been cleared for immediate take off: the first was expected to arrive at the viaduct imminently. Ambulance despatchers from the nearby Lister Hospital in Stevenage had also been notified. Although reports of casualties were low, two ambulances had been despatched to Welwyn North station and another three were being held on standby. Forensic experts and dog handling teams were on their way to the scene of the incident: the dogs' immediate priority would be to check for any other explosive devices or residues that might still be on the train.

Meanwhile, buses were in the process of being tracked down in order to ferry passengers from the train to a nearby school so that they could be interviewed and have arrangements made for their onward journeys. The co-ordination exercise was complicated since the presence of an explosive device meant that officers from Counter Terrorism command, part of

Special Operations branch in London's Metropolitan Police, had to be contacted. Several specialist investigators were being driven under fast motorbike escort from central London to Welwyn. They again would want to interview some, if not all, of the passengers. Finally, whilst the operation of the rail network was the responsibility of Network Rail, responsibility for policing of the railways in the UK was down to the British Transport Police. Both of these bodies needed to be fully part of the incident response. Specialist engineers were going to need to assess the extent of structural damage, if any, caused to the viaduct by the bomb blast. They also needed to consider what length of time it would take to conduct any necessary repairs: they then needed to advise rail passenger groups accordingly.

In amongst this planning and co-ordination activity, Twitter feeds began arriving directly from passengers still stranded on the stationary train. A specialist team at the emergency response centre was monitoring these. A man had been seen throwing a device off the train before escaping and running down the track back to Hertford North station. A blonde-haired woman in her early to mid twenties had followed him, soon after. A few passengers had taken pictures with their mobile phones. Although most were out of focus, they still allowed a description of these two individuals to be made available to mobile police units in the area. A police car had been despatched to Welwyn North station: a man fitting the description of the person leaving the train had been reported as having assaulted the driver of a Honda motor scooter and had stolen his machine. Within fifteen minutes of the explosion, the abandoned and damaged Honda had been located and the adjacent lane cordoned off. Officers at the scene were waiting for a fingerprint specialist to arrive. Reports also began arriving about a black Mercedes 'M' - class that had been stolen outside a school no more than a few hundred yards from where the moped had been abandoned.

Details of the car and its registration were broadcast to all units across the county as well as to London's Metropolitan Police and neighbouring forces. The driver was thought to be a young male in his late twenties or early thirties. Units were advised that the man might be armed and dangerous and instructed to take all reasonable and necessary precautions when apprehending him.

25

The *vaporetto* had been in the middle of the canal. It had been attempting to cross over to the right hand bank in preparation for its arrival at Rialto when the suitcase bomb had exploded. The force of the blast had been devastating, the carnage and destruction massive. People on board the vessel had been killed instantly. Various body parts were amongst the debris that had been flung far and wide into the canal. The scene was one of total destruction.

The Italian police later reported that, as best as they could judge, about two hundred people on board the ferry, and on other boats close by, had been killed. There were unlikely to have been any survivors from the *vaporetto*. Numerous pedestrians in the vicinity had also been seriously injured; flying glass from surrounding windows and falling masonry had also inflicted significant amounts of secondary damage. Many pedestrians had suffered cuts and lacerations, a significant number requiring medical attention.

It was sometime later before politicians from around the world had spoken out unanimously condemning the attack. They had called the bombing an intense act of cowardice – a senseless waste of human life. Surprisingly, no one had claimed any responsibility at first, leaving both journalists and counter-terrorism police guessing who might have been behind it. It wasn't until several hours later that a reporter working for Le Figaro in Paris had received an anonymous email. It was posted from a mail server whose IP address ceased to exist moments after the mail had been sent. The message had been stark but very clear.

The Venice bombing had been the work of Islamic State.

Venice, it announced, had been the first of many planned reprisal attacks across Europe for the West's continued arrogant foreign policy interventions in Iraq and elsewhere in the Middle East.

The West had been warned. More attacks would follow imminently.

Within minutes, a second untraceable email, similar to the first, was received by a different journalist this time working for The Times newspaper in London. It claimed that the Welwyn viaduct bombing had been a similar act of reprisal against the West by Islamic State. It also warned that further acts of reprisal were to follow.

26

From an early age, Hakim had been smart: much more worldly-wise, more resourceful, and better able to get others to dance to his tune than his cousin, Fouad. He had also been much more devious. The Jordanian had the natural talent-spotter's ability to remember disarmingly tiny pieces of, seemingly, irrelevant data about people – and then to recall them at a later date.

When Islamic State had taken the decision to wage *jihad* against the British in London, Hakim had been an obvious person to mastermind one component of such a campaign. It had been he who had first dreamt up the whole idea; he who had been the one to convince the high command that the plan would work; and he who had known how – and where – to source both the people and the C-4 explosive that would be necessary to make it all happen. His source of inspiration had been a loyal devotee to their cause and a friend of cousin Fouad: a man he had met only a couple of times but whose details had been salted away. A Pakistani by the name of Sadiq Akhtar.

Sadiq had been living and working in London, leading otherwise a very ordinary life. It had been the nature of Sadiq's job that had given Hakim the germ of the idea. And something that Sadiq had mentioned, in a reply to a question from Hakim, that had given him the real inspiration.

Back in Jordan, Hakim's brother, an increasingly well-connected importer and exporter, seemed to know just about everyone of any significance in the country. Over a lunch one day in an Amman restaurant, his brother had introduced Hakim to a Russian called Vladimir. Vladimir, a supposed arms trader, had been sitting just two tables away from them. Introductions over and pleasantries exchanged, Hakim had taken the Russian's proffered business card. Rather than file it and forget about him, later he had studied the card and had concluded that a contact like Vladimir might prove extremely useful to their cause. As a consequence, he started to invest quality time in getting to know the Russian. For the Jordanian, it was to prove a highly opportune, and profitable, investment.

Two months, and several meetings with Vladimir, later and the two men had reached agreement on a new business transaction. Vladimir was to source the importation of a large shipment of C-4 explosive into the United Kingdom – for a suitable price that the two had haggled over. Hakim, in turn, had secured approval for the deal from those higher up the rather ill-defined chain of Islamic State command.

The routing for the C-4 shipment was necessarily complicated. The goods were sent via Warsaw and Dublin, before finally landing at Liverpool docks. The product, in its familiar olive-green outer wrappers, and presented as rectangular-shaped blocks, about a foot in length, had been heavily disguised. Each stick had been concealed inside an empty photocopier ink toner cartridge. When the plastic cover on the cartridge had been snapped shut it had been, from the outside, indistinguishable from the genuine article. Each cartridge had been individually wrapped in foil-sealed packages before being placed in cardboard boxes with the manufacturer's labels stencilled on them. This charade had given the whole shipment added authenticity.

On arrival in Liverpool, the boxes of 'toner cartridges' had been taken by container lorry to a disused warehouse outside Bradford. Here the next stage of Hakim's secretive operation had begun. Hakim's cousin, Fouad, had arranged for two Pakistani faithful, flatmates of Sadiq, to begin the laborious task of removing the C-4 blocks from each toner cartridge, one by one. They had then arranged them into pairs before placing each pair inside its own hessian sack: every sack being topped up with a small amount of sand, before being sealed.

Once complete and the sack sewn together, they were virtually indistinguishable from a genuine sandbag. Finally, each completed 'sandbag' had been stacked, carefully and neatly, in the back of Fouad's white minivan for its onward journey to London.

27

Olena was gradually becoming aware of her predicament. Her jostled body had been shaken back to consciousness as the car took various corners at speed. Her neck felt incredibly sore and tender. It was slowly dawning on her still befuddled mind what must have happened. The car was a hatchback, that much she was aware: the lid over the boot space a simple parcel shelf hinged along its long edge. She reached above her head and felt it move. She rattled the boot lid some more and started yelling.

"Let me out of here! I think I am going to be sick."

"Shut the fuck up, bitch," was what she received back for her troubles. It was a strange accent. It had sounded partly French, but with a hint of Russian. "Or maybe you'd like me to come back there and beat the shit out of you, eh?"

"*Otyebis*," she muttered sufficiently loudly for the man to hear. If he was Russian, her swearing at him abusively in the slang language known as 'mat' was unlikely to be helpful to her current predicament – even if it temporarily made her feel better.

Virenque was approaching a roundabout: it was also, in part, a junction with the motorway. He had a decision to make: whether to head north, south or keep off the motorway altogether? On balance it was an easy choice. The man called Lewis was no longer on his tail. No one else knew about this VW Golf apart from the girl, and she was tucked away from view in the boot. As an operational headquarters, Polunin had rented a secluded farmhouse to the south of Cambridge. It was to here that Nemikov's son was being brought later that evening. Cambridge was to the north and east of his current position. Therefore, the most logical option was to head north on the motorway back towards Cambridge. Because only southbound cars were able to join the motorway at this particular junction, it meant that Virenque had a little further to drive before he could join the motorway.

28

The road is a dual carriageway. Lewis is travelling at nearly one hundred miles an hour as he approaches the junction. He brakes hard, feeling the electronic traction cut in as he turns on to the roundabout. All four tyres grip the road during the rapid deceleration, the action bringing his speed down to nearer the limit. Driving past the first turn off to the left, the slip road heading on to the southbound carriageway of the motorway, he can see no sign of the silver Golf: on either the slip road or the carriageway itself.

Beyond this junction the traffic continues as two lanes. Access to the northbound carriageways of the motorway is at a different intersection about half a mile further along. There is still no sign of the other car. Then, just as he is about to give up hope, he finally spots it: turning on to the northbound motorway slip road, almost one hundred metres in front.

Finally, Lewis is in position on the motorway, three cars behind the Golf. The traffic is down to two lanes at this point, the flow moderately heavy as they approach the outskirts of Stevenage. It is definitely the same man – the bomber from the train – who is driving the Golf. Lewis can see no sign of Olena. Either she is lying on the floor, perhaps unconscious, or, more likely, bundled into the boot. In different circumstances, Lewis might be tempted to hang back and follow the other car: to find out where it is heading and who the bomber's accomplices, if any, are. Olena's kidnapping, however, changes everything. There can only be one priority: to get her out of the car as quickly as possible. Nothing else matters.

People write fantasy about car chases: Lewis had once attended a one-week close-protection driving course in order to learn for himself what was fact and what was fiction. Popular fiction tells you that if you are in a chase vehicle, there's little you can do to stop the car in front without significant risk to all parties. Lewis now knows this to be factually inaccurate. There is one intervention that can work. It is not without risk. All that Lewis needs is a clear road, and a decent width of hard shoulder.

He finds both a couple of miles later on.

Just beyond the town of Stevenage.

Where the carriageway changes back from two lanes to three.

To begin, Lewis needs to get in position. He does this by overtaking the two cars ahead of him, allowing him to move into the space directly behind the Golf. Both cars are in the nearside lane – the separation between them about two car lengths. Each is driving at the speed limit: seventy miles an hour. Lewis checks his mirror. The two cars behind him, the ones he overtook recently, have already both dropped back some distance.

It is, as Lewis likes to think of it, a now or never moment.

'Nunc aut nunquam', as the Dutch Marines would say.

Lewis begins the manoeuvre by accelerating, steering the four-by four into the empty hard shoulder to the left of the main carriageway. In this manner, he starts to overtake the other car from the inside, positioning the front of the Mercedes so that it overlaps the rear of the Golf by about two feet. Speed is of the essence. Lewis wants to get the Mercedes in position before the other driver can figure out what is happening.

With his foot on the accelerator, Lewis begins the next stage: steering deliberately to his right. The front, driver's side, wing of the Mercedes makes physical contact with the nearside back end of the Golf, just behind the rear tyres. The collision is very real and very deliberate. Contrary to what his instincts scream at him, Lewis continues steering to the right, still pushing the other car: the physical contact being maintained. The Golf's tyres have no option but to lose grip

97

on the road. The car spins out of control, moving in an anti-clockwise direction around the front of the Mercedes: a pirouette through one hundred and eighty degrees into the hard shoulder lane. One second it is facing forward; the next backwards. There is little the Golf driver can do other than take his foot off the accelerator – and avoid hitting the brakes. By contrast, Lewis finds himself back in the nearside lane of the motorway, the two cars having, in effect, swapped places.

Lewis brakes sharply. He needs the forward speed of his car to be no faster than the rapidly slowing speed of the other. This is important: the other car, although technically still having forward momentum, in practice, is pointing rearwards. Its engine thus is fighting to drive the Golf in the opposite direction to the Mercedes; the tyres battling to re-establish grip on the road's surface. The instant the Golf becomes almost stationary is the precise cue for Lewis's denouement: steering the Mercedes, directly and aggressively, into the Golf's front passenger side wing. The Golf's steering and front suspension system is thus quickly disabled – the car immobilised, unable to be driven any further.

Reversing the Mercedes on to the hard shoulder behind the Golf, Lewis climbs out of the car. He leaves the door open and the engine running – but freezes when he sees the bomber from the train pointing a gun directly at him. It is a Russian-made GSh-18 pistol. Lewis knows it well. It was Oleg Panich's weapon of choice. It takes nine millimetre rounds. Fully loaded, it weighs well over half a kilogramme. It is a professional's weapon of choice.

"Get away from the car. Move ten paces back and hit the deck." It is an unusual accent, each word spoken with a deliberate inflection. A sudden flurry of traffic causes the man to waver: whether to shoot Lewis in cold blood or escape to save his own skin? In the distance, the sound of police sirens can be heard. They appear to be getting nearer. His mind appears to be made up. With a final glance to check that

Lewis is not about to attack, he races to the Mercedes's open door. Seconds later he is accelerating away, directly into the oncoming flow of traffic.

With no time to lose, Lewis is around the back of the Golf and opening the boot. Olena is there: alive and in one piece, albeit badly shaken. She clambers out and they embrace. The moment is short lived. Two police cars, sirens sounding and blue lights flashing, are fast approaching. Overhead, the noise of a police helicopter coming in to a hover above them is almost deafening.

It has been a busy afternoon. Lewis knows it is about to get worse: he will doubtless have to suffer his second police interrogation in thirty-six hours.

29

Virenque was watching the black Mercedes in his rear view mirror. It had overtaken the two cars immediately behind him before settling onto his tail. He couldn't see the driver because of the angle of the windscreen glass. The action itself was not particularly noteworthy. Satisfied that there wasn't an immediate threat, he focused on his breathing, forcing himself to relax. He began thinking about how he might kill the girl when they got to the farmhouse. Panich wanted her death to look like an act of Islamic Terror. Well, perhaps he would slit her throat for the cameras? Come to think of it, he liked the idea. They could make the younger brother watch. That would surely terrify any father into submission?

The next junction was the turn off for Cambridge. He checked his speed. He was travelling almost exactly on the speed limit, seventy miles an hour.

He sensed something was wrong. Before his brain fully had time to register what it was, the black Mercedes was overtaking him – but from the wrong side, from the hard shoulder lane. One second it had moved off the motorway's main carriageway; the next, it was deliberately ploughing into him, pushing the rear end of his Golf to the right. He tried to accelerate out of trouble, but he was too late, powerless to stop his car from spinning out of control. He knew not to hit the brakes, his training telling him that such a reaction would cause an even greater loss of control. Instead he took his foot off the accelerator. He found himself grappling to control the steering as the car rotated through one hundred and eighty degrees on to the hard shoulder. The residual momentum was still in the original direction: the tyres burnt rubber as they tried to drive the car in the other. As the Golf slowed rapidly, Virenque glanced momentarily to his left. It was Lewis! Just as his own wheels were regaining traction, the bastard suddenly ploughed his car into him once again. This time, it was a killer blow. The left-hand wheel assembly on the Golf crumpled under the impact and the car came to a crashing halt.

Virenque was out of the car, on to the hard shoulder, in a heartbeat. He might not have been quick enough to prevent the crash, but he wasted no time in removing his gun from its shoulder harness, brandishing it directly at Lewis.

"Get away from the car. Move ten paces back and hit the deck."

For a moment, Virenque was tempted to shoot Lewis in cold blood. Then he hesitated. Professional assassins weren't normally opportunist killers: Virenque preferred to choose his own time and location to kill his victims. There were too many potential witnesses on the busy motorway. Right now, his priority needed to be to escape, not to get caught. The sound of two police cars fast approaching seemed to decide it. Then he heard the helicopter and knew he was out of time. With the Mercedes's engine still running and its door wide open, he made a snap decision. Racing to the car and jumping in, he immediately drove away, pulling onto the main carriageway, narrowly avoiding a fast-approaching lorry. It, in turn, blared its horn, the lorry driver forced to brake hard in order to avoid a collision as Virenque sped away.

30

After disembarking the *vaporetto*, Oleg Panich's immediate priority had been escaping the island city as quickly as possible. Making his way to the main railway concourse, less than ten minutes away on foot, he had retrieved several items from a left luggage locker, courtesy of the unattributable help that Volkov and his agents had provided: a pre-paid car park ticket; fresh identity papers; and a set of car keys. He had then walked to the public parking garage on the adjacent island of Tronchetto. The car that Volkov had left for him – a Fiat Punto – had been easy to locate. Thus it had been that within fifteen minutes of the *vaporetto* bomb having exploded, Panich was driving across the causeway that linked Venice's islands to the Italian mainland. His destination had been Treviso airfield, some forty kilometres away by road. This was a mainly military airport that also shared its runway with a small number of civilian and private charter flights.

Waiting on the tarmac had been a crewed and fuelled Gulfstream G650 jet with a flight plan filed for a direct routing into London's City Airport. Parking the Fiat at the airport's VIP parking, Panich, now travelling under a new identity of a West German businessman, Anton Gerber, had easily cleared immigration and was soon boarding the steps of the aircraft. As the wheels lifted from the runway at five-fifteen in the evening Venice time, Panich had allowed himself a moment's satisfaction of a job well done. More to the point, no more than forty minutes had passed between the time that the bomb had exploded and the time he was leaving Italian airspace bound for London. He reclined his soft, leather, seat, briefly wondering whether Virenque had had an equally successful afternoon. He felt a stabbing pain deep in his chest, causing him to rub his rib cage. The sensation disappeared after a few moments and Panich tried to shrug it off. He'd been conscious of several aches and pains recently: this one felt deep inside of him, as if a knife were piercing his core. Perhaps he really might have that cancer after all? He dismissed the thought. He couldn't sit and worry about all that now: he had work to do. Reaching instead into his pocket to turn on his mobile phone, the device had buzzed in his hand. He had brought the screen close to his face, reading the string of loosely coded text messages that had been sent by Virenque.

All apparently had not gone well – in fact, it very much looked to Panich as if he was going to have his work cut out as soon as he got to London.

31

They had to speak in code because Panich knew that calls would be monitored – especially given the events of that afternoon. The signal strength on board the Gulfstream had been intermittent but sufficient. They had both kept the conversation short and to the point.

"Staying above any of the detail, tell me what happened," Panich began with no other introductions or pleasantries.

"The man you were interested in locating was also at the scene," Virenque had said obliquely. "His intervention was only just-in-time, but it was disruptive."

"Did both parties get away?"

"Yes and no. When I left them, the police were arriving. They will both be tied up answering questions for hours. The short answer is yes."

"Any collateral damage at the scene?"

"Very limited."

"That's also disappointing."

"Quite. I am heading to our location near the University and will meet up with our other colleagues as planned."

"Okay. I will stay in London and re-establish contact with the other two when they are released."

"Assuming that you can track them down."

"That usually isn't something that causes me problems."

Panich had ended the call abruptly. The whole conversation had lasted less than thirty seconds. It was unlikely that possible listeners, either at GCHQ or the NSA, would have picked up any flagged keywords. Panich closed his eyes, planning what he was going to do next. An idea began forming in his mind almost immediately: over the next few minutes, the more he toyed with it, the more he liked it. He looked at his watch. It was just after five-thirty in the evening London time. They should be landing within the next thirty minutes. There might not be a lot of time. However, there had to be a fair chance that, if luck were on his side, both Lewis and the Nemikov girl would yet be dead before the day was out.

32

"This is becoming something of a habit."

Saul Zeltinger is once more sitting opposite Ben Lewis in another featureless holding cell at Paddington Green. He is wearing the same suit and the same coloured shirt as the last time. Only the tie is different: it is the same colour but with a different pattern.

"Couldn't keep away, was that it, Saul?" Lewis asks. "The last time you and I spent any serious time together, we both bit off more than we could chew."

"I've been hearing about what happened this afternoon. You and trouble seem to have this magnetic attraction for each other."

Lewis simply shrugs, a hint of a smile on his face.

"Where's Olena? Is she still here or have they sent her home?"

"She's in the adjacent room. I've just got off the phone speaking to Jake Sullivan. Apparently, the team here are about finished with all their questions. You'll be on your way soon, or so I gather." He pauses, to see if this piece of news gets any reaction from Lewis. Seeing none, he continues. "If you recall, you were meant to be coming round to play chess this evening? You know: to meet Hattie and the Boys, to have some supper, that sort of thing. I suppose that's now out of the question?"

"I need to take Olena back to her father. We'll do it another time, Saul. Thanks, anyway."

"Who was this bomber? Did you recognise him?"

"Never seen him before. But I recognised the type. He was definitely ex-military – most likely from some elite troop, if not Special Forces. It's the walk. It's a dead giveaway." He spends a few moments telling Zeltinger briefly his version of events on the train that afternoon.

"It doesn't sound much like an Islamic State sponsored event from what you've been describing."

"I don't think so. The man wasn't British, I am sure of that. When he spoke, he had an accent. There was an undertone that sounded French."

"Doubtless you gave the SO15 team a full description?"

"Several times. And I've scanned through numerous mug shots, all to no avail."

"Who was he trying to kill, do you think? Olena or yourself? Or was he trying just to be as unpleasantly disruptive to everyone?"

Lewis looks surprised by Zeltinger's line of thinking.

"That's not a bad question, actually, Saul. My working assumption thus far had been that he had been out to kill Olena, with me just the innocent bystander in all of this. Otherwise, why stop and kidnap her after the failed bombing?"

"Suppose you weren't just the innocent bystander, as you put it. Is there anyone out there who might also have wanted you dead?"

"Enough to place a large bomb on a train, in the process killing loads of innocent people? No, I don't think that's very likely. Not anybody currently alive, at any rate."

"Did you hear what happened in Venice this afternoon?"

Zeltinger tells him about the bomb on the *vaporetto*, and the significant loss of life that it caused. Lewis looks visibly shocked.

"That can't be a coincidence: two bombings on the same afternoon and with Olena's mother, Valentyna, meant to be in Venice as well. I hope to God that she wasn't caught up in that."

"Back to my question, Ben. There are plenty of people who might want to inflict harm on Nemikov and his family. Is there anyone who might be keen to do the same to you? Everywhere you go, you seem able to attract people who end up trying to kill you. Especially after the public beheading you stopped the other day."

"Thanks," he says with yet another shrug and a smile. Zeltinger's question does make him stop and think, though.

"I upset a few Russians and Chinese over that business with the Iranian dossier, as you know," he says. I doubt that any of them are still minded to come after me for revenge."

"Well, let's hope so for your sake, Ben. Ponder it some more. None of it quite gels for me at present. The moment there's a whiff of a terrorist attack here in the UK, my mysterious friend, Ben Lewis, just happens to find himself smack bang in the middle of it all. It's too much of a coincidence for my peace of mind."

"It could just be my bad luck."

"Or perhaps it might be our good fortune."

33

It is just after nine in the evening when Lewis and Olena are allowed to leave the Police Station. They walk out on to the busy Edgware Road and find a black London taxi waiting on the curb. Its orange 'for hire' light is on. Anxious to get Olena home to her parents' house in Kensington as quickly as possible, they jump in. Olena tells the driver the address. The taxi performs a quick U-turn and heads off along the Edgware Road in a southerly direction.

"How did you get on?" Lewis asks. Olena is sitting to Lewis's left, her right arm interlocked with Lewis's.

"They asked endless questions, especially about the bomber. What about you?"

"More or less the same. I couldn't find his photo in any mug shot gallery."

"Me neither."

The traffic is light as they approach Marble Arch. For a moment, they sit and watch the passing nightscape, lost in their own thoughts.

"Did you speak to your father? To let him know what happened?"

"Briefly. They allowed me five minutes at the beginning, before I had to turn my phone off. I told him that you had saved my life. He wanted to send someone to come and collect us. I said not to bother, that you were with me."

She looks across at Lewis and smiles. Then, moments later, her face is filled with worry and consternation.

"It was me the bomber was trying to kill, wasn't it?" she asks, looking directly at Lewis. Her eyes flicker from side to side as she searches his for some glimmer of truth.

"Possibly."

She seems satisfied by the honesty of the answer and turns

to look out of the window once more.

"Or it might have been me." She turns her head sharply back towards him. "Or, indeed, anyone else on the train. Or nobody. I guess we may never know."

Lewis is not about to mention anything about the Venice bombing for the moment. He would like to check with her father before rushing to false conclusions.

"Could it have been someone from Islamic State?"

"It's doubtful. The man didn't look the part."

'What do you mean?" she asks.

"He was a professional soldier, I'm certain of it. He didn't look or speak like your average terrorist."

"Well, my father does have many enemies."

"Who can say?"

Out of the corner of his eye, Lewis notices a small orange light on one of the switches in the rear passenger compartment: the intercom connecting the driver to the passenger compartment. It is switched on. It hadn't been earlier, when they had got into the taxi. Lewis had checked. This means that the driver can listen – and has been listening – to their every word. Lewis glances directly at the man in the rear view mirror. The driver catches Lewis' eyes before swiftly looking away.

Lewis feels the hairs move on the back of his neck. An ice-cold feeling is forming in the pit of his stomach.

It is impossible!

This is someone who Lewis knows is meant to be dead.

How can it be?

The eyes are the giveaway: Lewis would remember those eyes anywhere.

If you think before you act, most times you'll end up dead before you get started.

The last time Lewis had seen these eyes, it was in a mountain chalet above the Swiss ski resort of Champéry. Then, as now,

110

they had belonged to a Russian killer. Someone Lewis had believed then to be unconscious, on the verge of death from injuries caused by two separate gunshot wounds.

Someone, then as now, who had been hell-bent on killing Lewis.

Someone whom, if he were to be back from the dead, would unquestionably be wanting to take up with Lewis exactly where he had left off before.

Could it really be that Oleg Panich was alive and driving this London taxi?

34

Viktor Plushenko shuffled his heavy frame off the rear seat of the stretch limousine. With a certain amount of inelegance, he managed to emerge on to the Moscow pavement with a modicum of dignity still intact. The presence of two very pretty and very blonde girls, both barely out of their teens, standing on the curb and waiting to take an arm, was enough inducement for the overweight Russian to sharpen up his act. In Moscow, whether stray paparazzi or one of the many FSB agents, one never really knew who might be watching.

Two bouncers, dressed in thick, fur-lined, leather jackets, had the task of greeting guests expecting to enter the exclusive Soho Rooms nightclub. They cast Plushenko a cursory glance before recognition kicked in and the large Russian VIP and his two escorts were ushered inside. A senior attendant, dressed in a dark-grey, hand-made suit, a curly-wired security earpiece in one ear, stepped forward to greet him.

"Good evening, Mister Plushenko. It is lovely to have you back here with us. Your guest is already waiting. Shall I lead the way to your private room?"

Plushenko nodded curtly. With a girl still on each arm, he flicked both hands away from his body gently at the wrist. The gesture made it clear to both his escorts that they were dismissed: he, Viktor Plushenko, had more important business to attend to. He followed the flunky through the crowded bar area, past several private booths, and then out through a door to one side of the large dance floor, watched over by two more uniformed guards. Despite the low light levels, both wore aviator sunglasses.

"Mister Plushenko? It's a pleasure to meet you."

Plushenko's companion was a petite Eurasian. She was wearing a long, slender, black dress with a scooped neckline showing off a modest cleavage. With sequins around her ruched middle, pendant diamonds and pearls in her ears, and several strands of black pears in a choker, she literally shimmered in the overhead lights as Plushenko came forward to kiss her hand.

"The pleasure is all mine, Miss Tian."

"Most people call me Kristina."

"And most call me Viktor," he said laughing, his whole body shaking as he did so.

A waiter entered the room bearing a silver tray with two tall champagne flutes and a bottle of Roederer Cristal Rosé.

"Ah, drinks. What an excellent idea. I trust you will join me, Kristina? I thought you could be tempted to try a glass of the finest rosé."

"Why, certainly, thank you." They watched as the waiter expertly uncorked the bottle. He poured a little into the tiny silver sommelier's tasting dish that was hanging around his neck. After sniffing, and then tasting it, he seemed satisfied, and proceeded to fill both champagne flutes expertly to just below the brim. Viktor didn't wait to be offered. He picked up both glasses and handed one to Kristina.

"Cheers!" he said, and took a sip. "Absolutely delicious, thank you," he said to the waiter, who took his cue and left them alone.

The room was very ornate and over-done, with onyx and marble everywhere. Three large, burgundy-red sofas piled deep with soft cushions surrounded a rectangular table on which the waiter had left the half empty bottle of Cristal in an ice bucket. There was also an oval platter containing various nuts, olives and an eclectic assortment of canapés. Plushenko indicated that they adjourn to one of the sofas. Without waiting for Kristina, he sank his heavy frame into a corner seat, letting out a big sigh as he did so.

"You come with quite a reputation, you know that?" he asked, looking at her as if sizing up an oil painting. This evening, the world-renowned hacker had shoulder-length, jet-black hair that, on this occasion, was wavy at the edges rather than curly.

"As most certainly do you, Viktor," she said with laughter in her eyes. She was naturally very confident. Plushenko knew that most people he met for the first time were usually quite nervous in his company. Not this one.

Then, to the Russian's surprise, she became more brazen.

"So, why don't we cut straight to the chase? If you tell me exactly what it is that you need help with, I'll tell you whether I am the right person for the job. Is that fair?"

Plushenko raised an eyebrow. He had been warned that Tian was special: he hadn't quite anticipated that she would be quite so forward so early on. Undaunted, he decided to continue.

"Very well. There is a man, in a senior, very privileged, position. By reputation he is a very private person, highly unlikely to succumb to financial inducements. This man is in possession of certain information that I want. I already have certain plans in progress that should get me some, if not all that I need. However," he paused, taking a large gulp of champagne, "I find myself in need of a little contingency – in case we run into difficulties." He glanced at her face to see whether there was any reaction to what he was saying. Kristina remained impassive.

"Is this information solely in the man's head or will it be on a computer somewhere?" she asked.

"Likely both. It will certainly be on a computer, but I don't know exactly which one or what it looks like."

"Then let me ask a different question. If it is on a computer, do you think there is a chance the man has a secure laptop? Or will the information be on some hard drive, the file server itself hidden deep inside some anonymous building somewhere?"

Plushenko thought about this before answering, in the process taking another large gulp of champagne. He reached for the bottle in the ice bucket in order to refill their glasses.

"I've no idea, I am sorry."

"Don't worry," she said, offering her glass for a refill. "I'll be able to find out. If you can get me in the same vicinity as the man and his machine, I am confident that I should be able to help you find what you are looking for."

35

Time seems to stand still, Lewis taking stock of several things at once.

The taxi is heading southwards down Park Lane. The road is wide, an urban four-lane carriageway, the traffic moderately busy. The speed of the taxi is at, or close to, the maximum permitted of forty miles an hour. Too fast, if Lewis had been thinking about getting Olena to jump out whilst it was moving. In any event, the doors are locked on both sides. Another light, this one red, next to each door handle indicates that the locking mechanism is activated. The lock will only release when the driver pulls to a halt and engages the hand brake. For the time being, both Lewis and Olena are trapped, unable to get out of either door.

The rear passenger compartment has a glass partition that separates it from the driver's cabin. In the middle, a glass panel can be slid opened or closed by the driver: currently this is closed. Lewis looks once more at the man behind the wheel. He is wearing a cloth cap and gloves on both hands. The last time, when he had left Panich for dead, the Russian had suffered a serious gunshot wound to his right elbow. Assuming that the taxi driver is Panich, he would almost certainly be using a prosthetic right arm. From Lewis's current position, directly behind the driver's seat, the gloves prevent Lewis from being able to tell.

On either side, the windows are electrically operated. An override switch will exist, located in the front of the cab: most likely on the driver's side door panel, next to his right hand. The electric windows give Lewis an idea. In the mirror, the driver is looking at Lewis again, a grin forming on his face.

It is definitely Panich.

And he knows that Lewis now knows.

He also knows that his two passengers are trapped. If Lewis doesn't act soon, he and Olena are going to end up very dead, very quickly.

The taxi filters across to the right hand lane. Close by the Intercontinental Hotel, just before Hyde Park Corner, Panich turns right, crossing the northbound traffic and heading westward into South Carriage Drive. Compared with the bustle of Park Lane, this feels like a minor country road as it skirts the southern end of Hyde Park. The neighbourhood is in relatively unlit darkness, with little, if any, other traffic on the road.

Lewis leans across and whispers something in Olena's ear. At first she appears not to understand. Lewis's repeated, terse, whisperings bring her to her senses. Following his lead, and now very frightened, she buzzes the window down on the left hand side of the taxi. Lewis does the same on his side.

"Get ready to jump when I say," he whispers into her ear.

Suddenly it is cold in the cab. In the front, Panich also hears and feels the change in air pressure and temperature. Lewis watches as the Russian struggles with his right hand to operate the window closing mechanism. The taxi slows as Panich fumbles to make the switch work.

It is now or never: '*Nunc aut nunquam*'.

"Go!" he whispers loudly to Olena. "When you hit the ground, curl up tight, let your body roll with the forward momentum. Go now!"

Too numb with shock to argue, Olena dives headfirst out of the open window, Lewis pushing from behind to help her on her way. Panich, seeing what is happening, brakes hard, and turns around in his seat to look over his left shoulder. A GSh-18 handgun has appeared in his left hand. He aims it in Lewis's direction and fires: the angle is difficult, the first shot wild. The roar of the handgun is deafening in the enclosed space. Lewis, seeing the appearance of the GSh-18, drops to the floor, ducking out of sight beneath the shattered glass screen. Looking up, as the small barrel of the weapon pokes through into the rear of the cab, Lewis knows that the next shot will be angled downwards – and thus much more likely to be on target. So instead he lunges upwards, grabbing the weapon with his left hand and then Panich's left wrist with his right: using both to push the weapon upwards, away from his body. As the weapon fires a second time, Lewis feels a flash of searing heat as the empty shell casing is discarded. The shot again misses, the bullet disappearing through the roof of the taxi. Lewis tries wrestling the weapon away from Panich, mindful of the need to keep the barrel pointing away from his face and body. Panich swivels around in his seat, both hands off the steering wheel and his foot off the accelerator. The taxi slows to a crawl as the two men struggle, both fighting to gain control of the weapon. In the middle of this, Lewis becomes aware of the strength of Panich's grip on his own right wrist. There is no longer any doubt whether the Russian has a prosthetic hand or not: he can feel its vice-like strength on his wrist. He knows that it will crush his bones to a pulp unless he acts soon.

Lewis is unable to match the strength in Panich's new motorised fingers. In seconds, the bones in his wrist are going to shatter. Almost out of options, it is then that he thinks about the broken glass screen, immediately above where their hands are wrestling.

There are jagged shards of glass near the top.

For every action, there has to be an equal and opposite reaction.

With no time to lose, Lewis changes tack and starts pulling Panich's gun hand in a downward direction. The surprise change in tactics achieves the intended objective, namely causing the Russian to counter this new downward thrust from Lewis. Feeling strength in Panich's countermeasure, without warning Lewis changes from pulling downwards to pushing in the opposite direction, forcing the Russian's hands and arms to shoot upwards momentarily towards the top of the glass screen. On the first attempt, Panich's left wrist narrowly avoids the razor sharp glass shards: on the second attempt, the glass cuts deeply into the flesh behind Panich's left wrist. The Russian cries out in pain, letting go of both the gun and Lewis's hand.

Using the moment of Panich's distraction, Lewis needs no second invitation: he dives out of the window headfirst in the same way as Olena had done. His torso clear, he feels, rather than sees, Panich finally succeeding in making the electric window-closing mechanism work. As the glass closes around his legs, Lewis responds by twisting his legs at the knee in an attempt to prevent them getting trapped. To compound the difficulty, in the middle of this manoeuvre, Panich presses the accelerator to the floor. Lewis's twisting movement, combined with the sudden increase in speed, causes him to land clumsily and painfully on the curb. Nothing is broken, but he knows he will be badly bruised. Several metres away, Olena is back on her feet and looks unhurt. Lewis runs towards her, conscious that Panich has brought the taxi to a halt a few yards further along the road. Any moment now and he will be reversing in their direction.

"Quick, follow me."

Together, they race across the road into the darkness and gloom of Hyde Park. Behind them, a single shot rings out, causing both Lewis and Olena instinctively to duck as they run. Stopping in the dark next to a large oak tree, Lewis watches to see if Panich comes after them. After several seconds of listening intently, they see or hear nothing.

"Are you up for running?" Lewis asks. Olena nods silently.

"Then let's continue across the park to Marble Arch. With luck we can, perhaps, pick up a more friendly cab when we get there."

36

The taxi drops them outside the gated Kensington mews entrance. As they stand facing two security cameras, Olena presses her electric key card against the special reader that unlocks the side gate. Seconds later, Sergei Fedorov is opening the front door to let them in. Fedorov no longer subjects Lewis to body searches each time he enters the Nemikov's London property. However, a *frisson* of animosity lingers: Fedorov's failure to discover Lewis's knife the other day still rankles.

Oblivious to this mood music, Olena rushes into the main living room.

"Where's Papa?" she calls out, surprised not to find him there.

Fedorov appears at the door. "He's just back from the charity function you were meant to be attending. He's upstairs, at the moment."

Lewis enters the room and stands a few paces behind Fedorov. He stretches the muscles and ligaments in his right hand. He has bruising to his skin and tenderness in his wrist bones: all courtesy of Oleg Panich, the man who is somehow back from the dead. How exactly did he achieve that, he muses?

"I've anti-inflammatory gel in my room upstairs," Olena says watching him, interrupting his thoughts. "Let me get it. It'll reduce the pain and inflammation."

"Okay – but don't be long. We need to be away *pronto*. Lest we forget, Panich knows exactly where we are: we gave him this address when we got in his taxi."

Olena hurries out of the room. Lewis hears her climbing some stairs to the upper floor.

"Has Nemikov heard from Valentyna?" Lewis asks Fedorov, once Olena is out of the room.

Fedorov turns slowly to look at Lewis, his stare cold and unfriendly.

"Nothing."

"Any news from Gregor?"

"About what?"

"Don't be so obtuse, Sergei! You and I have to work together. We're meant to be on the same team. Given the bombing in Venice this afternoon is what I meant."

He shakes his head a little.

"Nothing."

"What do you mean, nothing?"

"She lose Gregor in Venice."

"How can he lose her, for fuck's sake? He's meant to be her security detail."

"She disappearing is not unusual."

"Doesn't she ever call or anything?" Lewis asks.

"Today no. It is not unusual."

"So she might have been on that *vaporetto* this afternoon after all."

Fedorov considers this before replying.

"She might. But she might not. Perhaps we never know."

"What about Borys? Who is babysitting him this evening?"

"Pavel. I speak ten minutes ago. Borys is at Cambridge flat. He is sleeping. All is okay in Cambridge."

Fedorov then turns and walks out of the room just as Olena arrives back. She heads over to where Lewis is standing and looks at him quizzically.

"What was Sergei saying?"

"Not a great deal. I don't think he appreciates me being on the Nemikov team."

She smiles at him. "Well I do, for one. If it weren't for you, I would be dead."

"You and me both," says Lewis.

She holds his eyes for a moment, smiling. Then, leaning forwards, she kisses him, gently but deliberately, her kiss carefully planted to one corner of his mouth. Her lips feel soft. To Lewis it feels great, lasting as it does, perhaps a second more than might have been expected.

"Just for the record, thank you." She smiles at him, her head coyly on one side, reminding Lewis of how pretty she is.

"Just for the record, it was my genuine pleasure."

They stare for a moment or two longer, saying nothing, before she seems to remember something.

"Come on, give me your wrist." She squeezes some cold clear gel onto her fingers before massaging the ointment over his bruises. "It should feel cold, but it will help stop the swelling."

"All part of the training, is it?"

"Something like that." They hear a new voice in the outer hallway. "That sounds like Papa," she says, massaging the last of the gel onto his wrist, replacing the cap on the tube. "We have so much to tell him."

37

Kristina Tian had been busy following her meeting with Viktor Plushenko. Having agreed her usual fee of one million dollars, plus expenses, the money payable only upon successful completion of the project, the next morning she had flown directly to Zurich. Her first task had been to learn as much as she could about the man with the keys to the Nemikov private office: the Swiss banker who went by the name of Rudi Hildebrandt.

Hildebrandt Private Bank AG was a family owned and run business. It had first been established in the nineteen-twenties and set up as an *Aktiengesellschaft*, a company limited by shares. Rudi Hildebrandt, the grandson of the founder, Tomas Hildebrandt, had lived and worked all his life in Zurich. Prior to the demise of the Soviet Union, the Hildebrandt family firm had become increasingly involved in assisting wealthy Ukrainians in managing their clandestine wealth; in particular, how to keep it well-hidden from the eyes of the communist rulers at the time. Franz Hildebrandt, Rudi's father, had been the man who had first established links with the Ukrainian elite. When his son, Rudi, had joined the firm as a young lawyer newly graduated from the University of Heidelberg, Franz had decided to introduce Rudi to one of the youngest, and wealthiest, Ukrainians that he'd recently come across: a highly successful entrepreneur called Arkady Nemikov. The two young men had hit it off immediately. Over the years, the growing strength of this relationship had created a strong bond of trust between them. When Nemikov had decided that he needed someone to run his private office and administer his estate after his death, there was only one person he had turned to: Rudi Hildebrandt. Available twenty-four hours a day, seven days a week – each and every day of the year,

Christmas and holidays included – Hildebrandt had served Arkady Nemikov faithfully, always endeavouring to treat him, and his many demands, like royalty.

Hildebrandt's life outside work had suffered. He had married late, his bride a young secretary who had been working at the office with him. They had one daughter, currently in her late teens and living alone with her mother. Hildebrandt and his wife had never divorced, but there had been little love between them for many years. This explained why he had chosen to live on his own, in an exclusive serviced apartment that overlooked the Zürichsee.

Rudi Hildebrandt currently led a fairly dull and routine life. Apart from walking to and from work each day, he occasionally shopped for groceries on his way home but otherwise rarely went out except at weekends. On those Saturdays when he wasn't working, and nearly every Sunday, he would stroll from his apartment to buy the weekend papers. He would then sit and read them over a leisurely coffee, usually at one of a small number of local coffee shops that he favoured. Afterwards he might stroll the city's streets or go for a boat ride across the lake to find a suitable lunch spot. Here he would usually choose poached perch caught fresh from the lake that morning with a glass or two of *Petite Arvine*. In the evenings, there would be occasional dinners out with friends or perhaps a concert or play that he wanted to attend: otherwise he would be at home, usually working. The only exception to this pattern was that on at least three nights every week – not always on the same night and often at different times – he would make his way to his local gym. Here, after a typical workout of no more than forty minutes, he would shower, head to the bar for a quick rehydrating drink, before returning home to his apartment, five minutes walk away.

Tian had been waiting at the bar by the time Rudi Hildebrandt had emerged from the locker room. He appeared with his receding grey hair swept back over his forehead, the hair still damp from his shower. She had been minding her own business, quietly winding down, sipping a mineral water and reading a book. Close by had been the self-service counter with jugs full of various juices and water for guests to help themselves. There had also been half a dozen clean glasses set aside for the purpose. Hildebrandt had opted for the elderflower and mint spritzer. He had poured a generous portion into a tall, thin, glass and had then come and sat at the stool next to her. She had watched out of the corner of an eye as he had lifted the glass tumbler and taken a sip.

Almost immediately Hildebrandt had begun searching for his mobile phone in an inner jacket pocket. Finally located, he had spent the next minute or so checking for messages. Tian had been excited. It was, as she had thought, an iPhone 6 model, the version with the TouchID fingerprint recognition system: it meant that Rudi hadn't needed to enter a security code when unlocking his phone: placing his thumbprint on the bottom button had been all that had been required. She had watched as he had used the phone, noting with satisfaction that he used his right thumb to unlock the device.

With barely a passing glance at Tian, five minutes later Hildebrandt had been ready to go. Bidding her a polite *gute nacht*, he had swivelled off his bar stool, picked up his gym bag and made his way silently out of the building. Tian would soon be following – but first she had one final thing to do. Picking an ultra-thin latex glove from out of the bottom of her capacious handbag, she had carefully pulled it over her right hand and fingers. Next, ensuring that no one was watching, she picked up Hildebrandt's glass, placing it inside a small cardboard container also in her bag especially for this purpose. She had taken special care not to smudge any finger – and, most importantly, any thumb – prints. She needed a perfect print for what she had in mind, pleased that she had been able to apply the odourless and colourless spray to each glass before Hildebrandt had emerged from the locker room.

38

Back in her hotel room, the equipment Tian had needed had been set up earlier. The bulkiest item had been the laser printer, currently connected to her laptop by means of a simple USB connection.

Donning another pair of thin latex gloves, this time one on each hand just to make sure, Tian had lifted the glass tumbler containing Hildebrandt's fingerprints and set it on the desktop in front of her. There had been two un-smudged thumbprints that she had found, both towards the lower half of the glass. One of the prints, in particular, had looked perfect.

From a small zipped bag she had taken out a clear plastic jar of dusting powder together with her favourite dusting brush, a Zephyr, made up of microscopically thin fibreglass strands. She always preferred to make her own powder: it never ceased to amaze her how easy it was. Over a burning candle the previous evening, she had held a smooth bottomed saucer until the bottom had become blackened with soot from the flame. The soot had then been carefully scraped off with a sharp knife into a plastic container. Repeating this a few times until she had sufficient, the resultant soot had been mixed with corn flour in a jam jar in the proportion: one part soot: three parts corn flour. The lid had then been screwed on and the jar shaken. That was it: homemade dusting powder, ready and waiting to be used.

The trick with dusting was not to use too much powder. For that reason, her preferred method was to shake the jar before unscrewing the lid and then swirling the Zephyr brush very gently around the inside of the lid in order to lightly coat the fine fibres. Next, very gingerly, she would dust fibres all over the area of the print. The essence of a good print was achieving good contrast. One trick she had learned over the years, therefore, was to fill the glass with milk once she had completed the dusting process. Conveniently, there had been a small carton in her hotel minibar. Once this had been completed, it was time to take some crystal sharp photographs.

The camera she had used was a Canon EOS 700 D, well able to produce a digital image at the required resolution of at least two thousand, four hundred pixels per inch: any less than this and the resultant thumbprint would not have been useable. She had placed the half-filled glass containing the dusted thumbprint on the desktop and angled the table lamb in order to create the right lighting contrast. Several digital photographs had been taken of the print from various angles. With her camera connected to the laptop, the digital images had swiftly uploaded onto her computer screen.

The next part was always the most tedious – but also the most essential. Choosing her best image, she had used Photoshop painstakingly to clean up the digital image. The reason for this was all down to the dusting powder. On the one hand it was an excellent medium for capturing the various ridges and contours of a thumbprint: the traces of human oil retained by Hildebrandt's thumbprint trapping the microscopically fine powder perfectly. On the other hand, when enlarged, the image quality was understandably grainy, the lines and contours of the image much more uneven than in real life. After several minutes of adding or deleting individual pixels, dot by dot across the whole thumbprint, she finally had what she thought – and hoped – was a clean image. Scaling this back to actual size, the software had, on her command, then inverted the entire image: the black dots became white and vice versa. Now she needed to print it. The print medium she had used was not paper but a transparent acetate slide. With the toner settings adjusted on the laser printer so that the contrast was set to maximum, this resulted in the thickest deposit of toner being baked onto the acetate as the thumbprints were printed.

Just to be safe, Tian had made four copies, letting the acetate slides cool before the final and most important part of the whole process: making a serviceable duplicate thumbprint. From her zipped bag, she had taken a bottle of ordinary latex wood glue. She squeezed a generous measure of the white liquid directly over the image on each transparency. As the latex began to dry, the ridges formed by the toner on each acetate slide would be captured within the crude latex mould that had been created. In effect, once dried and peeled away, each should, in theory, be a perfect replica of Hildebrandt's thumbprint.

39

Arkady Nemikov sits listening to Olena's account of that afternoon's events. He doesn't interrupt, his torso bolt upright. Nemikov's thin face exhibits fatigue and worry in equal measure. His dark brown eyes hold his daughter's without any waver in concentration.

"Weren't you hurt? When you fell from the taxi?"

"Not really. We weren't going that fast. I think Ben took the worst of it." She looks at Lewis and smiles. He in turn looks at Nemikov and shrugs silently. The meaning of the gesture is clear: *'I'm alive; we got away; it wasn't a problem.'*

"I'd be happier if you went away for a few days, my darling. Until all this dies down. Let me talk to Ben. I'll ask Sergei to escort you to the yacht. In Venice. No one will find you there."

"Isn't that where Mama is at the moment?"

"Yes. Sergei can organise the jet first thing tomorrow morning."

"This can't wait until tomorrow morning," Lewis interrupts. Nemikov looks at him, surprised.

"The taxi driver," Lewis continues. "He knows exactly where this house is."

"So does half of London," Nemikov replies. "Certainly anyone who might be interested."

"Trust me. This is not someone about to head home to lick his wounds before coming back at daylight after a nice restorative sleep. He was trying to kill us both earlier. He'll be on his way here to complete the job any time soon. Olena isn't safe here. Neither, really, are you. We have to be out of here immediately – there's no time to lose."

"I'm meant to be in an important paediatric training session all-day tomorrow," Olena protested.

"Forget it," Nemikov says firmly. "There'll be opportunities to do all that later. Ben's right. You need to get away. I'm staying. I can more than handle myself, trust me. Let me have a quick conversation with Ben whilst you go and pack a bag. On your way out, tell Sergei that you'll be leaving very shortly."

She gets up from the sofa and kisses her father on the forehead. Turning to look at Lewis, she hesitates, her cheeks colouring.

"Thanks for everything, Ben," she says eventually, not moving from her position beside her father. "I owe you for today."

"Don't mention it. Just keep safe and out of trouble. I'll see you soon enough, once this has all died down."

"Have you heard from Valentyna this evening?" Lewis asks Nemikov once the door to the living room is closed. They can both hear the sound of Olena's footsteps as she makes her way upstairs.

Nemikov stares expressionless at Lewis and shakes his head.

"Sergei implied earlier that she is prone to break loose from her bodyguards when she is on these overseas trips. Is that true?"

The Ukrainian lets out a loud sigh before answering.

"Valentyna is a free spirit. I cannot, and do not, try to control where she goes all the time. It would be a pointless, if not futile, exercise."

"How long is it usually before you hear from her?"

"Typically?" He sighs again, thinking about the question. "Usually she calls me once a day."

An antique clock in the middle of a marble mantelpiece softly chimes eleven o'clock.

"When? Morning or evening?"

"Usually before she goes to bed. Most often not later than midnight."

'Which would be about now in Venice?"

131

"Correct."

"Do you think it's possible that your wife was on the *vaporetto* that was destroyed this afternoon?"

There is silence in the room whilst Nemikov considers this. His eyes stare at the gas fireplace in one corner, before he looks up, shaking his head.

"What do you think?" the Ukrainian asks in return.

Lewis doesn't reply immediately. Instead he asks a seemingly unrelated question.

"What do you know about a very unpleasant former-SVR killer named Oleg Panich?"

Nemikov considers the name for a moment.

"I have never heard of him. Why?"

"What if I told you that the man driving the taxi this evening – the man who was waiting outside Paddington Green police station specifically for Olena and me, so that he could lure us both into his taxi and kill us – was none other than this man, Panich? He's the reason why Olena needs to get way from here in a hurry. Do you believe in coincidences?"

"Not especially, no."

"Good. Neither do I. When I saw the man on the train this afternoon, I knew that this wasn't another Islamic State suicide bomber. He was an ex-soldier, one of a small elite: someone with specialist training. It isn't hard to spot. A few hours later, a Russian agent who I had left for dead half way up a mountain several months ago, suddenly appears out of thin air trying to kill us both. Coincidence?" He shakes his head. "It's very unlikely."

"Added to that, at precisely the same time as the Welwyn bomb was intended to wreak its havoc, another bomb explodes, this time in the middle of Venice. Another coincidence? Was Islamic State really responsible? When taken together, it all sounds improbable - especially with the sudden appearance of Oleg Panich on the scene. I think Venice happened precisely because Valentyna Nemikov was there. I suspect that she

132

probably was on board that fatal *vaporetto* this afternoon. I'm sorry for being so blunt. Perhaps we'll never know."

Nemikov remains impassive throughout this. Lewis can see moisture in the Ukrainian's eyes as he thinks things through.

"If I was determined to coerce several billions from you, what would I do? I would go after your wife and children. You said it before. They are your Achilles heel. I think you have to accept the very possibility that your wife was killed this afternoon. And if we don't act swiftly, both your son and daughter are in very real danger of ending up dead as well."

40

Alexei Polunin was huddled in the shadows of a sports retail outlet, just off St. Andrew's Street, close to the centre of Cambridge. He was smoking a cigarette to calm his nerves, trying his best to be patient. He always became anxious when on a mission. The time was eleven-fifteen in the evening. Some while earlier, Vince, the two hundred and twenty pound hired muscle that Panich had taken on for this project, had parked the get-away vehicle. It was a battered old red transit, suitably nondescript: ideal for ferrying hidden cargo. Vince had found a parking space a few hundred metres away, just off the green parkland known as Christ's Pieces. The two of them were waiting for any one of the residents of the apartments above the sports shop to return home. Entry to this exclusive block of flats required an electronic key. Vince had wanted to break the lock. Polunin had been insistent on there being as little evidence of their breaking and entering as possible. That had meant waiting for someone else to open the door for them. Polunin's reasoning had been that the entrance was exposed, located as it was in a public thoroughfare: there had also been a security camera above the door. So instead they had waited – on balance, the better option.

They didn't have to wait long.

Within minutes, a lone male started approaching the apartments' entrance. He was in his mid-twenties, a mature student on his way home after a night out. The man was drunk, lurching unsteadily along the pedestrian precinct as he approached the security door. After two failed attempts, he succeeded in making his key fob work. The man then staggered inside the lobby, weaving unsteadily toward the elevator directly ahead of him. Whilst the outside door was closing, Polunin and Vince slipped into the building unseen.

They took the stairs to the first floor, making their way along the corridor that wound its way around the building. The corridor was open to the elements on one side, providing a clear view over various college rooftops and church spires. They reached the Nemikov apartment without meeting anybody. It was number twenty-five. Checking that there were no further security cameras, Polunin removed a Walther P22 pistol from his shoulder harness. He had fitted a Gemtech adaptor to the barrel before leaving the parked transit. Now he took an AAC Element Suppressor from another pocket and screwed this on to the adaptor. He had always liked the suppressed P22 for close quarters work. It was virtually silent when used indoors. At close range, it was also deadly accurate: especially if, like now, it was fitted with a Veridian laser sight.

They stopped outside the apartment and listened for sounds. They could hear nothing untoward. There were two locks on the door: a deadbolt and a cylinder. It took Vince less than a minute, using a specialist tool, before he had unlocked the deadbolt. The cylinder took less time. He eased the door open a fraction and then waited, listening carefully.

The light in the hallway was on. From the apartment's upper floor there came the sound of late-night television on low volume. The two men went inside and silently closed the door. Turning on the Veridian sight on the P22 pistol, Polunin bade Vince to remain downstairs, by the door, whilst the Russian inched his way up the stairs. Cast in concrete and covered by thick carpet, Polunin never made a sound as he made his way up. A concrete balustrade provided additional protection as he neared the top. He was entering a large open plan living area that, on this level, comprised the entire floor of the apartment.

Pavel, the security guard that Fedorov had referred to, was standing across the other side of the room, next to a kitchen worktop. His back was to Polunin, busy helping himself to an espresso from a machine installed on the counter. Visible from across the room was a shoulder harness: in it, tucked under his left armpit, was a Makarov 9mm pistol.

The man never stood a chance.

One noise-less shot from the P22 was all that was required before Pavel began sliding, gracefully, to the floor. He took the bullet cleanly in the back and it followed through into his chest cavity. The gun was so silent that it was barely audible above the noise coming from the television. Polunin fired one more round, just to make certain. He then retraced his steps to the lower level. Vince was waiting, a pair of knuckle-dusters on his right hand.

It was time to take care of Borys.

41

Nemikov and Lewis are sitting in silence. The Ukrainian appears deep in thought.

"You think this man Panich is SVR?" Nemikov asks eventually. "Can you be sure?"

"He certainly was. I'd be surprised if he still is, though, given his field injuries."

"In which case someone has hired him. Someone like Victor Plushenko, for example."

"It certainly seems plausible."

"While Sergei takes Olena to the yacht, will you go and find Borys and escort him there as well? If I lose my family, I will have lost everything."

"Let me help get Olena safely on to your plane first. I know Panich. He will stop at nothing to try and get at her – or me for that matter. I wouldn't want Fedorov to let his testosterone get in the way of underestimating the peril your family might be in."

"Don't you trust Sergei?"

"Put it this way. If I were Panich, right this moment I would be on my way to this very house, plotting a way to kill or kidnap your daughter. Goodness knows what he has in mind for me. Fedorov may be good. However, I don't think he's that good."

"Maybe Panich is here already. Perhaps he's waiting outside as we speak?"

"Quite likely. Tell me, how many cars do you have?"

"Three. An Audi S3 and a Range Rover that are both parked on the street outside, and a yellow Lamborghini in a lock-up garage adjoining the house here in the mews."

Lewis raises his eyebrows in silent admiration.

"So here's a plan. I drive Olena to the airport in the Audi.

Initially she can hide in the front passenger foot well. At the same time, Fedorov departs in the Range Rover. Fedorov goes one way and I head another. If we're lucky, we might be able to organise a police escort. I should make a call before we leave in any event. Where is your jet at the moment?"

"Luton. Unlike most other UK airports, it's open twenty-four seven if you pay enough money."

"So, Fedorov heads directly northwards as if heading to Luton and I go in a different direction. That way, if there are more than one of them, we half the risk that they will end up following the car that Olena's in."

"Why not take the Lamborghini? You'd be faster than anything else on the road."

"Because it'll stand out a mile. Besides, the Audi will be very fast. Around London, it should be more than adequate. Whilst I am gone, who else is around to look after you?"

"Just my housekeeper and a driver. Stop worrying, I am more than able to take care of myself for a few hours."

"I'll see if I can organise something." Lewis locates his mobile phone and starts searching for a number. "Once I've made a few calls, I'd like to take a walk around the neighbourhood. After that, Fedorov, Olena and I must be on our way."

42

"Show me your hand."

Virenque had brought medical supplies with him. They were both sitting in the back of the taxi. With a small Maglite torch held between his teeth, the former Spetsbureau 13 agent carefully peeled away the makeshift bandage that Panich had applied to his injured wrist. The Russian winced in pain but said nothing. Virenque took the flashlight out of his mouth and shone the beam from different angles.

"I think it looks worse than it is. Can you bend your fingers?"

Panich clenched his fist a little, the pain evident in his eyes. He made no sound. He was feeling unusually breathless and it was bothering him: usually he was super-fit. He dismissed the thought and tried instead to block out the pain in his wrist.

"I don't think you've any serious ligament damage. I'm going to clean the wound, and then apply paper stitches and a bandage. You'll be good as new."

Both knew this wasn't true, but neither was in a position to say anything different.

"What happened on the train this afternoon?" Panich asked.

Virenque told him as he cleaned the wound with some rubbing alcohol.

"That Lewis is a lucky bastard," Panich said through clenched teeth as Virenque positioned two paper stiches. "I've had goodness knows how many chances to kill him. Every time, somehow he manages to slip away unscathed. No one does that to me and gets away with it."

"So, we both have scores to settle with him. Do you know where he's taken the girl?"

Panich nodded, smiling for the first time that evening.

"Not far from here. A small and exclusive garden mews in Kensington."

A knocking on the window caused both men to look up. A police officer in motorcycle leathers was standing on the pavement next to their taxi.

"Shit," muttered Virenque under his breath. "That's poor timing."

"Or maybe fortuitous," said Panich quietly.

"I need both of you to step outside the vehicle, please." The policeman was speaking to them in a loud voice through the still-closed passenger window. He had spotted something suspicious: what appeared to be a bullet hole in the roof of the taxi. He was in the process of depressing the button on his lapel microphone, presumably about to report in the details over his radio.

Virenque's speed, agility and strength was surprising, even to Panich. No sooner had the Frenchman placed his hand on the door handle than he was out of the taxi. Using power stored in his bent knees, he moved rapidly from a sitting crouch to a standing position, raising himself up to face the policeman in one swift movement. This small amount of upward momentum was sufficient to cause the right-handed punch that Virenque delivered to the tip of the policeman's jawbone to land with knockout force. The man's head snapped backwards. He fell to the pavement deeply unconscious.

"Quick, I'll help you get him in the back!" Panich shouted at Virenque through the open door. After hauling the body inside, Virenque stripped the man of his fluorescent jacket before putting it on himself.

"This one's armed!" Virenque held up a Glock 17 pistol.

"Special Escort Group. They protect VIPs and diplomats. Another gun could prove handy."

"Come on then," Virenque said by the time he had finished donning the bare essentials of the policeman's uniform. He had also handcuffed the man, even though he was unconscious.

Panich was, by this stage, back in the driver's seat. "It must be time to pay the Nemikovs, not to mention our friend Lewis, a house call, don't you think?"

Panich gave Virenque a smile through the broken glass window partition.

"My thoughts exactly. You've got a powerful police BMW bike to play with and I have a London taxi. What better cover? It's time to have some fun." Panich restarted the taxi's engine.

"What are you going to do with this one?" Virenque asked, climbing out of the cab, referring to the still unconscious policeman with a nod of his head.

"For now, just leave him tied up in the back. I'll drop him down some dark side street en route to the Nemikov place. Are you all set?"

Virenque nodded.

"Then I'll see you in Kensington in a few minutes.

43

The time is several minutes after eleven in the evening. Lewis has ventured onto the street in order to familiarise himself with the layout of the neighbourhood. He wants to see whether he can spot Panich lurking in the shadows: perhaps the bomber from the train might be here as well?

A short while earlier, Lewis had been speaking firstly to Jake Sullivan's rather surly section head, Laura, and then subsequently to Saul Zeltinger. MI5 were not, it seems, interested in providing any field assistance to Lewis: Nemikov wasn't currently on their operational radar. Whilst Laura appeared vaguely interested in hearing about Oleg Panich's return from the grave, she was unable to offer Lewis any help on the ground. Which is why Lewis next calls Saul Zeltinger. The half-German Detective Inspector, to use a degree of exactitude that Zeltinger himself would have been proud of, is at home when Lewis rings. He answers Lewis's call on the second ring.

"I have just finished eating a very nice lasagne, as it happens, Ben. It is the same one that Hattie, my darling wife, made for you, Ben. You were meant to be here, playing chess if you recall?"

"I trust you sent my apologies, Saul?" Lewis says.

"My long-suffering wife is well used to it. What can I do for you at this hour, Ben?"

Lewis explains his current predicament, in particular Oleg Panich being alive and once more in London.

"Very interesting," Zeltinger says once Lewis has finished. "You think Panich is working freelance?"

"I can't see the SVR keeping him on with a prosthetic arm, can you?"

"It's unlikely: certainly not as a field agent. Do you think the kidnap threat to Nemikov's daughter is real?"

"Totally – and, equally as likely to his son. He's currently in Cambridge. I'm heading there once the daughter, Olena, is safe."

"I'll make some calls and see if I can organise an escort for you up to Luton. Would that be helpful?"

Lewis assures him that it would and ends the call.

Nemikov's Kensington residence comprises four separate houses. Originally they had been purchased as separate dwellings before being joined together to form one large property. It is located in a private, gated mews at the eastern end of Lexham Gardens. This is a West London residential neighbourhood of smart, terraced houses. The road itself runs parallel with the major London westbound artery known as the Cromwell Road.

Because of its location, Nemikov and his family are able to leave their property in one of two ways. Either via the front door directly onto the mews: thereafter, once through their own security gate, they are out into Lexham Gardens and from there, indirectly, they have access to the Cromwell Road. Or the secondary way is out of the back of one of the conjoined properties. This lets them out in another, smaller, private mews linked to a completely separate, residential square called Cornwall Gardens. There is no direct road linking the two garden squares, only a pedestrian walkway. Nemikov explained to Lewis earlier that he finds the location of his Kensington house hugely convenient. He is able to leave one car parked on the mews off Lexham Gardens and another in the similar mews off Cornwall Gardens: anyone wanting to keep him under surveillance never knows which car or which exit route he is going to be taking when leaving the property. This evening the Range Rover is parked in front of the house itself, within the gated mews. The Audi is a short distance away in the side mews off Cornwall Gardens.

Lewis feels his phone vibrating in his pocket once again. He removes it and answers the call.

"Saul. What news?"

"Not good. I have been trying to find a police motorbike escort to keep you company on your journey to Luton."

"Well?"

"There's a flap on. One of the Special Escort Group riders and his bike have gone missing. Just over an hour ago. The rider was waiting outside an embassy near Hyde Park Corner when he saw a taxi parked up with its light off. The last we heard, he was on his way to investigate."

"I wonder whether it could have been Panich's taxi?"

"That's a possibility. Look, because of the way that so much appears to be linking to Nemikov and his family, a police car is on its way over to Kensington right now. Finding the missing policeman and his bike are a bigger priority than baby-sitting you all the way to Luton, I'm afraid."

"Understood. Keep me in the loop, can you?"

Lewis walks out of the gated mews and into Lexham Gardens itself. The road at this point encircles a large rectangular-shaped garden that is fenced and locked: for the use of residents only. Cars are parked tightly packed together: every available curb space adjacent to the roadway has been used. Walking briskly in the cold, night air, Lewis heads around the outside perimeter in a clockwise direction. As he passes, he looks briefly at each vehicle and the surrounding buildings. He wants to know if any cars are occupied – or whether anyone is loitering in one of the balustraded entrances to any one of the Victorian terraced houses.

He is about two-thirds of the way around when he spots two people: a man and a woman, sitting inside a Vauxhall Astra parked up ahead. The car is facing forwards, giving the two occupants a clear view directly towards the Nemikov property ahead. As he gets closer, Lewis hears voices. He can't see much of the man who is sitting in the driver's seat. The woman in the passenger seat has short blonde hair and is wearing a thick duffel coat. Her voice is loud and sounds American. He keeps walking, right past their car. Out of the corner of his eye he notices the woman has her mobile phone on her lap: the screen is lit. It tells Lewis that her phone may be on. Lewis notes the registration of the car and commits it to memory.

A few yards further on, he sees two other things that catch his attention. In the distance, beyond the mews entrance and on the short road heading directly to the Cromwell Road, are two London black cabs. They are parked in front of a small private hotel with their orange 'for hire' lights off, both with drivers sitting waiting. Could one of these be Panich?

The second thing he sees is more concerning. As he walks around the right-hand bend back towards the gated mews, to his left is the pedestrian walkway connecting Lexham and Cornwall Gardens. Bollards have been set in the pavement to prevent cars from using it. Just visible, jutting out from between two houses, are the front forks of a motorbike. Walking past, he catches a glimpse of the blue and fluorescent yellow chequered flashes of a Metropolitan Police motorbike.

44

Chess players are typically one of two types: natural born attackers or natural born defenders. Lewis considers himself a natural born attacker. On the front foot, thinking several moves ahead. Deceiving opponents by feigning an attacking move here, before coming on strong in another completely different direction there. It is why he plans to send Fedorov off in the Range Rover. To use him as a decoy. It will draw Panich's eye in the wrong direction. It might be enough to give Lewis a life-saving advantage.

Lewis is itching to discover whether one of the two taxi drivers is Panich. If so, his natural disposition would ordinarily be to find a quick and permanent way to remove him from the field of play. Likewise with the person sitting on the hidden police motorbike. If it were, indeed, the Welwyn bomber, then Lewis would like nothing better than to be circling around behind him, in the shadows, and slitting his throat. The man deserved nothing less. There had been children on the train that afternoon. Not to mention Olena. Any man who tries to explode a bomb on a crowded train earns himself the death sentence, in Lewis's mind. End of discussion.

Uncharacteristically, Lewis feels compelled to make his moves with more caution. There are too many unknowns making the entire neighbourhood not simply hostile – but potentially deadly. For one, he is on his own and without backup: he doesn't know who the pair in the Astra are, and what their connection to Panich, if any, might be; and he has no knowledge about whether anyone else might be watching – for example, from an upper storey window, perhaps with a night scope attached to a long-distance sniper rifle?

So Lewis decides on an alternative gameplay. He will call Saul Zeltinger. Perhaps the mobile police unit that Zeltinger referred to earlier as being on its way could flush both parties out? That would leave it clear for Lewis and Olena to make their way, unseen, out of the side entrance of the Nemikov's property and into the waiting Audi A3, currently parked in the mews off Cornwall Gardens.

Lewis reaches the security gate at the entrance to the mews and Fedorov buzzes him through. Once inside, he reaches for his phone to dial Zeltinger's number. The time is eleven-twenty in the evening.

45

"Target three is returning to base."

The blonde-haired woman was speaking. All parties – the fellow agent next to her and those listening in on the call – were listening intently.

"Are you certain no one's following?" It was a male voice coming through loud and clear over the speakerphone.

"Affirmative. At any rate, from where we are, his tail looks clean. The geography of the neighbourhood makes it hard to tell. I can head out and try and take a look, if it helps?"

"Not yet. What's the view like from up top?"

Another voice, this time another male, came on the line.

"There are two black cabs waiting outside a small, private hotel not far from the entrance to the property. Other than that it looks clear."

"Okay, people, listen up. The time is fast approaching. Once target three and the girl are gone, target one will be alone in the property. Perhaps not for long. We have to plan on having a very narrow window."

The man described the next steps in the plan. "Does anyone have any questions?" he said at the end, a few minutes later.

"Should we follow target one, when he eventually leaves the property?"

"Negative. By that stage, everything should all have been taken care of."

The blonde woman interrupted the conversation. There was a heightened sense of urgency in her tone.

"We've got trouble. A police car has just arrived. It's driven right by us, now it's stopping: a few yards ahead of us, next to the pedestrian cut-through to the neighbouring square." She checked her watch.

"This could change things," came the male voice over the

loudspeaker. "Keep the line open. We should reassess in a few minutes."

The time was eleven twenty-eight in the evening.

46

"Okay. Time to go." Lewis is checking his watch as he speaks. It is almost exactly eleven-thirty. He, Olena, Fedorov and Nemikov are standing together in the main hallway. On either side is the meandering corridor that connects each of the four interlinked houses. Nemikov has just been having a private conversation with Lewis in his study. It has not been a conversation that included Fedorov. The expression on the Ukrainian security guard's face shows that he is not happy about Lewis's newfound intimacy and favouritism with his employer.

"Sergei, you're taking the Range Rover. Olena and I will go in the Audi. Remember to keep all phones turned off until we reach Luton."

"That's crazy! How we speak with each other?" Fedorov asks gruffly in his poor English.

"The last time I was up against this particular Russian, he proved adept at knowing where people were by tracking their mobile phones."

Fedorov grunts but says nothing.

"Everyone ready?"

Fedorov nods, casually tossing the Range Rover's keys in the air. It is his attempt to demonstrate how calm he can be under pressure. He then turns towards the door that leads directly onto the Lexham Gardens mews. "See you at Luton. Don't keep me waiting."

He opens the door and is gone. The time is eleven thirty-one.

Olena turns to give her father a huge hug. Her eyes are moist with tears. A few minutes earlier her father had told her about the bombing in Venice and the possibility that her mother was missing.

"I'll track Mum down when I get to Venice. She often goes walkabout. You'll see. Will you promise me that you won't do anything stupid whilst you're left on your own?"

"I'll be fine. It's you I am more worried about. I am relying on Ben here to work his magic." He briefly touches Lewis's arm. "For the love of God, Ben, please don't let me down."

47

The driver of the Hyundai i30 incident response vehicle was unarmed, although that in no way diminished his bravery. Wearing a protective bulletproof vest under his fluorescent zip-up jacket, with various handcuffs and restraining devices clipped to his belt, he approached the stationary BMW R1200RT without fear or hesitation. If he had known the deadly situation he was about to walk into, he might perhaps have used more caution.

The pedestrian walkway was lit but not brightly. There was enough light to see everything on the footpath itself: even the fluorescent flashes on the BMW stood out clearly – although it was too dark to see into the shadows. Which was why the advancing policeman had turned on his small pocket flashlight. He was pointing the tiny beam to the left and right as he approached the alley where the bike was parked.

Stopping by the entrance, immediately in front of the bike, was his biggest mistake. If he had carried on walking a few yards further, he might have noticed the unmistakeable shape and form of a man concealing himself in the shadows. Virenque had guessed, correctly, that the half-hidden motorbike was going to be the magnet that drew the advancing man to a halt. It gave the Frenchman the opportunity he was looking for. With a deadly speed that the policeman never saw coming, he came from behind. Putting an arm around the unsuspecting man's neck, he executed a full arm lock with all the strength he could muster. The man wriggled and fought, but that simply made Virenque squeeze tighter: the life was draining from him as he struggled to breathe. Gradually, Virenque felt all resistance weakening. Choosing his moment, he finally snapped and twisted his locked arm in a counter-clockwise direction. The grizzly sound of the policeman's neck being broken was all that could be heard.

Virenque hauled the policeman's dead body into the alley beyond where the BMW bike was parked. The arrival of the policeman potentially gave him two transport options: the Hyundai car or the BMW R1200? For Virenque, it was a no-brainer. For manoeuvring around the London streets, the BMW was going to win every time. He checked his watch. It was eleven-thirty one in the evening. Lewis and the Nemikov girl had to be leaving shortly. He rocked the police motorbike off its stand. Then, flicking the electronic ignition to the 'on' position, he inched the machine out of the alley and into the back mews behind Cornwall Gardens.

48

A small concrete staircase leads down to pavement level from a nondescript door at the back of the house. The black Audi car is parked metres away. Lewis clicks the electronic key fob; the car's headlights come on automatically as the doors unlock. He directs Olena to the front passenger seat before climbing in behind the wheel and hitting the electronic ignition.

"Pull your seat backwards. Rake the seat incline and squeeze yourself down into the foot well."

"Are you serious?" Olena asks.

"Totally. If Panich has a team out there waiting, we are a much more likely target if they see two people in the car rather than one."

Olena reluctantly obeys, disappearing below the dashboard with difficulty.

The car is fast. Lewis finds that they soon reach the junction with Gloucester Road. He checks his mirror. He sees nothing that immediately catches his attention.

"Where are we going?"

"I thought you knew. Luton airport. The private jet terminal. I thought we would take the scenic route."

"Why?"

"I need to take care of you, apparently."

She looks up at him from the footwell and smiles weakly.

"You've been doing that all day, Ben. I've never had my life saved so many times in one twenty-four hour period before."

Lewis turns left on to the Cromwell Road, heading towards Knightsbridge and the West End of London.

"Did your father tell you what happened in Venice this afternoon?"

Olena doesn't reply immediately, lost in thought as Lewis drives.

"Papa says that he has given you Mama's security codes," she says eventually. "As a precaution. Is that right?"

Now it is Lewis's turn to remain silent. Before they had left the Kensington House, Nemikov had indeed entrusted Ben with Valentyna's security codes. He sighs as he remembers the conversation of a few minutes ago.

"Ben, if Valentyna really is dead, I need someone I trust to take her place. I'd like you to be that person."

They are standing together in Nemikov's study. There is a large chess table in the centre of the room, but no game is in play. Expensive-looking oil paintings adorn the walls; two are of young ballerinas on stage. Lewis is no expert but they appear to be by the French painter, Degas.

"Why me and not Fedorov?" Lewis asks.

"Because I instinctively trust you. You have shown today that you are totally loyal and thoroughly professional. In fact, the less involvement you have previously had with my family, the more confident I am that I can trust you to help me. Much more than someone like Fedorov who has been working with my family for years."

"Don't you trust Fedorov?"

"Ukrainian loyalties are tough to get to the bottom of," he answers cryptically. "I do trust him, but, at this particular moment in time, I have my reasons to trust you more."

He is dressed still in a double-breasted dinner jacket and black tie from the charity function earlier in the evening. He fixes Lewis with a long, penetrating, stare.

"As I explained when we first met: in the event of my death or disappearance, my affairs automatically revert to the control of my Swiss lawyer, Rudi Hildebrandt. The offices of Hildebrandt Private Bank AG are in Zurich. Should anything happen to me, I have given individual and unique access codes to Valentyna, Olena and Borys. Anyone trying to gain access to my money will soon discover that Rudi is unable to release any monies from my estate unless, and until, he is in possession of all three codes." He moves across to one of the ballerina paintings, hanging on the wall behind a mahogany desk. It is mounted on a hinge. As the picture swings away from the wall, there is a small safe behind it. A few moments later, Nemikov hands Lewis a piece of paper.

"These are Valentyna's codes. Do you think you will be able to memorise them?" He is smiling as he hands Lewis the piece of paper: shortly the former Marine understands why.

"If this is what you want," he says looking at Nemikov. "I am happy to play my part. As you say, for someone like me, remembering these should be very straightforward."

He glances at the paper one more time before handing it back to Nemikov.

"I have spoken this evening to Hildebrandt. You are now officially standing in for Valentyna, on the assumption that she may, God help us, be no longer alive."

Beyond the Natural History museum, Knightsbridge is fast approaching up ahead.

"What your father has put in place is actually a clever arrangement."

"How so?" asks Olena.

"If anyone is desperate enough to get their hands on his money and either kills or kidnaps him, it provides a layer of protection for you and your brother."

"And now you."

"Or your mother, assuming she remains alive."

"What do you think happened in Venice today?" she asks him.

Lewis doesn't answer. In his rear mirror, he can see a police motorbike fast approaching, heading towards the Audi, its blue lights flashing.

More to himself than to Olena, he mutters, "I think we have company."

The time is eleven thirty-four.

49

Oleg Panich was doing what he always did when he was anxious: smoking one of his – often described by former colleagues as foul – Turkish cigarettes. His new right hand was good for many things; however, the fine motor skills required to curl mechanised fingers around a slender cigarette was a step too far. Nowadays, he was reconciled to smoking with his left hand. Even though bandaged and sore from his recent interaction with Lewis, Panich had learnt over the years to block out pain. Now, as so many times before, he drew comfort and temporary peace of mind through inhaling the warm smoke into his lungs.

He checked his watch. It was eleven twenty-eight in the evening.

Only a short while earlier, he had watched as Lewis performed a reconnaissance circuit of the neighbourhood. Panich had been tempted to leave the cab, tail the former Marine and kill him on the streets with his GSh-18 pistol. Four things had stopped him. Firstly, all said and done, his primary mission was to take care of the girl. Secondly, Volkov, damn him, had been adamant: no private enterprise against Lewis! Thirdly, he had no idea who else was in the neighbourhood watching the Nemikovs. Killing Lewis on a London street in cold blood without reconnaissance was reckless, bordering on the insane. The real clincher, though, had been that, deep down, Panich felt that killing Lewis with a bullet to the back of his head on a London side street, was too simple: too painless an ending for someone who had caused him so much grief. In any event, wherever the girl seemed to be heading, Lewis on current form would be close by. There would be other, better chances to get Lewis, of that he was convinced: especially ones that allowed Panich no small element of retribution.

So, he had remained parked up outside one of the small, run-down, private hotels adjacent to the Nemikov property. There was one other cabbie waiting like himself: most likely a pre-booked, late nighter to somewhere far away – a clandestine affair between two parties with a free cab ride home for one of them. Panich's position provided a good vantage point over all comings and goings to the Nemikov property. He also knew that Virenque was waiting just around the corner on the police motorbike.

His mobile phone gave a muted buzz. With the cigarette held in his mouth, he took out his phone and saw a brief text from Polunin. The Nemikov boy, Borys, had indeed been taken alive. Excellent. Polunin was on his way to the safe house with him now, cuffed and sedated. Very good. One dead, one captured: all that remained was for the girl – and Lewis – to be taken care of.

A police car raced past Panich's parked taxi, its blue lights flashing. It drove around the garden square, parking close to where Virenque was hiding. Panich found Virenque's mobile number on his phone and hit 'dial'.

"The police have just arrived. One is about to come your way," was all he said.

A few minutes later, Panich was still debating what to do when his phone buzzed for a second time. He looked at the screen. The message read: '*RR is decoy. You want Audi from Corn Gards.*'

Panich started his engine as the security gates to the Nemikov property began sliding open. Moments later, a metallic-grey coloured Range Rover burst out of the driveway, the noise from the powerful V8 engine clearly audible as it accelerated away from Panich in a westerly direction. Panich dialled Virenque's mobile number once again.

"Any problems?" he asked the Frenchman.

"No, all taken care of," was the reply that came back.

"Good. It's the Audi we want apparently. They should be

leaving any time now,"

50

"Target one is finally alone in the house." The man in the driver's seat of the Vauxhall Astra was speaking. His accent was hard to call. It sounded oddly mid-Atlantic. He had an unusual shock of silvery-white hair to one side of his otherwise thick, black hair: apart from that there were few other distinguishing features.

"How long do you need?"

"Five minutes." The man checked his watch. It was eleven thirty-three.

"Do you have all you need?"

"Sure. It's not going to take long to convince him. It's the fallout we have to worry about."

"What's happening with the police car?"

"Still here. The driver went to investigate something on foot. He hasn't yet returned to his car."

"Should one of you go check it out? We can't risk being seen with target one."

"I'll go." It was the blonde-haired woman.

"Okay."

"I have you covered." It was the sniper on the roof. His vantage point was a fifth floor balcony across the street.

Three minutes later, the blonde-haired woman was back in the car.

"There's a police officer down in the alley," she called out once the door was closed.

"Dead?"

"I guess."

"You'll have to abort then." It was the man on the phone speaking.

"Not necessarily. There may be a short window right now.

Before the shit hits the fan," the man in the driver's seat replied.

"It's your call. But it feels high risk to me."

"This whole fucking thing is high risk." The man's mind was made up. "I'm going in. The rest of you, watch my back." He donned a black woollen beanie hat that covered his hair and ears. It made him look almost unrecognisable. "Remember. Five minutes."

Walking briskly towards the property, he took out a separate cell phone and hit the one and only number pre-programmed into the device. The call was answered seconds later. Sure enough, no sooner was he approaching the locked security side gate adjacent to the Nemikov private mews, than it 'clicked' open to let him in.

51

Virenque had watched the Audi drive away at high speed whilst he was emerging from the mews behind Cornwall Gardens. The bike's lights were switched off as he pulled onto the roadway, Virenque wanting to remain concealed until he knew in which direction Lewis was heading. There was little fear of losing him: the bike's acceleration was always going to be much faster than the Audi's. Virenque had secreted his mobile phone so that it was wedged inside his police bike helmet: the earpiece was thus close to his ear, the line open directly to Oleg Panich. It allowed them both to talk freely to each other whilst on the move.

"He's on Gloucester Road heading south. Are you sure he's got the girl?"

"Positive."

Virenque turned right at the road junction, his headlights now switched on. In the distance he could see the Audi turning left on to the Cromwell Road, heading for the centre of the city.

"Where are you?"

"Leaving Lexham Gardens. The Nemikov Range Rover has just driven away at speed, heading in the other direction. That's the decoy vehicle, apparently."

"I hope to God you're right. The Audi's heading east on the Cromwell Road. I'm going to try and stop them. Where are you?"

"Less than a minute behind you."

"I'm turning my blue flashing lights on. I want Lewis, as well as you, to be able to see me coming."

52

Lewis checks his mirror. The police motorcyclist is less than fifty metres away and closing. The rider is positioned on the road immediately behind him, hugging the lane centre line. Its blue lights are turned on and flashing.

"Keep your head down, Olena. We've definitely got company."

As the bike draws nearer, Lewis maintains a constant speed: he resists the temptation to apply the brakes. They are passing Brompton Oratory church, heading towards Knightsbridge. The traffic in their direction is free flowing; the lights thus far have all been green.

Lewis keeps one eye on his mirror. He knows that the biker won't be Panich. Riding a bike with a prosthetic hand would be impossible without serious modifications. The question is: is this a genuine policeman? Or could he, perhaps, be one of Panich's accomplices? Maybe the man from the train?

The biker starts to draw parallel with the Audi. Lewis considers it's time to change tactic: he hits the brakes. The Audi decelerates quickly, causing the bike to overshoot and take up a new position in front. For a split second Lewis thinks the biker might, after all, be genuine.

Then he sees two things that persuade him otherwise.

The rider's uniform for one. The biker is dressed in a fluorescent jacket and helmet that are totally appropriate for a Metropolitan Police Special Escort Officer; but his trousers and shoes aren't. Despite the dark, Lewis glimpses jeans and heavy-duty combat boots: not the waterproof trousers and special boots that they normally wore.

The second is the gun. Hurriedly pulled out of an inside jacket pocket as soon as he shoots past Lewis's Audi, the gun is the giveaway. This is no ordinary policeman. The gun may be a genuine police Glock 17 pistol. London's police force, however, do not patrol the streets of the capital on their motorbikes, waving Glock 17 handguns as though they were in the Wild West.

53

He was driving with his foot flat on the accelerator, the Manganese Bronze taxi closing the gap on both Lewis and Virenque. Panich tore through a red light at South Kensington, narrowly avoiding a collision with another car at the junction. This burst of speed meant that he was able to close the gap on the flashing blue lights of Virenque's bike up ahead.

"I'm about one hundred metres behind you, and closing," he said to the Frenchman over the open channel. "What's your plan?"

"I'm going to try and blow out his tyres. If I do that, can you ram him from the rear?"

"Good plan. Any sign of the girl?"

"Not yet. She may be in the back – or hiding in the front. I'll try and see as I get closer." There was silence and then swearing. "Fuck! He just hit the brakes. I've overshot. It is definitely Lewis. I'm going to try and take a shot."

The distance from Panich's taxi to the Audi was twenty metres and closing. The Russian's foot was still on the accelerator. He could see Virenque reaching into an inner pocket and removing a gun with his left hand. Panich knew how problematic firing a gun from a moving motorbike was going to be. If anyone stood a chance, it had to be a Moscow-trained assassin such as Virenque.

The Audi was accelerating once again, closing the gap on Virenque. Without warning, the car veered sharply to the right, narrowly missing Virenque's rear tyre. Instead, the Audi swung across the wide boulevard immediately in front of the Harrods department store, heading down a side road. It avoided hitting a crowded bus coming in the opposite direction by a hair's breadth. Panich, trying his best to follow suit, was just a second or two too late. He had little option but to slam on his brakes in order to avoid driving straight into the bus. The Russian swore loudly, losing precious seconds until a gap in the traffic allowed him to drive off. Virenque was in no better position. He too cursed Lewis loudly having been forced almost to a stop. Finally able to execute a sharp U-turn, he twisted the throttle to maximum, accelerating rapidly through the gear changes. He overtook Panich in the taxi, intently focused on closing the gap on the Audi, now some distance ahead.

54

"Bloody hell, Ben. Are you trying to get us killed?"

Olena lifts her head above the window for a moment. She can see, as well as feel, Lewis taking evasive action.

"Keep your head down. There are two on our tail. I'm trying to lose them. Hold tight."

Lewis floors the accelerator, feeling the enormous power from the Sportsback's engine kick in. He zigzags across Basil Street at speed, making his way eastwards towards Belgravia. His knowledge of the streets of Central London should give him the advantage: it is certainly likely to be better than the Russian's. Whether it is better than the biker's remains to be seen.

The traffic is light as he crosses Sloane Street. He checks his mirror. The police bike is doing its best to keep up, but is still some fifty metres behind. Lewis guns the two-litre turbo diesel injection engine. The car responds by accelerating to almost eighty miles an hour. Lewis takes a left hand bend as he enters Belgrave Square. Behind him the bike has begun to gain ground once more. As he continues around the square in a clockwise direction, Lewis hears two shots ring out behind him; one bullet actually ricochets off the door panel behind him.

"The bastard's shooting at us. Hang on."

Lewis floors the accelerator again, this time taking the slip road off the roundabout to the left, in the direction of Hyde Park Corner. Stationary cars are queuing at traffic lights up ahead. So instead, he cuts across three lanes of traffic at high speed to take up a position in an empty right hand lane, just as the lights turn green. Behind him the police bike, its blue lights still flashing, finds itself caught having to weave its way in and out of the traffic in his wake. For the time being Lewis has the advantage. It is unlikely to last for long. Continuing around the huge Hyde Park Corner roundabout the Audi turns into Piccadilly. Lewis believes this to be a better option than the possibly clearer roads around Buckingham Palace. In theory it provided more options to cut in and out of side roads.

He has a sudden idea.

"I want you to get ready to leap out of the car, Olena."

"Are you bonkers? With the Russians trying to kill us both?"

"Trust me. They won't know where you have gone. They will continue believing that you are in the car with me – until they learn that you are not. Climb into the passenger seat and get ready to jump out. Coming up soon on the right is the Ritz Hotel. Run in there, find somewhere to sit quietly, and wait. If I'm not with you in thirty minutes, ask the night porter to organise you a taxi to take you to Luton. It's the last thing anyone will be expecting."

"What about you?"

"I'm going to try and lead our friends astray."

Up ahead, adjacent to the junction with St. James's Street, the traffic light is set at red. There are three cars sitting stationary at the junction. There is no way to manoeuvre around them. The flashing blue lights of the police bike are some distance behind him but getting nearer. Lewis has little option but to slow the car to a halt as he waits for the traffic lights to turn green.

"Okay. Time to go. The entrance is just across the street there," he says pointing with one hand. He remembers to turn off the interior door light so that the lamp doesn't glow in the dark. "Be quick. If I'm late for any reason, jump into a cab, send me a text once you're safe, and then turn off your phone. Go!"

Too confused to argue, Olena does as Lewis orders. No sooner is she out of the car and into the shadows of the hotel, than the Audi is accelerating away, turning right across into

St. James's. The police motorbike, its lights flashing, is closing in on his tail.

55

"I'm having trouble keeping up," Panich was saying over the open channel line to Virenque.

"Don't worry, the stupid bastard's turned into Piccadilly. The late night traffic will slow him down."

"I heard a couple of shots back there. Did you hit anything?"

There was a sigh from the Frenchman.

"Negative."

"It's never as easy as it looks."

"I'm still hoping to take out his tyres. I'm relying on you to provide transport away from here for them both."

"Okay. I'm currently just coming off Hyde Park Corner roundabout and about to head down Piccadilly."

"We're less than a minute apart, then. Hold on, I may have spotted something." The line went silent for a moment.

"The Audi's turning right, into St. James's Street. I can't be one hundred per cent sure, but I think the girl just jumped out, back at the last set of traffic lights."

"Say that again?" Panich asked.

"The girl. I think I saw her get out of the car just after Green Park tube station. I was some distance away and the light wasn't great. However, I am fairly confident it was her that I just saw make a sudden dash across the road making directly for the Ritz Hotel."

56

Thus far, Lewis knows that he has been lucky. As he enters the long straight road known as Pall Mall, he senses that his luck might be about to change.

Taking the sharp left hand corner from St. James's Street into Pall Mall at over forty-five miles an hour, there are two police bike riders waiting in the darkness. Each is sitting astride their Metropolitan Police BMW motorbikes by the entrance to St James's Palace, watching the passing traffic intently. Part of SO14, the Royal Protection police unit, they are waiting as the remnants of an official function at the Palace draws to a close. From out of nowhere, they see Lewis's Audi careering towards them at high speed; they then see another police bike with its lights flashing evidently giving chase; it is all the incentive the two of them need to abandon their vigil and to take up the pursuit.

Pall Mall is long and straight. It is perfect for a motorbike, chasing a car, to make up lost ground; the bike's superior acceleration is the key. Lewis finds himself desperately needing a plan B. He contemplates taking the right-hand cut-through into the Mall. He rules this out, knowing that this will likely bring him into contact with yet more police, given the proximity with Buckingham Palace. Instead, travelling at close to seventy miles an hour, he slams on the brakes and turns left into St. James's Square. With three bikes on his tail, their lights and sirens still blaring, Lewis knows that he has only a small chance of coming out of this ahead, let alone alive. He even considers turning himself in to the police but rejects that idea almost immediately. He hasn't got the time to waste yet another twenty-four hours in even more pointless police interrogations.

Still searching for a different game plan, he accelerates

172

around the square and emerges on the east side. The Audi neatly ducks and dives across the late evening traffic on Lower Regent Street before continuing along the back streets towards Trafalgar Square. Looking in the mirror Lewis sees that the pursuing bikes are no longer gaining ground; all the manoeuvring and weaving is compelling them to slow down as well.

Lewis checks his watch: it is eleven fifty-seven in the evening.

An idea starts to take shape. Like a complicated entrapment manoeuvre in chess, it is one that, assuming he makes the right moves, could possibly lure his attackers into a dead-end. To make it stand a chance, he needs two things to play out simultaneously. The first is that Lewis's knowledge of London Streets and cut-throughs might actually be better than his pursuers. This, Lewis knows, could be problematic: two out of the three of them are fully trained police officers, and thus likely to know London streets as well as, if not better than, many cab drivers. The second will simply require good timing and no small amount of luck: namely that when something is meant to happen at midnight, it actually does – and not a few minutes before or a few minutes after.

When Lewis reaches Trafalgar Square, the noise from the pursuing bikers fills the entire area. The sound makes late night revellers turn their heads, the blue stroboscopic lights causing people to stop and stare. Firstly the Audi and then, shortly afterwards, three police motorbikes; the latter chasing the former around the southern side of Nelson's column and thereafter racing away to the east. Lewis cuts the corner at the south-eastern end of Trafalgar Square, passing straight into the Strand. He checks his watch. Eleven fifty-eight in the evening.

Just beyond Charing Cross Station, Lewis is handed a lucky break. A bus tries to pull out almost directly in front of him, only stopping when Lewis stands on the horn; even then he has to mount the central dividing pavement, narrowly missing two pedestrians before accelerating away. The bus does, however, succeed in slowing down the three bikers. The time is eleven fifty-nine in the evening.

The road he wants is up ahead on the right. Accelerating, Lewis heads into Adams Street, turning right again soon after before taking another sharp left-hand turn, down Lower Robert Street. This is a one-way street – and the Audi is driving down it in the wrong direction. It is an old London cabby's back route. In the past, it allowed traffic to cut through from Victoria Embankment next to the river Thames, to the upper levels of the Strand and vice-versa. The route passes along the rear of the Savoy Hotel, up through a small, wiggly, tunnel cut into the middle of the Adelphi Buildings towards Adams Street and the Strand. These days, city planners have made the route one-way only – and it is not the direction that Lewis is planning to take. Further, at midnight under an old bylaw, the road becomes closed until seven in the morning; a metal shutter at one end drops down, preventing traffic from using the route and disturbing the neighbourhood.

For the entrapment to work, Lewis needs to have timed it to perfection. He swings the Audi into Lower Robert Street, heading down the dimly lit tunnel within the Adelphi Building to the lower levels below. He can only hope that there is no traffic coming in the opposite direction. If there is, his plans will be scuppered: there is absolutely no room for two cars to pass.

Olena wasted no time. Without stopping or pausing, she ran across busy Piccadilly and hurried inside the entrance to the Ritz Hotel. She barely noticed the night porter holding the door open for her as she passed inside. The hotel's tranquil ambience hit her full on, bringing her back to the reality of where she was. A uniformed concierge stepped forward to ask if he could help. With a practiced air of sophistication and familiarity, she simply nodded at him, smiled and then walked elegantly into the interior of the hotel. Drawn by the muted sound of a grand piano being played softly, she headed toward the Rivoli Bar, hoping to find somewhere she could sit in peace for a short while. The bar was getting ready to close at midnight. Olena, checking her watch, suddenly had an idea.

Why didn't she take a taxi to Luton and not bother with waiting for Ben Lewis?

That surely had to be a safer option than waiting around in the hotel's lobby for thirty minutes for a man who might not even make it in time? Her mind made up, she turned on her heels. Moments later, she was walking out of the lobby entrance once more.

"Can I get you a taxi, madam?" the uniformed night porter asked her.

"Please. I'm heading to Luton Airport. Is that going to be a problem at this time of night?"

"Almost certainly not. Not every cabbie may want the journey: outside the M25, they are not obliged to. Let me ask. I am sure I can find you one."

The porter approached the first cab in the small rank.

58

"I've got company. Two other police riders."

"I can hear their two-tones over the line. Where're you heading?"

"He's taking us on a wild goose chase through the back streets. We've just emerged beyond Trafalgar Square, now travelling along the Strand."

"I think you should call it a day for the moment. You don't want to be answering police questions when they catch up with Lewis."

"I was thinking the same thing myself. Any sign of the girl?"

"I thought I would rank up at the Ritz Hotel and see if she came out looking for a cab. I am there at the moment."

"I like the thinking. How long have you been waiting?"

"Less than a minute. Hang on. Well, aren't I the lucky one tonight? Here she comes now."

"How many cabs ahead of you in the rank?"

"Two. The hotel porter's just gone to the first cab. Hang on; it looks like he's refused her fare. He's trying the next cab now. Come on, come on: let's hope he refuses her as well."

"One more and she's climbing into yours."

"Damn, the second cab is taking her. She's getting in. I am going to have to follow."

"Good luck. The Audi's just turned off down some weird side street towards the river. It'll be a dead end. I've let the other two bikers follow him. I think I can see another turning ahead. I'll dump the bike and catch up with you later."

Lewis drives clear from the depths of the Adelphi Building just as the metal shutters clatter closed behind him. The time is exactly midnight. His descent through the narrow tunnel has brought him out right beside the River Thames, adjacent to the wide urban carriageway, Victoria Embankment.

He is not minded to hang around to see whether some or all of the police bikes have followed him. Perhaps all three would be stuck behind the metal gates at the bottom? It is going to require a certain amount of explanation from the bogus policeman if the other two start asking questions – especially with the hunt already on for a police motorbike that went missing earlier that evening. Perhaps there wouldn't be time for any questions – particularly if there were a few rounds still left in the Glock 17?

Lewis's concern is for Olena's safety. His immediate and pressing objective has to be to make his way back to the Ritz Hotel to find her. He drives a short distance along the Embankment before turning off to the left into Temple Place right next to Temple tube station. From here it will be only a short drive up to the Strand, then along St. James's and back to the Ritz Hotel. He reaches for his mobile phone and turns it on. It is an opportune moment to call Nemikov. Instantly his phone is switched on, however, he feels it vibrate. He has a text. It is from Olena, sent exactly one minute earlier. He pulls into the side of the road to read it briefly.

'Decided not to wait. Sorry! Safely in a taxi en route to Luton A. At least the driver is not Russian! Keep safe O xx'

Lewis curses. He tries calling her but her phone is switched off. Damn her impatience. Why couldn't she wait? Perhaps he won't call Nemikov, after all. Where to now, that's his next question? Before he reaches a decision, his phone starts ringing. He looks at the number, briefly, sliding the white button on the screen across to the right in order to accept the call.

60

Oleg Panich knew exactly what he was going to do and how. His only uncertainty was when. Following the black taxi away from the Ritz Hotel, he hung back initially, able to keep on the other taxi's tail without being too close. They were heading northwards, ultimately in the direction of the M1 motorway, the traffic at midnight in the West End quite light. At Marble Arch, they joined the Edgware Road. Here the traffic was heavier because of the multitude of Asian and Middle Eastern shops along the route that remained open all night. Panich reduced his separation distance from the other taxi, confident that he would not be noticed: there were plenty of other black cabs on the road, all plying a similar route.

It wasn't until they were beyond Kilburn, before reaching Cricklewood, that Panich sensed the time was right. There were fewer shops and the traffic was more intermittent. There were also very few, if any, pedestrians. He checked that he still had his gun tucked in his right hand jacket pocket. Satisfied that it was time to act, he began accelerating towards the other taxi.

Olena's driver was completely oblivious to the threat coming from behind. As soon as he felt the impact of the other taxi ramming his own vehicle, he and the other driver applied their brakes and slowed to a halt. Both vehicles pulled into the side of the road, not far from a bus stop.

Panich sat watching as the other driver hurried out of his cab in order to inspect the damage. The look on the man's face was one of anger and disbelief. Panich waited a full ten seconds before getting out to join him.

"You clumsy idiot!" the driver began remonstrating. "Look at what you've done to my cab. I've only had it six months. There's never been a scratch on it. What were you thinking?

Did you fall asleep? Have you been drinking or something?"

Panich stood there in silence, quietly inspecting the damage. Bending down to look under the other car's rear bumper, he pointed with his hand as he did so. The taxi driver bent down to look also. He never saw Panich's gun swing backwards and upwards; never knew what was about to hit him. One moment he had been peering underneath the rear bumper, hands on knees, staring at what was being shown to him: the next he was lying on the roadside behind his vehicle, unconscious.

Leaving the body where it lay, Panich walked calmly to the driver's door. Without saying anything to Olena in the rear, he climbed in and began driving away. Only once they were underway did he turn around to face the frightened-looking passenger in the back seat.

"Hello again, Olena," he said calmly. The look on her face was one of pure terror. "I'm sure you're pleased to see me again," he said, a broad grin on his face. He pointed his gun at her through the gap in the window glass.

"Please hand me your mobile phone."

Too frightened to argue, she placed the device in the small tray beneath the dividing glass screen designed for coins and money. Panich in turn picked up the phone with his prosthetic right hand, his left hand remaining on the wheel. He then, slowly, squeezed his prosthetic fingers closed around the device. The immense strength in the motorised digits crushed the phone into a mangled, useless, wreck of twisted metal and shattered glass.

"Now, it's time to go for a little ride. Just the two of us. Can we agree that this time there is to be no jumping out of windows, please?"

He laughed as he said this, depressing both the rear door and window locking mechanisms as the car began picking up speed.

"Sit back and relax, enjoy the journey. I am certain your friend Ben Lewis will be coming to save you. In which case,

I will be so looking forward to meeting him again. You see, I owe Mister Lewis quite a lot, actually," he said, holding up his right hand for Olena to see.

"I want his death to be very laboured and so extremely painful. It will be deliciously exciting for us both to watch him suffer before I kill him, don't you agree?"

61

"I'm presuming that it's a bit late for this to be a social call?"

"Correct, Ben. But then, it's not every day that finds the Ben Lewis name linked to, amongst other matters: a bomb going off on a London-bound train; an incident with a stolen moped and a stolen car somewhere near Welwyn; another incident in a stolen taxi near Hyde Park where a gunshot was, apparently, fired; and a major car chase through the streets of Central London. Any of that ring any bells?"

"I spent several hours earlier answering police questions over at Paddington Green, as you well know. Did they forget to ask me something, is that the reason you're calling?"

Saul Zeltinger exhales loudly before speaking again.

"Have you, by any chance, been out and about driving Nemikov's black Audi, Ben? It's just that there's been a lot of radio traffic in the last few minutes. Someone, fitting your description, was seen driving such a car at high speed around Trafalgar Square. Being pursued by three police motorcyclists. Sound familiar?"

"Black Audis are a popular make of car, Saul."

"Much more seriously, a police officer has just been found dead, his neck broken, in a pedestrian alleyway next to Nemikov's Kensington property."

"Not guilty. But you should know: one of the police motorcyclists chasing me was bogus, Saul. You mentioned earlier that a police bike had gone missing. I have a hunch that it was the bomber from the train. At the moment, though, I have no way of proving that."

"So it was you in the Audi, you don't deny it?"

Lewis describes what happened that evening since leaving the Nemikov property in Kensington.

"If you were a cat, Ben Lewis, you'd have lost about eight of your nine lives this last twenty-four hours. What's happened to the Nemikov girl that you were meant to be escorting?"

"She bailed out by the Ritz. I told her to wait but I've just received a text saying that she's already in a cab heading to the airport."

"Okay. So listen up. Many of my colleagues in the Met suddenly want to ask a whole load more questions all of a sudden. The death of this policeman changes everything. We've been on the highest state of alert since that ISIS video surfaced threatening London and its transport network. You were involved, like it or not, with all that happened on the train this afternoon. With one policeman murdered and another one still missing, everyone's looking for a common link. Surprise, surprise, your name is connected with all of the above. Guess who's gone straight to the top of the 'wanted urgently for questioning' pile?"

"They'll have to wait, Saul. Once I know Olena is safe, I've got to head to Cambridge. I must try and prevent the Russians from getting to Nemikov's son, Borys."

"Your name and photograph are all over the police wires, Ben. You're going to have to turn yourself in. Either that or you'll be stopped and arrested. This time, you'll be detained for a whole lot longer, I'm afraid."

"It's not going to happen, Saul. Not yet, at least."

"I had a feeling you might say something like that."

"So why the phone call?"

"I thought you might appreciate a private heads up before the crap hits the fan, so to speak. One friend to another."

Lewis looks through the front windscreen towards the Aldwych up ahead. Three police cars, sirens blaring, have just shot past the entrance to the road he is parked on.

"I do. Thanks, Saul. I owe you. What happens next?"

"On the assumption that you are not prepared to come in voluntarily? I think you need to watch your back; very, very, carefully."

183

"It's bad enough having several Russians out to get me. Let alone the home team. Can't you have a quiet word, Saul?"

"It doesn't work like that and you know it, Ben. All I can advise is that you keep the channels open between you and me. If I can help, I will. Unofficially, of course."

One more police car has just raced past along the Aldwych and is now reversing to a halt at the entrance to this road: the police car is about fifty metres in front of the Audi.

"I'm going to have to bail now, Saul."

"Okay. One final piece of advice."

"I'm listening."

"Don't be foolish. Simply ditch the Audi. Anything to do with Nemikov is hot property." With that he rings off.

Lewis needs no further prompting. He closes the driver's door and walks back towards Temple tube station. As he does so, the police car starts reversing down the road in the direction of the now abandoned Nemikov vehicle.

62

The farmhouse Polunin had found was set back from a quiet, minor road linking the Cambridgeshire villages of Newton and Harston. Surrounded by fields on all sides and with no immediate neighbours, it was completely isolated – and yet, only about a fifteen minute drive away from the centre of Cambridge. Polunin had visited a local estate agent and been shown around six properties. Feigning interest in, and a preference for, a different house, he had nonetheless memorised the burglar alarm code for this particular farmhouse: all he had had to do had been to stand behind the agent and look over her shoulder as she had keyed it in. It had been that simple.

The house had been empty for some time. By the agent's own admission, it was an expensive rental. Because of this, and also due to its relatively poor condition, no one had, apparently, been shown around the property for a while; which had been another indicator that this location could be perfect. Panich had wanted somewhere that could be used for three or four days at most. The risks of being discovered by anyone in such a rural location seemed minimal. Given who was going to be in occupation, Polunin was confident that any risks of being discovered – such as they were – could, in any event, be easily taken care of.

There was a large farmhouse kitchen and downstairs living area on the ground floor, and several bedrooms on the first floor: however, it had been the cellar below ground that had convinced the Russian that he had found the right place. The cellar was only accessed by means of a single, solid oak door: stone stairs led down to the dark and dank-smelling basement, with no access to natural daylight.

On a wet afternoon, two days later, Polunin had returned to the farmhouse, parked his minivan out of sight from the road, and then picked the locks on the front door. Within minutes, the door was open, the alarm disabled and the house was theirs.

Polunin's next task was to prepare the house for its forthcoming houseguests. He went shopping, purchasing various pieces of equipment, and busied himself getting the cellar, in particular, ready. Later that same afternoon, Vince, the local muscle that he had hired, arrived in his beaten-up, red transit. The two of them had played cards, before heading into Cambridge for a curry in Vince's transit until it had been time to go and collect Borys.

The young Nemikov was something of a fighter. On two occasions Vince had needed to whack him, the second being whilst he was being forcibly marched to where the red transit had been parked. When he had tried to make his escape, Borys had nearly collapsed under the force of the belting that Vince had given him. The two of them had needed to half carry, half drag, the dazed young man before throwing him unceremoniously into the back of the van. Polunin had climbed in after him, for good measure. He had sat on the van's floor, pointing his Walther P-22 pistol at the Ukrainian to make sure there were no further misunderstandings.

They had arrived at the farmhouse a short while later. Vince had unlocked the rear door, and Polunin had helped drag a now frightened Borys from out the back. Vince held him whilst Polunin opened the front door, the two of them roughly shoving their new prisoner inside. They led him through the solid oak door leading to the cellar, down the stone steps, and into the makeshift prison area. Various metal chains lay waiting for him: they had been securely fastened to bolts drilled into the stone floor by Virenque earlier.

Once Borys was handcuffed and secured, Polunin had returned to the ground floor. He reached for his mobile phone and checked the time. It was nearly thirty minutes after midnight. Time to call Panich and tell him that Borys was safe and secure. Polunin took a lot of personal satisfaction of a job well done. His old friend and colleague would be well pleased: once more, Polunin had delivered, as usual, on time and in the manner prescribed.

63

The next time Rudi Hildebrandt had visited his gym was two days later. There had been a new Chinese girl working on the desk that evening. She had been wearing the standard, all white, club uniform and had smiled at him agreeably whilst handing him his normal locker key. Changed into his gym kit, Hildebrandt had then headed into the gym to begin his normal routine. As usual, he started by using the Tunturi cycling equipment first. One of the machines he liked had been vacant, so he had set the programme that allowed him to cycle six kilometres over rough terrain: then he had begun cycling.

Tian had wasted no time before heading into the male changing room to access Hildebrandt's locker. Using a master key, she had opened Hildebrandt's locker and searched his jacket, locating his iPhone in the same inner jacket pocket where she'd seen him secure it two days previously. Closing the locker behind her, she had retreated from the room and went to find the ladies' toilets. Finding a vacant cubicle, she had closed and locked the door and set to work. Taking from her pocket one of the acetate sheets that contained the dried latex thumbprint, she carefully bent one of the sheets to allow the latex print to come away from the transparency. Breathing on to it, to make it slightly moist, she had firstly pressed the button on the bottom of the iPhone to activate the screen, before placing the latex print onto the circular TouchID sensor at the bottom of the phone.

It had been the moment of truth.

She needn't have worried. Seconds later, and Hildebrandt's phone was unlocked. All that remained was to sync it with her own device and she would be done. From a jacket pocket she took a palmtop device of her own, complete with its own iPhone connecting cable attached at one end. She pushed this directly into the bottom of Hildebrandt's iPhone until it clicked into place. Since his phone was now unlocked, she was able to connect with, and interrogate, his phone without any further passwords being required. She touched the screen on her device in various places, initiating a routine that copied the entire contents of Hildebrandt's iPhone across to hers. A progress bar appeared showing the time remaining: it told her that the data transfer was going to take twelve minutes.

Fifteen minutes of fast cycling later, Rudi Hildebrandt's Tunturi programme came to an end. He decided to call it a night. It had been a punishing workout and he felt exhausted. Filling a blue plastic cup with cold water from the water cooler, he headed back into the locker room. Although he often completed a longer work out, it was getting late: Arkady Nemikov wanted an urgent call with him later that night. It was something to do with changing his wife's security codes apparently.

Back in the locker room, he collected a towel from the pile near the washbasins and began undressing, wrapping the towel around his naked body. He was about to open his locker and put his gym kit inside when the pretty Chinese girl from the front desk came into the room carrying some towels. She looked visibly shocked when she saw Hildebrandt standing there, half naked.

"I'm so sorry," she said bowing to hide her embarrassment. She made a swift exit. Hildebrandt, in turn, decided to leave his gym kit where it was and went, instead, directly to the showers.

Tian had been caught completely off guard. The download was completed successfully in twelve minutes exactly. By the time she was back in the main reception area checking on Hildebrandt's progress, he had been in the gym exactly eighteen minutes. Less than half his normal workout session. More than enough time, she had thought, for her to slip back into the locker room and replace his phone. Luckily, she had decided to carry some towels with her as she quietly knocked on the door and entered the men's dressing room.

To her complete surprise, when she opened the door and stepped into the room, Hildebrandt was changing out of his gym kit. Damn it! What should she do next? One idea she considered was whether she should inform Hildebrandt, when he was leaving the gym later, that his phone had been found by another male guest in the locker room and been handed in. It was a plausible option. Tian didn't favour it, however. It drew too much attention to the fact that the phone had been out of his control in the first place. There was another possibility. Since Hildebrandt had not yet had his shower, perhaps if she left it two minutes, she could slip back into the room once again whilst he was in the shower? She only needed thirty seconds at most to undo his locker, replace the phone, then leave. If that couldn't be made to work, for whatever reason, she would resort to the first idea.

Hildebrandt's phone began to ring. It was an incoming call, the ring tone loud and distinctive. Tian pressed the button to divert the call to voicemail. She had precious little time remaining before it would be too late. Picking up the towels once more, she entered the locker room. To her relief, Hildebrandt appeared to be in the shower still: she could hear the water running. She left the towels on the side and crossed to the locker. It took less than twenty seconds to open it, replace the phone, and then lock it once more. She turned to leave just as the distinctive ring tone began ringing once again.

Hildebrandt could hear his phone ringing even from within the depths of the shower. He quickly turned the water off, grabbed his towel, and headed across the locker room naked. His locker key was on a rubber band around his wrist. By the time he had unlocked it and found his phone, the call had rung off. It had been Arkady. There had been another missed call only two minutes earlier. He sat on the bench and decided to call him back. As he did so, he noticed the pile of fresh towels that had been left on the side. They hadn't been there when he'd begun his shower. Perhaps the Chinese girl had ventured back in again after all?

64

The tedious work had been trawling through the contents of Hildebrand's iPhone. The emails had been the easiest, although it had soon become clear that they contained nothing of any great importance. Tian nonetheless had scoured through hundreds of mails in both his 'sent' folder and various mailbox folders that had been set up. They had all looked very irrelevant and innocuous.

Next came the calendar entries. Again, there had been nothing in here that had caught her attention.

The address book had been where she had hoped she might find what she had been looking for. She had waded through all the entries, taking especial care to look at any notes that had been written. They had been surprisingly unrevealing. She had known that this was the place where many usually hid their electronic secrets: passport numbers, bank account IBAN's – and especially codes and PINs that they worried would otherwise be forgotten: tucked away as some innocuous footnote to an electronic address book entry; and synced with the cloud, available on all devices, as and when they were needed. It was, of course, a thieves' paradise. Except that Rudi Hildebrandt appeared to be one who had been reluctant to play that particular game. Damn, damn and damn!

She had tried wading through his photos, but again had found none that had been revealing. Despondent and on the verge of giving up, she had one final place that she wanted to check: the 'Notes' application.

Less frequently used by many, these were a serious of electronic pages that could be filed and synced in the cloud, which contained whatever anyone wanted them to: recipes, shopping lists, to do lists, diary jottings. Tian had prayed that Hildebrandt was a user. When she opened the application and saw what was there, she had known almost immediately that she had struck gold.

There, in amongst various debit card PIN numbers, personal tax reference numbers, life policy references and such like, had been one note that had the simple title '*Wohnung*'. It was the German word for 'apartment'. Faithfully recorded, month-by-month, were the door entry codes for Hildebrandt's apartment block: evidently these were changed each month, the latest code having been dutifully typed in. More importantly, it had also showed the alarm code for his apartment. It had been hidden right at the bottom of the long list; Tian had had to scroll down several lines before she had found it. Against the word '*Alarmanlagecode*', was an eight-digit number: it had been precisely what she had been searching for.

65

The next morning had seen Tian begin what she considered to be the cleverest phase of her operation. Developed over many months and field-tested several times, it was a unique protocol for capturing a particular target's laptop: in effect, it allowed her to control both it and the information contained within it. All without the individual concerned being the slightest bit aware.

She had taken up a position in a coffee shop directly opposite Hildebrandt's apartment. She had waited a full hour after seeing him head to work at the usual time before deciding that it had been safe for her to leave. She had crossed the road from the café, her large handbag, fully laden and with the zipper closed, slung casually over a shoulder. Seconds later, she approached the apartment entry lobby. The time had come when she needed to key in the entry code that had been found on Hildebrandt's iPhone. There had been only a moment's slight hesitation. Some people, she had known, were more security conscious than others about their electronic records. Some wrote codes and numbers as they should be written: a few, usually the more security conscious, wrote them differently – often writing the numbers in reverse order; a small minority performed an even more complicated juggling of the sequence. The door entry code was to be a good test: if it didn't work first time, she would try reversing the digits. If that didn't work, she would be forced to try other permutations. She would worry about the alarm code in due course.

She had taken a deep breath, before entering the code as it had been written. The door latch had clicked open immediately: she was free to enter the building.

One down, one more to go.

On the sixth floor, she had waited until the elevator doors had closed before she approached Hildebrandt's front door. She was an expert at using skeleton keys to pick a lock. Within three minutes she had both the dead bolt unlocked and, shortly thereafter, had been ready to push open the front door, having first released the tumblers in the cylinder lock: it had only take her a few deft twists of her skeleton keys. She had, she knew, only a short window of time, seconds only, to key in the correct security code once the door was open.

Taking a deep breath, she had taken the plunge. The alarm began bleeping its warning almost immediately. Closing the door behind her, the alarm panel had been easily to locate within a small cupboard to one side of the door. Inside, there had been a small keypad with an LED display on the alarm box. She had entered the eight digits, one by one, carefully.

The words '*Falsche Eingabe*' had instantly displayed on the panel, the beeping continuing.

Incorrect code!

Taking a deep breath to calm her nerves, she had tried once more, this time reversing the eight digits. As soon as the final number had been entered, the beeping miraculously ceased. Steadying herself, she exhaled with considerable relief.

She had wanted to break into Hildebrandt's apartment for one reason, and one reason only: to find his wireless router and the connection to the cabled broadband supply. It didn't take her long to find both, located as they had been behind a television set on the floor of the main living room. They had both been tucked into a corner out of sight. Unzipping her handbag, she had withdrawn a rectangular-shaped device about the size of an airport edition paperback novel. This was battery powered, the battery life typically lasting more than one month. It would be more than sufficient for the job in hand. She had connected the device to one of the ports on the back of the wireless router and flipped a small rocker switch on the side of the device to turn it on. A tiny green light had illuminated on the front. She had finally placed it on the floor, underneath the router itself; to all intents and purposes it would be completely invisible.

Her job done, all that had remained had been for her to reset the alarm, lock the door on her way out, and head back to sit in her hotel room and wait.

66

Arkady Nemikov was pacing anxiously around his study. The worry lines on his long, thin face had become prominent. As if the recent house call hadn't spooked him enough, he had just ended yet another call with Gregor in Venice. There was still no word from Valentyna. No one seemed to have any knowledge at all of her whereabouts. The Italian police were going to take days, if not longer, before they had recovered most of the bodies from the canal. Perhaps no one would never truly know who had perished and who hadn't? Would she really have been on a public *vaporetto*? Nemikov thought it possible, knowing his wife – the truth was, he simply had no way of telling.

He stopped next to the chessboard and picked up one of the onyx pieces, examining it idly. His world was in danger of falling apart. He looked at his watch. It was nearly one o'clock in the morning. Ordinarily he might have expected to have heard from Lewis by now, telling him that Olena was safely on the plane. That would only leave Borys. He'd been about to call Pavel to check that his son was still safe, but he had caught himself moments before dialling the number. It was, after all, one o'clock in the morning. Fedorov had checked in with Pavel only two hours earlier.

He replaced the chess piece on the board and decided he needed a drink. He was mid-way to the drinks cabinet in one corner of the room, about to pour himself a glass of white wine, when the sound of the house phone ringing stopped him in his tracks. People rarely called him on the house phone. Not many knew the number: especially not at that time of the morning. With some trepidation he reached for the cordless phone that was in its charging cradle on his desk and picked up the handset. The loud ringing instantly stopped.

"Hello." It wasn't either the hour, or Nemikov's usual style, to start with pleasantries.

"Papa," came the all too familiar sound of his daughter's voice. Instantly, Nemikov knew something was wrong. He could hear the plaintive cry in her tone, the strain as she tried to remain calm, the tearfulness as she spoke.

"You have to help. They've taken . . . ," she pleaded before the phone went silent for several seconds.

"Olena, Olena, can you hear me?" Nemikov found himself shouting into the mouthpiece. "Where are you? What's happening?"

He continued this persistent questioning for what seemed ages, hearing only silence on the other end. Then, there was a 'clicking' noise in the earpiece and another voice began talking to him. This one was male and, by the sound of it, very Russian.

"Arkady Nemikov. Your daughter is safe. For the moment, that is. Her fate, and in time her brother's, now lies in your hands, not mine. The price you will pay for her release is eight billion US dollars."

There was a slight pause before the same voice continued.

"If this is not paid in twenty-four hours, the price increases to ten billion. If this still remains unpaid in forty-eight hours, then she will be killed. Just like her mother today. You will receive a text message shortly with the payment instructions."

"Who are you? Why are you doing this, you bastards?" Nemikov yelled into the mouthpiece but the line was dead. In a moment's rage, he threw the handset against the hard wooden floor, watching as it smashed into pieces. His eyes were wet with tears. Distraught, he slumped into his favourite armchair, his head in his hands, quietly sobbing.

It slowly began to dawn on him.

The time had come: no other course made any sense. It was what he had been dreading, but it was the only way.

Reluctant to admit it, he remained slumped in the chair,

time and again testing to see if there was another way, always coming back to the same conclusion: he had to go through with it, if only to save his children.

He composed himself before reaching for his mobile phone. Scrolling through his contacts, he eventually found the number he was looking for. His finger hovered over it for several seconds. Then, with a sudden finality, he pressed the entry on the screen and the number was dialled.

A male voice answered on the second ring.

"Hello, Arkady."

"It is time," was all he said initially.

"Are you sure?"

"Certain. Please make the necessary arrangements. Two requests: one that the deed be done quickly; and secondly, that no one else gets hurt."

With that, he ended the call and sat back in his chair, the once great Arkady Nemikov a resigned and broken man.

67

By the time that a terrified, and shaken, Olena had emerged from the basement cellar, she would have considered doing virtually anything that Panich asked of her – if it was going to spare Borys any further pain. She had been shocked to see her brother's swollen left eye, puffed up so large that he could barely see out of it. The cause had been what Vince had described to Polunin as a 'playful tap'. In truth, they had both agreed that giving Borys a gentle work-over early on might be helpful – as a form of insurance; to help to encourage him to be as compliant as possible for the duration of his stay in their care.

Panich had forced her to sit at the kitchen table whilst he scrolled for the number on his mobile phone. He was smoking a cigarette, and coughing badly as he searched his directory for the number.

"We are going to call your father," he said, struggling to say the words as his cough refused to clear. "I want him to hear your voice," was what he went on to say, the words spoken in a dry-throated way, once the coughing had abated. Olena had merely nodded, watching in terror as Panich waited for the call to connect at the other end. After several rings, a male voice at the other end could be heard to say, "Hello." Panich had then handed the phone to Olena.

"Papa," she cried out, fighting to keep her emotions in check. "You have to help. They've taken . . . , ," and then the phone was snatched away from her hand by Panich. He pressed the 'mute' button, signalling to Vince that he wanted the girl taken back to the cellar. He waited until she had left the room before he unmuted the phone and began speaking

"Arkady Nemikov. Your daughter is safe. For the moment, that is. Her fate, and in time her brother's, now lies in your hands, not mine. The price you will pay for her release is eight billion US dollars."

He looked across at Alexei Polunin's disbelieving face at hearing of such a large sum of money, and winked.

"If this is not paid in twenty-four hours, the price increases to ten billion. If this still remains unpaid in forty-eight hours, then she will be killed. Just like her mother today. You will receive a text message shortly with the payment instructions."

With that, he ended the call.

68

It takes Lewis fifteen minutes to reach his rented apartment, located on a side street behind Earls Court. In no time at all after that, he is on his Honda CB750, heading north towards Luton airport. Bought several years ago when he was, by his own admission, in his 'funny' period – in reality grieving for the death of his young bride – he had lovingly restored the bike over a period of many months. As a result, the machine is tuned to perfection, providing ample competition for many of the more modern and more expensive models on the road.

The traffic is light at this time of night: it takes Lewis less than an hour to cover the distance to the airport. He makes his way directly to the private jet terminal. There he finds no sign of Fedorov or the Range Rover anywhere. He parks his bike in the VIP parking area and goes in search of anyone who might be able to tell him whether the Nemikov jet had left yet or not. Inside the customer reception area, there is one lone employee dressed in a navy blue uniform, seated at a desk. The man looks up when he notices Lewis and smiles.

"Can I help you?"

"I am looking for the Nemikov party. Has their plane left for Venice yet?"

The man peers into a small television monitor set within the table in front of him.

"Not yet. The jet is still on the apron, waiting for one passenger. Are you that person, sir?"

"No. It's Olena Nemikov, the daughter, who they are waiting for. She hasn't turned up yet, I suppose?"

"Not that I'm aware, I'm sorry."

"How about a man, a bit older than me – a Ukrainian, by the name of Sergei Fedorov? He's driving a Range Rover."

"Not since I've been on duty, sir. I came on at midnight.

You're the first person I've seen all evening."

Lewis thanks him and walks outside the building. He tries raising Fedorov on his mobile but the call rings through to voicemail. Next he tries Olena's number. Hers too is turned off, routing to voicemail. He walks towards where his bike is parked. Standing in the shadows and about to switch his own phone off, it suddenly rings in his hand. It is Saul Zeltinger.

"No sleep for the wicked, is there, Saul?"

"You and me both, it would seem. I thought you should know something. A London cabbie's been found unconscious, his cab stolen. It happened on the Edgware Road, about forty-five minutes ago. The cabbie told police that he'd picked up a single woman from the Ritz Hotel at just before midnight. He was taking her to Luton Airport when another taxi rammed him from behind. When he stopped to inspect the damage, the other driver whacked him from behind and stole his vehicle."

"Shit," Lewis mutters, more to himself than to Zeltinger. "It has to have been Panich."

"Sounds ominously like it."

"Oh, bugger. Do we know where he went? Can ANPR records tell us anything?"

The police's automated number plate recognition camera system was a little-known tool in the UK police force's arsenal of weaponry against criminals driving on the UK's major road networks.

"I have someone checking. I wouldn't hold your breath."

"If that bastard lays a finger on her," Lewis begins before stopping himself.

"This is a police matter now, Ben. Don't get yourself any further into trouble than you already might be."

"That's easy for you to say, Saul. I was meant to be looking after her. And her brother."

"There's something else you might be interested in. I'm probably not meant to tell you all this, but I am going to. It concerns your current employer, Arkady Nemikov. We've

203

been watching his house, given everything that has been going on these last few hours. About ten minutes ago, he left the Kensington property in a tearing hurry. In his Lamborghini sports car. Apparently it's bright yellow. Ring any bells?"

Lewis starts wondering where on earth Nemikov would be going at this time of the night.

"It is a very distinctive car. We should be able to track it down without too much difficulty."

"Yes," Lewis says, still distracted. Might Nemikov have received a call from Panich? Was he *en route* to a rendezvous with the Russian?

"One favour, Saul. If you do find out where he's headed, can you let me know? I am going to try and call him."

Lewis hangs up. He searches for Nemikov's mobile number in his address book and hits 'dial'. He is not looking forward to the conversation. After five rings, the call, like everyone else's that evening, is routed through to voicemail. Lewis decides not to leave a message.

He is on the point of switching off his phone, lost in thought, when he feels the unmistakeable cold, hard, shape of a gun barrel being pressed into his neck.

"Hands behind your back. Where I can see them. Forget any fancy moves, Marine scum."

Sadly, for this particular aggressor, Lewis recognises the voice.

69

Lewis has been here before – and not only during his training at Lympstone. Hostile, attacking moves are nothing unusual. He closes his eyes, using his senses to tell him how much trouble he might be in. Judging by the pressure of the weapon on the back of his neck, not much: this feels like one confrontation that is going to be over quickly.

People with a genuine cause – or intent – to use a gun don't normally worry about fine-tuning their motor skills. If the aggression is genuine, their actions will be driven, if not by anger, then by revenge or some other powerful motive. In this state of mind, when pointing their gun, their focus will be binary. Things will be typically 'on' or 'off': 'hard' or 'soft'; 'black' or 'white'; 'dead' or 'alive'. There will rarely be room for 'medium' in the range from any one end of a particular scale to the other. Someone with intent to use a weapon – when they sneak up behind and take their victim by surprise, for example – what do they do? They jab the barrel of their gun hard into the other person's neck, or back. They are trying to compel the other party to do something. The person with the gun will be fired up; their heart will be pounding and the adrenalin will be flowing. In a public place, or if there are security cameras nearby, this might diminish the degree of outright aggression on display. However, at one-thirty in the morning, with poor light, with no one around and with no obvious cameras in the vicinity: these are ideal conditions.

Especially for an aggressive assailant with an intent, literally, to get away with murder.

Under these conditions, Lewis expects his aggressor to use considerable force. The pistol should be pressing into him: with menace, the force being maintained – and with the person's index finger half-on the trigger itself.

Not, as now, with the barrel barely touching Lewis's skin. The messaging in this scenario is completely different: more akin to: '*I want you to feel the presence of the weapon, to scare you, to allow you to feel that I am in control. But then we are going to relax, for a while, so that we can all sort this out together.*' It tells Lewis that the other person is either overly confident, or simply naïve.

Perhaps both.

Which is all to Lewis's advantage. The other person's finger most likely will only be grazing the trigger.

Ordinarily, Lewis might have played along: for a short while, at least. At this particular moment, though, he is not in the mood for games. Not at one-thirty in the morning.

Especially with Olena missing, presumed kidnapped.

Especially since he recognises the voice – and he knows the person with the gun to be both overly confident and naïve.

Is his attacker right or left-handed? The answer determines the optimal direction in which Lewis is to spin around in order to disarm the person. It's not crucial if he gets it wrong. However, choosing correctly can really improve the chances of wrestling the gun away safely. If he is up against a right-handed opponent, Lewis prefers to spin clockwise. That way, rotating rapidly, he grabs his opponent's right wrist, the one holding the gun, with his left hand. At the same time, the palm of his right hand swings round to connect with the gun itself, both hands now able to exert considerable rotational force to push the weapon away from Lewis's face and upper torso. The speed in which this is done, combined with the momentum that the manoeuvre provides, usually takes the aggressor by surprise. More often than not, it allows the gun to be moved out of the intended victim's immediate danger zone before a bullet can be fired. With a right-handed aggressor, and with Lewis spinning clockwise, there is also less resistance when forcing movement in this direction – unless the attacker is deploying a more stable, double-handed, gun grip. The fact that Lewis can feel the gun wavering about loosely at the nape of his neck is a good enough indication that this person is holding the gun with one hand only.

So, is this person a left or right-hander?

He already knows the answer.

Only a few days previously, he had been following the man as he had led the way from the Sikorsky S-92 helicopter towards Nemikov's house. He had guessed then, correctly, that Sergei Fedorov was indeed right-handed. Which means that the gun currently at his neck will be in Fedorov's right hand. The Ukrainian will be standing there, arm-outstretched, enjoying Lewis's moment of discomfort, toying with him, pleased with himself for having got one over the former Marine.

Which in Lewis's mind means only one thing: it is time to set the record straight.

70

Five seconds is all it takes. In that brief amount of time, Lewis is able to deflect the gun away from his own neck and inwards towards Fedorov's body. The Ukrainian never sees the move coming; never considers that Lewis would be so foolish as to try and wrestle the Glock 17 away from his fingers; even less believing when he succeeds. What he especially doesn't see coming is the sharp jab to the face with Lewis's left elbow as soon as Fedorov's gun is on the deck, having been kicked away by Lewis.

"What the fuck do you think you are doing?" Lewis sneers at him, his face up close to Fedorov's now bloody nose, his right hand gripping Fedorov's jacket lapels. "I thought we were meant to be on the same team."

Lewis lets go of Fedorov. The man draws breath and regroups. His nose looks broken; there is a distinct kink in it beneath the bridge.

"Where's the girl? You keep me waiting one hour. Where is she?"

Lewis views Fedorov with contempt.

"If you ever, ever, pull a stunt like that on me again, I promise I will kill you."

"Where's Olena?" The man is holding his nose, feeling the broken cartilage, dabbing at the blood with a handkerchief.

"Fuck knows," Lewis says, the contempt for the other man making him spit the words out. "She took a taxi. Someone crashed into it. I think she may have been kidnapped. Or perhaps you knew that?"

To Lewis's surprise, he sees the Ukrainian smile momentarily before he seems to catch himself, eventually shaking his head.

Fedorov pulls out his mobile phone.

"So, I call Nemikov," he says, pressing a button and holding the phone to his ear.

"You won't get him," Lewis says, watching as Fedorov's call is routed through to voicemail. "He's off the grid. It is nearly two in the morning."

Fedorov simply grunts in disbelief.

"Nemikov never sleeps," is all he says, pocketing the phone and looking at Lewis with loathing.

"What next, arsehole?" is the question that eventually comes in Lewis's direction, the fingers still testing his broken nose.

With terrifying speed, Lewis grabs Fedorov roughly by the collar and pulls him close, the man's frightened face right up against his own.

"If you," he spits angrily, "don't start showing some courtesy, the next time you call me an arsehole, I promise I'm going to break your jaw." He finally releases the Ukrainian's collar. "I'll tell you what's next. You are going to wait here. To see whether Olena turns up after all. Sleep on the plane for all I care."

He is about to leave then turns back, as if remembering something.

"The Cambridge flat, where your man is babysitting Borys. You have a set of keys, don't you?"

Fedorov nods, not bothering to say anything. Lewis, equally belligerently, holds out his hand, waiting. Fedorov fumbles in his pockets. After a few moments spent digging around, he pulls out a large bunch of keys. Painfully slowly, he removes a small set from off the bigger bunch. He tosses them to Lewis, in a manner deliberately designed to make Lewis have to pick them off the floor. Except that the former-Marine's reactions are better than he anticipates: Lewis catches them and puts them in his pocket. Turning, he begins walking back to where his bike is parked, on the way stopping to pick up the Glock 17 pistol that Fedorov had, moments earlier, been pointing at him.

He almost reaches his bike when his phone starts vibrating. He looks at the caller identification. It is Saul Zeltinger once more. Lewis slides his finger across the screen to take the call.

"What news?"

"Bad, I'm afraid. You may be out of a job." Zeltinger pauses.

"Why?"

"Because Arkady Nemikov is dead."

71

Sadiq had not been at home the night the team from SO15 had raided the house in Kilburn principally because he had been working. Sadiq was a maintenance contractor working for Transport for London. TfL was the local government body responsible, amongst other things, for operating the entire London Underground rail system.

Sadiq worked nights. That was the time when the tube network was typically shut down to passenger traffic, the occasion in each twenty-four period when most maintenance work was carried out. Whenever Sadiq was working, his routine never changed. He would sleep, with earplugs in and eyeshades on, until just after four in the afternoon. At this point, the alarm on the phone that he kept under his pillow would vibrate him awake. He would get up, go for a run, have a meal at around seven in the evening, and then prepare a snack to take with him to work in the large rucksack that he always carried.

Ordinarily, Sadiq left for work at eleven in the evening. He would dress in his TfL uniform and then travel by tube, or bus, to wherever on the network he happened to be working that night, returning usually after daybreak the next day. For the past month, Sadiq had changed his routine, now leaving home at least thirty minutes earlier than previously. The reason had all been down to his newfound friendship with Hakim. Over the course of a number of meetings in London, Sadiq, under encouragement from Fouad, had felt obliged to share with Hakim certain pieces of information about his work that had seemed on the face of it trivial – but to Hakim had been of inspirational significance. In no time at all, Sadiq had become central to Hakim's plans. Fortunately for him, Sadiq had been only too eager to cooperate.

As a direct consequence, for the last month Sadiq had been taking himself and his large rucksack on a small diversion on the way to work each night. Starting at his local tube station, Kilburn, he had ridden the Jubilee Line train to Bond Street before changing trains and heading east on the Central Line, to Tottenham Court Road. Always to the same station: Tottenham Court Road. Regardless of where on the network that night he was actually working, Sadiq had been making the same detour. Once at Tottenham Court Road, he made his way in along the twisted labyrinth of underground tunnels at the station, heading for the platforms where the trains on the Northern Line arrived and departed. There, he walked along the platform until about two-thirds of the way down: to where there was a cut through linking the north and southbound platforms. This passage was no more than twenty metres in length. In the middle, set back in oddly dark-blue-painted brickwork, was a dark-blue painted door with a lock. To Sadiq's knowledge, there was only one living person who had the key to this particular door lock: himself.

Refurbishment work had been underway at Tottenham Court Road for about three years before the advent of Crossrail, the massive, east-west tunnelling project that was still under construction beneath London's busy streets. The planned-for enlargement of the station complex at Tottenham Court Road, as part of the Crossrail works, meant that many on-going improvement works had overnight been halted and become reprioritised. Sadiq had been working onsite for about two of those three years. One evening, his boss at the time had introduced him to an old storeroom located behind the dark-blue door. Long since forgotten about, no longer appearing on any architects' plans, it was a tribute to how complicated and full of history these old tunnels really were. In reality the room existed. On paper, it didn't. It had been a small place that had simply been forgotten about. Sadiq's boss had, until the works had been reprioritised, been planning simply to brick it up, and then tile the wall over. The pair had used this room, in reality a four metre square box-shaped space with a two metre ceiling, as their own secret rest room: somewhere to come in the middle of the night for a beer or two and a quiet kip; a private space where no one would find them. They had wanted to keep prying eyes out. Rather than put up 'Danger, Keep Out' signs, or similar, on the door, which they had felt at the time would be an invitation to the curious minded to discover what was behind it, they had devised something different:

'On Entering, Please Mind the Step.'

To their knowledge, never once whilst using the room had anyone had the curiosity to try opening the door to see what was behind it. The rectangular-shaped piece of paper on the door was old and slightly soiled; it looked like something from a different age. It had been taped in place with torn pieces of black electrical tape: exactly the sort of thing that a concerned health and safety person might have put in place.

Thus it was that when Sadiq's boss had suffered his fatal heart attack whilst pushing a trolley along the station platform one evening in the height of winter, it had left Sadiq being the only person at the time with knowledge about – and the key to – the room.

72

When the nine hundred metric tonne Crossrail tunnel-boring machine had been digging its path, centimetre-by-centimetre, below the surface of central London, every second of its journey it was being monitored by a complex system of wall-mounted lasers. These lasers, combined with GPS, had provided both the machine operators and the planning engineers, in their offices several metres above them, pinpoint-precision information about the exact location of the machine: and, most critically, whether it had been pointing in the correct direction.

The various machines used by Crossrail had been exceptionally sophisticated. Not only did they have mechanisms that allowed the waste and spoil from the digging process to be passed to the surface, along miles of conveyors, in their wake; but no sooner had the seven-metre-wide tunnel cavity been created by the cutter head, than behind it, other machines were soon sealing in place the tunnel linings that made the tunnel safe and secure. Seven curved pieces of lining were bolted into place before a final keystone was positioned. This had ensured that the circular 'ring' of the tunnel was intact: the lining slabs being akin to curved pieces of a jigsaw that had to be carefully slotted together.

If there had been one place along the Crossrail tunnel route that engineers had been particularly concerned about, it had been at Tottenham Court road. At this location, the path of the tunnel needed to be bored with deadly accuracy. Termed 'the Eye of the Needle,' the tunnel route had required the immense boring machines to pass exactly eighty-five centimetres immediately overhead the Northern Line tunnels at the station – whilst simultaneously tunnelling thirty-five centimetres below an escalator tunnel leading down to the Northern Line itself. In a tribute not only to the engineers, but also to the strength of the old tunnels – and their original linings – the machines had drilled the new tunnel with remarkable precision; and, more amazingly, at platform level there had been no cracking or collapsing of the old tunnels evident at all. This had been despite the immensely heavy tunnel digging equipment that had inched its way less than a metre above both platforms at the station.

No cracks at all.

Not even in the ceiling of the small four-metre square box room, lost and forgotten about by everyone apart from Sadiq. Which for some reason he had chosen, in a moment of foolishness, to mention to Hakim.

The proximity of the small, secret, chamber so close to the newly bored tunnel, had been precisely the reason Hakim had been so excited: it had been his 'light bulb' moment, the occasion when his whole, hideous, plan had suddenly started to take shape and purpose.

As a direct consequence, Sadiq had deliberately changed his nightly commuting routine. Every night for the previous month, he had made his way along the Northern Line platform at Tottenham Court Road station late in the evening. Approaching the dark-blue door set in the connecting passageway he had checked that no one was watching. Carefully and cautiously unlocking the door, he had entered the small room. Once inside, he had set his rucksack down on the floor and dutifully removed two sandbags. Each had been placed against the end wall of the room. One by one, adding to the considerable pile already building from floor to ceiling: exactly as Hakim had instructed him.

In another few days, the remaining sandbags would all be in position. The room would then be ready.

Insha'Allah, the devastation, when the time came, would be truly catastrophic.

73

Sadly for Hakim, neither he nor Sadiq were structural engineers. If they had been, they might have realised that, cunning though their plans might have been on the face of it, the effect of setting off explosions in tunnels was not likely to cause the kind of devastating destruction that they anticipated.

Surprisingly, tunnels are immensely strong structures. The physics is not dissimilar to the surprising strength of an egg: despite the thinness of the outer shell, the curved surface, in particular at the dome, allows an egg to withstand a large amount of weight being borne down on it. The same effect, only more so, was inherent with tunnels; especially given the composition of modern tunnel linings.

The linings used within the Crossrail tunnels, comprised three composite layers: a primary lining layer, about three hundred millimetres thick and a secondary layer that was slightly thicker; both made from steel reinforced aggregate mixes. The final, much thinner, finish layer contained no steel but consisted of polypropylene fibres and calcareous aggregates. These had all been bonded together, providing specific protection against both fire and explosions: for instance, exactly the sort of sudden and dramatic pressure variation that might be caused by a large terrorist device.

Vladimir, who had supplied Hakim with the RDX explosive, C-4, had known quite a lot about the science of tunnelling and the impact of explosive devices at depth. Sadly, Hakim had never thought to ask Vladimir for his advice.

Which was a pity.

In fact there was quite a lot about Vladimir that most people didn't ordinarily discover. On the surface an arms dealer, he was also an SVR field agent. Vladimir diligently worked the complicated channels and connections within the

Middle East theatre; sniffing out opportunities and conduits that might benefit mother Russia here; providing pieces of intelligence back to Yasenevo, there. In point of fact, his relationship with Hakim had been established, and built, with the full connivance of the planners back at Yasenevo. Mikhail Volkov, Oleg Panich's one time controller and now Vladimir's, had wanted to learn more about the Islamic State threat to the West. Given this, Hakim had seemed a sensible man for the Russians to befriend. Volkov had been the one who had given the final approval to supply the large shipment of RDX into the UK. Volkov's only condition had been that he needed to know, chapter and verse, about where it was going and what it was to be used for. A small SVR field team had therefore been assigned to the UK to try to find out. It didn't take them long.

Tracing the delivery of the toner cartridges to the Bradford warehouse had proved remarkably straightforward. From here all that was required had been patience, and two hidden cameras. Fouad's white minivan had been discreetly but easily followed all the way to Buckley Road in Kilburn. Thereafter it had only been a matter of a few days, and some fairly simple surveillance, until all had become clear. The Russian field team, closely observing the comings and goings at the Buckley Road house, noticed that one of the occupants, a Pakistani male, commuted to work each night carrying a heavy rucksack. When the same man returned home again the following morning at the end of his shift, the rucksack appeared lighter. Sadiq had been put under close watch. The very next night he had been photographed entering the secret room between the two Northern Line tunnels at Tottenham Court Road. The following night the surveillance team had recorded Sadiq's comings and goings at the dark blue door on video. One of the team had then continued tailing the Pakistani, whilst his two other colleagues had picked the lock and ventured inside. Facing them along one end wall of the small room, carefully stacked from floor to ceiling, they had found the pile of sandbags that Sadiq had, night after night, been building. Photographs had been taken. Only a few hours later, these had been closely scrutinised by Mikhail Volkov and his team back in Yasenevo.

74

The Lamborghini Aventador was a seriously fast road car. A six and a half litre, V-12, engine powered the sleek carbon fibre monocoque outer body with its aluminium front and rear frames. It enabled the car to go from a standing start to sixty miles an hour in less than three seconds – thus potentially losing an owner their driving licence in one simple, careless moment of misjudgement. Designed with a sleek, aerodynamic body shape, it was a rare – and much coveted – vehicle whenever sighted on London's congested roadways. Despite its gull wing doors and Formula One-style side air vents, when Arkady Nemikov had taken delivery of his three hundred thousand pound car, it had been the colour that had immediately caught the eye. Finished in what the manufacturers described as *Giallo Orion*, a glossy yellow colour with black trimmings, it was never going to be a car driven by someone who didn't want to be noticed. Which might have explained why Nemikov had kept his parked in a lock-up garage beside his property at Lexham Mews and not on the street outside.

By the time that Saul Zeltinger arrived at the crash scene, it was almost exactly two-fifteen in the morning. By that stage, the fireball that had engulfed both the Lamborghini and the navy-blue transit into which it had collided had been extinguished. The whole of the southbound carriageway of the A3 was closed. Two fire trucks that had first attended the blazing wreckage were parked in the nearside carriageway, adjacent to the cindered remains of both vehicles. Their crews were busy tidying away various lengths of fire hose. An ambulance from nearby Kingston Hospital was also waiting. It had soon become clear upon arrival at the scene that there would be no survivors; the crew were waiting final permission from the senior traffic officer at the scene, Adam Hitching, to be allowed to leave.

Strong arc lights, positioned on the roof bar of a breakdown lorry that had been summoned to the scene, flooded the area. This artificial light enabled Zeltinger, once out of his car, to locate Hitching relatively easily standing, as he was, close to the burnt-out remains of the Lamborghini. Introductions over, the two got down to 'brass tacks', as Hitching, a Yorkshire-man by birth, put it.

"What do you think happened?" the Detective Inspector began.

"As far as we can make out, the driver of the Lamborghini was, one," Hitching looked at his notebook to confirm the pronunciation, "Arkady Nemikov, I think it's pronounced."

"That's correct. Nemikov is, or rather was, Ukrainian."

"Very good. Well, we reckon he must've been travelling at a fair old lick. At this time of night, folks are usually heading home from the clubs and restaurants in town. Once past all the speed cameras up at Hook underpass, they come round the bend, see this unlit stretch of road, put their foot down and go for it. Often they are doing well over a hundred miles an hour when they pass by where we're standing right now, especially at this time of night. In a car like this," he said, pointing to the wrecked Lamborghini with a gloved hand, "he might only have had to tap the accelerator and he'd be doing more than that, easy." He bangs his hands together to get the blood flowing through chilled fingers. The night air was cool; there was almost a frost on the ground.

"Whether this poor fellow has a blow-out, or whether he falls asleep at the wheel, we're not sure. However, at approximately one forty-six in the morning, as best we can judge, he comes around the bend up there," he said pointing back towards the direction of the Hook Underpass. "For whatever reason, he then veers off the nearside carriageway, on to the hard shoulder, and straight into the back of this

Mercedes van. Boom!" he says, once more banging his hands together. "Why it was where it was, on the hard shoulder at that time of the night, we're not yet sure. The Lamborghini was definitely shifting it a bit, though. You can tell by the rubber skid marks on the hard shoulder, here," he points with a handheld flashlight. "Both vehicles were shunted forward during the collision by several metres. The compression at the Lamborghini's front end, and the degree of buckling of the Mercedes's rear chassis – they are also tell-tale signs of his excessive speed."

"Likely to be over a hundred miles an hour?"

"Making an educated guess, I reckon well over that."

"Have you been able to recover the body?"

Hitching shook his head, adjusting his peaked cap with his hand as he did so.

"It was a hell of an inferno. My guess is that death was pretty much instantaneous. There was nothing much left of him by the time we got here."

"You're sure it was Nemikov who was driving?"

"Who can say? They might run various tests: DNA, dental records, that sort of thing. Likely as not, however, if this Ukrainian was reliably witnessed leaving his house a short while before the accident, driving this particular car; then, minutes later, the same vehicle is involved in a total write-off, there's unlikely to be much dispute about the identity of the dead body behind the wheel."

"Anything suspicious about the accident? You must have seen a fair number of these in your time, Adam."

Hitchings thought about this for a moment, before shaking his head.

"No, nothing really. High impact collisions at speed are invariably fatal." He paused for a moment. Zeltinger's silence seemed to egg him on.

"One thing's a bit curious: the Lamborghini has its engine mounted at the rear. Its petrol tank is behind the driver. The

221

Mercedes van also has a rear fuel tank, but it was a diesel: much less flammable that petrol. I don't yet fully understand why there was so much combustion when the two vehicles collided."

"Probably it was exacerbated by the speed of the collision, don't you think?"

"Yes," he said pensively. "You're may be right."

"Won't forensics be able to tell us, in any event?"

"Probably not. There may be little point in any event. Once we find out who the owner of the other van was and why it had been left on the motorway hard shoulder, I suspect that the case will be closed. We only do forensics these days if we're concerned about a potential crime having been committed. It's all part of the cuts."

Zeltinger thanked Hitching and returned to his car. He hadn't wanted to say it to Hitching: however, given who Nemikov was, and the recent circumstances surrounding what had been happening to his family, Zeltinger thought it highly unlikely that the case would be closed that quickly.

75

News travelled fast. Within minutes of accident investigators arriving at the scene, a journalist working for the UK's Daily Mail newspaper had received a tip off. Less than twenty minutes after the accident, a short story had been posted online. As yet unconfirmed, it speculated that Nemikov had been killed during the early hours on the A3 to the south of Surbiton, driving his yellow Lamborghini. There was speculation that he might have been driving too fast. Shortly after two o'clock the same morning, the story was hitting several of the major international news wires. At ten minutes after four in the morning Moscow-time, Viktor Plushenko was being woken from a vodka-induced slumber to be told the same story by his personal valet. Viktor had been lying in his large king-sized bed, snoring loudly, with a pretty blonde Russian girl gently purring beside him when he'd been awoken.

Despite the alcohol undoubtedly still in his system, Plushenko became awake instantly. Instinctively realising that he should be trying to connect with Panich, he reached for his silk dressing gown. He grabbed one of three mobile phones on his bedside table, and waddled out of the room into the living room next door. Finding Oleg Panich's number easily, he hit 'dial', surprised when the call was answered on its third ring.

"Da."

"It's Viktor. I am told Nemikov may be dead. Did you know anything about this?"

"When?"

"How the fuck do I know when? Not long, apparently. In his car so the story goes."

"Shit. That could be disastrous."

"Tell me something I haven't already worked out for myself!"

"I spoke to him only an hour ago, on the telephone. I had his daughter make the call, if you follow me?"

"Sure. But she's going to be fuck-all use to us now if her father is dead."

"What do you want me to do now?"

"How the fuck do I know? Did you have any hand in this, assuming it's all true?"

"Me? Of course not. He and I had just begun our negotiations, as it were."

"Be in no doubt. It is absolutely, one hundred per cent, non-negotiably imperative: we need to get our hands on Nemikov's money. None of it can be allowed to find its way to Kiev. See what you can find out for yourself about Nemikov, whether this story has any truth in it. I am going to call someone and then I'll ring you back." Plushenko hung up, and began searching for another number.

Ten minutes later, Viktor Plushenko called Panich back on his mobile.

"Any news?" the oligarch asked Panich.

"We're still checking. There are definitely reports circulating online about Nemikov's death."

"Well, I might have something. All may not be quite as bleak as we feared. As you are aware, Sergei Fedorov's been working for me on the inside of Nemikov's operation for several years. Perhaps Fedorov may already have been helping you a little bit as well?"

"He has. He texted me information about which car the Nemikov girl had been in. It proved invaluable."

"Good. As it should have been. Fedorov's father and I did a lot of work together, in Donetsk, several years ago. He also worked with Nemikov. However, for reasons that are, shall we say, complicated, the father owed me a huge personal debt. Ten years ago, I called this in. Ever since, the son has been working for me, in secret, passing me information from time to time. I've just spoken to him. Nemikov apparently put in place certain arrangements that were specifically intended to keep his fortune safe in the event that he was either kidnapped or was killed. Would you like to know how it works?"

"I'm listening."

"He gave his wife and two children each their own unique code. Each doesn't know the others, apparently. If Nemikov dies or goes missing, his assets get frozen; the only way to get access to them is for the wife and two children to give their individual codes to Nemikov's Swiss banker. Only then, when the banker has all three, can the money be released."

"But the wife is dead. She was killed this afternoon in Venice. That had always been part of the plan."

"I know. However, and you are not going to like this: apparently, before he died, Nemikov was already beginning to wonder whether his wife might have been amongst those who perished in yesterday's Venice bombing. As a precautionary measure, Fedorov believes that Nemikov may have deliberately passed his wife's codes to someone else. It was something the daughter let slip to Fedorov earlier this evening, apparently."

Panich said nothing, letting the implication of what Plushenko was saying sink in.

"The bottom line is this. With Nemikov dead, if we want to lay our hands on his money – and trust me on this, Oleg, we most certainly do – then we certainly need both children, as well as this new person, not just found, but kept alive. They need to be in a co-operative frame of mind: willing and able to share their secrets freely, if you understand my drift?"

Panich knew what was coming next.

"I thought that sounded like something right up your street, wouldn't you agree, Oleg?"

76

"I've just been speaking with Virenque. He's acquired a motorbike from somewhere and should be with us, here at the farm, within the half hour." Panich was buzzing, drawing nervously on a Turkish cigarette. A half-finished cup of strong, black coffee lay unfinished on the table in front of him. Even Alexei Polunin, who had worked with the legendary killer over several years, had rarely seen him this fired up.

"What next?" Polunin asked him.

"During the period I was recovering from my field injuries," he said, waving his prosthetic arm in the air to make a point, "I learnt to play chess. I studied many Russian grandmasters. I learned a lot of their games by heart. This assignment is fast becoming like one of those complicated games – perhaps more than anything I've worked on before. We had all the moves to checkmate planned out; every move has been going down like clockwork. Then Nemikov gets killed, and the whole game has been fundamentally changed. It's as if we're almost back at the beginning."

He ground out the thin stub of his cigarette on a saucer. In the next breath, he reached for another one from the carton in his shirt pocket, placing it in his mouth and using a lighter with his left hand.

"So, at two-fifteen in the morning, we start again. Our two Nemikov hostages now need to be kept alive. They have each been given a code, which they have, apparently, committed to memory. We now need those codes. As soon as Virenque gets here, he and I are going to start our own little interrogation. We also need a third code, from someone as yet unspecified. Nemikov's wife had it: as I have just been led to believe, following her presumed death this afternoon, Nemikov has assigned it to someone else. Apparently, the girl knows who has it. Give Virenque and I a little time, and I am confident that she will tell all." He drew on his cigarette, inhaling the acrid smoke deep within his lungs.

"Do you think he might have given it to our friend, Ben Lewis?" Polunin asks.

"Funny, I've been wondering the same thing. There has to be a chance. I know Lewis is meant to be off limits, but it would be so convenient and not a little ironic. Not that I need any excuse to find and nail that bastard, but it would have a certain symmetry. Imagine the fun we could have trying to persuade Lewis to give us his code?"

"You and me both, Oleg."

"Just think. If that bomb really had gone off on the train today, the girl would have been killed – then we'd really have been in the shit."

"Yes and no. Perhaps her death might have compelled Nemikov to give her code to someone else as well?"

"Perhaps. Anyway, we've got two out of our three people in custody. Once Virenque is here, we'll soon know the identity of the third person, assuming Olena really does know who it is." He drew on his cigarette and Polunin watched as Panich continued pacing.

"So I've been thinking. If we wanted a way to lure Lewis to us, whether he's the mysterious third code carrier or not, the way to do it is to let him think he stands a chance of rescuing either the boy or the girl, perhaps both."

"Do you have a plan?"

"Of sorts. Put yourself in his shoes for the moment. What is his next move likely to be?"

"He'll want to know why Olena never showed up at Luton airport."

"Correct. But assuming he believes Olena is missing, most likely kidnapped, what next?"

"Will he know yet about Nemikov's death?"

"Even if he does. What, besides finding the daughter, will

be uppermost on his mind?"

"Checking that Borys is alive."

"Precisely!"

"But we have him here."

Panich looks momentarily exasperated. "Yes, but Lewis doesn't know that. He thinks Borys is still in the Nemikov apartment in Cambridge. That's where Lewis will be heading next."

"It's a possibility."

"It's more than that. I may not have told you this before, but Plushenko has had a deep cover asset working for Nemikov for several years: his head of security, Sergei Fedorov. Fedorov has already helped us earlier this evening whilst we were waiting for the girl at Lexham Gardens. I've just spoken to him again. He was with Lewis, literally moments ago, out at Luton Airport. Lewis has just left, taking the keys to the Nemikov apartment in Cambridge with him. Lewis is heading there right now." He looked at his watch. "He'll most likely be there within the half hour. You and Vince need to get over there right away. He won't be expecting anyone, so surprise the bastard. Then restrain him, and either keep him in the apartment or bring him back here. Whatever is easier. Do you think you can manage that?"

"Nothing would give me more pleasure."

"Good. Be very careful, my friend. In particular, please remind Vince that we need Lewis kept alive. If he really does knows Nemikov's third and final code, I want him to sing like a canary before he is allowed the chance to die."

77

Lewis is back on his bike, passing the outskirts of Hitchin. He is heading towards the A1 motorway before cutting across country on the A505 towards Royston and then Cambridge. His location is very close, once more, to where he had, only hours earlier, rammed the bomber's vehicle and then rescued Olena from out of the car's boot space.

It is just after two-fifteen in the morning. A huge burden of responsibility hangs on his shoulders – and it is not simply because of Olena's kidnapping.

Arkady Nemikov's death has been the game changer.

Whether it is Viktor Plushenko, Oleg Panich or whoever previously had been planning on getting to Nemikov's money by means of his wife and children: each will have had their game plan completely turned upside down. No longer will killing or kidnapping members of Nemikov's family, to extort money from the father, be the order of the day. For the time being, everyone needs both Olena and Borys alive – and, for that matter Lewis, assuming it becomes more widely known that he is in possession of Valentyna's codes.

It was starting to feel like a complicated, real-life game of chess. One or two major pieces had been taken out of the game; various key pieces were still in play; the game had been turned on its head by a series of unexpected moves; almost akin to castling. The upshot was that a different winning strategy was urgently required. Which, given his prowess at chess, should be to Lewis's advantage.

If he were Oleg Panich, what would he be doing next? The answer depended on two related questions: does Panich yet know that Nemikov is dead; and, if so, has he become aware of the contingency arrangements that Nemikov has set up to protect his money in the event of his death? Not to mention whether, if yes to both of these, Panich is also aware that Lewis is in possession of Valentyna's codes?

Lewis toys with various moves and countermoves in his head before coming back time and again to one over-arching conclusion: whatever other imponderables there might be, his next move, surely, has to be to head to Cambridge, to check that Borys is safe.

It is more of a defensive play really. Not really his forte. However, it is something that he knows needs to be done.

78

Cambridge at two forty-five in the morning is quiet. The centre of the city is especially deserted. Most student parties and clubs have long-since finished for the night. Lewis hauls his Honda motorbike off the road and on to a pavement not far from Christ's College. He parks it outside a branch of a bank, close to where undergraduate bicycles have been padlocked to iron railings. Rather than walking the direct route to the Nemikov apartment, he takes a small detour; around the back of a church on the corner of Petty Cury before slipping into the bottom end of the Lion Yard shopping precinct. This small, anti-clockwise, circuit brings him to a vantage point: one that allows clear line of sight directly into the narrow pedestrian precinct on the other side of St. Andrew's Street: the passageway where the entrance to the apartment block is situated.

He waits in the shadows, next to the church. He stands, barely moving, for a full ten minutes. All the time his eyes scan back and forth, looking for movement. He sees nothing. All of which is expected, but it helps to have confirmation. Feeling in his pocket for the keys that Fedorov had passed him, he moves slowly out of the shadows. He crosses the deserted street, and walks into the passageway leading to the entrance lobby. When he holds the small key fob over the magnetic panel, adjacent to the door entry intercom, there is a satisfactory 'clicking' sound. The lock releases. Without waiting, Lewis heads inside.

Similar to Alexei Polunin and his accomplice, Vince, a few hours previously, Lewis takes the stairs rather than uses the lift. Inching open the door on the first floor landing, he lets it close behind him, moves out of the light from the stairwell into the darkness, and pauses. Apart from the distant humming sound of college heating systems in operation, all is quiet. Nothing out of place can be heard at all. Lewis moves in silence towards apartment twenty-five, the open-air corridor meandering around the outside of the building. Lewis has a birds-eye view over the city centre streets and courtyards: college buildings, church spires and shopping arcades. He stops suddenly; his face looking down at an oblique angle into the pedestrian precinct by the ground floor entrance. He has seen something; a man moving stealthily: carefully but deliberately. Two things strike Lewis about the individual. First is his furtive behaviour: at two forty-five in the morning it stands out. Secondly, and more worryingly, Lewis recognises him: from another time and another place. The location had been London's Green Park a few months earlier. Lewis had had cause to dislocate the man's shoulder after he had been followed all the way from Berkeley Square. The man was Russian. Lewis had nicknamed him 'Scarface' due to a long, thin, knife wound he had down one cheek. As Lewis had known on that first occasion, such scars come from knife fights. He should know. In hand-to-hand combat situations, many would testify that in Lewis, there was rarely any one better.

Several questions come to mind, none with any immediate answers. What is a Russian SVR agent doing skulking around the back streets of Cambridge at this time of night? Next, if he was here in order to keep an eye out for Ben Lewis, how does he know that Lewis is about to show up? Lastly, if Scarface is indeed following Lewis, is he alone or will there be anyone else with him?

79

Olena was sobbing: uncontrollably – like a child, almost. The transformation from confident adult to emotional wreck had been rapid. The cause had been Virenque: he had just told her about her father's death. She was sitting on a chair with her hands and elbows tied roughly behind her back. The wrist ties had been Panich's idea: the elbow ties were Virenque's. It was a Spetsnaz trick, designed to prevent prisoners from shuffling tied wrists under their body – otherwise achieved by wriggling their feet through the gap between wrist and shoulder.

In the adjacent stall, within earshot but out of direct line of sight, Panich had just given the same news to Borys. He, too, had been physically restrained in the same manner as his sister. His emotional reaction had been more controlled: less believing, possibly; less overtly emotional, definitely. This had intrigued Panich, likely, as it was, to shape the way the interrogation would progress.

"Your father gave you some codes, Olena."

It was Virenque speaking, each word clearly audible by both Borys and Panich nearby. He spoke softly at first, his tone even, and with no hint of menace. "And to Borys as well." He waited to see if there was any reaction. She continued sobbing, her head bent down low.

No reaction whatsoever.

"In the event that he died. In order to protect his money."

Still no reaction.

"We need those codes, Olena," Virenque continued, his voice unexpectedly raised; less patient and more authoritative. "Assuming that you don't want me to hurt you or your brother?"

"Don't tell them anything!" Borys yelled from the next stall. Panich was quickly off his seat. He hit Borys with a clean left hook, right across the bridge of his nose. Borys screamed.

Blood began to pour. It was a slow, steady dribble; down on to his upper lip and chin before splashing on the table in front of him.

"Another word out of you, and I promise you there'll be much worse to come," Panich said through gritted teeth.

In the next stall, Olena looked up, terrified: her eyes red, her cheeks wet with tears.

"Don't hurt him. Please! I beg you."

"Your father gave someone else your mother's codes tonight. Is that correct?" Virenque asked her. Once again, his tone was soft, his voice not raised.

He waited. Olena still refused to say anything; she was weighing up her options. In reality, she had none and Virenque knew this.

"I think Borys needs more treatment," Virenque eventually called out in a loud voice to Panich.

"Okay. But don't say we didn't warn you," Panich replied.

"Wait," screamed Olena finally. Virenque knew that long interrogations were for the movies. In real life, all you needed were the right pressure points.

"So who has your mother's codes, Olena?" Virenque asked, softly and gently. "Is it Ben Lewis? Does he have them?" He was staring hard at her whilst she looked at the table, her body shaking, the tears continuing to roll down her cheeks.

"Oleg," Virenque called out. "I don't appear to be . . . . no wait," he said, seeing Olena nodding her head. "My mistake. Finally we might be making progress. Are you nodding your head because the person is indeed Ben Lewis?"

Virenque waited. For several seconds, there was no sound in the dark basement other than their breathing. He was staring hard at Olena, willing her to speak.

"I'm waiting," he said, his voice rising once more.

"Yes," came her answer. Very softly, hardly audible, but nonetheless there.

"I didn't hear that."

This time she spoke more confidently. "Yes. My father gave the codes to Ben.

80

"Finally we're getting somewhere." It was Virenque talking. "Perhaps it's time to bring young Borys over here," he calls out to Panich. "I have a chair for him, all ready and waiting."

Panich arrived, holding on to Borys's arm. The young man's nose was a bloodied mess. Olena looked up.

"Oh my God!" she screamed, seeing her brother's face. Ignoring her, Panich thrust Borys into the vacant chair before positioning himself behind him. As ever, he had a cigarette in his mouth. He was drawing on it, heavily, ignoring where any ash fell.

"Your brother's fine," Panich said in between puffs, using a tone that indicated that he was bored by her the fuss. "I didn't hit him hard. You're meant to be the doctor. These things look worse than they really are. He'll be okay. That is, unless you decide not to co-operate. In that case . . . ." he paused, his sentence deliberately unfinished. He shrugged his shoulders, turning down his bottom lip and tilting his head on one side at the same time. He glanced at Virenque and saw the Frenchman copying the gesture: the implication was abundantly clear.

"So, Olena," Virenque continued. "Now that we are all together. Perhaps you should be the first to give us your code?"

Olena was staring at her brother. Just for one, brief, moment, he gave an imperceptible shake of his head.

"We're waiting," Virenque said, his voice rising.

Olena still said nothing. She sat, head bowed, shaking gently from side to side.

"This is it. You won't get any more chances, Olena. From now onwards, things are going to get unpleasant for you both." He pushed his face very close to hers. "You really don't want to see my friend over there get angry."

Olena began to shake, her eyes still locked on her brother's. Once more, he gave an almost imperceptible shake of his head. It was the signal that Panich had been expecting – and waiting for.

"Are you right or left handed?" Panich whispered into Borys's left ear. It caught the young man by surprise. He swivelled his head around sharply to try and look at Panich. Instead the Russian placed his prosthetic hand on Borys's right shoulder blade, just close to his neck. His fingers began to squeeze, the mechanically induced pain instantly excruciating.

"I'll ask one more time," Panich said menacingly into Borys's left ear. "Left or right handed?"

"Right," Borys gasped, writhing in agony.

Panich released his grip. The young Ukrainian breathed out, his body trying its best to relax and recover. It was only a momentary respite. Before he realised what was happening, Panich grabbed Borys's bound wrists with his left hand, pulling them taut behind him so that they were straining the shoulder sockets. Borys instinctively curled his fingers into a ball, trying to block out the pain. Anticipating this, Panich placed his prosthetic right hand over Borys's, letting his mechanical fingers encircle the bunched fingers of the young man's right hand. Borys tried to wriggle the fingers free; even uncurling them would have helped. It was no use. Panich's ever-tightening grasp made any movement impossible.

"So now, Olena. The time has come to stop playing games," Panich said. He was slightly breathless, but nothing in comparison to the effect his exertions were having on Borys who was sweating profusely, his breathing ragged, his eyes full of fear. He could sense what might be about to happen and he was terrified. The pain was building in his fingers and shoulder sockets as Panich increased the pressure on both.

"The codes please, Olena. Or your brother will find himself needing an artificial hand in future: just like me. It's your choice."

Again Borys shook his head. This time he was more overt.

"Don't tell them Olena. If they kill me, they can't get Papa's money. Let them do it. If I die, their plan is finished."

Panich didn't wait to see if Olena responded in any way. He was not renowned for being patient during interrogations. Instead the electrical impulses from his arm muscles were directing the motorised digits in his right hand to close. Borys began to scream. The Russian was oblivious and the pressure continued to build. He had rehearsed this many times during his rehabilitation. The screams became more agonised; something was about to break, everyone in the cellar could sense it. Having curled his fingers into a ball, it arguably had made Borys's predicament much worse. Without warning he felt his index finger snap at the knuckle; soon after, so did another; with the pressure refusing to abate, the remaining knuckles soon all dislocated, the joints squashing and becoming useless. Borys's screams were ear-curdling. Panich tuned out this sound. He was even oblivious to Olena's high-pitch screaming at him to stop.

When he finally reduced the pressure, he looked across at Virenque and nodded.

It was Frenchman who spoke next, after a suitable pause: his voice was once again soft and gentle.

"Now, perhaps, you have something to tell, Olena?"

The tone was in such contrast to the aggression and noise that Panich had induced, that Olena simply nodded, then started to speak almost immediately.

"I'll tell you," she said. Tears were trickling down her cheeks as she looked across at her brother. He was unconscious, having blacked out with the pain.

"We're listening."

"Pavel Eljanov," whispers Olena. "In the World Cup in 2013 in Tromsø. When he defeated Sergei Karjakin."

Virenque looked bemused. It was Panich who showed the only sign of recognition.

238

"Karjakin eventually went through, but the Ukrainian, Elijanov, defeated him earlier in one of the rapid fire games."

To his surprise, Olena interrupted him.

"They are both Ukrainian born. Karjakin, for his own reasons, decided in 2009 to become a Russian citizen. Therefore, we Ukrainians enjoy seeing him lose."

"What has this got to do with the code, Olena?" It was Virenque, speaking. He still was looking puzzled.

"When Elijanov beat him, he was playing white." She was speaking in a flat monotone voice. It was as if the life was draining out of her as she spoke. "It was the nineteenth move. Knight to g5. Thereafter, Karjakin had no way back. Black played pawn to e5. White responded with bishop to b7. Black took white's rook on d4. White ended the game by moving his bishop to d5. The code is in the moves: Ng5 e5 Bb7 ed4 Bd5."

She lowered her head in exhaustion. Panich looked at Virenque and flicked his head briefly over his right shoulder. The message clear: it was time to leave their prisoners alone. The two of them needed to talk.

81

Vince dropped Polunin on the corner of St. Andrew's street. He then continued around the back of the apartment block to park the red transit in the same place he had parked previously. This meant, once again, approaching the ground floor entrance from the north. Meanwhile, Polunin walked a broad sweep of the area to the south. Without realising it, he was covering exactly the same ground, along Petty Cury and into Lion Yard, that Lewis had walked only minutes earlier. Their reconnaissance complete, the two met back at the ground floor entrance. They were confident that Lewis wasn't lurking in the shadows. Polunin used the key fob on the set of keys that they had found on Borys Nemikov to open the door.

Their first imperative was to check the apartment. Only once they were happy that Lewis was not there, waiting for them, would they begin their stake out. Vince had already agreed that he would position himself outside the front of the building; Polunin was going to remain inside, on the first floor landing, close to the door where the stairs emerged. That way, they could execute a pincer manoeuvre on Ben Lewis: let him get inside the building; before trapping him on the stairwell. Perhaps give him a much-deserved working over, before taking him to the apartment until Panich arrived.

Polunin checked the silencer on his Walther P-22 pistol, switching the safety catch to the 'off' position. They then began climbing the stairs to the upper floor.

Lewis hears them, long before he can see either: Scarface and another man. This newcomer sounds heavier than the Russian. He can tell by the breathing. Lewis has found a dark recess, tucked into an inner wall, adjacent to some cupboards. In the dark, he is certain that the other two will walk past and not see him. Which suits Lewis just fine. He wants to see who he's up against – and to watch what they are up to. The latter, he believes he knows; however, he still prefers to check.

The Russian with the scar down his cheek is tall and thin, exactly as Lewis remembers him. He is wiry rather than stocky. Lewis remembers that the man's right shoulder blade had dislocated with relative ease. His companion is the opposite. Well over two hundred pounds, probably more. A lot of it muscle. The man moves like a gym workout specialist: great strength in his muscles but already out of breath from climbing one flight of stairs.

This is likely to be a push over.

The door to apartment number twenty-five is ten metres further along the corridor from Lewis's hiding place. He can hear the Russian searching for keys. It is intriguing that he doesn't try to pick the lock. Scarface is in possession of the right keys for the Nemikov apartment. As is Lewis. Except that Lewis acquired his from Sergei Fedorov. So how did the Russian and his overweight companion get theirs? Was it from Olena? Or had someone been here earlier in the evening? For example, a snatch team? Perhaps even these two? Had they taken Borys, and his set of keys, into safe custody? It seemed probable.

Concluding it futile to rush into the apartment after them, Lewis decides it is better to wait outside. He wants to see who, or what, eventually emerges.

He's not kept waiting long.

82

Inside the apartment, the front door closed, Vince waited downstairs whilst Polunin went to check the status of the upper floor. Exactly as he had done earlier that evening, the Russian inched his way up the stairs, his P-22 pistol out in front. At the top, he peered gingerly over the concrete balustrade to see into the main living area. The body of the dead security man was on the floor, precisely where he had fallen earlier. The television is still on, exactly as before. A pool of blood had oozed onto the wooden floorboards beside the dead man. Apart from that, everything appeared to be unchanged and undisturbed. Retreating downstairs, Polunin covered Vince with his gun as they checked the bedrooms: one by one. The flat was empty. There was no sign of Lewis anywhere.

It was almost time to begin their stake out. Before taking up their agreed positions, Polunin, being the professional that he was, made Vince wait whilst he walked a full circuit of the entire first floor corridor. Polunin did this carrying his gun: he wanted to make certain Lewis wasn't waiting for them around the next corner. The circuit didn't take long, Polunin stopping a short distance beyond the stairwell, beckoning in silence for Vince to come and join him.

Lewis has chosen his position well. Twice the Russian and his muscular friend walk right by where he remains hidden. He hears the other man speaking as they pass him the first time. He is a Brit; a Londoner from the sound of it. Scarface then stops almost directly in front of Lewis on his subsequent reconnaissance of the corridor: still with no inkling that Lewis is just inches from him. Lewis sees the Russian's gun. It is a small semi-automatic: a Walther P-22. It has a silencer attached: most likely a Gemtech suppressor. Silent and quite deadly at close quarters. Beckoning to his overweight colleague to follow, Scarface heads back towards the lift stairwell. Lewis has a decision to take: whether to follow; or firstly to check out the apartment? Lewis feels in a mood to follow.

He is about to move from his hiding place when the Russian stops suddenly, about thirty metres away, taking up a new vigil adjacent to the stairs down to the ground floor. His colleague has gone on ahead, presumably down to street level. Lewis watches intently. The other man is pacing. He has the look of someone expecting action, but doesn't know when. The time is almost three o'clock in the morning. People don't normally creep around apartment blocks at this hour of the night. Scarface is waiting for something to happen. He doesn't know where it is going to be coming from; but he knows it is coming. And he's not waiting for the good guys either. Scarface is nervous. His body language and entire demeanour indicate that he is expecting trouble: his gun is drawn; it is silenced and ready to fire; and he continues pacing.

So, who is he waiting for?

Lewis knows. An SVR agent, already known to him, turns up out of the blue in the middle of the night, armed with a gun. Not one, but two of them, both arriving almost exactly the moment that he gets here on his motorbike. Is this all a happy coincidence? Not likely. Lewis doesn't believe in such things. They are here because of him. The million-dollar question is this: how is it that Scarface and his friend know that Lewis is going to be here?

A lucky guess on their part? Like happy coincidences, Lewis doesn't believe in such things.

It wouldn't be because of Saul Zeltinger either, of that Lewis is totally confident. He briefly considers Jake Sullivan or Laura, the department head whom he had recently met – but quickly rejects both as non-starters. MI5 wouldn't be sending a Russian agent to lie in wait for Ben Lewis to show up.

So, that really only leaves one possibility. If the Russian and his friend truly are part of a Ben Lewis reception committee, there could only be one person able to inform either of them about Lewis's impending arrival: Sergei Fedorov.

Fedorov certainly had a bone to pick with Lewis. But Fedorov, working for Plushenko or the Russians? That feels bizarre. Could Arkady Nemikov have had Fedorov working for him all these years whilst the man was simultaneously working for the opposition? It is certainly a possibility, Lewis concedes.

For the moment, Lewis has more pressing issues to deal with. For instance, how to take out a Russian armed with a Walther P-22 pistol?

He knows the answer to that.

The Russian is too far away for what Lewis has in mind: Lewis first needs to be a little nearer. He also needs to find something small and reasonably heavy. Once he has accomplished both, Scarface is definitely going down.

Peering over the top of the lockers next to him, he spots something that looks ideal. Tucked away at the back, hidden next to the wall, is an old, discarded, brass padlock. It is about two inches square, with a simple combination lock: three brass number wheels that rotate down one edge. It is broken but that is of no concern to Lewis. He swings the metal clasp around into the closed position before feeling the weight of it in the palm of his hand. It seems perfect.

He sets off in a crouching walk, edging stealthily around the corner of his hiding place, into and along the corridor, halting when no more than ten metres from the Russian. It is time to wait; until he can be confident that the other man's back will remain turned away from him for a sufficient period.

Lewis has this knack of throwing objects with pinpoint accuracy. Cricket balls at a wicket; coconuts at a fairground shy. Nearly always he is deadly accurate. Whether throwing them gently, or hurling them with deadly force – he seldom misses. It is an innate talent – and one that he uses to great effect. Scarface is talking. He has an earpiece microphone in one ear, most likely speaking with his buddy outside. Open channel communication. Out goes the element of surprise. It's a risk Lewis can live with. It might even help. Choosing his moment, he extends to full height, hurling the padlock at the Russian with maximum force. It hits exactly where Lewis had intended it to: directly behind the ear, in the soft fleshy tissue: the most dangerous and lethal place. The man sinks to the floor like a stone.

Quickly on his feet, Lewis runs towards the fallen man. The P-22 handgun has dropped to the floor beside the body. Lewis picks it up, contemplates using it for a second before thinking again; instead, he places it in the rear waistband of his trousers. He feels for a pulse. It is very faint – the Russian is out cold, and will be for a while. Calmly, Lewis locates the Russian's earpiece microphone. He yanks the ear bud out of the dead man's ear and brings the microphone closer to his own mouth. It is time to send the other man outside an urgent SOS.

83

Vince was pacing as he was talking with Polunin. Outside, the temperature had fallen, his breath condensing heavily in the cool night air. He had located a good place to watch and wait for Lewis: the cold, however, meant that he needed to keep moving.

"What's the plan once we've nabbed him?" Vince was asking.

"Keep him here in the flat, initially. Possibly they'll want him brought back to the farmhouse. Either way, they'll want to interrogate him, for sure."

"There's a lot of interrogation going on. What's that all about?"

"Some things that are best not asked," Polunin said.

"What's this Lewis gone and done to annoy you lot, anyway?"

"He's a nasty piece of work. A few months ago, he nearly killed me. I had to quit my job because of him."

"Want to tell me about it?"

"Not real . . . ." The line went dead.

"Hello," said Vince into his mouthpiece. "Alexei, can you hear me? Hello."

Vince heard muffled noises and a crackling sound that lasted several seconds before hearing what he assumed was still Polunin's voice in his ear.

"Help . . . . you've . . . got . . . to . . . help. . . . me . . . quickly . . . need . . . you . . . here . . . " The voice sounded strained, faint and anxious, hardly like the Russian's at all. Vince reached into his pocket for the key fob, already running towards the front door of the apartment block.

Running up the staircase, two steps at a time, takes its toll.

Despite his sessions at the gym, the man arrives at the first floor landing out of breath. Pushing open the door at the top of the stairs, he nearly falls over Polunin's inert body.

Soldiers have it drilled into them: thinking on their feet and not freezing when confronted with the unexpected. It means the difference between life and death – especially when, emerging from a lit stairwell into a darkened corridor, you discover your comrade lying motionless on the deck in front of you. A good reaction would have been rolling out of the light into the relative safety of the darkness to one side. Another might have been slamming the door wide open – in case Lewis, or whoever, happened to be hiding behind it.

Not behaving as Vince does: freezing in the doorway, slowly taking stock; silently looking for unknowns; and patiently listening for the unexpected.

It is not a wise countermeasure.

Especially since Lewis has the padlock back in his hand.

It is going to be a repeat performance, but with some very minor variations.

Lewis is once more back in the shadows, this time on the other side of the corridor: but again in a dark recess, a place that makes it difficult for him to be noticed.

As he did with the Russian, he waits to pick his moment: when the man decides that it is safe to bend down to inspect his fallen colleague.

Which Lewis predicts should be within the next few seconds.

Which, in point of fact, turns out to be wrong.

The man surprises Lewis by his inertia. In all other respects he is a sitting target, the light from the stairwell illuminating him so clearly from behind. He remains like this for almost a minute, his heavy breathing gradually subsiding.

Finally, after what seems like an age, he considers it safe to snatch a quick look. Stepping forward, out of the light, he bends down to check the Russian's pulse.

Which is the moment when Lewis, too, steps forward, taking careful aim. This second time around he doesn't need the man unconscious. Questions need answering urgently. So he plans to throw the padlock with slightly less force.

The man senses something is wrong. Unwisely, he chooses to raise his head just as the padlock is in mid-flight. So that, when it hits him, it is not the glancing blow that Lewis had planned. It makes contact directly on the right temple causing the man to collapse.

Rushing forward, Lewis tries to keep the man conscious by shaking him, slapping him hard around the face several times. The man groans, groggy and confused by what has just happened. After further vigorous shaking, he opens one eye. Lewis places the P-22 pistol hard against the man's throat to avoid any ambiguity.

"Name?"

"Vince," comes a weak response.

"Who told you I would be here tonight, Vince?"

The man tries to swallow but the pressure from the gun at his throat prevents him. The very act of trying makes him wince involuntarily. Pain receptors in the area around where the padlock hit him are starting to send danger signals into Vince's nervous system. Close to the edge of a complete melt down, his eyes start sliding behind the eyelids. Lewis responds by slapping him hard on the cheek with the palm of his left hand once more. Lewis needs Vince focused and still conscious. Temporarily, it does the trick.

"Panich .... someone .... told .... him .... I .... don't.. .. know."

It had to be Fedorov. He is the only person who would have known.

"Where are Olena and Borys?"

The man shakes his head weakly, his face grimacing. Lewis needs a fast change of tactics. He moves the P-22 away from the man's throat and fires one shot into Vince's left hand. The gun hardly makes a sound. The same is not true of Vince. His whole body jolts, as if a surge of electricity has just flowed through it. He lets out a cry of pain. Changing gun hands, Lewis uses his right forearm to exert downward pressure on Vince's throat: placing the gun, now in his left hand, hard against the man's other hand, pinning it to the ground.

"If you don't want to lose this hand as well, I suggest you talk. Where are Olena and Borys?"

Vince grits his teeth but doesn't answer. Lewis's face is now very close to his. He contemplates a head butt – but rules this out for the moment. Time to start a countdown.

"I'm counting down from five. Ready? Five. . . . four . . . . three . . . . I'm serious, Vince, I will pull the trigger, ... two . . . . "

"Wait," Vince gasps. It's . . . . a . . . . farmhouse . . . . south . . . . of . . . . Cambridge. . . . near . . . . Newton . . . . and . . . . "

The man is fading. Lewis releases the pressure on Vince's throat momentarily.

"That's better. Come on, Vince. Between Newton and where, exactly?"

Vince starts coughing involuntarily, the physical movement causing the pain in his head to intensify. He is about to pass out. Lewis tries shaking him: it is no good. The man slips into unconsciousness. Lewis is not about to get anything more out of him in a hurry.

84

When Mikhail Volkov had learnt that the Russian-made RDX explosive was being used to build a bomb deep underground at London's Tottenham Court Road station, he had known that Hakim's London operation was a potential liability. When he heard that London's anti-terrorist police had arrested three Pakistani males at the location where the RDX was being stored, he knew the liability was in danger of becoming a full-blown disaster. Discovering several blocks of Russian-made C-4 explosive sewn into sandbags at the Kilburn flat might be one thing: linking these same explosives to a massive terrorist tunnel bomb, currently under construction beneath the centre of London would, politically, be quite another. Chemical analysis of the explosive would link the RDX back to Moscow. The public humiliation caused by Russian state sponsorship of terrorism in the heart of London would be devastating – especially at a time of sanctions and increased tension with the West. For Volkov personally it had all the hallmarks of being a career limiting, if not life shortening, experience. His orders from the highest level had been quite specific: nothing overt to be carried out against the West that could be linked back to Moscow.

At the time, there had seemed only one appropriate course of action: Sadiq had to be eliminated – and quickly. Fortunately, Volkov had just the operative. The Russian trained assassin, Rafiq Virenque, had just arrived on the ground in London, about to start his assignment with Panich. An urgent instruction had been transmitted and Virenque had rapidly set to work. Adopting the disguise of a TfL maintenance worker, he had travelled late at night to Canary Wharf underground Station where Sadiq had been working as part of a track repair crew. Within three hours of starting his shift, Sadiq had mysteriously slipped and fallen under the wheels of his maintenance train, his body crushed to a pulp.

Volkov was an early riser – which on this particular day proved to be a useful habit. Over his first cup of coffee, he was using the time to trawl through various emails on the subject of Arkady Nemikov's unexpected demise. He was drinking his second cup when he took the call from Viktor Plushenko. By the time he had listened to what Plushenko had to say about the subject, he was fully awake.

"Cunning bastard." Volkov said. He had been listening to Plushenko explaining Nemikov's secret arrangements for protecting his assets. "That could be a game changer."

"Maybe yes, maybe not," Plushenko replied. "We have certain contingency plans kicking in. Oleg Panich is, as you promised, indeed hugely resourceful."

Volkov smiled when he heard this. Panich was indeed very resourceful – he had, after all, been the one to request Rafiq Virenque be made available to work with him. Together, the pair made a formidable team.

"I appreciate the heads up. Given that Panich is officially your property on this Nemikov operation and not mine, I need to ask: is there another reason you are ringing me, Viktor, or is this simply a courtesy call?"

There was a grunt from the other end of the line. It was only because of Volkov's immense power and authority within the SVR that Plushenko wasn't shouting down the phone at the Yasenevo deskman for his impertinence. People normally showed much more deference to such a powerful oligarch.

"Nemikov's demise, you can appreciate, makes aspects of our little field operation more complicated. It might prove enormously helpful to our cause if the boys and girls of the SVR were willing to increase the level of field support you felt able to provide: without attribution, of course. I suspect we might only be talking about a small amount of specialised equipment procurement here, the occasional exchange of information there, that sort of thing. Is that likely to be a problem? I, for one, would be hugely in your debt."

This last remark made Volkov smile. Was he mistaken or had one of the most powerful men in Russia just come to him, cap in hand, asking for his help?

"Without attribution? Of course we'll do our best, Viktor, we're always happy to. As a matter of fact, we have been providing quite a lot of help in one or two areas already, you might be aware?"

"I wasn't for one moment suggesting that you hadn't. We are all immensely grateful for everything you have been doing."

"Very good. I'll see what additional things we might be able to do. No promises, but I'll have a quiet talk with Panich and see what might be helpful." With that, he ended the call. Volkov took a final gulp of coffee. A germ of an idea was forming.

Whether it would be helpful to Panich's operation or not, he couldn't say. However, he still had to work out what he did about the significant pile of Russian made RDX that was currently sitting in a locked storeroom deep underground at a certain London tube station. Those explosives had the power to cause widespread havoc in London: fear, panic and severe disruption. The fact that, if they were ever detonated, they were unlikely to do any significant structural damage, would give it the look and feel of an amateurish operation. Not something sponsored by any state organisation. Especially not by people as intelligent and sophisticated as the Russians. Quite the opposite. In fact, it would display all the hallmarks of something that a small terrorist cell might indeed have planned.

He recalled his conversation with Panich at the Dacha in Peredelkino:

"... we Russians have always been the masters of subterfuge. We practically invented the word. So, to plant a seed, how about *this, Oleg? What if certain fanatics, planning hideous acts of revenge against the West, were to do our job for us? Certain religious fanatics, for example. Perhaps even the nutcases who call themselves Islamic State? It would be unfortunate, wouldn't you agree, if one or two Nemikov family members happened to become innocent victims of such terrible crimes?"*

So, why didn't Volkov mention this room and the presence of the explosives to Panich when they next spoke? Perhaps he could find a way to put them to good use. He was, after all, a hugely resourceful operator, as Plushenko had been only too keen to remind Volkov.

It had a certain symmetry, like finding two pieces of a complex puzzle that surprisingly fitted together. It might also, at a stroke, remove another problem of his – how to get rid of the RDX. He reached for his cell phone, about to dial Panich's number when he paused. It would be wise to have this call rooted through secure channels: it was a conversation he would make from his office at Yasenevo and not over the cellular network from home.

85

Oleg Panich finished speaking to Volkov and turned to stare at Virenque. He had just put the phone down. The Frenchman was sitting in the kitchen chair opposite, nursing a mug of black coffee similar to the one that Panich was drinking from. Panich was discovering that drinking whilst smoking – at the same time as holding a phone to his ear – was a precarious juggle, given that he had only one good hand. Even the function of that one had been impaired, courtesy of Ben Lewis. His other, his prosthetic, was not dextrous enough to hold a mug of coffee; nor was it fine-tuned sufficiently to be that helpful when smoking. Instead, Panich had developed a posture that allowed his prosthesis to rest on a table, with the hand, lightly gripping the cigarette in its motorised fingers, angled towards his face. This allowed him to lean forward and draw on a cigarette whilst holding a mug of coffee in his other hand. It wasn't ideal; but at least it gave him the fuel – nicotine and caffeine – that his body craved.

The time was shortly before four in the morning. Nearly six o'clock Moscow time. Virenque was the first to speak.

"What was all that about?"

"You had an assignment a couple of days ago. Before this Nemikov thing kicked in. A Pakistani male. He died late at night, apparently, crushed under an underground train. Ring any bells?"

"I don't usually discuss my case work with other people." Virenque's chiselled, square-set, jaw was a prominent facial feature. As he spoke, he rubbed his chin with his thumb and forefinger, as if filing the jawbone down further. "Is it relevant to our current operation?"

"I'm not interested in the details of what you may or may not have been up to. I have just been informed that the same

254

Pakistani had apparently been building a terrorist bomb. Night after night, over a period of time, he'd been filling a secret storage room, deep underground in London's tube network, with a stash of RDX. My former SVR colleagues were wondering whether we might be able to make any use of it."

"What, the room or the explosives?"

"Both."

They didn't speak for a while, each lost in their own contemplations. The only sound was the background hum of the electric fridge – that and the noise at one stage of Panich's zippo lighter as he lit another cigarette.

"So, lateral thinking time. What are we going to do to persuade Lewis to come to us and tell his codes?"

"What, you mean if Alexei and Vince don't deliver him to us in the back of the van in the next hour or so?"

"Correct."

"Do you know something that I don't?"

Panich shook his head. "No, but I am making an intelligent guess. Lewis, by all accounts, should have made it from Luton to Cambridge over an hour ago. We have heard nothing from Alexei or Vince in that time. I view that as ominous."

"Let's give them a call?" Virenque said, reaching for his mobile.

"In a moment. Let's just think things through. Never underestimate this man, Lewis. He is extremely irritating at times, annoyingly clever. Assuming that he is not about to arrive here, bound and gagged, what next? How do we persuade him to come and pay us a visit voluntarily?"

"Well, obviously by letting him think he stands a chance of saving the boy and the girl."

"Correct. I am just not that sure that this place is the perfect hideout anymore: the risk of discovery here is quite high."

"I agree with you. Vans and bikes arriving at odd hours of the day and night get noticed. The police will be hyper-active looking for us. And this property is still on the market: an agent could drop in at any time with a prospective tenant."

"So, let's assume that, like his sister, Borys is willing to part with his codes fairly easily. Recent evidence would suggest that our powers of persuasion continue to be effective. That would leave us only needing Lewis's code before we had our hat-trick." He paused for a puff at his cigarette, swirling the dregs of his coffee around the bottom of his empty mug as he did so.

"Go on."

"What would have more impact? Us sending a 'come and find us' picture text to Lewis that shows a bound and gagged, slightly the worse for wear, shot of the two of them in our cellar downstairs? Or perhaps a similar shot but with both wearing explosive vests with timers on them, both sat in front of a pile of C-4 plastic piled from floor to ceiling, location unspecified?"

"The latter has more of a photogenic appeal to it, I have to admit. Do we need the added complications of blowing up half of London as part of simply finding a way to get to Nemikov's money?"

"Just to remind ourselves. Our orders, coming directly from Russia's richest and wealthiest are not only to get Nemikov's billions: but also, as you will be aware from your near-miss bombing on the train yesterday, to cause as much misery and mayhem under the disguise of terrorism as possible. This whole operation is being bankrolled by some deeply unhappy oligarchs, highly resentful about what the West is trying to do with their money currently."

"Okay, I'm up for this if it can all be made to work – and if the risks to ourselves are manageable. But not at any price. Whereabouts is the bomb?"

"Beneath Tottenham Court Road tube station apparently."

"Why there?"

When Panich told him, Virenque raised an eyebrow.

"Even if the Crossrail tunnels are unlikely to collapse, a bomb at that particular location is certainly going to produce chaos and mayhem."

"Precisely. Look, why don't you call Alexei and see if you can find out what's happening with Lewis?"

Virenque nodded and picked up his mobile and dialled. He waited for over a minute, but got no answer. He next tried calling Vince, again with no reply. He put the phone back on the table and looked across at Panich.

"That seems to confirm it," was all he said. "Chances of Lewis having learnt about this location?" he asked.

"Medium to high," Panich replied. "It's another reason why we probably need to bug out and move on."

"Should we use Fedorov? Is he reliable?"

"That's not a bad thought. We could certainly use his car. I am not sure about his loyalties. What do you think?"

"I never trust double agents. I instinctively feel they make life much more complicated. You never really know whether you can depend on them when the chips are down."

"I agree. Let me call him. If he brings the Range Rover, that's all we need."

"Okay. You ring him, and I'll go downstairs and check on our guests. When do you want to be moving out?"

"Assuming that Fedorov has wheels, as soon as he gets here."

"Okay. Let's try and finish our interrogation before we leave. The logistics here are so much more amenable."

"I'll be down to join you in a moment."

86

Lewis is navigating his way out of the city centre, trying to find the best road that will take him south. He is unfamiliar with the area, in danger of getting lost. He certainly doesn't know anything about a place called Newton. Locating a quiet layby just beyond an interchange with the M11 motorway, he pulls in and turns off the Honda's engine. He needs to check the map: equally importantly, he has a call to make. Removing his mobile phone from his jacket pocket, he presses the small round button on the bottom to wake it from its sleep. Flicking upwards with his thumb, he locates the small 'airplane' symbol in its small, white circle. He taps it once. The colour turns from white to grey, reconnecting his phone to the mobile network. Lewis is paranoid about leaving his phone disconnected as much as possible. Especially with people like Oleg Panich trying to locate him.

With the signal restored, he finds Zeltinger's number and dials. Zeltinger answers the call on its second ring.

"Saul, we need to talk."

"It's four in the morning, Ben."

"This can't wait. I've just been at the Nemikov flat in the centre of Cambridge. The boy is missing, and Nemikov's security detail, Pavel, is dead from a gunshot wound to the chest. Two other goons tried to ambush me whilst I was there. One's a Russian, the other sounded like a Brit. They are not dead, but they won't be doing any clear-headed thinking for a while."

"Bloody hell, Ben. This is madness. With every passing hour there seem to be yet more dead and injured turning up here, there and everywhere. They all have one thing in common. You. Do yourself a favour. Turn yourself in. I'll do my best to help sort things out for you, but the longer you leave it, the more difficult it gets."

"I can't, Saul. There's too much at stake. This isn't some gangland tit for tat. These people are out to kill, make no mistake."

"Then leave it to the security services and the police to sort it out. That's our job."

"Saul, you and I both know that this thing is moving much too fast to start involving everybody now. Cranking the machinery that you're talking about into action takes hours, if not days: they'd want to get everything properly planned, all the paperwork sorted, search warrants obtained and so on. Whilst all that bullshit is going on, it'll be too late. One of the goons who tried to kill me at the Nemikov apartment in Cambridge volunteered that Olena and Borys are being held in a farmhouse to the south of the city."

"So, only a few thousand properties for us to go looking at then. Is there any other information to be going on?"

"Apparently it's close to a place called Newton. Do you know it?"

"I'll take a look whilst we talking." The line goes silent for a few moments as Zeltinger puts the phone down.

"Here it is," he says eventually. "I've found it. Where are you at the moment?"

"Not far from a place called Harston. Just by the M11 interchange."

"Then you're virtually there. It's only two or three miles away."

"Is it a big place?"

"No, it looks tiny: lots of open farmland on all sides. I'm taking a look on Street View as we speak."

"I think I'll go and have a nosey around."

"What are you hoping to find at four in the morning?"

"I don't know, Saul. I can't sit around and do nothing. There are two innocent young people whose lives are on the line at the moment. I'd like to try and keep them alive. I'll take my chances."

"Aren't you in enough trouble already, Ben? Don't go adding breaking and entering to the list that the police are going to be wanting to ask you questions about."

"I was thinking about that. Surely it would be easy to check whether any farmhouses in the Newton area are, or have been, on the market recently?"

"At four in the morning?" Zeltinger chuckles, his tone one of disbelief.

"It only needs someone to scan through a number of local estate agent's websites, surely?"

"Okay, point taken. I'll ask someone to get on to it right away."

"Great. If you do that, I'll call you back within the half hour."

87

Virenque found them both exactly as he had left them: huddled together, leaning one against the other on the floor. Their wrists and elbows were still bound behind them. By now, Borys's mangled hand was badly swollen and bloodshot.

"My brother needs medical attention." Olena spoke with contempt, the moment she saw Virenque returning. "It's urgent."

"I don't think you're exactly in a position to issue demands, my dear."

"He's going to need reconstructive surgery, otherwise he'll lose his hand." She glowered at him. "And I am not 'your dear': not now, nor will I ever be."

Virenque came and squatted down on his haunches next to where the two of them were resting. He held her chin in his right hand briefly before she twisted it away. He grabbed it back and twisted her face viciously towards him.

"You, bitch, I shall call you what the fuck I want," he said angrily and with emphasis. "For the record," he continued, back to speaking softly and evenly, "I don't actually give a damn about your brother's hand. Anyway, *my dear*," this time saying the words with deliberation exaggeration, "you saw for yourself how well my Russian colleague seems to manage with his new prosthetic. In time, and assuming we all get what we want, your brother will be able to have the same."

"Philistine," was all that she muttered, causing Virenque to laugh.

"Is that the best you can do?" he said. Then, completely unexpectedly and with rapid speed, he hit her hard with his right hand on her left cheek. He used the open flat of his palm to make contact, the impact sickeningly loud in the confined space of the cellar. It caused Olena to cry out in pain.

"Leave my sister alone, you bastard," Borys said, speaking for the first time.

Which was the reaction that Virenque had wanted. He grabbed Borys by the hair and drew his face painfully close to his own.

"If you ever, ever," he said with vehemence, "speak to me like that again, I will personally stand on your broken hand until you pass out with the pain, do you understand me?"

Borys nodded in silence. Tears were streaming down his sister's face. Her left cheek was red: large welts were beginning to form where Virenque's fingers had hit her.

"Now then," Virenque was back standing, pacing around the small space where they were huddled. "Soon we are going to have to have another discussion about those secret codes, yours especially, Borys. Your sister had the sense to be helpful earlier. Now it is going be your turn. Do I make myself clear?"

To his surprise, Borys nodded: Virenque had anticipated some form of stubborn refusal. Perhaps this wasn't going to be so difficult after all.

It was at this moment that Panich hurried back down the stone steps to join them in the cellar. He looked at Virenque and spoke in simple shorthand.

"The man was already on his way. He should be here any moment."

"That's very good. Because I was just explaining that the time was fast approaching when we were going to need to ask Borys to share some of his secrets."

Panich was looking at the red welts on Olena's face.

"What happened to you, my lovely woman?"

"I am not your lovely woman," she spat, her anger resonating in every word.

"Oh, I think for the time being you are," he said, stroking the red welt with a prosthetic finger. He too squatted down next to her. "All mine," he said, smiling lecherously at her, his eyes wandering deliberately all over her breasts, her body, her legs and then back slowly to lock on to her eyes once more. "Don't be under any misapprehension, Olena. " he said, stroking her other cheek now, his finger wandering so that it tilted her head directly towards him. She had little choice but to look him directly in the eye. "Whether you like it or not, you will do anything and everything that we ask of you. You'll see."

She shuddered, and Panich stood up. Whether it was the cold air in the cellar or the sudden movement or for whatever reason: Panich began to cough. It was the phlegm-filled cough of a smoker, rattling around deep within his chest, and it continued for several seconds. Virenque waited for it to subside, looking at Panich to check he was all right before continuing. Panich simply nodded, his body slowly gathering breath.

"Borys, let me ask a simple question." It was Virenque speaking. "On the assumption that you are unlikely to hand over your codes without additional persuasion, I am going to give you three options. Option one is that my friend here," he said, pointing at Panich, "provides some symmetry to your current infirmity and does to your left hand exactly the same as he did to the right. Option two is that he and I take it in turns to tread very carefully and repeatedly on your right hand. This will render it completely useless as well as being very painful for you. Option three," he said, pausing for dramatic effect, "is what I fear my friend over there," he said pointing at Panich, "really wants. Option three sees us tying your sister up against the wall over there, completely naked, and then we both take it in turns to enjoy ourselves whilst you are forced to watch. How does that sound, Borys?"

Both Olena and Borys began shaking visibly, fear and tension wracking their entire bodies.

"Of course, there is always a fourth option," Panich was speaking, his head on one side, looking at them both pityingly. "The fourth option is that you tell us what we want and there will be no need for any unpleasantness."

"But then you will simply kill us," Borys blurted. It was a brave, yet foolish, thing to have said. It caused an instantaneous reaction from Virenque. With lightning speed he bent down and picked up a terrified Olena under both armpits as if she was a child, as light as a feather. With her in his hands, he thrust her backwards towards the wall immediately behind where they had been sitting. The impact of her body crashing into the wall made her scream, the force making the cellar walls reverberate. Virenque thrust his right hand directly against Olena's windpipe and pressed it hard against the stone behind her. Olena struggled desperately to breathe: choking sounds emanating from her throat.

"How about option five, assuming that you really want to go there?" Virenque was shouting, the adrenalin in his system pumping fast and furious. "Why don't I simply kill your sister now, Borys? She's already given us her codes. She's now excess baggage. No longer needed – so we kill her, just as you suggested."

Olena's eyes were bulging. She was fast becoming desperate: unable to breath, unable to swallow, the pressure on her throat intolerable.

"I quite like option five, actually, Oleg." Virenque said, deliberately addressing Panich. "It's one less to worry about. What do you think, Borys? Do you have any last words to say to your darling sister? Your silence is going to be the thing that kills her."

"NO!" Borys suddenly screams. "No! I'll tell you,' he starts sobbing. 'Don't kill her. I'll tell you what you want."

Virenque looked at Panich and the two of them nodded. The Frenchman released his grip on Olena's throat, letting her fall to the floor where she gasped and coughed, heaving for breath.

"Okay, Borys." It was Panich speaking now. "You've earned Olena a reprieve. You've got two minutes to tell us all we need to know. Otherwise, my friend will not hesitate to kill your sister. Killing is his particular expertise."

The game that had been chosen for Borys had been the Ukrainian grandmaster, Alexander Areshchenko against the Russian grandmaster, Sergei Rublevsky in the 2009 world cup held in Khanty-Mansiysk in Russia. Rublevsky, playing white, had made a tactical error on the seventy-sixth move. White Queen to g6. Areshchenko had moved his black knight to f4. Thereafter, the Ukrainian trapped the white queen and used his pawn to put Rublevsky's king in check and force a resignation. The code was in the final four moves of the game: Kg3 Rh5 Kh3 g4. Borys gave up his secrets without any further encouragement. The time was almost exactly four o'clock in the morning.

88

Before disconnecting his phone from the network, Lewis uses the map function to plan his route to Newton. As Zeltinger had suggested, the village is close to his current location. There are two roads running through the middle; one roughly north-south and the other east-west. About to arrive from the north, Lewis decides to make a quick sweep through the village and explore the entire area by bike first. Then he will park up and perform a secondary scan on foot.

By four-fifteen, his first scan is complete. The village is indeed small. There are possibly no more than ten houses that, in Lewis's mind, fit the description of being a farmhouse. Of these, all bar two have cars in their drives, indicating some kind of possible human presence. Four have lights on in one part or other. It is like searching for a needle in a haystack. Two stand out as being places that he would have chosen: one is on the road heading east from the village; the other is on the road to Harston, heading west. Both are isolated, both about a mile from the village centre and thus quiet. He decides to modify his secondary scan on foot by starting with these two first. He begins with the property on the west side.

He parks his bike in a small turning to the left. It is the entrance to a field, allowing Lewis to tuck his Honda behind a hedge and out of sight. He approaches the house on foot from the road. The main building is set back some distance and hidden by trees and bushes. At this time of year, the leaf cover has disappeared: in the pale moonlight, Lewis can see through them directly onto the property. A Range Rover is parked in the drive. Lewis did not see this on his first drive past the property: probably because it is tucked in, tight next to the hedge, adjacent to the road. Lewis salts away the number plate. His one nagging thought is that Nemikov had a Range Rover.

Earlier the same evening, Fedorov had driven off to Luton Airport in it. Could it be the same vehicle? Lewis dismisses the idea as an unlikely coincidence: too many people in this part of the country drive the identical make and model. There are two lights on downstairs, but no movement he can detect. He decides to get closer. The drive is laid with pea shingle, causing him to tread carefully so as not to make a sound. To one side there is a small open-fronted garage. As he gets closer, Lewis finds a motorbike parked up. He feels the engine block. Despite the cold night air, there is residual warmth there. This machine has been used in the last few hours. No more than three or four, perhaps less. He tries looking through the windows of the house, but the curtains are drawn and he can hear no sound. He waits, listening, smelling the air. Nothing. There is no letterbox on the main door to look through either. Still stepping carefully, he checks the garden: again finding nothing. The time is four twenty-five. Time to check the other property.

Retrieving his Honda, he heads to the other side of the village, leaving his bike parked once more behind a hedge. This second property is more exposed to the road than the other. There are two cars in the drive: another Range Rover and an old, 'T' registered Volkswagen. Once more faced with a driveway covered in pea-shingle, Lewis creeps carefully up to the house so as to get a closer look. There are three lights on: two upstairs and one downstairs. This time, there is a letterbox on the front door. Lewis pushes it open and peers inside, letting his senses eke out anything unusual. He neither sees nor hears anything. He does, however, smell lingering tobacco smoke. Could this be Panich? It is possible.

The time is four thirty-five in the morning. He should be calling Zeltinger once again.

Backing away from the property as stealthily as he is able, he pulls out his phone. Zeltinger answers it on the second ring.

"We might have found one property," the half German Detective Inspector tells Lewis. "It's a rental property, on the west side of the village. It's on the road to a village called Harston."

89

Fedorov found the farmhouse without any difficulty. He reversed the Range Rover into the drive and parked it next to a thick hedge, where it wouldn't be seen that easily from the road. The time was five minutes after four in the morning. He had no keys to the property. Without any doorbell to ring, he instead banged loudly on the door a couple of times. After waiting in the cold night air for what seemed like an age, he was about to knock again when he felt the blade of a knife being pressed hard against his throat. He had never heard a thing.

"Who the fuck are you?" came a voice from behind him. "What the hell do you want round here at this time of night?"

Already sporting a broken nose from his earlier encounter with Lewis, the last thing Fedorov wanted was another confrontation.

"My name is Sergei Fedorov," he said weakly but with a tinge of pride, his poor English clearly audible.

The man behind him seemed to consider this for a while before releasing the pressure of the blade.

"Okay, we were expecting you. Do you have a gun?"

Fedorov shook his head. He did earlier, before Ben Lewis had confiscated it from him.

"So first thing, I am going to check to make sure. No funny tricks, Sergei. It looks like you've been in the wars this evening. Who did that to your nose?"

He was patting him down expertly whilst he was speaking. He even checked behind him, in the small of his back, to Fedorov's chagrin: the place where the Ukrainian had failed to find the knife on Lewis.

"A man called Ben Lewis." He pretended to spit on the ground having spoken the name.

"Ha!" the man laughed, the body search complete. "Then we have common enemies, even if we don't know one another. I am Virenque, by the way. And your arrival is most timely. We are shortly to be leaving, and you are going to be our designated driver. Follow me and I'll show you around."

Virenque let Fedorov lead the way down into the cellar. He wanted to observe the Ukrainian's reaction when he saw both Olena and Borys tied up. It would help make it clear where the man's loyalties really lay.

The light in the cellar was dim and it took a while to adjust to the semi-darkness. When he was finally able to make out what was going on, Fedorov let out a cry.

"What have you been doing?" he asked Virenque, pointing to where Olena and Borys were lying with their hands and elbows restrained. "They are no threat! This is barbaric!"

Virenque turned to Fedorov and smiled thinly.

"If you want to see barbaric, I'd be happy to show you." He turned to face the Nemikov pair and waved with his arm. "Why are you so concerned about them both anyway, Sergei? You're meant to be on our team, not theirs." He looked at Olena and Borys, and saw that he had their attention. "Yes, that's right. Your friend Fedorov has betrayed you. All these years, he's secretly been working for the Russians. Isn't that right, Sergei?"

Fedorov said nothing.

"You've gone very quiet all of a sudden, Sergei. Why not explain to Olena here who tipped us off that she was leaving Kensington with Lewis in the Audi, and not with you in the Range Rover? I am sure she'd love to hear the truth."

"It's complicated," is all that Fedorov said.

"Too bloody right it's complicated," retorted Virenque. "Everyone has their own secret agenda. These two included. Or at least they did." He laughed as he said this. "In any event, it no longer matters. They have told us all that we need to know."

"Then let them go."

"Sergei!" It was Olena speaking. "You've got to help. They are going to kill us, I know they are."

"Shut up, woman," Virenque snapped. A Glock 17 pistol had suddenly appeared in his hand: it was pointing directly at her.

"Unless you'd like to take the first bullet?" He turned to face Fedorov, tapping the man's chest with the barrel of his gun.

"So, Sergei, just to prove finally that you and I are on the same side. I'd like to hear you explain how you've betrayed these two, and their father, all these years. That's all."

Fedorov said nothing. He was staring at Borys and Olena, a mixture of anger and sadness on his face.

"We can wait all night, if you'd rather," Virenque said, casually moving his left sleeve cuff with the barrel of the Glock to check the time.

Time stood still for several seconds.

Then, as fast and as unexpected as a lightning strike, he spun the Glock pistol abruptly towards Fedorov's face and pulled the trigger: at point blank range, directly between the eyes. The sound was deafening: blood, sinew and bone fragments of what had been Fedorov's head splattered far and wide in the bullet's wake. Olena and Borys both screamed, but in the depths of the brick-lined cellar, with nothing but earth and stone on four sides, the noise was barely audible, even to Panich on the floor above.

"Pull yourselves together. The man was a traitor. He betrayed your father." Virenque assessed the petrified look in their eyes. He bent down on his haunches so as to be at their level. "Nobody trusts a traitor. We're better off without him, don't you think? At least you now know what happens to those who piss me off."

He raised himself back up to full height again.

"We shall be leaving very shortly. If you need to use the bucket," he said with a nod to the white plastic receptacle in the corner, "now is the time to do so. I am about to undo your wrist bindings. Don't start getting any smart ideas. If you plan on messing me or my friend around, you've seen now how I'm likely to react."

90

Already suspicious because of the information that Zeltinger had passed him, by the time Lewis approaches the house on the Harston Road for the second time, his hackles are well and truly raised.

The Range Rover is no longer there.

Also, since his earlier visit a few minutes ago, all the lights in the property have been turned off.

It is time to look inside.

Still treading stealthily on the pea shingle, he reaches a side entrance and tries the handle. The door is unlocked. Another bad sign.

He closes the door behind him and listens. There is no sound to be heard anywhere. Once again he can smell smoke. Cigarette smoke. This time it is a brand he knows: Turkish. This is the place, he feels sure. Reaching for his phone, he flips the screen with his thumb and turns on the flashlight. He is in the kitchen, and there is evidence that people have been here. Two mugs are on the table. More importantly, numerous cigarette butts have been stubbed out on a saucer.

This is definitely the place.

He reaches for the Walther P-22 pistol still tucked in his waistband, moving the safety to the firing position. Inching his way into the hallway, he has the clear sense that the house is deserted. He checks from room to room to make sure. The ground floor first: there is no one: all rooms are empty. The stairs to the upper floor creak as he shuffles his way up. Lewis takes care to press his heels on the edge of the tread nearest the wall so as to minimise the noise. He checks each room methodically: again all are empty.

The only remaining place to check is the cellar. The steps are behind a door leading off a passageway from the kitchen.

He opens the cellar door and the smell of death rushes up to meet him. Emboldened by the absence of anybody in the rest of the house, Lewis flips the light switch on as he descends the stairs. Step by step, all the while listening. He makes an easy target, he knows, to anybody waiting with a gun. However, he is confident that no one is lying there in wait: no one alive, that is. When he reaches the bottom and sees what little there is left of Fedorov, his face and most of his head blown away, he knows that he was right.

Zeltinger answers the phone on the second ring once more.

"Saul," Lewis says with no introductions. "This is definitely the place. If you can mobilise all police units, there is a chance of catching Panich and the two young Nemikovs: possibly also the bomber on the train. I arrived about five minutes too late. They've taken off in Nemikov's Range Rover." He recites the car's registration details from memory.

"I've no idea where they're heading, but they can't be far from here. Why don't you call me back in a couple of minutes, once you've got that sorted, and I can give you a proper heads up?"

Zeltinger calls back in three minutes.

"I've set the ball in motion," Zeltinger says. "We're a bit early for the commuter rush hour into London, clogging the roads. With luck we might be able to catch them."

"Great. Look, Saul, you need to get the Cambridgeshire police out to this place. The house is completely empty, I've checked. Nemikov's head of security, Sergei Fedorov, is however, lying dead in the cellar. He's had half his head blown away by a gunshot wound to the face."

"Bloody hell, Ben. Did you do that?"

"It was tempting, but not guilty. There's also evidence in the cellar that one or more have been held here against their will. You'll need a forensic team. I am certain Olena and Borys

274

were here."

"I trust you haven't left prints everywhere, Ben?"

"I've been über careful. I'd like to beg a favour. A 'no' answer is perfectly acceptable. I need to come back London. If I go to my apartment, I am likely either to be arrested or, if Panich is still at large, to find myself dragged somewhere unpleasant and interrogated. Are you at home for the next hour or so? If so, could I drop by to freshen up, grab some fuel and recharge? Always assuming, you're not about to turn me in."

"Ben, I've had virtually no sleep tonight. What's another interruption going to change? I am not about to turn you in, I promise, if that's what you're worried about. The deal is that, in return you'll have to promise to give me straight answers to each and every question I may have."

91

Although mainly operating in daylight hours, pilots flying for the National Police Air Service that supports each of forty-three regional police forces across the United Kingdom are all trained to fly at night: as a result, NPAS had controllers on duty around the clock based in their headquarters in Dudley Hill, near Bradford. Following Saul Zeltinger's telephone briefing to SO15's duty commander, Alan Naisby, Naisby had contacted Dudley Hill controllers requesting immediate support in identifying, and following, a high priority target vehicle in the South Cambridgeshire area.

Two pilots were on standby that November evening, both based at Lippitts Hill, in Loughton in Essex. In order to reduce wind and night-time frost damage, their Eurocopter EC 145 aircraft were housed in hangers at the heliport, ready fuelled. This had the advantage of negating the need for de-icing or fuelling on start up; it had the disadvantage of requiring the hangar to be opened and both aircraft towed out onto the heliport apron before start up routines could be commenced. Since the heliport was otherwise shut down at four forty-five in the morning, it took at least fifteen minutes from the time that NPAS had authorised release of the two aircraft before the two pilots of call signs India 98 and 99 respectively were ready to commence engine start up. By the time they were airborne, it was nearly twenty minutes since Ben Lewis had first contacted Saul Zeltinger with details of the Range Rover's registration.

Virenque drove. Panich was next to him in the front, with Borys and Olena, their hands retied tightly, this time only at the wrist, in the back. Virenque was able to control the central locking from the front – and to be sure, he had also switched on the child lock on both rear doors before they had set off: they could no longer be opened from inside the car. Panich and Virenque had debated their destination earlier; time and again, Panich had found himself being drawn back to the storeroom deep underground at Tottenham Court Road station. He found the location exciting. It gave them an opportunity to plan something really special.

"What route are you taking?" Panich asked as they were fast approaching the A505 to the south of Fowlmere. He'd been coughing again, and felt quite drained by the experience. The pain was also coming back in his chest: he'd felt it several times that night already.

"I thought we would find ourselves alternative transport," Virenque answered.

"Why?" Panich asked, but the instant he said it he knew: this was a Nemikov vehicle and it would be flagged in the police database.

"Because I like to think we are professional," Virenque said, turning right on the normally busy main road. They were five miles from the commuter town of Royston.

"There is a large station car park at Royston. We'll be able to find ourselves a car there. It will prove a useful contingency, you'll see."

Ten minutes later, having parked the Range Rover in a dark corner, adjacent to an old Vauxhall Astra most likely belonging to a commuter who had not made it home the previous evening, Virenque had his contingency. Panich, despite his prosthesis, picked the driver's door lock in seconds and Virenque, bundling Olena and Borys into the back, hot-wired the engine. There was just over a half a tank of petrol in the car.

Fifteen minutes later, just as they were approaching the junction with the motorway, two police helicopters could be seen coming into a hover to the north and south of their junction, their searchlights on, slowly and carefully watching the traffic in both directions. They had, on board, Virenque knew, sophisticated ANPR tracking cameras, able to pick up targeted number plates automatically. He turned south onto the motorway and briefly glanced at Panich.

"Having this contingency might have been a good idea after all, don't you think?"

"God, they were on to us quickly." They were passing the hovering helicopter to their left. He began coughing once more. "Good idea about the contingency," he said eventually. "I don't think we'd have escaped the police otherwise."

"I agree. This whole place seems jinxed for some reason. Just for the record, I sincerely hope that I never have to drive on this particular piece of motorway ever again."

92

As they approached the suburbs of London, there were an increasing number of police vehicles on the roads. It wasn't normal for five-thirty in the morning. The commuter traffic was building: as they approached the Mill Hill roundabout at the bottom of the A1, there were three policemen in fluorescent jackets watching the traffic carefully.

"I'm not sure I like the look of all this," Virenque was saying. "If they start looking inside the wrong vehicle, we'll be in trouble."

"How about a different idea?" Panich had been studying the map as Virenque had been driving. "When we get to Hendon Central, in about a couple of miles, let's pull in. We can take the Underground into the centre of London. It's Northern Line all the way: no need to change trains even. The tube will be deserted at this time of the morning. All round, it'll probably make it easier to get to our destination as well. What do you think?"

"Smart idea," Virenque sounded impressed. "The police will eventually tow this vehicle but it'll take an age before they put two and two together. We'll need to ensure that our guests don't misbehave, though."

"Don't worry. You can take hold of Borys's right hand, and give it a reassuring squeeze if he starts to make trouble. I will have Olena in mine," he said, holding up his prosthesis. "I've been developing an agreeably strong grip, what with all the recent practice it's been getting. I can't wait to try it out on Lewis."

"Do you know exactly where we are heading?"

"Oh yes. The team at Yasenevo haven't completely forgotten us. I received a couple of highly informative text messages in the last hour. One even had a photograph. All thanks to our friend Volkov."

93

It is just after six in the morning when Lewis brings his bike to a halt on the quiet side street, just off West End Lane in Hampstead. He stands on the roadside with his helmet off, surveying the neighbourhood. There has been a heavy police presence everywhere on the roads coming into London. En route, he had passed two police helicopters. On the back streets of West Hampstead, it remains calm and dark, the damp and cold November night air lingering. It makes his breath condense as he exhales.

Houses on both sides of Ulysses Road are identical. They are Victorian terraces, the majority recently modernised. Each has large bay windows on both ground and upper floors. Most have a pocket-handkerchief sized piece of terracing in front, next to the fencing that separates the house from the pavement. The Zeltingers, like several other house owners, have a large box hedge alongside their fencing. As Lewis watches and listens, signs of life are beginning to appear along the street. Lights are being turned on; early risers are making tea; and people are letting their dogs out. Nothing looks out of place: no cars or bikes are parked with people sitting waiting, like him, watching and listening. As satisfied as he can be that he's not walking into a trap set by Zeltinger, he approaches the front door. Rather than ring the bell and disturb the whole house, instead he turns on his phone and gives Zeltinger a quick call.

As ever, it takes just two rings before it is answered.

"I'm outside your front door, assuming that you still want to see me."

Moments later, a sleepy Saul Zeltinger opens the door. He is dressed in his shirt and trousers. The two men shake hands in silent greeting and Zeltinger ushers Lewis inside, a finger on his lips indicating that others in the house are still asleep. They move into a room off the corridor and Zeltinger closes the door. It is the main living space, with sofas on two sides, a television in one corner, and toys strewn everywhere. It is evident that Zeltinger has been using this room to sleep in.

"Been banished from the family bed, have we, Saul?"

"Because of your various comings and goings all through the night, I thought Hattie needed to sleep undisturbed. I seem to find myself sleeping down here quite a lot."

"Any news on Olena and Borys? Has the car been found?"

"Not yet. The police have been scouring the roads around the north east of London for the past hour."

"They probably changed vehicles."

"What's that?"

"It's what I would have done. The car is Nemikov's. Or rather was. Even without the knowledge that someone might have seen it in odd circumstances in a house outside Newton, I would still reckon on it being on the police's wanted list. Therefore, if I were Panich and didn't want to risk being stopped, I would change vehicles."

"How, exactly, would you do that at five in the morning?"

"That's dead easy. Most probably, I'd go to a commuter station car park. There are always plenty of cars parked up in those places overnight: people away on business; people staying in hotels overnight after a boozy night on the town, that sort of thing. I'd pick a car, probably something old that could be hot-wired easily. In a place like that there'd be no end of cars to choose from."

"Bloody hell, Ben. How do you think of all this stuff? Policemen aren't trained to think like that. Our problem solving is much more linear."

"Once you've been on the run a few times, trust me, you soon learn how to work things out."

They talk for a while, Lewis describing in detail certain events of the last few hours. Suddenly, there is a sound like distant rolling thunder: footsteps, charging barefoot down the stairs.

"Six-thirty in the morning," Zeltinger says, looking at his watch. "Time for our wake-up call. We are about to be interrupted."

Moments later, the door is flung open, and two identical boys burst in.

"Daddy!" they shout, before realising there is someone else in the room. Instantly they go quiet, backing up close to the sofa where their father is sitting, feeling the reassurance of his arm around them both.

"Who are you?" one of them asks.

"Why have you been sleeping on the sofa, Daddy?" the other asks.

Zeltinger chuckles.

"Boys, this is Ben Lewis. Ben, meet Zach and Nate."

"Hello, Zach. Hello, Nate. I've heard a lot about you from your Dad."

The two youngsters wriggle closer to their father, still not convinced about the stranger in their house.

"Ben, here," Zeltinger continues, "is one of the country's top super heroes. Isn't that right, Ben?"

Lewis smiles.

"I guess. When I'm not saving the world from all those bad guys, occasionally I like to hang around with your Dad. He's a pretty good cop too, you know that?"

There are giggles from them both now. They are beginning to relax.

"No, he's not. He's useless," one of them says and the two of them collapse in more giggles.

"Why don't you two scallywags run upstairs and start getting dressed for school? Tell your mother that we've an unexpected guest for breakfast. I'll be up in a moment. Go on, before I have to set this super hero on you."

"He doesn't frighten us," one of them says, still giggling.

283

At which point, Lewis lets out a pretend lion's roar, sending both boys racing out of the room shouting and yelling, stomping up the stairs at great speed.

"That seemed to do the trick!" Zeltinger says. "I must try that myself next time."

Hattie Zeltinger greets Lewis warmly.

"I've heard a lot about you, Ben. We had been expecting you here for supper last night until Saul mentioned that you'd been detained."

"You missed a great lasagne," Zeltinger chipped in.

Despite the hour, Hattie doesn't look as if she has just woken up. Her curly blonde hair is neat and combed: and her blue eyes sparkle.

"I'm sorry about that. It's been quite a night, all things considered."

"Mummy, Ben here is a super hero. Daddy told us. He's been working to save the world and he's really, really good, apparently."

"Is that so, Nate? Ben, do you have anything you can say about that?"

Lewis looks at the two young boys, standing staring openmouthed, waiting for him to speak.

"I never discuss my work, I'm afraid," he says winking at both of them. "It's all highly confidential." He taps the side of his nose.

"That reminds me, Ben. I need to show you something," Zeltinger says. Lewis follows as Zeltinger heads into another room at the back of the house, this one containing a desk piled high with papers: a computer desktop machine sits on one corner.

"This is my study," Zeltinger explains. "Sort of. As you can see, it also serves as a general filing area for everything that we don't want the boys messing with. They know not to come in here." He moves the computer mouse, positions the cursor on a password login entry point and types in a long password.

On the screen are various photographs of Arkady Nemikov's mangled Lamborghini.

"Wow!" exclaims Ben when he studies the photographs. "You'd never believe a car like that would crumple that much. Poor Nemikov. On the plus side, death would have been instantaneous."

"I went to the crash scene myself, as soon as I heard what had happened," Zeltinger explains. "They reckon he must have been travelling at least a hundred miles an hour."

"In a car like that, I'm surprised he wasn't doing more."

"Well, the crash created a hell of a fire ball. Even the officer at the scene when I arrived was surprised by its intensity."

"What time of night did it happen?"

"At, or close to, one forty-six in the morning, based on witness information from the man who called in the accident. Every call is logged, so there can be no doubt about the time, give or take a minute."

"Do I hear a lingering doubt in your tone?"

"Not really. After I left the accident scene, I went on the police traffic information computer system. I pulled up the information that is automatically recorded by the Truvelo digital speed cameras when cars go past. Nemikov was driving well under the limit when he went through the Hook Underpass."

"So? He rounds the bend, sees the speed restriction is no longer in force, and floors the accelerator. He'd have taken off like a rocket. Over a hundred in a second or two."

"Yes, you're probably right. However, the time recorded on the last speed camera he passes, less than a mile from where he crashed, was only one-forty one. A full three or four minutes earlier than when the accident was meant to have occurred a short distance just around the corner."

Lewis laughs.

"You are showing your true half-Germanic side again,

Saul! Stop looking for ghosts. There'll be a simple explanation. A two-minute lull in traffic before the next car came along, maybe. Or, more likely, the clocks on the camera system are wrong," Lewis says. "Even the one on my phone is inaccurate from time to time." He takes his phone out and waves it symbolically. It is only then that he realises that he has forgotten to disconnect the device from the network after ringing Zeltinger earlier. He quickly remedies this and puts the phone back in his pocket.

"Do they know why the van was parked on the hard shoulder?"

"Not yet. We're having difficulty tracing it. The front plates were missing, apparently, and the rear ones have been pulverised by the collision and then destroyed by the blaze. In time, we should be able to find the chassis number, but it's early days yet."

"What a way to go."

"Tell you what: do you fancy breakfast? I don't know about you, but I'm starving."

"That sounds perfect. When I said I'd like to refresh and refuel, a decent breakfast was exactly what I'd had in mind."

94

They reached their destination in under twenty minutes. They sat in the rear carriage, all the way from Hendon Central, with only one other passenger for company until Euston station, when several more got on. Neither Olena nor Borys showed any attempt at escaping. Nor did they try to communicate with any other passengers. Two stops later, when the tube train pulled into Tottenham Court Road station, they were the only ones who got off.

Panich made the four of them wait on the platform until the train departed. He didn't want anyone to watch where they were going. It was only a short walk along the platform until Panich found what he was looking for: exactly as had been described, a small linking passageway connecting the north and southbound platforms. The blue door was indeed set in the middle of a blue-painted brick wall. On the outside was a white card: 'ON ENTERING, PLEASE MIND THE STEP'. The black electrical tape holding the card in place was beginning to peel away at the edges.

It took Panich exactly twenty-eight seconds to pick the lock. For a few seconds, he felt stupidly out of breath: the action of stooping down to wrestle with the tumblers actually making him momentarily light-headed. The pain in his chest was back once again. Shaking his head as he stood up, he pulled open the door: it swung outward into the small passageway. There was a light switch on the wall just inside. Once switched on, the pile of sandbags stacked from floor to ceiling immediately became visible.

When Virenque stepped inside, he understood instantly the potential the room gave: it was the ideal place to keep hostages.

When Panich stepped inside, he understood instantly the

impact the explosives would have: he considered it perfect.

When Olena and Borys stepped inside, they both understood instantly that they had reached the end of the line.

95

One of the benefits of living close to the office was that, during his lunch break, Rudi Hildebrandt often went home to his apartment for an hour, sometimes longer. It wasn't unusual for him to have a female accompany him. There was a pretty young accounts clerk he was currently very much infatuated with.

When Hildebrandt returned home at lunchtime on that particular day, he was alone and hardly thinking straight. He had never experienced a morning quite like it. With Arkady Nemikov dead, he, Rudi Hildebrandt, was suddenly the man in charge of administering the whole of Nemikov's vast estate. It was a huge responsibility. Whilst he had no doubts about his ability to perform the role, it hadn't stopped his anxiety levels from rising as soon as he heard the news upon reaching the office that morning. He had already tried, and failed, to make contact with the three holders of Nemikov's key codes. In the meantime, the entire Nemikov financial empire had been frozen: the assets of the estate held in a form of Hildebrandt-imposed suspended animation.

That lunchtime, he wasn't interested in food. He had something much more urgent that he needed to attend to: updating the bank's master records with the details of the new code that Arkady Nemikov had entrusted to Ben Lewis. At the time that he and Nemikov had spoken on the phone late the previous evening, Hildebrandt had taken copious notes on his laptop computer, completing the 'change of details' template that was necessary to update master password fields on the bank's main computer server. Due to the late hour and because he was at home, he had been working offline: this had proven much easier and quicker, avoiding the need for numerous password access controls to be completed. His thinking, late in the evening, had been that he would take his laptop into work the following morning and synchronise everything then. The only problem had been that, in his haste to leave for work on time that morning, he had forgotten to remove his laptop from the safe and take it with him. He was going to have to do this now, during his lunch break. It was critically important to do this as soon as possible given Nemikov's death.

Retrieving the laptop from his well-hidden, fireproof, floor safe, he powered up the machine and waited for it to connect to his wireless network. Before he did anything else, he wanted to see what was being said online about the death of Arkady Nemikov. He went to the SRF1 website first but found nothing. Next he tried the BBC news channel and soon found a video news clip detailing the high-speed car crash. He clicked on the link and an annoying pop-up window appeared telling him that first he needed to upgrade his Flash Media Player. Exhaling with mild exasperation, he clicked on the link and waited whilst the new software downloaded. When prompted whether he was sure he wanted to open the programme, he clicked 'yes' in response, typing in his system password on the next page to complete the installation. Less than a minute later, the install was complete. He reopened his browser and was swiftly directed back to the same page on the BBC site. He clicked the link to start the media clip and watched in grim fascination. Even he, Rudi Hildebrandt, gave an involuntary shudder when he saw Nemikov's wrecked Lamborghini. What a terrible way for anyone, let alone his biggest and most important client, to die.

A few streets away, in her hotel room, Tian was, literally, jumping up and down with happiness. Once again, her box of tricks had performed its magic. She, Kristina Tian, was now fully in control of Rudi Hildebrandt's laptop.

As a hacker, her challenge was always finding ways to upload software on to a target computer without the owner ever being aware. Some of the more basic rogue software, or malware, only recorded keystrokes. These simple programmes were easy to install on a computer by means of an email attachment or a web link. They worked in the background and didn't interfere with the computer operating system. More complicated malware, in particular any kind of software that attempted to take control of a computer, needed to permeate the heart of the computer's operating system. In these circumstances, the malware could only be made to work if, first, the hacker had access to the system administrator passwords. Without that, it was useless.

Several months ago, Tian had had a brainwave about how to do this.

Why not disguise the software that she was trying to install by pretending it to be something else? By making it appear to be something that the computer user might be expecting to install – such as a software update or, for example, a periodic Flash Media update? The beauty of this approach was that the computer owner was tricked into entering their system administrator password, as part of what they believed was a genuine software install. They thought they were installing a new Flash Media update: in practice they were uploading Tian's rogue software.

It was genius. In one fell swoop, Tian now owned Rudi Hildebrandt's laptop.

Including all the information contained within it.

96

Having showered and borrowed a spare razor, Lewis feels presentable.

"What's the plan?" Zeltinger asks him. The children have left for school with their mother, and he and Lewis are finishing up the remains of a cooked breakfast that Hattie had prepared.

"We have to think like the opposition," Lewis says, wiping his mouth with the back of his hand whilst munching on a slice of toast. "Their story, as best as I can make out, probably goes something like this." He swallows a mouthful of coffee before beginning.

"Certain Russian interests want to take control of Nemikov's billions. This is unlikely to be a full-blown, state run, SVR mission: that's too overt. No, a few powerful oligarchs are probably driving this whole thing – Nemikov mentioned one to me in particular: a man called Plushenko. Powerful Russians, with lots of money, all seriously pissed off about the West freezing their assets in their foreign bank accounts, as well as being barred from various commercial deals and the like. Make sense so far?" He takes another bite of toast and looks at Zeltinger, who nods in silent agreement.

"So, they commission some private enterprise. Who better to take the lead than Oleg Panich? This man is a former SVR hero, pensioned off due to injury, and with an outstanding track record as a field agent. In picking Panich, they also gain an additional benefit: they have someone working for them who has real anger in his belly. The mission objective? To try and coerce Nemikov into handing over his billions – and, in particular, stop the man from directing his money to Kiev, to help prop up the anti-Russian government there. Panich, in turn, recruits a few team mates: one or two former SVR colleagues like the one I bumped into in Cambridge in the early hours of this morning; and also the bomber from the train."

"What I don't understand," Zeltinger says, interrupting him, "is why, if that hypothesis is true, are they trying to disguise everything to look like a series of terrorist attacks? The bomb on the train: the Venice *vaporetto* bomb that killed Nemikov's wife? Why go to all the trouble?"

"We think it killed Valentyna: we don't know for sure, but let's assume it did. The reason, I think, is this. Panich's MO has been simple: kill the wife and daughter and then kidnap the son. Nemikov then has a choice: hand over his money or else the son is tortured and then killed and Nemikov Senior will have lost everything he holds dear. Arkady told me that himself: his wife and children are his Achilles heel. Dominant male syndrome being active in the Slavic cultures, Nemikov would be most worried about his son's fate and would have yielded to the pressure.

"Meanwhile, I think we need to imagine the pent-up frustration building amongst those oligarchs who have suffered sanctions. The sense of what they see as injustice against them gnaws away: who wouldn't be interested in some kind of private retaliatory action against the West? However, Mother Russia doesn't want itself, or its oligarchs, portrayed as a bunch of modern day gangsters. Maybe this desire for retribution has been bubbling away like an angry sore for some time, the pain and irritation getting worse day by day. Perhaps private enterprise against Nemikov is suddenly seen as a great mechanism for achieving two aims simultaneously: dealing with Nemikov – preventing his money from reaching Kiev – and exacting some revenge against the West? So they dream up the idea of a little subterfuge. Set off a few bombs here and there that cause widespread panic and destruction: make them look like the work of Islamic State – even if they aren't; and make them coincidentally kill off, injure or maim one or two

Nemikovs along the way. I 'd say that was a devilishly clever plan."

"It sounds a bit far fetched to me," Zeltinger was saying. 'Overly complex."

"Which to the Russian mind, makes it ideal. It is like a complicated chess strategy: the Russians thrive on them."

"Nemikov's death must have been something of a game changer, then?"

"Possibly. Or possibly not. Certainly no less complicated. For the moment, he needs to keep the two Nemikov children alive."

"And you too."

"Quite."

"I doubt that it will take him long to extract the codes from Olena and Borys. Once he has them, will he kill them?"

"Hard to say. What if they deliberately give him the wrong codes? If Panich has killed them before he has verified that they are indeed the right codes, then it would all have been a bit pointless. I guess that Panich may want to keep them alive, until whoever has his hands on the money."

"So what next?"

"Pound to a penny, Panich is here in London with Olena and Borys somewhere. I would also bet money that he has extracted the codes from them both. Guess who is the missing link?"

"You."

"Correct. Right now, he's going to be desperate to try and find me."

"How's he going to do that?"

"That, my friend, is what I've been thinking quite a bit about."

"I think you and Jake Sullivan ought to be having this conversation."

"I was thinking that earlier. Do you think he might be persuaded to make a visit to West Hampstead? If I step inside the solid stone walls of Millbank House, I might never be allowed out."

"I'll give him a call and find out. Help yourself to more coffee."

97

All things considered, Jake Sullivan arrives in remarkably quick time – once again, he has the same woman, Laura, in tow. Jake gives Lewis a back-thumping, 'Hail fellow well met' handshake. As before, Laura gives a cold, rather pointless, limp version, quickly sitting down at the round wooden breakfast table in between her boss and Zeltinger.

As the broker of this off-the-record meeting, Zeltinger kicks off the proceedings.

"Why don't you give the same re-cap you gave me earlier, Ben? Then, I thought we could ask Jake and Laura to provide us whatever updates MI5 think it appropriate for us to hear. Does that sound like a plan? Help yourself to coffee. Mugs are behind you and there's a fresh pot on the table."

Lewis repeats his potted version of what he thinks has been happening these last thirty-six hours. The two MI5 senior staff listen in silence. Jake nods at several points along the way; Laura is impassive. Once he is finished, Laura asks the first question.

"Did Arkady Nemikov really give you a set of codes, Ben?"

"Yes, he really did," Lewis replies. He notes the trace of doubt in her voice and chooses not to over-react.

"Are they written down anywhere?" she continues.

"No."

"So where are they?"

He taps his head.

"I've memorised them." This raises an eyebrow from Laura.

"Do you think Nemikov's wife is actually dead?"

"I hope not, but I don't know. I've got no insight as to what happened in Venice yesterday. Have they found her body?"

"I don't believe so." She looks to Jake for confirmation. He shrugs and shakes his head.

"What are you planning to do with the codes, Ben?"

Lewis considers this before replying.

"I don't have a plan at present. I am not about to reveal them to anybody any time soon, that's for sure."

"Why did you have to hit the Russian and the guy called Vince so hard? Those two are in a seriously bad way. They are not going to be any use to anyone for a long while. If ever."

"My heart bleeds, Laura. It's a tough world we play in. They were trying to kill me."

"Can you be sure?"

"Try escaping from the bureaucratic comfort of a government department once in a while and come and see how the real world operates. It's kill or be killed, trust me."

"Okay, you two: enough!"

It is Sullivan speaking and he is determined to change tack.

"This hypothesis of yours, Ben. About the Russians wanting to hide behind a smokescreen of supposed Islamic terror whilst performing evil deeds against the West. Is this simply conjecture, or do you have any proof?"

"The man on the train who had the bomb in his rucksack. He was no more an Islamic terrorist than you or I. He is, either currently or in the distant past, a highly trained soldier. I am sure of it."

Sullivan looks at Laura and nods once again. It is a nod of assent: she has just been granted permission to do something. On cue, she removes a photograph from the folder beside her and pushes it across the table towards Lewis. He takes one look. It is the bomber from the train.

"The man in that photograph, is Rafiq Virenque," Sullivan recites from memory. "Half French, half Algerian, he joined the French Foreign Legion before being spotted by the Spetznaz who trained him, as you rightly assumed, with the Russian Special Forces. How did you know, by the way?"

"It's the way we walk, those of us who've undergone the training: it's very distinctive."

"Virenque, it seemed, was pretty adept at killing people. He was headhunted by the KGB and transferred to their notorious Spetsbureau 13 division. Does that ring any bells?"

Lewis shakes his head.

"It's Moscow's assassin school. Virenque is a wet work specialist."

"Which, I guess makes my hypothesis about what Panich and Virenque are really up to seem more realistic, wouldn't you say?"

Neither Sullivan nor Laura reply. Instead, Sullivan waves a hand at Laura.

"Why don't you go on from here, Laura? Gentlemen," he says to Lewis and Zeltinger, "What you are about to hear is highly classified. On no account is any of it to leave this room. Do I make myself clear?"

Both men nod in silent agreement.

"Very good. Laura, over to you."

"About six weeks ago, we began to pick up snippets of information about a large shipment of RDX– that's C-4 plastic explosive to you and I – due to arrive in the UK. It was thought to be of Russian origin, but it was being routed via Poland and Ireland to lay a false trail. We tracked its arrival at Liverpool docks and traced it through to a warehouse just outside Bradford. It was cleverly and expensively disguised, hidden inside bona fide ink toner cartridges. Once in Bradford, the cartridges were disassembled and the sticks of RDX packed into Hessian sandbags, two sticks per bag. We maintained surveillance over the entire operation, for several reasons other than the obvious. Firstly, a lot of trouble and expense had been incurred to hide both the RDX and where it had originated. Secondly, the whole processing operation was also being watched over by a small SVR cell from the moment the product arrived in the UK.

"It was, and still is, our belief that this entire consignment of RDX was for the purpose of supporting a major terrorist attack, most likely in London. We had two reasons to believe London was the target. Firstly, once all the RDX had been unpacked and then repackaged, in pairs, into the sandbags, the completed sandbags were transferred by van down to a house in Kilburn in North London. The second reason is more complicated but provided the strongest evidence yet that London was the intended target." She looks at Lewis briefly before continuing.

"It was actually because of your intervention at Westminster Cathedral the other day, when you stopped the public beheading, that compelled us to reach out swiftly to our Islamic networks. We wanted to find out whether the statements about a new *jihad* against London were real or simply scaremongering rhetoric. One of our deep cover assets was living in the Kilburn house at the time. He advised his MI5 controller that something big was imminent."

Jake Sullivan takes over once more.

"This is where the joys of departmental boundaries kick in. Operational jurisdiction for raiding the Kilburn premises fell to SO15, now counter terrorism command but formerly the Anti-Terrorist Branch and Special Branch before they merged together. What they didn't know, when they raided the flat in the middle of the night, was that one of the four Asian males who lived there, a Pakistani called Sadiq, worked the night shift. Sadiq was employed as a contractor on London's Underground network. SO15 located only about ten per cent of the total shipment of RDX hidden in the flat. A large quantity of sandbags had disappeared somewhere. Subsequent interrogation of those arrested revealed that Sadiq had been carrying two sandbags with him in his rucksack into work every night and leaving them somewhere. His flat mates didn't know where. We don't know where. We have to presume that the location is somewhere on the London Underground network."

"Why haven't you been able to arrest Sadiq and interrogate

him?" Zeltinger asks.

Sullivan nods once more at Laura before she continues, permission given to reveal another secret.

"Sadiq was killed in mysterious circumstances that same night. His death was made to look like an accident: we are convinced it was murder. We can't be one hundred per cent certain, but we have video footage of someone approaching Sadiq moments before he died." He passes across another photo that Laura has withdrawn from her folder.

"As you can see, Sadiq's last minute visitor looks a lot like our friend, Virenque. Wouldn't you agree?"

"Which sort of implies that the Russians are likely to have a greater level of insight into what Sadiq has been doing, and where, than we do."

"It certainly looks that way."

98

"So you believe there's a stash of explosive stored somewhere on London's Underground network?" It is Lewis speaking, trying to get his thoughts in order.

"Correct."

"But you currently have no idea where?"

"Also correct."

"When this man Sadiq travelled to work each evening, do we know where he went? Won't his rail pass have logged him on and off the system?"

"Unfortunately, not. We know where he got on the tube network. Surprise, surprise, it was Kilburn. Frequently, he never actually left the tube network until the end of his shift."

"What you're saying is, that the sandbags containing the RDX could be anywhere."

"Correct."

"There are probably well over two hundred London Underground stations."

"Two hundred and seventy, to be precise."

"Have you tried examining various station video cameras about the time that Sadiq travelled to work each night to try and work out where he might have been going?"

"We're already on to that," Laura says. "With all the stations and video cameras that there are everywhere, it's an enormous undertaking. We're doing our best, but we're not hopeful."

"Do we think that Panich or Virenque know about the explosives and where they are located?"

"Pass. Assume yes. We simply don't know."

"If the Russian SVR cell was trailing the RDX, might they have twigged that Sadiq was carrying some of it to work each night, a sandbag at a time, and possibly followed him?"

"I like your train of thought, Ben," Sullivan says. He looks at Laura. "We ought to pursue that some more." She nods and writes something down on a pad of paper.

"What I don't get," Lewis continues, "is that if your team were also trailing the RDX, why didn't we pick up on Sadiq and his heavy rucksack? Two sandbags, in a rucksack, is potentially quite a weight. It should have been obvious that he was carrying something heavy to work each day – and then not bringing it home again when he returned, surely?"

Laura rests her head in her hands at this point, her fingers combing through her short, black hair.

"Basically, we screwed up, is the honest truth," she says looking up at him once the words are out of her mouth. "We were focusing on the flat being the destination, not that it might have been just another stopping off point. It's a good idea of yours, about the SVR cell. Maybe they did work out that Sadiq was the onward courier, even if we didn't. If so, I'm sure they would have followed him. It certainly might explain why Virenque was sent to kill him."

"I'm surprised you weren't all falling over each other in Kilburn High Road, with so much surveillance going on." It is Zeltinger, trying to lighten the mood, but his comments are ignored.

"Are any of the SVR cell still in town?" Lewis asks.

"At least one, possibly two," Sullivan replies. "Maybe we should invite them around to Millbank for a coffee?" It is a rhetorical question to no one in particular, another attempt at humour. Again it gains no traction. A mobile phone starts ringing: there is general relief at the welcome distraction. It is Zeltinger's. He takes the call without leaving his seat, answering it on its second ring.

"Saul Zeltinger," he says, and then listens to the person at the other end for about a minute.

"You're sure it's the same vehicle? Do we know if any other car has gone missing?"

He listens some more.

"Okay, very good. Please keep me informed." He ends the call and looks across to Lewis.

"You have an uncanny knack of being right, Ben Lewis. They found the Nemikov Range Rover. It was parked up at the bottom end of Royston Station car park. Out of sight of any security cameras. We've been looking for the wrong vehicle."

Lewis shrugs.

"I wouldn't worry. Right now we've got more important things to concern ourselves about. Let's start thinking like Panich: what's his next move? Assuming he's gone to ground somewhere and he urgently wants Ben Lewis to come and visit him, what will he be doing?"

"Finding a way to get your attention. Probably via the Nemikov boy or girl. Perhaps posting something online or on Twitter or similar." It is Zeltinger speaking, thinking tactics, like a good chess player. "Or why not a simple text message? Direct and to the point."

"Okay, so spin it on its head. If I, Ben Lewis, wanted to lure Panich or this Virenque person to me, what would I need to do?"

Zeltinger thinks for a moment.

"Well, for a start you'd be leaving your mobile phone switched on so that they might stand a chance of actually finding you."

"Absolutely right. We need to try and make them come to us, not the other way around. Offense rather than defence. We need a suitable location."

"Have you anywhere in particular in mind?"

"As a matter of fact, Jake, I do."

99

Oleg Panich was beginning to realise that he might not be well. Even the relatively simple task of securing and gagging his two prisoners in their subterranean room had brought on an onset of violent coughing. Fortunately, Virenque had been on hand to help so it hadn't been a problem. It had, nonetheless, been a warning: another glimpse of worse things yet to come.

Leaving Virenque behind, he had walked a few hundred metres up the road to meet with Vasily, the SVR London station chief, at a small, cheap, all-day diner located just off Goodge Street. It was run by a burly Greek and his wife, usually frequented by students at the nearby University of London. At that hour, just after seven-thirty in the morning, the place was empty. Even walking the short distance, he felt weary. He sat down and ordered a coffee, berating himself for his physical weakness: he was on an operation; he needed to get a grip.

Panich and Vasily knew each other of old. They had virtually grown up in the service together. Whenever Panich had cause to visit London, it was always Vasily he turned to for assistance. The Greek proprietor was serving Panich his coffee when a large, muscular, man wearing a black leather jacket and a cloth cap, walked through the door. The reason for the latter soon became clear once he removed the cap and waved a greeting at Panich: underneath, he was completely bald.

Vasily asked for a coffee before sitting down, at the same time ordering some breakfast pastries, toast and jam. The two men exchanged pleasantries until Vasily's coffee arrived in a mug. He took a sip, his hands clenching the outside to keep warm.

"How can I help, Oleg?"

"I need some supplies, Vasily."

He went on to describe the equipment he wanted. The request caused Vasily to raise an eyebrow.

"Volkov had forewarned me that you might be wanting something along those lines. Sounds like quite a gig you've got going here."

"Can you help?"

"You can have them both within the hour. How do you want to take delivery?"

"I'll send Virenque. Where does he have to go?"

Vasily told him and Panich committed the address to memory.

"I'd heard you were using Virenque. He's a ruthless son of a bitch. Sounds right up your street, Oleg!"

Panich ignored the comment.

"Any joy in locating Ben Lewis for me? That man's become really tiresome."

"Ah, yes. The man who gave you so much grief last time you were here. Volkov is worried that you might be heading off-piste with your personal vendetta against the man."

"I know he is. Happily or otherwise, Lewis has made himself central to the current operation. So you can tell Volkov, everything's back on-piste. I can't say that I am unhappy about that, though: that bastard owes me for quite a lot."

"At this particular moment, he's at a house in West Hampstead. It belongs to a policeman called Saul Zeltinger. Ring any bells?"

Panich grimaced. There was a sudden stabbing pain in his chest and it took several seconds before it receded. "I do indeed, Vasily."

"Everything all right, Oleg? You seem in some difficulty."

"No, it's fine," he said, although he evidently wasn't.

"Moscow Tracking tells me that he and Lewis have been on the phone a lot this last twenty-four hours."

"Well, the pair were thick as thieves during my last

305

operation in London. The one that caused me so much grief," he said, holding up his prosthetic arm.

"Are you planning to head over there now?" Vasily asked. It was an apposite moment: the pastries and a pile of warm, white toast, butter and jam were just arriving.

Panich thought about this before answering, eyeing up a sticky-looking pastry and picking it up with his fingers.

"I want Virenque to bring him in, not me. He's in better shape for starters, for when it gets rough, which with Lewis it most certainly will. If that doesn't work, I'll resort to some poignant emotional blackmail: that usually does the trick." He bit into the pastry and began chewing. "That's where the equipment you're going to supply will come in handy. If Virenque needs a little unattributable field support later in the day, by the way, can you help him out?"

"We'll do our best, Oleg. Background only, as I'm sure Volkov has explained. But as much as we can, for an old friend and former colleague, of course."

"Virenque is busy right now. Assuming Lewis's visit to the policeman's house is only temporary, can Moscow Tracking keep me informed about where he goes?"

"We can do better than that. I have an asset on the ground watching the house right this minute. Everywhere he goes, we – and through us, you – will be kept fully in the picture. You see, Oleg, I like to think ahead and plan, just like you."

"You're a good and loyal Russian, Vasily. Tell me, if I use the underground rail network later today, are you still able to get messages to me?"

"Certainly. Most tube stations have wireless networks these days. London's changed a lot since you were last here."

"Good," Panich said, taking another mouthful of his icing-covered pastry. "That," he went on cryptically, "actually opens up all sorts of interesting new possibilities."

100

The location he believes is perfect.

Liverpool Street Station.

It is a major London concourse, humming with people. It also has lots of vantage points. There is the main concourse, below street level. This is where the railway platforms are, where travellers mix and mingle, waiting for the departure of their train to be announced. On an upper level, immediately above the concourse, are various shops. These are positioned around the concourse perimeter on two sides, with four pedestrian walkways that traverse the upper level from one side to the other: two at either end, and two evenly spaced in between. Other than that, the rest of the upper level is open space, giving the area a light, roomy feel. It is thus possible to sit at a coffee shop on the upper level and look down, through the glass sided walkways, to see almost everything going on down below.

At such short notice – given that it is, as Sullivan describes it, something of a fishing expedition – only a small team have been assembled. They are all from Laura's section, although a unit from SO15 is also on standby not far away: in case, as Sullivan puts it to Zeltinger, the heat gets turned up. All ten of Laura's team are undercover around the station: five on the lower level and five watching from up above. Their only distinguishing feature is an earpiece microphone: so small it can hardly be seen. Even Lewis is wearing one. Laura has assumed command, sitting this one out from inside a black Renault van parked immediately outside the station on a double yellow line. Various feeds from station security cameras are being streamed live on the television monitors in front of her.

At ten o'clock in the morning, Lewis is sitting at a table in the coffee shop on the upper level. He has been here for nearly thirty minutes. For some time, his cell phone has been on and connected to the network, the signal strength high. He has a clear view, across the upper level walkways, to those arriving at the station from the south. Down below, he can look out over a significant proportion of the main concourse area. Including the young female operative, Naomi. He can see her clearly – and for good reason. Naomi has his mobile tucked inside her shoulder bag. She has been chosen as the decoy. It is Laura's idea: an attempt to draw the opposition into the centre of the field of play. Lewis is sceptical. He is rapidly going off the idea of working in Laura's team.

"Lima one, anything to report."

Lima one is Lewis's call sign.

"Negative," Lewis replies, with just a hint of insolence. On balance, he would have preferred to be here on his own. Not as part of someone else's stakeout. He is pretending to do the Telegraph Crossword, a pot of tea on the table beside him. If the Russians really were desperate for him to surrender the Nemikov codes, someone would have traced his signal location by now. So, who will be sent to find him? Lewis thinks he knows: Virenque. Whether he will be on his own or whether he comes with Panich is tough to call. It depends whether they need a baby sitter for Olena and Borys. With Scarface and Vince out of action, and Fedorov dead, the opposition's numbers must be getting thin.

It is another reason why Lewis is sitting where he is: he wants to give Virenque a good chance of spotting him. He doesn't need this to be too difficult.

Looking around the concourse, he is able to spot several of Laura's team. It hits him how much they all stand out. They are either in the shadows, watching from a static position like he is; or they are moving about, hiding in plain sight. Both have pros and cons. Knowing what to look for, Lewis thinks he finds at least six. The majority are not moving around that much: either they are loitering in one place or sitting without purpose, usually on their own. It's what they don't do that is revealing. Normal passengers at a railway station check their watches and look at the departure boards frequently. People on a stakeout don't. They tend to be looking everywhere but the departure boards; and, from time to time, they talk to themselves, mumbling into hidden microphones to speak with one another – a form of conference call for spooks.

Virenque realistically has one option: to keep moving. The moment he becomes static, checking out what may or may not look out of place, he becomes vulnerable – especially if he's outnumbered ten to one. He probably adopts some crude disguise, allowing him to move around undetected. So that he can check out the opposition. Once Virenque knows what he's up against, he'll try to lure Laura's team down a blind alley, by creating a diversion. Perhaps a fire alarm, or some kind of explosive or incendiary device placed in a rubbish bin to cause panic and confusion; which will give Virenque time to make his direct move on Lewis. Assuming he knows where Lewis is; which, given that Lewis has deliberately been sitting in the same place for nearly forty-five minutes, is increasingly likely.

Time to move on, Soldier.

He stands up, and a smartly dressed young woman with a rolling suitcase bumps into him. She apologises, before rushing away towards the platform area. She seems in a hurry. She turns around a short while later, ostensibly to check that he's okay. Then, with a brief smile and a wave, she is gone.

Lewis heads in the opposite direction, towards the far end of the concourse, still on the upper level walkway.

Which is when he feels something buzzing in his jacket pocket.

He's just fallen for the oldest trick in the book.

Placing his hand inside his pocket, he removes a small pager. Dropped in there whilst he was distracted. By the pretty woman, now long gone, her appearance changed already. He looks at the message on the screen, and smiles.

101

The device is simple, similar to those worn by doctors in a hospital. Crude but effective. About three inches by two, it gives the bare minimum of information.

Entrance to platform 10 in 2 mins.

Lewis is faced with a choice; comply or deny.

He also faces another decision: inform Laura or not.

Four options to choose. This could be interesting.

If he complies and he informs Laura, then the other guy is going to be watching with amusement as Laura's team start converging around platform 10. The other guy will be watching as the cordon is tightened. In this game play, the other guy is going to start having some fun, bouncing Lewis from one destination to another, probably whilst he starts picking a few of Laura's team off. Lewis will be like a puppet on a string, at the beck and call of whomever. Come to think of it, the other guy's got to be Virenque. It feels just the sort of adventure he would enjoy. An assassin's game: picking your foes off, one by one.

If he complies without informing Laura, then what? This would be similar to the first option, but probably less time consuming. He, Lewis, will still be subjected to the same pattern of being bounced around, but it will be shorter, given the absence of Laura's people. Lewis will eventually be directed somewhere where Virenque thinks it will be easy to trap him: then he will most likely be sedated, bundled into a van and taken off to the same sweet location they are holding the other two.

Which leaves the two denial options. Ignore the message completely and deny that it ever came his way – and, for good measure, say nothing to Laura. If the other guy is Virenque, he will be thinking like a soldier. Soldiers obey commands.

So when Lewis is ordered to head to platform 10 and sharp, Virenque will be expecting Lewis to comply. Especially because of the pager gimmick. It makes the whole communication piece feel more personal: more one-to-one, one elite soldier to another. Virenque will be expecting activity, but see none. This option has the very real danger of pissing Virenque off. Which is why Lewis likes it so much.

He likes the fourth option even better.

Lewis knows that whichever option he chooses, the other guy, Virenque, has to be concealed on the station concourse somewhere. As the two minute deadline expires, under the fourth option, Virenque will be watching as a number of Laura's assets start to converge on platform 10. It is just that Lewis won't be one of them. Which will make Virenque firstly puzzled: and then secondly, angry.

Under these conditions, Lewis is hoping that Virenque will risk emerging from his hiding place, to find out whether Lewis actually has made it to the *rendez-vous*: in time, he might yet be tempted to pick off one or more of Laura's team. Before doing that, he will probably type another instruction, his mood visibly changing. He will be fast becoming pissed off. He will watch as the worker bees that are Laura's team start swarming around this new destination. Still with no sign of Lewis, Virenque's angry mood will only be getting worse.

Under option four, Lewis won't be where Virenque expects him to be. He'll be using this window of confusion, and Virenque's growing infuriation, to try and locate exactly where Virenque is hiding. If he can do that, he might just be in with a chance.

It is time to give Laura's team a heads up.

"This is Lima One," he whispers into his hidden microphone. "I'm instructed to head to platform 10 within two minutes. I'm going to need some cover."

102

Virenque hated seat of the pants operations. With virtually no time to prepare, let alone plan, he'd been forced to improvise as soon as he arrived at the station. He'd had two lucky breaks: firstly, in spotting Lewis so easily; and secondly, in Moscow agreeing to supply the girl and certain equipment at short notice. For a last minute operation, he'd also been pleased with his disguise: that day he was a newspaper deliveryman, wheeling unused copies of the free Metro morning newspaper off the station concourse. He wore a baseball cap and a zippered fleece, and had a tilting hand trolley as a prop. He had found this, folded and tucked behind one of the newspaper kiosks on the concourse.

He urgently needed data about what – and who – he might be up against. It was possible that Lewis was here on his own: he'd already spotted one or two people he felt were potential watchers. Therefore he wanted first to flush them out. His current plan was to draw Lewis into the open and see who followed. Eventually he'd lead him out of the station, to a place he could be bundled into the van that was waiting. He had even contemplated the direct approach to Lewis in the coffee shop: pointing a gun into his ribs, marching him out of the station like a convicted criminal. That idea didn't last long: Lewis was never going to let himself be taken as easily as that. Hence the idea with the pager. It had actually been the girl's: simple but effective.

Two minutes goes very quickly when you want them to go slowly. Lewis is walking around the upper floor perimeter, directly above the entrance to platform 10. He is completely fed up with Laura and the team's pointless chatter.

"Where are you, Lima One?"

"I can't see you, Lima One," and such like.

Ignore them. Concentrate on what you can see, Lewis.

On this level, there is the shop attendant who is standing outside his shop giving a big yawn, his hands and arms outstretched above his head. Further along a mother and child stroll along, window shopping before their train departs. Down on the floor below, there are crowds of people milling about: a pair of uniformed British Transport Police patrolling side by side; business men and women – some emerging from the Underground railway: others about to go down into it. A number of passengers are standing below the massive train departure information board; staring to see what platform their train will be leaving from. A few people are sitting down: some reading newspapers; one or two tucked into a book. Then there are the railway workers: train drivers making their way to and from various trains, ticket inspectors heading to their appointed trains; men with trolleys delivering boxes of goods to various shops; and a newspaper delivery man pushing a pile of newspapers.

His two minutes are up and he can, as yet, find no trace of Virenque. He keeps walking, deciding that it is time to descend to the lower level. As he does so, he feels the pager buzz in his pocket. Carefully picking it out of his pocket, he catches a sudden movement out of the corner of his eye. When he looks up, the pager in his hand, the moment has gone. But there was something, he feels sure of it. He looks at the message.

Where were you? 2 mins Boots the Chemist next to platform 1 - last chance.

Does Lewis imagine this or is this person sounding angry?

"Lima One, I am now being ordered to head to Boots by platform 1, in two minutes."

Again another barrage of questions rains down on him from Laura and her colleagues.

"Are you in trouble, Lima One?"

"I still can't see you, Lima One."

"Where exactly are you, Lima One?'

He finds himself walking directly past Boots and heading west, on the pedestrian walkway out of the station. He passes three of the watchers, for sure: he can see their lips move. One of them sees Lewis. Lewis blanks him and continues as if nothing has happened. There are more businessmen and women now, fast approaching the Broadgate exit from the station. This is the enclave where large numbers of different office buildings reside. Lewis stops near the exit and, turning back around, almost collides with a man pushing a pile of newspapers on a two-wheeled trolley. A newspaper man. That's what he'd seen moments earlier. When he'd caught movement out of the corner of his eye. A man in a baseball hat, setting off from a stationary position pushing a pile of newspapers. Except this isn't a newspaper man.

It's the bomber from the train.

It is Virenque.

103

Fight or flight?

Lewis wants to fight; he loves fighting. If he's allowed the chance, he should win: one on one is his speciality.

Virenque drops the trolley and starts to square up in front of Lewis. The man moves effortless on the balls of his feet. Just like Sergei Fedorov had done the first time he and Lewis had met. Virenque's is a boxer's tread, dancing feet, everything is being kept fluid and flexible. The two size each other up. Lewis can sense Virenque debating: fight or flight?

"What's the matter, Virenque? Too afraid to throw the first punch?"

Lewis always tries to goad his opponents. The man is evidently surprised that Lewis knows his name.

People are starting to make space for the pair of them, their aggressive posturing drawing a hesitant crowd of onlookers. This suits Lewis fine. If they want to watch a fight, it's not going to last for long. On further reflection, a street fight with spectators is not going to suit Virenque. There'll be little room for escape afterwards. The police will be arriving sometime soon, and then it will be game over. What tips the balance is the sudden arrival of one of Laura's helpers, although this man hardly helps. He makes Virenque realise that he really only has one option: to run for it. The decision made, without warning, he bolts, taking off like a fully-fledged sprinter.

Lewis is no slouch, either. He, too, is quick off the blocks, following close behind. Virenque has about a two second time advantage. Lewis has no idea about Laura's man – he's just not interested. In Lewis's ear he hears a sudden burst of noise: people all talking at once. It is Laura's team-mates scrambling in an attempt to come to his rescue. He rips the earpiece out of his ear, stuffing it into his pocket and keeps on sprinting.

316

Virenque races towards Broadgate circle, a pedestrian only area that in winter has an ice rink in the middle. He skirts the perimeter and veers around to the right. An office building is under construction immediately ahead. Virenque makes a running leap, grabbing hold of a lower piece of scaffolding and pulling himself up. He begins scaling the scaffolding, one floor after another, eventually reaching a level where there is a concrete floor that has been laid down.

Lewis is close behind. As he reaches the concrete platform, Virenque takes a shot from the Glock-17 pistol he stole from the traffic cop. The shot goes wild and costs him almost a second of time advantage. Lewis, seeing a bullet coming, does a forward roll on to the deck to avoid being hit. Both these actions keep the two of them still no more, no less, than two seconds apart.

The building floor plate is L-shaped. Virenque heads to the right-hand corner of the construction and, grabbing hold of another piece of scaffolding, starts sliding back to the ground. As his feet hit the deck, he turns, taking aim with his Glock again, pointing it directly towards Lewis's rapidly descending body.

Lewis senses rather than sees the imminent danger. Whilst only halfway through his descent, he leaps off the pole to his left, landing heavily on the ground in a forward roll to cushion the impact. Hearing the deafening roar of the gun, he narrowly escapes being hit by the bullet as it whistles past his jacket. Lewis knows that he has had a lucky escape.

Virenque is off and running again, this time around the side of Exchange Square and along a pedestrian cut-through to Bishopsgate. Lewis, despite bruises and grazes from the fall, still manages to keep up. The traffic on Bishopsgate is light. Virenque darts across the road looking for inspiration. He finds it in a motorcycle courier who is about to get off his bike to deliver a package. The man is in the wrong place at the wrong time. Virenque takes aim with the Glock and fires at point blank range. He drags the dying man off the machine, stopping the bike from falling to the ground as he clambers on. Casting a rearward glance at Lewis, he opens the throttle and takes off at speed.

Now it is Lewis's turn to look for inspiration. Another terrified but anxious courier comes to his aide. Having seen his colleague killed in cold blood, he offers Lewis his machine, its engine running. Lewis, needing no second prompting, takes the bike, jumps on and accelerates after Virenque.

104

Around the back of Houndsditch and heading towards Aldgate, Lewis keeps Virenque in his sights. Lewis loves being on a motorbike. He would pitch his handling skills against most bikers and expect to come out on top: but Virenque is good. Whether out of skill or desperation to stay alive, he sets a tough pace as the two bikes head into the Aldgate one-way system. Virenque ignores traffic lights, darting down Mansell Street towards the Tower of London, heading the wrong way down the busy one-way street. Cars, buses and lorries blare their horns at him. He ignores them, ducking and weaving in and out of the oncoming traffic.

Lewis is closing in. With Virenque in the lead, gaps have already been made in the oncoming traffic making Lewis's life, as pursuit bike, easier. Horns continue to sound as they both hurtle around the Tower at speed, ignoring the red lights.

Virenque is faced with a decision: head south over the river by crossing Tower Bridge; or continue west on the northern embankment? He chooses Tower Bridge, for reasons that are soon to become clear. The traffic on the approach road to the bridge has come to a halt. The warning lights immediately in front of the bridge are blinking red.

The bridge is being raised.

Over to the west, a tall ship is waiting to be allowed to pass through it. As Virenque turns into the bridge approach, the right hand lane of traffic is empty; the oncoming traffic long since departed.

Virenque is going to jump the gap.

The ramp is of a height where Lewis cannot see the other side, already about one third of the way raised. The gap between the two bikes is less than three seconds. By the time Lewis makes the jump, the bridge will be almost half way raised.

Easier than when Robbie Maddison did his backflip over the fully-open bridge in 2009: but nonetheless challenging. Lewis is game, if Virenque is.

It appears he is.

Both bikes accelerate down the empty right hand lane towards the end of the bridge. Lewis knows he must angle his approach so that he is pointing slightly to the left. Otherwise the bike will crash directly into the lead vehicle waiting to cross on the other side. In his head, he goes through the mental checklist: approach speed, fine; angle of the ramp, okay; position on the road, good. He watches as Virenque clears the gap. At the very last second, loud warning bells start to sound in his head: Virenque's departure position on the road looked too straight. Lewis compensates by consciously steering to the left, pointing his bike at about the eleven o'clock position, just as he leaves the ramp: ready for a safe landing, he hopes, on the left hand lane on the other side.

105

Even whilst he is in the air, Lewis knows that Virenque has made a fatal blunder. He sees, before he hears, the massive fireball, the result of nearly five hundred kilogrammes of bike and rider travelling at over seventy miles an hour crashing head first into a container lorry waiting to cross on the other side.

Lewis lands pretty near perfectly and brakes hard, bringing his bike to a halt in the narrow confines of the bridge. He walks back as close as he can to the burning wreckage. There are, however, no questions that need answering. Virenque will not have survived that by any stretch of the imagination. Walking back to his bike, Lewis digs in his pocket for Laura's microphone and sticks the earpiece in his ear.

"Lima One back on air," he says into the ether.

"Where the hell are you, Lima One? What's been happening?"

"Tower Bridge, Laura. Virenque is dead. I repeat dead. A massive head-on collision with a lorry whilst trying to leap Tower Bridge. I'm on my way back to the van. I'll see you in about ten minutes."

Lewis arrives in five. The traffic over London Bridge is light. He zigzags his way through the back streets to where Laura's van is parked up. Banging on the van's rear door, Laura fumes at him as she opens it.

"What the hell did you think you were playing at?" she rants once the door is closed. "Trying to get us all killed, yourself included? Why didn't you stay on air as we agreed? Why didn't you answer when we were trying to talk with you? You put the whole team at risk, you know that?"

"I think the only person I put at risk was myself, apart from the poor bugger Virenque shot dead when he stole the bike."

"What? Who was shot dead? For God's sake, Ben, we're in London, not a war zone."

"You could have fooled me," he says and lets his eyes wander around the inside of the van.

"Is that my phone there on the desk?"

Laura doesn't answer. Lewis picks it up and checks.

"Please thank Naomi for looking after it," he says, putting it back in his pocket.

He turns and puts his hand on the door handle to leave.

"Where do you think you're going?"

"I've got two hostages to try and find."

"It's a pity you couldn't have kept Virenque alive: then you might know where they are."

"I don't think it was me that killed Virenque. One of your team did. He tried to intervene when Virenque and I were about to fight each other. The thought of two against one seemed enough to scare the shit out of Virenque. That's why he ran for his life. I wasn't, I'm afraid, about to let him get away. You and your team need to get real, Laura."

With that, he turned and left her to it.

106

There was a muted knocking at the door before Plushenko's valet entered the room, coughing twice before crossing the threshold. The pretty blonde, who had been sitting astride the Russian oligarch, quickly rolled off, covering her nakedness with the sheet.

"I am sorry to intrude, sir, but I have a Miss Tian on the phone for you. She suggested it might be extremely urgent."

Plushenko scowled, disliking intensely being interrupted during such moments of intimacy. He then remembered who Tian was.

"Of course. I'll take the call in the next room." He rolled out of the bed and began searching for his dressing gown. The valet, anticipating this need, was holding it for him.

"I'll put her call through right away," the valet said. Then, with a knowing wink at the blonde, he withdrew from the room.

"Kristina," Plushenko said. "I hope you are calling with good news?"

"Viktor, my apologies for interrupting your busy day. However, yes, I have some very good news! I have located one of the codes you have been looking for."

"Only one?" said Plushenko, his voice sounding concerned.

"At the moment, yes. It was the one that previously belonged to Nemikov's wife – now, passed to someone called Ben Lewis."

"What about the other two?" Plushenko said impatiently. He was not about to let on that he already had those, courtesy of his call with Oleg Panich a short while earlier.

"I need a little more time. I thought you said that you were interested in having a periodic progress report?"

"I am, Kristina. You are to be congratulated on your progress. Why don't you read out the code you've uncovered? I've got paper and pen to hand." He listened as she read out the mixture of numbers and letters, carefully recording them on a sheet of headed notepaper.

"When will you have the remaining two, do you think?"

"Probably this evening."

"Excellent work, Kristina. Thank you. I am very pleased with what you've achieved in such a short period of time. Once I have all three codes, I shall of course settle your bill immediately. Payment on completion was what we agreed, I recall?"

"It was indeed, Viktor. All things being well, you'll have the final two very shortly. I'll call you as soon as I have more news."

Viktor smiled to himself as he replaced the receiver. His contingency planning appeared to have paid off handsomely. Now that he was in possession of all three codes, he would arrange to travel to Zurich in the morning on his private jet. There was a certain Swiss banker that he needed to visit. Once Nemikov's money had all been transferred, he would find someone to take care of Miss Tian. That way, he would be able to save himself an additional million dollars, plus her expenses.

107

"I can't believe what you did, Ben! It was incredibly dangerous and incredibly foolish."

"Saul, I'm a good biker. I know what I am capable of, what my limitations are. Virenque obviously didn't."

They are speaking over the phone. Lewis is on foot, walking out of the financial district, heading westward towards Holborn.

"It is out of my hands, now, Ben. Officially, I am obliged to instruct you to turn yourself in. Perhaps it might be better if you came here, to Savile Row police station. At least I can try and ensure that you're detained in a comfortable police cell."

"It's a tempting offer, but for the record, not at the moment, thanks."

"The more dead bodies that keep appearing, Ben, the tougher this whole thing is getting for you. Remember that."

"I need a good lawyer, is that what you're saying?" Lewis laughs.

"Don't joke. I'd turn that phone off if I were you, my friend. Even I can see that you're walking along London Wall at the moment."

"Point taken."

Lewis ends the call and looks at the handset, about to disconnect it from the network. As he does, an incoming text message arrives.

It is from a withheld number. It is a picture and a text message combined. When Lewis clicks to open it, he sees the photograph.

He then reads the text message.

His blood once more is turning to ice.

108

Saul Zeltinger answers Lewis's call on the second ring.

"Having second thoughts, Ben?"

"Saul, I'm about to forward a picture text that I have just received. Look at it, then call me right back." Ending the call he forwards the message on. Less than thirty seconds later, Zeltinger rings back.

"My God, Ben. Who is this lunatic?"

"Someone I should have taken care off a long time ago."

"Where's all this leading?"

"Where do you think? I've got no choice: I've got to follow his instructions. Otherwise a lot of people are going to die."

"He might be bluffing."

"Saul, by this stage of the game, Panich will not be bluffing. Not after what just happened to Virenque."

"Why Trafalgar Square?"

"He wants to play puppet on a string with me."

"Just like Virenque tried to do with you earlier?"

"Precisely. Only suddenly the field of play has got much, much bigger. When I get to Trafalgar Square, in my allotted fifteen minutes, I will get another instruction: sending me somewhere else; then another after that; and so on. He's going to be making sure I have no one on my back. And, you wait: the time separation is going to be reduced each time. I am going to be running around London like a blue-arsed fly, at his beck and call. And then, when he deems it right, he will try his best to kill me."

"What about the girl in the photo? I presume that's Olena?"

"Correct. Notice the sandbags she's leaning on with her explosive vest? We have the potential for a monumental catastrophe."

"We should be shutting down the tube network. Thousands

of lives could be at risk here."

"That's a call for you and the authorities to make not for me. Until we know what we're up against, it might be hasty. If you do, it'll create widespread panic and disruption – which could be playing right into Panich's hands."

"So, what are you going to do?"

"As discussed, I'm going to Trafalgar Square to find this bastard once and for all. Only this time, once I find him, be under no illusion. Once he and I are through, he is most definitely going to end up dead."

109

Trafalgar Square, North side, by the National Gallery. Fifteen minutes or the girl dies.

It is a big place. There is a wide pavement in front, stretching from St. Martin's-in-the-Field's on the East side to the Sainsbury Wing of the National Gallery to the West. Mime artists use this as their playground. The place is busy with tourists, even on a cold November morning. The time is shortly before noon. Lewis makes it with three minutes to spare. Technically he made it with seven minutes to spare: he has been using the last four minutes quietly completing a circumnavigation of the area.

He sees nothing. He is expecting to see nothing. It is not evident that Saul has mobilised the world and his wife: overt police presence is no higher than normal; and Lewis is unable to detect any increased volume or frequency of police sirens or helicopters. He thinks he sees three who might be part of a plain-clothes surveillance team: they show no recognition when he passes them.

Lewis's mobile phone will now be the hottest number in town. Where he goes, others will be following. Whatever mails or texts he receives, they will see them at the same time.

One minute remaining. There is no sign of Panich. Where will he be? On the top deck of a tourist bus, sitting with field-glasses making sure Lewis has turned up? Already heading to the next *rendez-vous*: perhaps in the back of a black cab, having checked to ensure that Lewis is in position? Next time Lewis resolves to cut his arrival much finer. Assuming that he is given a next time – and not about to receive a Russian sniper's bullet in the head. He thinks that unlikely. Panich will want to exact some personal revenge, before killing Lewis. Besides, there is a certain code that Panich needs – and only

Lewis has this.

He checks his watch. The fifteen minutes are up.

As if on cue, his mobile phone buzzes. It's a text message.

Harrods Department store. Western entrance on the Brompton Road. Twelve minutes. Just you, Lewis.

Lewis feels no satisfaction in being right. He knew it was coming.

What he needs is his bike.

What he gets is Jake Sullivan in the back of a London black taxi.

110

"Do you still have the pager on you?"

Lewis reaches in his jacket pocket and pulls out the device. Sullivan takes it from him and affixes a small, thin, black disc to its rear before returning it.

"In case he tells you to ditch the phone. That's what I would do. Give me your watch."

Lewis hands his over. It is of the cheap, functional rather than pretty, variety. The one he gets back in return looks worn: but an upgraded version.

"We're working on finding the room. All London Underground operations and maintenance managers are being contacted. We're showing them the picture. I'm not holding out much hope, but we're giving it our best shot. Police units are on standby at all major railway stations. SO15 are also active. Transport Police are being reassigned to patrol the major central London interchanges."

"Thanks, Jake. With due respect, we're all fishing in the dark."

They are already at the roundabout by Buckingham Palace, about to head towards Hyde Park Corner. Seven minutes out of the allotted twelve remain.

"You've known about the explosives for some time. What have the MI5 analysts come up with?"

"Not a lot. Explosives in tunnels don't make nearly as much damage as people like to think."

"Have you no ideas?"

"We think the most likely places are the major interchanges. Piccadilly Circus; Holborn; Kings Cross; Euston; Oxford Circus and so on. As soon as you think of another one, you feel compelled to add it to the list."

"Why those stations in particular if explosives in tunnels

don't do much damage?"

"Because of the numbers of people who pass through them. It's the collateral damage they'll be after."

They are at Hyde Park Corner and turning down Knightsbridge.

"I want you to drop me at the next lights. I'd like to give the appearance, at least, of having got here under my own steam."

The taxi obligingly pulls into the curb.

"Jake, I think you need to change the angle. You should be thinking more like the opposition, not what your theorists says the opposition ought to be doing. Get Saul Zeltinger into your inner circle. He's a good chess player. Let him put a cold towel over his head. Don't be hanging around me, waiting for the next message from Panich either. Find the room! Nothing is more important."

With that, he gets out and sets off running down the Brompton Road in the direction of Harrods,

Ten minutes gone, two remaining.

111

The next message arrives exactly twelve minutes after the first. Lewis is standing with his back to the storefront windows, his eyes scanning in all directions. What if Panich isn't here: what if it's someone else doing all the fieldwork for him? Lewis stands no chance of spotting them in that scenario. The phone buzzes in his pocket once more.

Drop the pager, your wristwatch and any other electronic device apart from your phone into the rubbish bin immediately to your left. Once you have done this, you will receive another text. No tricks, or the girl suffers.

Lewis has to smile. So much for Sullivan's state of the art electronic tracking tools. He walks to the bin and, very purposely and visibly, drops his watch and the pager inside. He wants to find Panich's look out. There is no one he can see at street level. They could be anywhere: in a shop across the road; on a passing bus; watching from a first floor window somewhere. He is given no time to work it out either. His phone is buzzing once again.

Go to the Underground Station at the other end of Harrods store. Take the Piccadilly Line train to Green Park. Wait on the platform to be contacted. Drop your phone in the rubbish bin. You have ten minutes.

Things are starting to get complicated.

112

Saul Zeltinger was sitting in the back of a different taxi as he listened to Jake Sullivan on the other end of the phone.

"What exactly did Ben Lewis suggest?" The taxi was heading west along Pall Mall.

"He said we should be thinking more like the opposition, not what us theorists believe the opposition ought to be thinking. If you can work your way through that one, you're a better man than me."

"I'm less than two minutes from Green Park station. Let me give that some thought and I'll call you back. I was planning to go and keep Ben company on the subway platform. I suspect that half of London's police may be about to converge on the same place."

Zeltinger rang off and closed his eyes, trying to fit all the various strands of thinking together. He liked nothing better than solving problems using logic. Two words kept swirling around in his mind from what Sullivan had just said. He had actually used them twice: 'the opposition'.

Who exactly were the opposition?

Right this minute, it was this Russian, Panich, and his rapidly depleting army of deranged thugs. However, it had been Sadiq who had first had the idea of putting the explosive somewhere on the London Underground. If Sadiq hadn't been killed, and if Panich hadn't hijacked the explosives that Sadiq had planted, then whatever terror group Sadiq had been part of would still be the opposition, not the Russians. So, to solve the puzzle of where the room was located, perhaps one needed to think more like a terrorist than a former Russian spy? Perhaps that was what Lewis was hinting at? Remembering the Islamic State video that had been released in Jordan in the last twenty-four hours, it had promised '*a bombing campaign*

333

against the capital's transport system intended to drive terror into the heart of every man, woman and child living in, or visiting, the city'. The Welwyn Viaduct could have been one such strike against the transport system. Which out of the many potential targets on London's Underground System had Sadiq chosen as the next? Which would create the most damage and cause maximum terror in its wake?

113

Lewis runs to the station entrance and purchases a ticket. Racing down the escalators, two steps at a time, he soon reaches the depths of the underground tunnels below. He no longer has a watch. By the train indicator board on the station platform, he has five minutes of allotted time remaining. The next train is a minute away. He looks around the platform. It is a mixed group: people with shopping in expensive-looking bags; and a few business executives carrying briefcases or shoulder bags. No one pays him much attention apart from one man at the other end of the platform. Lewis thinks he recognises him as one of Sullivan's watchers from Liverpool Street station earlier.

Something is nagging in his mind. Something that Sullivan had said in the back of the taxi.

Explosives in tunnels don't make nearly as much damage as people like to think.

The train arrives. A few disembark before Lewis and everyone else on the platform squeezes on. The train is crowded. It is the lunchtime rush. Lewis stands, one hand holding on to the vertical metal pole in the centre. Green Park is only two stops away. There are about four minutes remaining.

The train departs. As it picks up speed and enters the tunnel, Lewis works out what has been bugging him. *Explosives in tunnels don't make nearly as much damage as people like to think.* Sullivan is saying something that Lewis thinks, on reflection, could be profound; it is the informed judgement of an intelligence expert. The implication being that most people aren't experts.

Most people think differently.

Most people believe that a bomb placed in a tunnel *would* cause catastrophic damage. If you were a terrorist and thought like most people – and not like a well-informed agent working for a national security service – you'd be placing your explosives in a location you believed would cause maximum devastation.

Even if, in practice, they wouldn't.

The question is, which of several hundreds of possible places might that be?

114

The Piccadilly Line platform at Green Park Station is heaving with people. Lewis gets off and stands to one side of the carriage doorway to let departing passengers clear the train. He wonders how many of those on the platform are part of an undercover Ben Lewis reception committee: plain clothes policemen and specialists from the security services?

Warbling sounds indicate that the train's doors are about to close. Moments later the train departs, accelerating at speed as it clears the station platform. In its noisy wake is a contrasting silence. A number of people remain on the platform, ostensibly waiting for the next train. One of these, Lewis is surprised but happy to see, is Saul Zeltinger.

Putting his hands in his jacket, he casually starts walking down the platform in the direction of his friend, recoiling in surprise to find another unknown device lurking in the inner recesses of his pocket. Twice in one morning; and, once again, he had never felt a thing. Most likely, it had been someone on the train. It would have been so easy, with people jostling against each other in the tightly packed carriage. Nonetheless, it is a professional job. He takes whatever it is out to have a look. It is a cell phone: a cheap device with a simple flat screen able to cover the basics, including taking photographs. The next thing, the phone starts bleeping. A text message has come in. He works out how to read it on the unfamiliar device; when he does, his heart sinks.

Oxford Circus tube station. Victoria line northbound platform. Six minutes.

The puppet master is, once again, pulling the strings.

115

To get to the requisite platform, Lewis has to go up one long escalator, almost to ground floor level, before coming down a different, but shorter, one. He takes the escalator stairs, two at a time, in both directions. By the clock on the platform indicator board, this platform change uses up three of his allotted six minutes.

Few, if any, of Lewis's supposed watchers seem empowered enough to race after him; the one exception being Zeltinger who surprises himself by managing to keep pace with the former Marine. They arrive at the northbound platform of the Victoria Line within seconds of each other.

"I've been given a new phone," Lewis says, hearing the distant rumble of an approaching train. He is not looking at Zeltinger, trying to keep up a not particularly well-disguised pretence that the two do not know each other. "Oxford Street station in two and a half minutes from now. I think we are starting to get close. The time intervals are shortening."

"We have to be thinking like a terrorist: one who wants to severely disrupt London's transport system."

"I agree."

The next train bursts out of the tunnel and into the station.

"My thinking is this," Lewis says in a hurry. "Assume our terrorist, Sadiq, won't have been aware how resistant tunnels are to explosives. Assume that he believed, when he was alive, that a big blast underground was going to cause massive, long term, structural damage – as well as killing lots of people in the short term."

The train's doors open and Lewis climbs in. Zeltinger steps forward to follow but Lewis holds him back with his hand.

"I think it best if you stay here and let me continue alone," he says, and Zeltinger nods. "Go looking for somewhere like that, Saul. That's where the room will be, I'm certain."

The closing alert sounds and the doors slide shut. Now separated by the window glass, the two men can only eyeball each other. Lewis raises an eyebrow and gives his friend a slight shrug as the train begins to accelerate away.

Just one minute remaining, according to the platform clock.

Thankfully, Oxford Street is the next stop along the line.

116

For the moment, things seemed to be going according to the hastily improvised plan. Panich had been compelled to adjust and adapt everything following news of Virenque's death. For now, he was on his own: it was him against Lewis – rather apt, he had thought, in a perverse way. One on one wasn't ideal; but Panich felt confident in his own abilities. He always had. It was perhaps what had kept him alive all these years.

Oddly, he never had feared death: some might have argued that he'd been a better field agent for it. Now that his own life expectancy was measurable in weeks and not years, he was prepared to take greater risks than ever. Such as this newly improvised plan. The objective – bringing Lewis directly to him, alone – seemed to be achievable, thanks to the help he was getting from Vasily. The one-time Marine was already running, here, there and everywhere, completely at Panich's beck and call. Designed to wear Lewis down; to shake off any who might be following; and to deliver him directly into Panich's waiting arms. Vasily's small army of London-based foot soldiers had been brilliant: at their unattributable best – ensuring that Lewis kept to the rules and deadlines of Panich's deadly game of cat and mouse.

He, meanwhile, had nothing more to do than wait. Currently standing at street level, immediately outside Tottenham Court Road station, he was smoking a cigarette to calm his nerves. He looked at his watch. If all continued according to schedule, Lewis would be arriving at the station platform within the next half an hour.

His phone started to ring. It was Viktor Plushenko. Deciding to take the call, he discarded his cigarette, grinding out the stub with the heel of his shoe.

"How can I help?" he asked the oligarch.

"I thought you would like to know," Plushenko said, his breathing heavy in Panich's ear, "that I have found myself suddenly in possession of the missing Ben Lewis's codes. I've had someone working the problem from, how shall I put it, a slightly different angle. In conjunction with the two codes you provided earlier, I seem to have the complete set. Which is good news, I hope you agree?"

"Yes indeed," Panich said, his tone ambiguous, his mind spinning with the different permutations that Plushenko's information allowed him to consider.

"So, once your other concerns in London have all been taken care of, I look forward to welcoming you back home and thanking you in person. Until then, goodbye." The phone went dead.

117

In the wake of previous terror alerts in the United Kingdom's capital, a dedicated digital radio network for use by police officers had been installed throughout the London tube network. Whilst the public were only able to access the internet whilst underground at certain major London stations, uniformed Metropolitan Police officers, together with members of the British Transport Police, had the ability to use their specialist radios throughout the entire network – even in the tunnels.

Left on the platform watching Lewis's train depart, Zeltinger's first action was to locate a policeman with a radio handset that worked. He found two such people, both arriving out of breath on the platform just as the train was pulling out of the station. Zeltinger waved his badge and soon the message was put out into the ether: Lewis was, in the next few seconds, due to arrive at Oxford Street station where he'd been instructed to wait on the platform.

This message, routed through the Met Police's Command and Control centre based in Lambeth, was soon being distributed to various operational units in position across central London, now on the highest state of readiness. Time was not on their side. With a number of active units already diverted towards Green Park, the sudden change of focus to a different location was having the impact Panich had intended: creating confusion; and bifurcating valuable resources across multiple locations.

The one thing that Panich might not have thought about was that the message had also been sent to two other key people in London's emergency response decision-making process. One was the Metropolitan Police Commissioner; and the other was to the office of London's Mayor. At the time of the London Olympic Games, various strategic threats were analysed and a number of emergency response processes and protocols were rehearsed and implemented for the nation's capital. These came together under the umbrella of London Resilience, an umbrella partnership of various emergency departments and interested bodies. Their role, in an emergency, was to co-ordinate London's response to any major crisis. Two important decision makers in any such crisis response were London's Police Commissioner and the Mayor. Given all of the events of the last twenty-four hours, one pre-planned response under active review was whether or not to shut down the entire tube network in the interest of public safety.

At the time the message from Zeltinger was being relayed, the Commissioner was at her desk, evaluating various incident reports received during the last twenty-four hours. She had already formed a view that it was fast approaching a decision point. When she heard of the latest developments at Knightsbridge and Green Park tube station, her mind was made up. She simply needed the Mayor to agree with her recommendation. Unfortunately, the Mayor was less immediately available, at the time on stage, speaking to business leaders at a major conference being held at the ExCeL centre. It wasn't until a full ten minutes later, when an aide was instructed to walk to the podium and whisper urgently in his ear, that the matter received his rightful full attention. It was an important ten-minute delay: one that was to be very helpful to Oleg Panich.

118

No sooner does the train begin entering the station at Oxford Street than Lewis feels the phone vibrate again in his pocket; the wireless network signal is once more re-established.

Central Line westbound platform two minutes.

Immediately the doors open, Lewis begins to run. The transition from one line to the other necessitates a small maze of pedestrian tunnels. He hears someone running in his wake, trying to keep up. He has to believe it is one of the good guys: perhaps the police, who knows? He passes a surveillance camera, one of thousands positioned throughout the tube network. Assuming enough operators were able to keep track, Lewis tries doing the maths as he runs. Two hundred and seventy stations: large stations – say those with several interchanges – probably had seventy or more cameras; small stations, about ten; on average, say thirty to forty. In total, about ten thousand cameras across the whole network. That was a lot of close circuit television feeds to be watching. Lewis presumes the security services and police have the means to radio ahead in the tunnel network – but doesn't know for certain. Right now, his focus is on staying alive and getting to the next platform within the allotted time limit. He also has to assume that others, like the people in his wake, are able to keep track. He runs down the staircase to the platform level: to his left is the line heading east; to the right it heads west. Lewis turns right, as instructed. There is a train already at the station with its doors open.

Get on now.

The phone in his pocket buzzes its command. Lewis looks around, trying to see who has sent this message. Irritatingly, he can see no one. He jumps on board as instructed, just as the doors close, still looking to see who might be typing a message. There is no one. Too late, two of his pursuers arrive at some speed on to the platform, just out of time to grab hold of the closing doors. Lewis recognises one of them: it is the woman, Naomi, from Liverpool Street station earlier. One of Laura's team. He shrugs his shoulders at her futile attempt to bang on the door to halt the train: instead it picks up speed as it leaves the station and enters the tunnel.

Where to next?

The journey to the following station, Bond Street, takes less than a minute, the sensation of speed in the tunnels surprising. As soon as the train enters the platform, the phone buzzes once more; it doesn't even come to a halt before Lewis is reading the next message. This one has another photograph. It is of Borys. The pained expression on his face tells its own story.

Stay on board. His life is in your hands.

Lewis debates disobeying the instruction and leaving the train. Heading to the surface and taking his chances. He has the phone: Panich could track him down. After all, he, Lewis, has the code Panich craves. Then he looks at the photograph and reminds himself that such thinking is fantasy. Lewis has no intention of leaving the train.

The doors close and the train starts moving again, speeding westward, the next station Marble Arch. Lewis tries to imagine the ground resources on the surface and what they must be doing. A number will have been sent to Green Park. Then, almost immediately, Lewis is directed to Oxford Circus – so there's a mad scramble to get more people despatched to that station. However, very quickly, Lewis is on the move again: a different line, this time westward. But for how many stops? Each time, no one can predict the next move. The whole thing is akin to a massive three-dimensional chess game. Is there a strategy the police could adopt to ensure they didn't lose Lewis, given their starting position? By sending reinforcements to the next station, Bond Street, perhaps? Or even the one after? What if Lewis had been instructed to change trains at Bond Street? Every station presents a choice, a potential dilemma. Winning by conventional rules of play is likely to be impossible. Despite all of the CCTV cameras and clever police radios, Panich is likely to win: unless the authorities were suddenly to change the rules; such as shutting down the tube network or turning off the station Wi-Fi.

Seconds later, the carriage bursts out of the tunnel into the light of the next station, Marble Arch.

When, and only when, you hear the door-closing signal, jump out at last second and wait on platform.

That is clever: how to abandon your tail in one quick manoeuvre. The doors open, and a few passengers get off. Lewis waits. Hardly anyone is getting on board. Then the shrill warble begins. As instructed, Lewis steps onto the platform. The doors slide shut in his wake. He looks up and down the platform as the train departs. No one has got off after him.

He is on his own.

The station is in the middle of a major upgrade. There don't appear to be any closed circuit television cameras that he can see from where he is standing. Perhaps this is a temporary dead zone in the CCTV system? That's all Lewis needs.

The phone buzzes once again. How are they doing this?

Take next eastbound train from adjacent platform.

He must be getting close. There are no longer time limits in the messages.

As he boards the train less than one minute later, he starts to prepare mentally.

It is going to happen any time soon. He senses it.

He is ready.

Bring it on.

119

Another minute, and the train arrives back at Bond Street: same station, same line: but different platform, now heading in the opposite direction. The doors open but his phone doesn't buzz. Lewis peers out, seeing who is on the platform. Several people are about to board, none of them uniformed police: the CCTV cameras are thankfully back in evidence; Lewis hopes that a vigilant operator might yet spot him. He looks at the map. The next stop is Oxford Circus; after that Tottenham Court Road. When is this all going to end? Sometime soon, he is certain. He checks the phone again. The network strength is strong. Still no message.

The doors close and the train continues its journey eastward: towards the City of London.

Is the City of London where he is being taken? A bomb below Bank station would cause massive damage. Or would it? Lewis finds he needs to correct himself, even as he considers it. Massive damage in theory: perhaps not in practice. The City feels like an important commercial target: is it a serious enough terrorist target? He doesn't believe so but what does he know? He puzzles over what else might be a serious target, between there and here?

The train clatters into Oxford Street Station and draws to a stop. He checks the phone. Still he has good signal strength. Still there is no message. The doors close and the train starts to accelerate once more. Beyond busy Oxford Street, what next before they reach the City? The following stop is Tottenham Court Road. Nothing much happens there apart from a busy traffic intersection, the large tower block, Centre Point – and of course, suddenly Lewis remembers: the station is currently a building site. It is being transformed, as part of the Crossrail development.

Crossrail: Lewis feels the blood run cold in the pit of his stomach once more. Crossrail is a terrifyingly real terrorist target. He looks at the Central Line station map above his head to remind himself of the stations on this route that are impacted by Crossrail. Bond Street, now behind them; and on this tube line, both Tottenham Court Road and Liverpool Street stations up ahead.

At which point the train pulls into the next station: Tottenham Court Road.

Almost immediately, he feels the phone buzz in his pocket.

Leave the train and head immediately for the Northern line platforms.

Once again there is no pre-set time limit.

Is the puppeteer still pulling strings?

Or has the final performance already begun?

120

At the British Transport Police's CCTV control centre based near London's Euston Station, a small, dedicated, team had been attempting to track Ben Lewis's movements. Their starting point had been the moment Lewis had entered the Underground network at Knightsbridge station. It was exactly the sort of operation that they trained for repeatedly. It never was easy; however, this particular team of crime reduction officers, led by Superintendent Amanda Savage, were considered amongst the best at their job.

The problem with tracking individuals using camera surveillance was the multiplicity of image locations and camera angles that constantly needed to be synchronised and cross-referenced. One day London might have a fully automated facial recognition system: in the reality of today's world, Amanda Savage's team had been compelled to do most, if not all, of the hard graft themselves.

The Railway operators and London Underground were each responsible for their own camera networks. Across the entire London Underground system, there were some eight thousand, five hundred CCTV cameras in operation around the clock. One additional difficulty facing Savage's team was that, for a variety of reasons, not all the cameras at every location were in operation. There were various reasons for this: many times this was down to camera malfunction; other times it was due to planned maintenance or upgrades to the equipment. More recently, station refurbishment projects had also created a number of short-term surveillance 'black spots'. Marble Arch, currently in the middle of a station upgrade, was a good example. Here most, if not all, of its cameras had been removed pending the arrival of newer and better equipment at the completion of the works. Also affected were several of the stations impacted by Crossrail engineering works. One of these was at Tottenham Court Road. Here, early work to refurbish the station had been halted to allow station remodelling and rebuilding to begin. Camera systems at the station had, therefore, been in a state of flux for some time, significantly increasing the number of black spots throughout the station.

Surveillance of Lewis had proceeded well all the way to Oxford Street station. The team had tracked him as he had run to change from the Victoria Line to the Central Line train. They had seen him get on the train at Oxford Circus; they had, however, been unable to observe him changing trains and direction at Marble Arch station. Their working assumption, therefore, had been that Lewis had still been continuing in a westerly direction. It had only been when, after several minutes – and thus several feeds from other stations further down line the line – when no further sign of the man had been found that Savage had suggested a different possibility: could Lewis have disembarked the train at Marble Arch? If he had, then only three options were possible: firstly, he might have left the tube network completely; secondly, he might still be there; or thirdly, he might have switched trains and headed back in the reverse direction. It had taken a few minutes of frantic searching by the whole team before one team member found an oblique image of someone looking like Lewis peering around the door of an eastbound train at Bond Street Station.

121

Lewis stands on the station platform and waits for the Central Line train to depart. He is instructed to head to a different line. Lewis is going to take his time to get there.

Several passengers are walking in the same direction. The station is fully functioning, even though it has the look, in places, of a building site. He climbs up a staircase to an underground lobby where escalators out of the station head upwards: it is also where a pair of escalators down to the Northern Line platforms are located.

The station loudspeaker system unexpectedly comes to life, an automated male voice audible everywhere all at once.

'*Attention. All passengers, please leave the station immediately. I repeat, all passengers, please leave the station immediately. The station is now closed. No further trains will be operating until further notice. Please use the escalators and leave the station now.*'

The decision has finally been taken to close the tube. Lewis checks the phone. The wireless signal has also disappeared. At last, the authorities are trying to re-establish control.

Are they too late?

Lewis thinks they might be.

So: fight or flight?

Lewis hasn't come this far to run away.

All the 'down' escalators have stopped working.

So now he has to walk down – it's no big deal.

If he's right – and this is the station: will it be a fair fight? Somehow, Lewis doubts it. How to even up the odds, that is the challenge he faces?

He is unable to see a back staircase. There is probably one, but he doesn't believe it is worth his time to try and find it.

So, since it's fight not flight, he has only the one option: he begins walking down.

Several people are using the upward escalator, escaping the lower level platforms. London Underground don't realise it, but they are most likely playing into Panich's hands. They pass Lewis walking down and look back at him with frowns and worried looks on their faces. *Hasn't he heard the warning?* Lewis ignores them. It is not a long escalator. Ten more steps and he is at the bottom.

Left or right?

Left is the northbound platform: right for the southbound. Toss a coin time.

Lewis turns left.

The platform is deserted. The loudspeaker system continues its recorded message. It is on a continuous loop. The words echo and sound hollow in the empty station. Lewis looks around. It feels like a platform in mid-construction: the walls are stripped bare, the tiles removed; the ceiling void full of girders and brackets, waiting for cladding and finishings to be added; various cables and wires are also exposed. There are no CCTV cameras anywhere.

Lewis walks along the platform, not sure what to expect. Every sinew of his body is on alert. He checks the phone in his pocket: there are no new messages. The track has a slight curve to it, meaning that Lewis is unable to see from one end to the other. He gets to about halfway, and finds a passageway off to his right that connects this platform to the adjacent one. It is about twenty metres in length. He decides to take it. The passageway is narrow, the décor unusual: there is dark blue, painted, brickwork on both sides: a locked door to his left, the door having a tatty sign stuck on it with black electrical tape that is peeling away slightly. Up ahead, just a short distance away, is the other platform.

' . . . *please leave the station immediately. The station is now closed. No further trains will be operating until further notice. Please use the escalators . . . ,*' the recording continues as Lewis

steps onto the platform.
    Left or right?
    Lewis turns right.

122

Panich had never been so grateful to Vasily and his team of watchers. Lewis was on his way, right this minute, from the Central Line platforms to where he, Panich, was waiting. Estimated time of arrival: ninety seconds. Panich couldn't wait. The end game was about to begin: suitably close to where the Nemikovs were already in position and waiting. With a special place reserved specifically for Ben Lewis: right in the middle of them. They would be a happy threesome, enjoying the countdown together; all of them watching the clock as it got closer and closer to zero hour – each able to do absolutely nothing to stop the explosion that would soon be killing all three instantly.

Not that Panich wanted Lewis to have a pain-free ride to his death-bed. Nor did he expect him to either. Which explained the baseball bat. He'd acquired this at the sports shop across the road during a cigarette break. He wanted Lewis to die hurting: a broken man. The bat would soften him up; and then Panich would go to work on him with his prosthetic hand. He was looking forward to that especially. He would be starting with Lewis's hands, exactly like he had with the younger Nemikov. Next he would progress to other, more painful, parts of Lewis's anatomy. Then he would set the timer on the explosive device and leave.

The public address system announcement was something that he hadn't expected. It seemed to be on a continuous loop. The absence of passengers was, in hindsight, more a help rather than a hindrance.

'... *further notice. Please use the escalators and leave the station immediately.*'

After three or four repetitions, Panich was tuning the words out. Now in position, hiding and waiting, his back was resting

354

flat against the platform wall. He was tucked into a small recess, just to one side of where he predicted Lewis would emerge any time now. Very close to the special room. All he needed was to see Lewis. As he emerged onto the platform. If Lewis turned right, away from him, then Panich was ready to crush the man's upper forearm from behind. If he turned left, then Lewis would receive a baseball bat directly in the face.

' . . . *notice. Please use the escalators and leave the station now. Attention. All passengers, please leave the station immediately.*'

An elderly passenger distracts him up ahead to the right.

She is in the throes of trying to leave the platform. Her movement catches his eye, which cause him to turn her way in the first place. Ordinarily, he might have gone to help her: he advances one step and then stops.

'... *The station is now closed. No further trains will be operating until further notice.*'

Conceivably he hears Panich's muffled footsteps coming his way, positioning himself behind Lewis as he is about to swing the baseball bat. Perhaps he feels, or hears, the rush of air as the bat swings with all of Panich's force towards Lewis's right arm? The reasons are not relevant. Instinct has saved his life before; and it saves his life this time.

Reaction is equal and opposite to inaction.

It is his colour sergeant once again: one of the basic laws of fighting physics. The mottos keep coming back, time and again.

Unknown danger behind. Clear field of play immediately in front. Urgent reaction required, Soldier!

Lewis rolls forward on to the platform in front of him. He almost times it perfectly – but not quite. The speed of Panich's downward swing, its trajectory aimed directly at the place where Lewis's right arm had moments earlier been, allows it to connect with Lewis nonetheless: later in its trajectory than had been planned – with some of its energy dissipated as a result – but still contact is made. The points of impact for both sender and receiver are, however, different. Lewis, on the receiving end of a slightly more glancing blow than intended, gets hit on his inner left thigh: the leg directly in the baseball bat's swing trajectory as Lewis is rolling his torso forwards through three hundred and sixty degrees. For Panich, the blow connects with its target not in the centre of the baseball bat – but at its tip, creating a stronger counter-leverage effect than expected. Panich struggles to control the bat, the resultant torque along its length is strong; the weakness in Panich's left wrist caused by his shard of glass wound causing him to drop the bat.

Lewis rolls on to his feet but his left leg is severely weakened. His femur is not broken, but the area around it is screaming painful warnings: the muscle tissues are damaged and he will be bleeding internally. He sees Panich, stooping down to pick up the baseball bat. With the moment upon him, Lewis charges, using power from his good right leg to get him moving. It is a one-step, two-step, three-step manoeuvre.

Step one is the initial power lunge; the power being delivered by muscles in both his right calf and thigh. It is well executed, allowing well over a third of the distance between the two men to be covered in that first initial stride.

Step two is the problem, the weak link in the chain. In step two he wants to land, full force, on his left leg, needing power and strength within the leg muscles, to provide stability and strength at the landing point. Step two, however, is problematic. As he lands on what is now his bad leg, he feels the muscle weakness severely: involuntarily, his knee starts to buckle. Despite every conscious instruction from his brain to the contrary, the leg is unable to hold his body weight.

The result is that step three, the intended power-spring off his left leg that should have allowed his right knee to connect with Panich's stooped face, lowered as he bends to pick up the baseball bat, never gets delivered. Instead Lewis falls clumsily to the ground, his forward momentum causing his body to roll on to its left side, his head swivelling back to the ground and with his feet in front of him.

Not what Lewis had intended.

Although, it doesn't prevent him from executing an inelegant improvised version of step three.

No longer able to deliver a knee directly into Panich's face, he does the next best thing: he swings his right foot at the same target.

Lewis's heavy soled boot connects directly with Panich's nose, the strength of the kick sufficient to cause the sound of the nose cartilage breaking to make a sickening crunch. Blood starts to gush as the Russian, knocked off balance, now falls to the ground.

Panich reacts with surprising speed. Ignoring the pain and bleeding, he raises himself up, sending his prosthetic right arm in a downward chopping motion aimed directly at Lewis's left thigh. It is a clumsy move, and there is limited strength in the blow itself, but the motorised fingers succeed in clamping around the damaged tissue in the area around Lewis's thigh muscle. Panich then begins to squeeze. At the same time, he deploys his left hand to pin Lewis's right foot to the ground, using his body weight bearing down on top to help keep Lewis immobilised.

Lewis tries sitting up, the screaming pain in his upper left leg making this difficult. Panich's face is out of reach of both of Lewis's hands: his only available weapon is his right leg, currently pinned down by Panich's left hand and the Russian's body weight as the two men wrestle against each other. The pain in Lewis's leg starts to get a lot worse. Lewis needs to think, but his mind is fogging. His hands might be free, but Panich's face and body are out of reach; the only part that isn't is the Russian's prosthetic hand, currently squeezing the life out of his left thigh muscle and bone. Lewis is running out of options, close to blacking out.

He tries wriggling free, snaking about on his back to move his good leg. The pain in his other leg stops him progressing too far. It is becoming unbearable, Panich's mechanised thumb now mining deep into his muscle tissue towards bone.

Then he feels something. With a rush of gratitude, he remembers.

Behind his back; tucked into the small recess there.

His knife.

The same one that had evaded Fedorov on that fateful first visit to Arkady Nemikov.

Lewis fumbles behind his back with his left hand, keeping his right free in case Panich, in a moment of stupidity, brings his face within striking distance. Lewis grabs the shaft of the knife, wrestling the blade free from its harness, bringing it within an inch of being exposed underneath his left side. All the while he watches Panich's face: sees the winning glint in his eyes: and senses the pleasure the man is getting from the pain and suffering he is causing.

124

Panich never sees it coming. He has been focusing on the wrong things for just a few nanoseconds too long: in particular, getting his brain to send the right myoelectric signals from his upper forearm muscles to the electric motors in his prosthetic digits.

It is the difference between win and lose. Once the small but deadly blade has embedded itself deep in Panich's upper left arm muscle, Lewis knows that he is in with a fighting chance of winning back the advantage.

Panich does what Lewis hopes he would do. He releases the pressure that his motorised fingers are exerting on his left thigh and tries to grab the knife blade with his prosthesis. He shifts his body weight in the process, allowing Lewis to move his right leg so that it wriggles free. Instantly, he aims a punching kick right with this same right leg directly into the zone where Lewis is certain that Panich's prosthesis is connected to his upper arm. The artificial arm immediately detaches itself from the stump on Panich's forearm. Sensing a winning opportunity, Lewis pulls the arm away from Panich's body and hurls it, clumsily, towards the platform edge where it clatters over the side and on to the tracks below.

Panich, his face still bleeding badly and with Lewis's knife embedded in his upper arm, tries using his teeth to pull the knife blade clear. Lewis anticipates this. Sitting up, he aims a sharp right hook directly into the Russian's jaw. Panich flies backwards with the force of Lewis's blow, allowing Lewis to finally wriggle free and attempt to stand on one leg. The process of standing is difficult: putting weight on his left leg is another thing entirely. Taking his eye off Panich for a second, he tests his left leg and winces. It isn't broken and the bone doesn't feel fractured. On the other hand, the thigh muscles are badly traumatised, weak and unresponsive.

When he looks back at Panich, Lewis sees that the Russian is also back on his feet. This time he has something in his left hand. Surprisingly, it is neither a knife nor a gun. It is a small, plastic, black-coloured, box. On one surface, there is a tiny, hinged, lid. Panich has flipped the lid to the 'open' position, his thumb resting on the red button underneath.

"This is the end of the line, Lewis. For both of us, I am afraid."

"Not necessarily," Lewis replies.

"Don't fool yourself. You, me, the Nemikovs: we're all about to die. Just you watch." He presses the red button. Nothing appears to happen. Except that Panich's face, although covered in blood and despite the knife sticking out of his arm, is grinning.

' . . . *All passengers, please leave the station immediately. I repeat, all passengers . . .*'

"And so the countdown begins," Panich says in a loud voice to be heard above the tannoy. "In exactly five minutes, we will all be dead – and there's absolutely nothing you are going to be able to do to stop it."

Lewis takes a step towards Panich, gritting his teeth against the pain in his leg. Panich moves as well, this time towards the platform edge.

' ... *The station is now closed. No further trains will be operating until further . . .*'

"Where have you hidden the bomb, Panich?" Lewis calls out, he too raising his voice. "Where are Olena and Borys?"

"Getting anxious, all of a sudden? It's too late for that. Everything that is about to happen: it's as much for you, and all the pain you've caused. I'm not bothered about myself: I've got cancer. By all accounts, I should have been dead a long time ago. Just think of it as all being for you: for all that you stand for."

"Where is it, Panich?" Lewis shouts over the tannoy

361

announcements.

But Panich is no longer listening. Unable to intervene, Lewis watches aghast as the Russian gives a wolfish grin before, in one final dramatic move, jumping off the platform edge. Spreading his left arm and legs into a star-shape, he flings himself deliberately on to the live electrified rails below. The sound is sickening. The high voltage in the live electric rails creates a massive electric current that racks Panich's body. It twitches uncontrollably for several seconds, then stops. For some reason, the tannoy also stops at the same moment.

By the clock in Lewis's head, he has less than four minutes until the bomb will explode.

125

Saul Zeltinger emerged from Oxford Street station and was busy contemplating where to go next, when his phone rang. It was a young constable, Adam Cartwright, from his own police station at nearby Savile Row.

"Sorry to trouble you, Sir. You know you asked for off-the-wall ideas about where the bomb could be?"

"Go on."

"Well, I've just had a thought. How about Crossrail, Sir?"

"What about it?" Saul said a little impatiently.

"What if a bomb were placed in one of the tube locations close to the Crossrail tunnels?"

"Is this all idle speculation or do you have some reason for this hypothesis, Cartwright?"

"Well, Sir, at Tottenham Court Road in particular, the Northern Line and Crossrail tunnels pass incredibly close by each other. There was a programme about it on the telly just the other night, that's why I remembered it. Less than a metre apart, perhaps closer. Think of the disruption and havoc a bomb could wreak there."

"Well, it's a nice idea, Cartwright, but Lewis is sadly heading in the opposite direction on the Central Line. Sorry."

"Oh, okay. Well, it was only an idea. It just struck me as an ideal location, what with the station being redeveloped and everything."

"Meaning?"

"Meaning, that I suspect all sorts of old rooms and cupboards that people never knew existed get uncovered during station upgrades. You asked for ideas about where the room might be. I hope you don't mind my suggesting it. I'll have another think."

"You do that, Cartwright. Just a suggestion: next time, try

and back up your hypotheses with a few facts to support them, can you?"

He rang off and shook his head. Crossrail was, he had had to admit, an interesting idea. However, it was only one more to add to several that were already high on his worry list. Such as Oxford Circus itself. The truth was, that no one had a clue.

His phone rang again. It was Amanda Savage at the CCTV control centre on the Euston Road.

"Lewis switched trains at Marble Arch. About two minutes ago, we spotted him on an eastbound Central Line train back at Bond Street Station. I thought you'd like to know. Any time now, the order to close the entire tube network is about to be implemented."

"Good work, Amanda, thanks." He ended the call.

Zeltinger quickly performed the maths in his head. Assuming that Lewis had received no further instructions to change trains, by the time that the Underground network was shut down, Lewis would be at or near Tottenham Court Road. Something of a coincidence, given what Adam Cartwright had just hypothesised.

Especially since it was less than half a mile away from Zeltinger's current location.

126

"Ben!"

Lewis turns around and sees Saul Zeltinger racing towards him along the station platform.

"Saul! Thank God! We've got less than three and a half minutes before this bomb explodes. The room has to be close by. Panich primed the bomb with a radio-controlled device. In these tunnels, it wouldn't have a long range. We have to find it, quickly!"

They narrow it down to just two possibilities: the dark blue painted door that Lewis passed earlier; and a door that purportedly has electrical equipment inside it positioned further down the platform. Lewis hobbles to the dark blue door and is joined by Zeltinger. One hundred and eighty seconds left. They bang on the door, but hear nothing. Deciding not to use his P-22 pistol to shoot the lock in case explosives are inside, it takes Zeltinger twenty seconds to pick the lock.

Olena and Borys sit side by side on the floor, their arms and legs bound, their mouths gagged. They look petrified. They both wear explosive vests but, as in the photograph that Panich had sent earlier, only Olena's has a timed detonator attached to hers. The countdown is displayed on the face of the detonator by bright red light-emitting diodes in large format. Lewis was being overly optimistic. There are only ninety-five seconds remaining and counting.

Zeltinger undoes the gag on Olena first.

"Oh my God, Ben" she gasps. "You have to help, hurry! Please, please, hurry!"

Lewis is examining the device. Below the LEDs showing the countdown, there is a simple keyboard and various wires of different colours. He is not an expert: the chances of a booby trap have to be high. Pulling out various wires has to be a last resort.

"Did Panich say anything to you when he set the device?"

Olena shakes her head, but Borys is nodding vigorously. As Zeltinger releases his gag, words flow in a big torrent.

Seventy-two seconds remaining.

"He did say something," he says, looking at his sister. "I asked him, don't you remember? '*Only by following the greatest Russian chess move ever,*' was his cryptic reply. I thought it odd at the time."

Fifty-four seconds.

"Saul, the greatest Russian chess move ever? What do you think?"

"Kasparov. Against the Bulgarian, Topalov. Rxd4."

"I agree. It has to be. Arkady Nemikov also agreed. He and I discussed it. Let's try entering that."

Lewis keys in Rxd4 and hits the enter key on the keyboard. Nothing happens and the clock continues its countdown.

Thirty-two seconds.

"Shit. What else, Ben?"

"I don't know. Perhaps Karpov versus Korchnoi, the fourteenth move: Ng4." He keys in this combination and hits enter. Again nothing happens.

"Say again, Borys, What were Panich's exact words?"

"*Only by following the greatest Russian chess move ever will you stop this thing*, or words to that effect."

Lewis stops and thinks. Twenty-four seconds.

Only by following. Only by following. He has an idea.

"Saul, what moves came immediately after Rxd4"

"I've no idea, I'm sorry."

"Topalov takes the rook Kasparov sacrificed with his pawn: cd4. Then Kasparov moves his other rook to e7. It's worth a shot." Fifteen seconds on the clock.

He enters 'cd4re7' on the keypad and then hits enter.

Nothing happens. Perhaps he hasn't entered enough

moves? How many more should he enter? Nemikov's codes all had either four or five moves in them. Maybe Panich's code needed the same. What came next? Black moved his King. Was it to b6 or b7? Lewis tries to visualise it. It had to be b6. He knows this game backwards. White's subsequent move was Queen takes Topalov's pawn on d4.

Eight seconds left.

He is going to try entering four moves first.

He enters 'cd4Re7Kb6', holds his breath and presses enter.

The clock miraculously stops.

Only four seconds remaining.

The only sound in the room is one of a collective exhaling of breath.

First on site are the bomb disposal experts from 101 Engineer Regiment based at Carver Barracks, near Saffron Walden. Their first and immediate task is to remove, and safely take to the surface, both of the explosive vests being worn by each of the Nemikovs. It is not an easy task. Lewis is not surprised to learn that the vests had, indeed, been booby-trapped by Panich: if he had tried to remove them before the device had been disarmed, they would have exploded.

Next comes the job of removing the sandbags containing the RDX explosives. Since, in the absence of any detonation device, the RDX is considered relatively inert, various officials are given permission to venture down to the platform level. One of the first to arrive is a small team of paramedics from the London Ambulance service.

Lewis's femur bone is examined and the paramedic declares that the bone is, indeed, not broken; the thigh muscles, though, are badly bruised and damaged. Lewis asks for strapping and some painkillers, the combination of the two immediately improving his mobility. Borys's hand is more problematic. The paramedics administer a large painkilling injection and his hand is carefully bandaged. Arrangements are hastily made for him to be transported to a leading orthopaedic surgeon specialising in hand trauma. Before the two of them are led gingerly away, they both stop to say thank you to both Zeltinger and Lewis.

"Don't thank me," says a typically, self-effacing Zeltinger.

"This is the man," he says, one arm around Lewis's shoulder, "who you need to thank. He's the one who's responsible for us all being alive at the moment."

Borys gives Lewis a clumsy, but spontaneous, hug. Tears in his eyes, he avoids contact with his now heavily bandaged right hand as the two men embrace. Next is Olena, the stress of the last twenty-four hours evident all over her face. She gives Lewis a huge embrace, at the end of which she holds his face in both her hands and kisses him, firmly and deliberately, on the lips.

"I can't thank you enough, Ben. Can't you come with us? I am scared to be left alone after all this."

"I'll be back with you soon, I promise, Olena. Some of Saul's team will help you over the next twenty-four hours or so. I have something I need to do first. Something that I promised your father I would do for him."

They embrace once more, and then Olena and Borys are led away by the ambulance crew, two policewomen from Saul's team following close behind.

"How did you guess Tottenham Court Road, Saul? That was genius, you turning up when you did."

"We were lucky. One of the CCTV crew at the Met's Euston Road surveillance centre guessed that you must have changed trains at Marble Arch and then we had a break: you were spotted leaning out of the door of an eastbound train at Bond Street station a short while later. When you didn't get off the train at Oxford Circus and, with the tube network closed shortly thereafter, it seemed likely that you would be at Tottenham Court Road."

"So this wasn't the work of a genius super-sleuth who had worked out the room's location by deduction, Saul?"

"Well, to be frank, someone in my office did call me, only five minutes before I turned up at the station here, to tell me the reason why he thought the bomb was located here."

"What did you say?"

"I told him it was a crazy idea and that you were heading in the other direction. It turns out that he was right after all! What clinched it was that, as I was speeding in a taxi towards Tottenham Court Road station, one of the CCTV team rang to say that you'd been seen at this station on one of the remote cameras."

"I'm surprised there are any," Lewis says. "I couldn't see them. I was checking the platform everywhere."

"Not down here. On the upper level, along the corridor you took when you changed from the Central to the Northern Line platforms."

They were riding the up escalator, on their way out of the station.

"Tell me about Panich? Did he jump or did he have help, Ben? I won't take issue either way, I'd just like to know."

"He did that to himself voluntarily. For some reason he had a knife sticking out of his left arm and I'd given him a helping hand in removing his prosthesis. He responded by priming the detonator on the bomb and then leaping on to the live rails. He had cancer, or so he said. Probably all the cigarettes."

"Not a nice way to go."

"It would have been quick."

"Where are you off to in such a hurry? I would have thought you'd have been consoling Olena. She's lovely, by the way."

Lewis explains what he plans to do.

"My colleagues are not going to be happy. They have so many questions they want to ask, Ben. It's not helpful, you going AWOL."

"No, I'm sure it's not. But then, I'm sure that you'll be able to cover for me. One friend to another?"

"You're pushing your luck, Ben Lewis. The clock is ticking. I need you back here in twenty-four hours. Go, before I change my mind!"

127

Viktor Plushenko's Bombardier BD 700 jet left Moscow's international private airport at Ostafyevo shortly after five in the morning Moscow time. The three and a half hour flight direct to Zurich's Kloten airport was smooth and uneventful, the time difference such that it was a little after seven-thirty in the morning, local time, when the plane touched down on Swiss soil. Kloten ground controllers directed the plane to the airport's Private Terminal, the separate facility used by VIP visitors to the city. Formalities completed, Viktor was, in short order, ushered into a waiting Mercedes limousine for the brief drive into the heart of the city's financial district. Rush-hour traffic being what it was, it was almost exactly eight-thirty that morning by the time the limousine arrived outside the small and nondescript offices of Hildebrandt Private Bank AG.

Viktor Plushenko pressed the brass buzzer. It was positioned adjacent to a small, faded, brass plaque bearing the bank's name. Unaccustomed to being kept waiting by anyone, the Russian felt decidedly exposed as he stood waiting on the Zurich pavement: the chill November air, moist from the lake, icy on his skin. What seemed to him like an uncomfortable length of time later and a muted 'click' followed by a buzzing sound emanated from the door latch. Plushenko pushed the door open and gratefully went inside.

A male receptionist stepped forward to greet him. Plushenko preferred flirting with pretty female receptionists before most of his business meetings back home in Moscow. He wasn't about to make a fuss, however. It wasn't every day that he was presented with an opportunity to lay his hands on nearly ten billion US dollars of someone else's money. So instead, he shook the offered male hand warmly.

"Herr Plushenko. Welcome to Zurich. I trust your flight

was in order and to your satisfaction?"

When Viktor announced that indeed it had been and that all was well in his world, he was instructed to follow the receptionist to their private meeting room.

Somewhat to Viktor's surprise, the meeting room was not on the ground floor, but in the basement. The two men took a lift down one floor, and Plushenko was directed down a dimly lit corridor that wound its way in various directions until they reached the allocated room. The door had a sign on the outside: *Konferenzraum Zug: Privat*. Plushenko was ushered in and told to make himself comfortable. Hot tea, coffee and pastries on a trolley soon followed him into the room. Plushenko was on his second cup and third pastry by the time the door was pushed wide open and Rudi Hildebrandt came in to greet his guest.

"Herr Plushenko, it is my genuine pleasure to meet such a distinguished and honoured guest. Welcome to Zurich. I hope you didn't mind us using a basement room? It is so much more private."

Plushenko nodded, clearing pastry crumbs from off the table in front of him and wiping his hands on some paper napkins before raising his large body from the chair. He shook Hildebrandt's proffered hand before sitting down again.

"I see that you have helped yourself to coffee and pastries. Excellent. Is there anything else that you need before we begin?"

Plushenko shook his head.

"Very good. So, to business. How may I be of service, today?"

Plushenko sat upright and opened his calfskin leather portfolio.

"One of my former business partners and life-long friends, Arkady Nemikov, is, as I am sure you are aware, no longer with us. His death is a great sadness to us all. Already he is greatly missed." He looked across at Hildebrandt, pleased to see the Swiss banker following his every word, nodding sagely at appropriate moments.

"Arkady and I have had our ups and downs, over the years. Somehow, despite that, we have always maintained this long-term bond of trust between us. As I understand it, he put in place certain arrangements designed to protect his assets. He gave his wife, daughter and son a specific code. Three codes in total, each Nemikov family member not knowing the others'. Following his death, his assets were automatically frozen, this freezing order to remain in place until, or unless, you, his private banker, received all three unlock codes. Then, and only then, would you be in a position, as custodian of his assets, to release either some or all of them. How I am doing?"

"Herr Plushenko, I am not, as I am sure you will understand, in a position to either confirm or deny any of what you are saying about my client's instructions. It would be entirely inappropriate. However, is there some specific request or information you might have for me today?"

Slightly taken aback at the degree of frostiness, Plushenko decided not to take affront but instead carried on.

"Yes, there is." He reached into his calfskin folder and extracted a single sheet of paper. "I have in my possession, on this sheet of paper, the three codes. Each has been given to me entirely voluntarily. It is each code holder's express wish, and thus my specific instruction to you today, to effect a cash transfer from Arkady Nemikov's estate to my own bank account with immediate and irrevocable effect."

"How much money are we talking about, Herr Plushenko?"

"Ten billion US dollars," he said, sliding the piece of paper across the table to Hildebrandt.

Hildebrandt's facial expression never changed in the slightest. Instead, he stood up, picked up the piece of paper that Plushenko had passed to him, and walked towards the door.

"Please help yourself to more coffee and pastries. I have to

373

make certain investigations, as I am sure you appreciate. I will try not to keep you too long."

It was nearly twenty minutes later before the door swung open. Two people entered. Neither of them was Rudi Hildebrandt. One came and sat down opposite Plushenko, the other stood by the door. The one by the door was younger. In his late twenties, or early thirties, he was athletic, muscular, wearing a dark brown leather jacket and jeans, clothing that looked out of place in the offices of Hildebrandt Private Bank AG. The man who came and sat down was older. He was thickset with few distinguishing features other than a small shock of silvery-white hair to one side of his otherwise thick, black, mane.

"Who exactly are you?" Plushenko asked, taken aback by the lack of introductions from his visitors. The temperature in the room felt suddenly hot. The Russian was beginning to perspire.

"Part of the verification team," the man sitting opposite him said, his English sounding slightly mid-Atlantic.

"How long does verification take?" Plushenko asked. He received no reply to his question.

"Who is the man by the door?" Plushenko was becoming rattled, his voice louder, more imperious. Again, neither man answered. Becoming angry at their impertinence, Plushenko stood up. Without warning, the man at the door withdrew a suppressed Heckler & Koch HK P30 from a jacket pocket, pointing it directly at Plushenko. It was a powerful 9mm semi-automatic that made a clear statement. No words were exchanged: they weren't needed. Plushenko sat down, producing a handkerchief from a pocket and mopped his brow. The man by the door lowered the weapon, this time keeping it in his hand.

They stayed like this for five minutes, the temperature in the room rising. Still no words were spoken. At one point

Plushenko slammed his fist on the table, demanding to see Hildebrandt. Again, no one took any notice.

Then a remarkable thing happened. There was a knocking on the door. The man in the leather jacket holding the Heckler & Koch stepped to one side. It allowed the door to swing open.

Into the room walked none other than Arkady Nemikov.

128

It is the Saturday night. The twins are in bed, almost asleep, having been read the most exciting bedtime story ever by a real life super-hero: the new best friend of their father: Ben Lewis. Hattie is clearing away the supper, having enjoyed an evening mildly flirting with their guest who, in turn, seemed not to notice a single hair flick. Zeltinger and Lewis are sitting in front of a chessboard, both nursing a glass of the excellent German Spatzburgunder that Zeltinger has been serving all evening. Lewis raises his glass to his new friend.

"Thanks, Saul. You've cut me a lot of slack these last few days. By all rights you should have turned me in. I am glad you didn't." They clink glasses. "The Germans make decent red wines these days, by the way. Thank you."

"It's good isn't it?" Zeltinger says, picking up the bottle and pouring the remnants into their glasses. Lewis moves his bishop to a3.

"Check."

"I have a feeling I am going to lose this game. Why don't you tell me what happened in Zurich? I still haven't heard it all."

Lewis leans back in the simple wooden chair and folds his arms.

"Very well. I am, of course, sworn to secrecy. The very fact that you're asking me – and that I am about to tell you – what happened, is probably perjuring us both. Arkady Nemikov did not die in that car crash. It seems that for years he has been secretly working with the Americans. They cut him a deal. They would help him rise to power in a new Ukrainian administration as long as he pledged his money to prop up the cash-starved regime in Kiev. The Americans knew the Russians would do anything to try and keep Nemikov out of

Kiev. Without his money, Nemikov had nothing to bring to the table in Kiev. Therefore the Russian strategy was to go after the cash. They knew that Nemikov was clever, that he'd put in place various ruses to ensure his money would still get to Kiev, even if he was killed. So instead they planned to steal it."

He takes another sip of wine, moves another piece on the chessboard, and then continues.

"What no one saw coming was the Americans helping Nemikov fake his death. They helped him disappear. It was a masterstroke. You almost worked it out, though, didn't you, Saul? You were suspicious that the timings around his death looked out of sync, that the van his car crashed into seemingly burst into a fireball all too conveniently. No one else got close: next time, trust your instincts. You nearly cracked it."

He raises his glass in a toast and they both salute each other.

"What about Plushenko?"

"You don't really want to know the details, Saul. Trust me."

"How did he react when Nemikov returned from the dead and walked into the room with you in Zurich?"

"Let's just say that he knew immediately that his time on the planet had come to an end. He'd reached the end of the line."

"Did Nemikov really kill him?"

"No comment, Saul, I'm sorry. Official secrets and all that."

"Was it all orchestrated or did we just strike lucky in the end?"

"Saul: the one weakness in the whole plan was the Americans' failure to safeguard Nemikov's wife and children. That was left in part to me and, in part, to the fortunes, or misfortunes, of Oleg Panich. He very nearly succeeded. If he had, we'd both be dead and the Russians would have won."

"You came out on top, Ben. You're the hero of the hour. We all owe you. Especially the Nemikovs. Do we know for sure whether the wife really was killed in Venice?"

"I don't know. Jake Sullivan didn't know when I asked him earlier. The working assumption is yes. We may never know. At least Olena and Borys live to see another day."

"Go and see her, Ben. You would be good for each other at the moment."

"Who?" Lewis says, studying the chessboard.

"Olena, of course, don't be so obtuse. It's the perfect match."

Lewis shakes his head, then smiles, moving his queen to b6.

"Checkmate!"

He looks across the table at Zeltinger. Zeltinger studies the pieces and then sits back, nodding.

"You win, Ben. Congratulations!"

"Look Saul. Whether I happen to agree with your other assessment or not," he says draining his wine glass in one pull, "one thing I do know," he says pointing at the chessboard with his head.

"This particular match may not have been perfect: but it has been pretty good."

They both laugh.

"Perhaps that's a good omen, Ben."

The End

Acknowledgements

Nothing gets written without a lot of patience and support from so many people out there – not least to all those who bought my first Ben Lewis book, *The Dossier*. Thank you to all who gave me so much encouragement to write another. I hope that I listened to what you told me along the way!

Special thanks must go to the continued patience and never ending support of my wife and two sons, each tirelessly giving me feedback – good and bad – and ideas along the way.

I am also hugely grateful to Sonia Land, my agent at Sheil Land. She has nudged, cajoled and actively encouraged me to write and has helped enormously with my growing relationship with Amazon. For us independent authors, Amazon and Kindle provide a great outlet to a worldwide readership and I have benefitted hugely from their continued support and promotion.

Finally, I would like to thank all those who really helped with the production of this book – especially Gabrielle from Sheil Land – without her painstaking work, the book would not look as good in its present form. Sadly, it does not just happen automatically. Also to Ginny, Maggie and Helena for their help in proof reading, oftentimes at ridiculously short notice. I really do appreciate it.

About the Author

David N Robinson has flown the equivalent of eight round trips to the moon during his travels with a large international professional firm, a private equity business and latterly one of the world's largest law firms.

A graduate metallurgist from Cambridge, he has lived and worked both in London and Cambridge for most of his life, two locations that have, in particular, been a source of inspiration for *The Gambit*, his latest Ben Lewis thriller. David's fascination with, and professional interest in, cyber crime and identity theft led him to write his first thriller, *The Morpheus Network*. His detailed knowledge of many overseas locations, both in Europe, the Middle East and Russia, provided an important backdrop to his second thriller, *The Dossier* – the first book featuring Ben Lewis.

David currently lives with his wife of 30 years and divides his time between his home, near Cambridge and the Alps, where he both skis in winter and walks in the summer. He is currently trustee and Chairman of Addenbrooke's Hospital's Charitable Trust.